loyalty

book one

BETHANY-KRIS

Published by Bethany-Kris

www.bethanykris.com

eISBN 13: 978-1-988197-52-4

Print ISBN 13: 978-1-988197-53-1

Cover Art © Mignon Mykel

Editor: Elizabeth Peters

For all my readers who waited so patiently—and not so patiently—for John. I hope he is everything you wanted, and much more.

CONTENTS

BETHANY-KRIS

CHAPTER ONE

THE BLACK CAR pulled up and parked alongside of Johnathan. The sight of a dark vehicle with tinted windows was so familiar to him he almost smiled. *Almost.*

A good portion of his life was filled with memories of cars just like this one picking him up for one thing or another. Likely some situation he'd gotten himself in to and needed out of.

The passenger window rolled down and revealed the person who had come to pick John up this time. He *did* smile at the sight of Giovanni behind the wheel.

"*Zio*," John greeted.

Uncle.

Truth be told, Giovanni had always been more like a friend and brother to John than just an uncle. Especially now that John was thirty and not just a kid under his uncle's feet anymore.

Still, Giovanni was the one person in John's family that he connected with on a level of trust that he didn't have with anyone else. Despite the salt peppering the fifty-seven-year-old's hair, and the lines on his face that said Giovanni was not a young man, he somehow still gave off the air of youth. Antony, John's grandfather, always said that Giovanni had a young soul.

Whatever that meant.

"John," his uncle replied. "Get in. We're going to be late as it is with the drive. They told me you would be getting out at twelve, and it's already one."

"They had some kind of delay on the paperwork."

Giovanni pointed at the passenger door. "Don't care. Get in."

Johnathan knew better than to disobey Giovanni. Pulling open the passenger door, he tossed the large brown paper bag to the floor of the car and climbed in. He hadn't even shut the door completely before the Gio hit the gas, and the car lurched forward.

"Shit," John said, grabbing for something to steady himself and laughing. "Slow down. I'd like to see Ma at least once more before I die, all right."

Gio smirked. "Not your father?"

"You know how it is."

"I don't, actually. Lucian, like Dante, is my best friend. We've always been close, John. When I was younger, had no self-control and too many issues to name, I always had my brothers. When my father felt a million miles away, my brothers were still there. So, no, I don't understand."

"It's like this, he's not my brother."

Gio hummed under his breath. "He's your father, I know."

John had never seen eye to eye with his father on a lot of things. Lucian was a good father, as far as that went. He'd always been good to John and his sisters. He loved his children totally. But John had always felt misplaced somehow in his life. Or even out of touch with the people around him, his father included. It made it difficult to have a connection like his younger sisters had to their mother and father.

"What is in the bag?" Gio asked, passing the brown sack John had tossed to the car floor a look.

John shrugged. "Shit I went in with. Clothes, a watch, stuff like that. Nothing important."

"Let me see your band, John."

"Why?"

"Let me see it."

Sighing, John lifted his hand up to show off the leather wrist band he wore with his family's crest embossed across the middle. "Happy?"

"Just making sure you got that back, too."

"Everything that I took in came back out with me, *Zio*."

"I don't trust the system, John."

Neither did John, really.

"Thanks for sending a package to the prison for me to have clean, decent clothes to come out with today," John said.

Gio shot his nephew a look. "I didn't send anything, John."

"Who did?"

"Your father. He sent it up a couple of weeks ago, so you would have a suit to wear today. He thinks about you even when you're not thinking about him."

John wished that made him feel something, but all he got was a twinge in his chest that reminded him of how detached he truly was. It had always been this way for him. He never felt at home; he always looked at the people around him like he was on the outside looking in.

"So, what is your next week looking like?" Gio asked.

"Nothing unusual. I have to check in with the probation officer. Three years of that nonsense should be fun."

Gio laughed. "Or we could just pay the fucker off."

John scowled. "Bribing people was one of the reasons I spent three

2

years behind bars instead of the one year it would have been, *Zio*."

"Yeah," Gio said, wincing. "You're right. Better to let it lie."

Attempted bribery of officials to drop the charges he faced. Possession of an unregistered weapon. Discharging an unregistered weapon. Assault on a police officer. Actually, *several* police officers.

The charges had racked up one after the other on John. Before he knew it, a five-year term slammed down on him with the bang of a judge's gavel. Not even his family's money, status, or connections had been able to get him out of that one.

John was pretty sure his father and uncle, Dante, had a bit of a hand in it all. To Lucian, John was out of control. Or rather, out of his father's control. He didn't always follow the rules. He liked to do things his way, which wasn't always the Marcello way.

Wherever John went, trouble usually followed.

Lucian had said more than once that it was time for John to grow the fuck up. John supposed he finally had, in a way.

He just wished his father hadn't let him take a five-year rap to get his head straightened out. Thankfully, John served his time in three years with good behavior and probation for the foreseeable future, but it still stunk like shit no matter which way he looked at it.

"Hey," Gio said.

John fell out of his troubled thoughts and gave his uncle the attention and respect the man deserved.

That was the Marcello way.

It was a rule John didn't mind following.

Respect and honor.

Always.

"What?" John asked.

"What do you want to do right now?"

"We've got a party to make it to, don't we?"

"Fashionably late is the thing or so I hear," Gio replied. "Just tell me something you'd like to do, John."

"A beer. I'd like to have a beer."

Gio chuckled. "Are you supposed to with—"

"It's fine. One won't kill me."

"I think we can manage that without Dante sending people out looking for us."

John frowned at the mention of his uncle ... and boss. "It's my first day out. Are you seriously urging me to irk Dante? Dante, who has a shorter fuse than even I do?"

The older Dante Marcello got the less tolerable to bullshit he seemed to be. John was smart enough to know that his uncle, the Don of the Marcello Cosa Nostra, would kick his ass first and then ask questions later if need be.

Gio smiled. "It's not him you should be worried about."

"Oh?"

"No. Worry about when your mother gets her hands on you for not calling her for three months."

Shit.

Family first, John. Always.

His father's words were a mantra John couldn't forget.

John's mother, Jordyn, had gotten progressively more concerned the closer his release date loomed. She voiced her worries about his release, and a possible relapse into another one of his episodes enough that it started to grate on John's nerves. His focus was simply getting out of prison and what he was going to do after he was out. To do that, he had put a block of sorts between him and his mother.

It probably wasn't the right thing to do.

"Maybe we should stop at a flower shop on the way to Tuxedo Park," John murmured.

Gio nodded. "Maybe we should."

"And the jewelry store."

"Now you're getting it, man. Lucian taught you well, regardless of what you think."

John laughed. "I know my mother worries because she loves me."

"But?"

"She suffocates me," John admitted. "I'm an adult, not a child. She acts like I'm seventeen and not thirty. She still thinks I'm a boy."

"For the record, all mothers see their children as their babies. Jordyn isn't a special case. Cecelia still thinks she has to fix my damned tie if it's crooked."

"You know it's not the same."

Gio sighed heavily. "Or maybe you just don't understand your mother and father, John."

"I think I do."

"Do you? They almost lost you twice. Have you ever thought that letting you go too far ahead where they can't reach makes them feel suffocated? That being unable to keep you close takes away the security they have?"

John didn't answer his uncle, but he knew Giovanni had a good point. When he was just a baby, his aunt, Catrina, had been involved with a cartel that had taken John as a way to draw Catrina out. He'd nearly lost his life, as had his father, uncles, and aunt when they'd made the attempt to save him.

Clearly, his family won that battle.

The Marcellos always won.

And then John's first episode had happened when he was seventeen. In the process of losing himself in the manic chaos of his brain, and the torrent of his uncontrollable, rash decisions that led him to a bad place, he nearly died again. Self-medicating, living fast, and almost dying young.

He might as well have been a walking cliché.

Except he wasn't.

His life was real, and so was the manic bipolar disorder he had been diagnosed with at seventeen, and then severely failed to manage as an adult.

"John," Giovanni said quietly. "I'd like an answer."

"How close did my father keep me when he let me be carted off to prison for three years?"

"You didn't give Lucian a choice. You were running crazy, John, doing stupid shit. The faster you ran, the more frenzied you became. You were refusing to work with your father or the people set up for you. On more than one occasion, you put everyone in terrible situations that could have cost us all a lot. You were self-medicating between chemicals and prescriptions. *Cristo*, John, you went missing for two weeks!"

He had.

He had done all of that.

"I thought I had it under control," John said.

"That was your first mistake because clearly you were lost. Everybody was trying to help you, but you just kept pushing us away until we couldn't even see you anymore."

Not one word was a lie.

John wouldn't deny it.

His last manic episode had begun shortly after his twenty-sixth birthday, and the cycles of the disorder went on for weeks at a time, and lasted for over a year. It almost mirrored his first episode from his teenaged years when his family had finally gotten a diagnosis for what was wrong inside his head.

Chemical imbalances.

Bipolar.

John's biggest mistake back then was thinking he could manage his mental health without medications. Those pills labeled him crazy. He didn't need them. He was wrong, and the longer he was without them the more manic he became in his daily life. He'd go from stealing because of the rush, fighting because of the high, using substances to manage the highs and the lows, to fucking any female within arm's reach just to feel.

When he was in a high cycle of the mania, he'd be up for days, running non-stop, and obsessive to an extreme. When the lows of the cycle hit, he would do anything just to get out of it, if he could even manage to function.

Yeah, he'd lost that battle with a bang.

Literally.

His parents hadn't been able to step in like they had when he was a teen because he was an adult the second time around. When his episode came to a head and John finally hit bottom, he nearly killed his cousin, Andino, during an argument over territory and men on the streets. It should have been a simple discussion between Capos. John was far too lost in his own nonsense to fully understand what he was doing when he pulled that gun on his cousin in a busy restaurant.

How Gio was even sitting in a car with John after what he'd almost done to the man's son, John didn't understand.

Well, truthfully, he did know how.

Family first.

"I'm good," John said firmly.

"Now," Gio agreed.

John decided right then and there to end the conversation. He didn't want to talk about his mental health with his uncle, or anyone for that matter. He had a fucking doctor for that shit. Or he'd had before.

"Drop it, *Zio*," John said.

"You brought it up first."

"And now I'm done."

Gio glared at the highway they were driving down. "Your crew has been divided between a few of the family Capos."

"Better than Dante handing my position and men off to someone else entirely."

"You could say that."

Oh, for fuck's sake.

John could hear the hesitance in his uncle's tone, which wouldn't lead to anything good.

"What now?" he demanded.

Gio rapped his fingers to the leather-bound steering wheel. "Just to be sure that you're not going to have a relapse the moment you're out and free to do your own thing, Dante and Lucian decided that it would be better if you worked alongside Andino and Timothy with their crews for a while."

Anger surged through John like he hadn't felt in a long time. It was good. So fucking good. Like a shot of adrenaline straight to his bloodstream.

But that feeling was also addictive and bad for him. Bad for his mania and bad for the bipolar currents of his emotions that he fought with daily. He wasn't that crazy, out of control, unmanageable person. He got that his behavior and issues had put his family and *la famiglia* through hell, but he was good.

Wasn't he?

Now?

Did his family not trust him?

Christ.

It pissed him off even more.

"Just to be clear, I don't get a say here, right?" John asked.

Gio shrugged. "No, you don't."

Because that's how Cosa Nostra worked, and his family was knee-deep in that life and culture. Nobody could possibly begin to understand their life. With his uncle being the head boss of the family, his other uncle acting as Dante's consigliere, and John's own father being the family underboss, there was no escaping who he was.

Mafia.

Made.

Cosa Nostra.

When it came to family decisions, especially ones made about him, John didn't get a bone in the fight. His uncles pulled rank, as did his father.

Rules.

His life was dictated, surrounded, and determined by rules.

John stifled the familiar urge to push back against the walls closing in on him again. They were only in his own mind, after all.

"There's something else I have to do this week," John said, dropping the conversation. He didn't want to fight with his uncle about something that neither of them could do anything about at the moment. "I should do it tomorrow, but I need some contacts."

Gio cocked a brow and passed John a look. "What is that?"

"I need a new therapist. One that my father doesn't have on his payroll."

"John—"

"I'll follow his fucking rules and give him what he wants, but he's not having control over that. Not now. It's been three years since my last episode. Give me a fucking break here. I've earned that, Gio."

"You were wrong," Gio said quietly.

"About what?"

"Your father. He did give you a choice, John. You know he did."

John forced back his irritation. "Leave it alone."

"He gave you a choice. An institution to get yourself checked out and settled, or time behind bars. You made the choice, John, not Lucian."

"I'm not crazy," John said.

"No one ever said that."

But they might as well have.

"Putting me in an institution would have labeled me exactly that."

"We just wanted you healthy."

"I am."

Gio passed him another look. "Let's hope you stay that way."

"Thanks for that, asshole."

"I'm just being real, John. We both know if you don't keep managing this like you've been forced to for the last three years, you can easily relapse into another episode."

John knew that, but it still made his anger rear its ugly head. His saving grace was being able to control it now, whereas he couldn't before.

"By the way," Gio said as he pushed the gas pedal harder.

"What?"

"Happy birthday, John."

• • •

A drop of tension crawled down John's spine as his uncle pulled up to the iron-wrought gate. A long, twisty driveway led up to a mansion with two wings, three floors, a pool, and a guest house out back. The estate rested on six acres of property in Tuxedo Park.

The Marcello family home was massive.

"Passcode, please," a robotic voice commanded from the speaker Gio was talking in to.

"Seven, two, six, nine, five, five," his uncle replied.

"Please speak your name clearly for voice recognition."

"Giovanni David Marcello."

The speaker buzzed for a split second before the gate shuddered and began to open automatically. Gio pulled the car through the opening the moment the vehicle could fit through. It never failed to amaze John how careful and protective their family was about keeping their private lives hidden from public view. He understood, of course, but it was still amusing.

"Voice recognition?" John asked. "When did Antony have that put in?"

"A year ago."

"Why?"

Gio stilled in his seat. "Just because, I suppose."

"Are you being purposely difficult, or what?"

Quickly, Gio put the car in park at the mid-way point on the driveway between the gate and the house.

"He put it in because he's not young, John. He's eighty-seven, and he doesn't like to be reminded of the things he's not capable of doing at his age. He's not quick on his feet, his eyesight is terrible, and he wants his wife to feel safe."

"What happened to the guard he had?"

"You'll see," Gio muttered as he put the car in drive again. "Just don't say anything to him about his age or the changes. It bothers him and then Cecelia gets pissy."

"I got it."

"Good."

John found the guard in question the moment the front entrance to the Marcello home was in full view. Dressed in all black, the man rested beside a dark sedan with a cigarette in one hand and a gun at his waist. John knew the man had to be the guard because no one else was permitted to smoke in front of the Marcello home. They had areas designated for that sort of thing.

"He's keeping him closer," John noted.

"Yeah."

"Any particular reason why?"

Gio shrugged. "You can never be too safe."

Why didn't John believe that?

"Hey," Gio said quietly.

John gave his uncle a look. "Hmm?"

"You good?"

"Yeah."

His tension was still there, dancing hand in hand with his anxiety. Three years in lock-up was a long time to be gone. How many things had changed since he'd went to prison? How much more distance had he forced between him and his family in that time?

Gio turned the car off and put his hand on the door handle. "For the record, John ..."

"What about it?"

"I thought you made the right choice three years ago."

John's brow furrowed. "I don't know what you mean."

"When your father bribed the judge with the option of an institution or jail time. I thought you made the right choice."

Well, that was not what John expected to hear.

"Why is that?"

"Because despite how irrational everything you were doing seemed to be, I don't believe for a second that any hospital in the country would have sorted you out like prison did. Thirty days in an institution with a couple of therapists, new meds, and little else wasn't what you needed. Time was what you needed, John. You still got the doctors, you got the meds, but you also got the break. You made the right choice."

John let out a slow breath. "Who else feels that way?"

Gio laughed. "I know what you're asking without outright asking it."

"So?"

"Your mother is probably at the front door about ready to blow it down and come out here."

John nodded, knowing his uncle wasn't going to answer his question. "I better get my ass in the house before she comes out."

"Yeah, probably. I bet your father is waiting, too."

"We haven't talked a lot since I went in."

"All you had to do was pick up the phone, John."

John glanced at the mansion. "I know."

"Lucian thinks you made the right choice for you. In case you were wondering."

"I wasn't."

"Lying is a terrible habit, Johnathan."

It was.

But John was too damned good at it.

• • •

"Oh, *il mio ragazzo!*"

John barely heard the words come out of his mother's mouth before he was engulfed in tiny arms that squeezed him nearly to death. For such a tiny thing, his mother was strong as hell. She literally knocked him off balance forcing them both to spin in a half circle, so they were facing the front door and not the large entryway like before.

"Hey, Ma," John said, letting her crush him for all she was worth.

Gio grinned as he strolled on by.

Asshole.

He could have helped John a little. Physical expressions of emotions and John had never mixed well together. Not unless he was the one doing the expressing. And when he physically expressed emotions, it usually never ended well for anyone involved. Mushy, lovey nonsense didn't do very damned much for him, either.

Jordyn squeezed her son harder. "I missed you."

"You saw me a few months ago, Ma."

"So?"

John bent down when Jordyn finally loosened her grip around his chest and gave his mother a quick kiss to the cheek. "So nothing, Ma. I missed you, too."

Jordyn's face lit up with happiness.

Guilt stabbed at John's insides.

He didn't verbally express his feelings very well, either. He felt a lot of shit, and that was just the by-product of his disorder. Processing, understanding, and communicating his inner thoughts and emotions was difficult. It had clearly been too long since he'd given any affection to his mother if her joy over a simple admission was any indication.

"Liliana couldn't make it down from Chicago with Joseph," Jordyn said as she fiddled with John's crooked tie. "She tried, but she couldn't get out of the shifts at the hospital."

Liliana, John's younger sister, had married a man involved with the

Chicago Outfit. John barely remembered the wedding, as he'd been right in the thick of his manic episode.

"But she's coming down next month," Jordyn added.

"Lucia?" John asked.

"She's here," his mother said about his youngest sister.

"And Cella?"

John's other sister, also married but to a man who was unaffiliated to the mob, had never been very close to him. He wouldn't be surprised if she hadn't shown up for his welcome-home-slash-birthday party.

"She's here, sneaking food while everyone else waits to eat," came a darker, familiar voice from behind John.

Jordyn took a step back from her son. John spun on his heel only to come face to face with his father.

For John, it was like looking in an aging mirror. As he grew up, almost everyone he knew felt the need to point out how much he resembled his father. A twin, they said. Hazel eyes that matched John's looked him up and down. His father smiled a little, making the sharp lines of his features soften briefly. Even at sixty, Lucian Marcello stood tall and straight, matching John's height at six feet, three inches tall. Lucian commanded a room with his no-nonsense demeanor and his blunt attitude. He could also be intimidating with his quietness and watchful eye.

"Son," Lucian greeted.

"Hey," John replied.

"You look good."

"I hope so."

"Seems prison has its benefits, hmm?"

John let the comment roll off his shoulders, knowing his father hadn't meant it as an insult. "I think it did for me."

"How was the drive?"

"Long," John answered.

Lucian chuckled. "With Gio, any drive is long."

"He talks a lot."

"That he does." Lucian jerked a thumb over his shoulder. "As I said, Cella is here and sneaking food. We're letting it go what with the pregnancy and all. She has to feed the baby."

John cleared his throat. "I didn't know she was pregnant."

"Phones work, John, even in prison."

Ouch.

That comment didn't roll off like the first one did.

"Lucian," Jordyn said, coming to stand beside her son. "Don't."

Lucian's jaw tightened before he frowned. *Mi scusi*, I'm sorry. That was out of line, son. I'm happy you're home. We all are."

John wished he could say the same, but for a split second he was back to feeling like the outsider in his family again. No one in particular made him feel that way directly, but the disconnect he experienced with his own father made everyone else seem distant, too.

"John!"

The shout of his name drew John's attention away from Lucian.

John stiffened when his cousin, Andino, moved past his uncle with a wide grin. Andino stood toe-to-toe with John. Before the incident that landed John in prison and nearly took Andino's life, the two cousins had been inseparable.

Ride or die, their family said. Because the two cousins always found trouble together. They had always been close, best friends even, and one mistake ruined it all.

At twenty-eight, Andino was the closest cousin in relation to his own age that John had.

"Jordyn," Lucian said with a pointed look in his wife's direction, "… why don't we go let everyone know that the man of the hour has arrived."

"Sure," Jordyn replied.

With a squeeze of her hand on John's arm, his parents disappeared.

"It's good to see you, man," Andino said.

John smirked. "And you, *cugino*."

Andino grinned at the Italian word for cousin. "I would have made the trip up to see you, but I wasn't sure if that was good for you."

"I wouldn't have turned you away, Andi."

Andino held out a hand.

John passed it a wary glance.

"John?" Andino asked.

"Yeah?"

"We're good, man."

Just like that, three words ripped away the concern John had about his friendship with Andino.

"Are we?" John asked.

Andino didn't drop his hand. "Family first, John."

John shook his cousin's hand. Home started to feel a little more real. The distance keeping John and his emotional attachments to his family at bay began to close.

"I hope you don't mind a crowd," Andino said.

John cocked a brow. "I never do."

"Good, because the whole damn city might as well be here to welcome you home."

"Seriously?"

"Open invitation to anyone in *la famiglia*, man," Andino said, chuckling. "I don't think anyone refused it."

Huh.

• • •

"I have to start looking for a place," John said.

Andino took a drag off his cigarette, and eyed his companion in the Lexus. "I told you that it was all right if you stayed with me for a bit."

"I like being alone, Andi. It's not about you."

"Fine. You've only been home a couple of days, John. Give it a bit of time. You've got a lot of adjustment to do. Work in to it all slowly. You don't have to do it all at once."

John disagreed. He wanted to get back to his old routine of things as quickly as he possibly could. Part of that was not being under his cousin's watch all of the damned time. It wasn't Andino's fault because the man was just following orders. But John felt suffocated all the same.

"I still need to find my own place."

Andino tossed his nearly finished cigarette out of the window. "We can do that."

"Good."

"So hey, I've got to handle some business over at one of my restaurants. Are you interested in coming or do you have things to do?"

John shrugged. "I've got shit to do."

"I'm not giving you my car."

Laughing, John said, "I don't need it, asshole."

But he did need to get his own and soon. It was in the works.

"I'll take the bus," John added. "The warehouse is only a couple of blocks from here."

"Careful and clean, right?"

John glowered. "Back off."

"I'm just making sure."

"It's on the up. It's your goddamn guys I'm working with."

"I know," Andino said. "But not all of those fools are good, either. I'll see you later."

John climbed out of the Lexus without another word to his cousin. As Andino pulled away from the side of the road, John strolled down the sidewalk to where the bus stop was and waited. Less than ten minutes later, a bus heading straight into the heart of Hell's Kitchen pulled over, and John stepped in the vehicle.

Pulling out a phone from his pocket, John dialed his father's cell phone number as he walked toward the back of the bus with his eyes on the ground.

"*Ciao*," Lucian said when he picked up John's call.

"Hey, Dad."

"John."

13

"I'm not going to make it for dinner. Give Ma my apologies."

Lucian sighed heavily. "Why not?"

"Business in the Kitchen."

Technically, it was a lie. He didn't have to work today if he didn't want to, but he needed something to do other than be under his cousin's watch. John simply didn't want to go through another round with his parents and their concerns. He needed space and time to breathe. He needed to be his own person without everyone else's worries and influence.

His parents didn't understand.

"Breakfast tomorrow then," Lucian said.

"I—"

"It's not a request, John," his father cut in harshly. "When you flake on your mother, I expect you to make it up to her."

"Fine, tomorrow."

"Good."

Lucian hung up the call before John could.

Shoving his phone in his pocket, John took the first seat he could. Glancing up from his clenched hands that rested in his lap, he came face-to-face with sapphire eyes.

John blinked.

The woman smiled.

She had a tablet in her hands and one earbud in her ear. A messenger bag rested at her feet, drawing John's gaze down to the leather boots she wore. Skinny jeans showcased the length of her legs and the curve of her hips. He didn't recognize her, but something about her was familiar.

Tucking a strand of her caramel-toned curls behind her ear, the woman met his gaze again. His mouth went dry and he didn't have the first clue of why. Maybe it was because he'd spent three years in prison, and the only females he'd had contact with since he got out were family.

Or maybe it was because the girl was fucking beautiful.

Every part of him knew it.

"Hi," she said, still smiling.

"Hi." John grinned back. "Johnathan Marcello."

"*The* Johnathan Marcello?"

John chuckled. "There's only one alive in this city, as far as I know."

The woman's smile turned wider. "Siena."

"Like the city in Italy?"

"Just like that," she replied.

"A last name?" John asked.

"Calabrese. It's very nice to meet you, John."

Shit.

CHAPTER TWO

JOHNATHAN'S EYES widened, and Siena grinned at the sight. Surprise looked good on the man. His confident smile earlier had sharpened his strong jaw and chiseled cheekbones, and made her think, *I bet he could kill a woman with that smile. Stop her heart with a look, and restart it with a wink.*

The surprise, though?

That took his sexiness, and turned it almost boyish in a blink.

"You didn't know who I was?" Siena asked.

"Marcellos don't tend to … mix a lot of business with the Calabrese family." Johnathan's confident grin took over once more, and his gaze traveled over her form. "You must be Matteo's daughter."

"One of a few," she replied.

Johnathan cocked a brow. "I only know the Calabrese boss to have one."

"The three illegitimate ones don't get much recognition in the family."

Across from her on the bus, Johnathan cleared his throat.

"Ah, I see," he said.

So was the way of their life.

Nobody ever said being a *principessa della mafia* was an easy thing. In fact, it was one of the most suffocating things to be. All the rules and expectations that never ended. Having a Cosa Nostra boss for a father—and high-ranking brothers—left a young woman like Siena under their control and demands.

She was used to it, now.

Twenty-five years dealing with it all had done that to her.

"Kind of strange to see a Capo riding on a city bus," Siena said.

"And what do you know about Capos, *donna*?"

The way he called her woman, and his hazel gaze drifted down over her jean-clad legs left a heavy feeling thumping in her throat. Siena was used to men staring—a byproduct of having taken after her exceptionally beautiful, but cold, mother. She wasn't, however, used to a man like Johnathan doing it.

A man connected to the mafia. One that might face punishment from her father or brothers for disrespecting their family name by treating one of their women in any way that wasn't honest and pure.

Like she was some angel.

Or a saint.

Siena was *none* of those things.

She quite liked the way Johnathan was looking at her.

"Well?" Johnathan asked. "What do you know about the business, huh?"

A lot.

More than he probably thought she did.

Siena simply said, "Do you think I shouldn't know who is who when it comes to the Three Families in New York? Wouldn't that be a little dumb of me, considering who my father is and all?"

"Fair enough."

She mentally patted herself on the back for dodging that bullet. After all, one who dealt in the business did not discuss the business.

It was a rule.

Siena's father repeated it to her a little more often than he did to everyone else. She figured that was because she was a woman, and no made man in the mafia wanted other *Mafiosi* to know a woman was handling business.

Especially ... numbers.

"Isn't it always black cars, and ten under the speed limit for Capos?" Siena asked.

"For some, maybe." Johnathan chuckled. "My car is still in shipping somewhere between the Rust Belt and here."

"But is it black?" she asked.

Johnathan smirked. "Possibly."

"And do you drive ten under the limit?"

"Possibly."

"I knew it," Siena said, winking. "So, for now you're slumming it on a bus, then?"

"I don't mind the bus. I get to be around people without actually engaging with people."

Siena lifted a single eyebrow. "Is that a shot at me—I shouldn't be engaging you, or something?"

Johnathan's grin deepened, and he looked her over once more. "Nah, I don't mind engaging you, Siena."

"It's just a shame my last name is Calabrese, huh?"

He waved a hand, and said, "It is what it is."

Johnathan looked out the bus window, and stayed silent for a few moments. As the bus stopped to let more people on, and a few off, Siena took the chance to take Johnathan's profile in. A lax, easy smile. Strong lines shaped his jaw and cheekbones. A single dimple in his right cheek peeked out whenever his grin deepened. His bottom lip was slightly fuller than his top, and his olive complexion spoke of his Italian bloodline.

He had to be at least six-foot-three, or taller when standing up. The black suit he wore looked cut perfectly to his form—a lean, yet fit, form. The diamond incrusted Rolex on one wrist, a leather band embossed with something on the other, and black leather shoes gave credence to the wealth the Marcello family had.

Everything about Johnathan screamed handsome, bad news, and entirely interesting to Siena. His good looks certainly couldn't be denied, and his last name—without needing him to confirm or deny—was enough to tell her he was probably mixed up in *la famiglia*.

The interesting bit, though, was a little harder to explain.

Other than how he looked at her?

Something different from how his dark grin made her pulse quicken?

Maybe it was because the Marcello family kind of felt like an enigma to her. She knew they were real, and heard enough about them to respect how they controlled New York. Yet, at the same time, the Marcellos were also illusive. A crime organization just like her father's, but one her family only whispered about over the years.

Johnathan was, essentially, one big mystery.

Just like his family.

Straight, thick brows gave him a disinterested expression, except when he turned his hazel gaze on her. The cool, calm demeanor of Johnathan Marcello was shattered when someone got a good look at his eyes—a wild, lost man stared back.

Johnathan glanced away from the window. He caught Siena staring at him like a foolish girl, but she didn't look away.

"Yes?" he asked.

Lying really wasn't her forte.

She wasn't very good at it.

"You're very handsome, Johnathan," she said.

Those dark eyes of his flashed with something unknown before he said, "I prefer John."

"John."

"Yeah."

"What I said remains the same, John."

Siena was not usually so bold. Daring statements like those to a man like Johnathan could possibly get her in trouble, all things considered.

Still, she said it.

It had to be said.

He arched a brow. "Why did you call me *the* Johnathan Marcello earlier?"

Siena cleared her throat. "You're a little infamous, aren't you?"

"Me?"

"All the Marcellos, really."

Johnathan nodded. "I suppose."

Then, the bus came to another slow stop. Johnathan glanced out the window, and cussed before he stood up. His back was already turned to her, and he was heading for the door when he looked back over his shoulder.

All over again, with one single look, Siena's heart thumped hard in her throat. A rhythm that intrigued and frightened her.

How did he do that by only staring?

Why couldn't she control her own body?

"Maybe I'll see you around, *bella*."

Siena stilled.

He'd called her beautiful.

"Maybe," she agreed.

Johnathan didn't hear her.

He had already exited the bus.

• • •

"You're late."

Matteo's voice boomed over the bustling Brooklyn restaurant. Siena's father was a lot of things, but overwhelming was highest on the list. He towered over her mother who stood next to him at the table, and was wide enough that Siena's arms couldn't reach all the way around him when she hugged him.

"Traffic was bad," Siena told him. "Hi, Dad."

Matteo scowled at her when she stepped back. "Taking the bus again?"

"I like the bus. It's ... responsible."

And it gives me a little less time with you.

She didn't add that last part out loud.

Siena knew better.

"You have a brand new Lexus sitting in your apartment's lot," her father said, shaking his head full of dark brown hair, although it had started to thin a bit at the top. He didn't like for anyone to point it out. "I bought you that car for you to do your business, and get to places *on time*, Siena."

"Oh, leave her alone, Matteo. So, she likes the bus, who cares?"

Siena's mother—Coraline—smiled sweetly at her daughter. She returned the smile, but hers wasn't as honest or wide.

Sure, she loved her parents.

They had given her life, after all.

The two were still … difficult. Siena had grown up as the afterthought in her parents' lives. Her brothers, Kev and Darren, had always taken center stage with Matteo and Coraline. Siena, on the other hand, had simply been given direction and restrictions. Rules she was meant to follow with no questions asked, and a set path in life chosen by these two people in front of her.

It certainly left her with a bitter taste.

"Because riding a bus with the money she makes is undignified," Matteo said.

"Or economically and fiscally smart," Siena put in.

Matteo passed her a look, and narrowed his gaze. "No, I told you what it is."

Yes, undignified.

Heaven forbid she ride the bus with the rest of the lowly people. She might catch their poor people cooties, or something.

Siena had all she could do not to roll her damn eyes. Matteo wouldn't like that, either. Respect needed to be shown at all times when it came to her father. He expected nothing less from his children.

At least that was one thing she had in common with her brothers where their father was concerned. Matteo treated them all equally in that respect. One of the only fucking things.

"Sit, sit," her father demanded with a wave at the table.

Matteo didn't bother holding out a chair for Siena, but he did for his wife. Siena pulled her own chair out, and sat down. She was hoping this lunch with her parents would be over quickly enough because she had a million other things she'd rather be doing.

Coraline reached across the table to tap the napkin in front of Siena. "You'll be staying a while—act like it, sweetheart."

Damn.

Siena picked up the napkin, flicked it open, and set it on her lap. At least the place had decent food, and that would make this lunch slightly more bearable. For now, anyway.

Matteo waved at a waiter who was handling another table. At the sight of her father gesturing for him, the man instantly left the couple whose coffees were not yet poured, and came their way.

So was the way of Matteo Calabrese.

He did not like to wait, or be left waiting.

He did not like to be ignored.

He was king of the room, always.

Luckily for her father, Matteo owned this particular restaurant. Actually, he owned quite a few businesses, and so did Siena's older brothers. Between restaurants, clubs, used car dealerships, a couple of barber shops, pizza joints, a laundry mat, and a pub in Manhattan, they had more businesses than they knew what to do with.

None of the men in her family seemed particularly good with numbers unless it included counting up their profits for the month. Taxes were a thing to be avoided at all costs. Every single nickel and dime needed accounted for at the end of the day.

Given how they used their legal businesses to hide their illegal profits from the criminal side of their lives, her father and brothers needed someone good with numbers. Someone who could scrub books clean, and hide dirty cash.

They needed her.

Siena was … exceptional with numbers. She could take a business's books, hide a couple of hundred grand in dirty money through different receivables accounts, and push the cleaned money straight out the other end.

It was the one thing she could do that her brothers could not. It was the only reason why Siena suspected her father hadn't tried to force her into some arranged marriage to get the responsibility of her off his hands.

After all, a girl was only useful if she wasn't useless.

Without numbers … without her talent of scrubbing books for her father's Cosa Nostra, that's all Siena would be. Entirely useless to the men in her family.

It gave her a little bit of control. She had no problems running with it every chance she could. It wasn't her fault if Matteo and her brothers couldn't see that she was manipulating them sometimes to get what she wanted.

"Mr. Calabrese," the waiter said with a smile. "Good afternoon, sir."

"Yes, yes, I'm ready to order now."

"Pen's ready, sir."

Like always, Matteo ordered for himself, his wife, and Siena. Had her brothers been there, he would have ordered for them, too.

Anything her father could control, he did. Even if it was something as simple as what they wanted to eat for lunch.

"Shoo," Matteo told the waiter with a flick of his wrist. "I'm hungry."

"Yes, sir."

The young man—who didn't look old enough to be serving liquor, likely—darted off, and headed right for the kitchen. He didn't even go back to the table where the couple was still waiting with their still-empty coffee cups.

"New boy," Matteo told Coraline. "I like him so far."

"He seems quiet," her mother agreed.

"For now."

Then, Matteo turned his dark eyes on the phone he had pulled from his inner jacket pocket. Just like that, Coraline and Siena were dismissed from the man's attention. Coraline didn't really seem all that bothered, as she simply stared out the window at the passersby on the street.

Siena was never more aware of how much she took after her mother in appearance and behavior than in that moment. Sure, her slyness and attitude came from her father, not to mention her determination to get shit done.

The rest?

All her mom.

From the blues of her wide eyes, to the caramel of her long, wavy hair. Standing side by side, the two only reached five-foot-seven in four-inch heels. Their full lips curved the same way when they smiled, or smirked, and even the button nose was compliments of her mother's delicate features.

The physical appearance was about as far as it went, though.

Coraline was quiet, and quick to bend to the whims of the men around her. Siena was far more likely to find a way out of it, or speak loudly enough for someone to listen.

Her mother was happy in her place, spoiled and content. She never batted an eye at the three daughters her husband fathered with a mistress over the period of twenty years, or the fact that mistress lived in a bigger house than she did.

Siena was not the kind of woman to stick her head in the sand.

She just couldn't.

She certainly wasn't going to turn her cheek, and pretend like the men in her life were some kind of good, godly creatures who gave back to society, and attended church every Sunday. Sure, they did those things— they also sold drugs, laundered money, blackmailed anyone they could, and murder was always at the top of someone's to-do list.

Coraline could pretend all she wanted about her family, and live in her gilded cage of clouds where the bad stuff didn't touch her.

Siena's feet were still firmly planted on the ground.

She liked it here better.

"Don't pull this tardiness nonsense on your brother later," Matteo said.

Siena's attention was back on her father in a blink. "Pardon?"

"Later—you're heading over to Kev's club, aren't you? You've got books to scrub for him."

"Of course."

"Don't be late again. It's rude, Siena."

"I know, Dad. I won't be late."

Lies.

She would make sure to be late.

Besides, she did need a couple of new books to put on her nightstand.

The old bookshop a couple of blocks away from her brother's club sounded like a good place to get lost in for an hour or so.

If she could do it, and get away with it, then what was stopping her?

It was the Calabrese way.

• • •

Siena thumbed through the brand new paperback of a romance she had asked the old shopkeeper to order in for her well over a month ago. Sure, she had an e-reader and could have purchased a digital copy instantly, but she still liked a good old paperback once in a while.

"How long are you gonna caress that book, girly?"

Siena gave Eugene a smile.

Well in to his seventies, Eugene had been supplying Siena's addiction to romance and thrillers since she was seventeen or so. Sometimes, she came in the shop just to help him rearrange shelves, or unload the new releases for the month. He didn't need to be lifting things, anyway. His aged face showed more wrinkles when he smiled, and told the story of his life.

"I'm going to touch it and love it for as long as I want to, thank you," she said, smiling sweetly.

Eugene sighed. "You and those damn romances. You're going to give yourself an unhealthy outlook on men. No real life man will stand up to the kinds of heroes in those books."

Siena shrugged. "My standards are already pretty sky-high."

The man chuckled hoarsely. "As they should be, Siena. You take the book, and have a good day, sweetheart."

"You didn't ring me up yet."

From the other side of the counter, the man winked. "Call it even for you doing my books last month for the quarter."

Siena gave him a look. "Yeah, and I saw how much you're making, too. So, let me pay for the damn book."

"No way. It's all yours. I already paid for it. You thought I would forget, I bet."

"Eugene."

"I remembered your birthday was today. Twenty-five."

"*Eugene.*"

The old man smiled. "You didn't ask for a thing to do my books, girly. Plus, you filed my taxes last year and wouldn't let me pay you for that, either. Consider it payback, and a birthday gift. It's just a book."

"I didn't want anything," she replied, giving him a look.

It literally took her all of an hour to do his books, and twenty minutes to file his taxes.

Eugene shrugged. "The least you could do is allow me to buy you a book—one you've been waiting a long time for me to get. I know you have one of those fancy e-reader thingys. You could have just as easily gotten yourself a copy on that reading thing, and not from me. It's one book. Don't worry about it. Your reading addiction keeps me in business."

Siena knew that was only partly true. She still adored Eugene for saying it. Both sets of her grandparents had died—one after the other over the span of a decade. Before she ever even reached sixteen years old.

Now, at twenty-five, she kind of felt like she had found a stand-in for a grandparent with Eugene. Seeing him once or twice a week made her whole day.

Leaning across the counter, Siena pulled Eugene in for a tight one-armed hug. "Thank you, Eugene."

"Ah, no need for that. You let me know if the book is as good as you wanted it to be, okay?"

Siena tapped the paperback against her palm, and cocked a brow. "Even though you think romance novels are just trashy sex scenes now?"

The old man laughed. "Now, I read some … mostly because you made me, but they're okay."

"Just okay?"

"How about you don't go getting unrealistic ideas in your head about what a real man is, huh?"

Siena nodded. "I won't."

"But make sure he treats you like a queen."

Exactly.

"Got it."

Eugene waved at the door. "Have a good day, Siena. By the way, I know that's a series, and I have already ordered the following two for you. This time, *you* can pay. They should get here in a couple of weeks."

"*Grazie.*"

"*Ciao,*" Eugene replied in kind, butchering the Italian greeting.

It still made Siena smile as she headed out of the bookshop. Eugene didn't need to make her feel special by saving or buying her books, or greeting her the way she greeted him every time she entered or exited his shop. Yet, he still did all of those things.

She suspected he was the one and only reason why people like her kept going back to him, and his bookshop. Because he was so sweet, he cared, and he never forgot to make someone who came into his business feel important while they were there.

The man should have retired years ago—he wasn't willing to give up his shop, though. Never was married, apparently, so he didn't have a wife or kids to pull him away from work and show him the world.

Siena thumbed through the first few pages of the paperback as she headed out of the bookshop. Her attention was fully engrossed in the opening paragraph introducing a CEO heroine getting ready for what was intended to be the biggest meeting of the woman's life.

She was so engaged in the book she had waited forever for, that she wasn't even paying attention to the people blowing by her on the street. It was only a couple of blocks to her brother's club. Kev had texted her four times and left one voicemail asking where the hell she was and why she was late.

Siena didn't bother to respond.

Who else was going to cook and scrub their books?

Nobody but her.

He could wait.

Siena flipped to the second page in the book, and not a breath later rammed straight into something hard. Her book went sprawling to the—thankfully dry—pavement, and landed with the cover up. She stumbled backwards, and almost fell herself.

A dark chuckle and a hand wrapping around her back kept her from hitting the ground as well.

The spicy cologne of the man helping her up was the first thing Siena noticed about the guy. His familiar black suit was the second thing.

She stared Johnathan Marcello right in the face as he helped her to stand straight. He flashed her a smile, showing off straight, white teeth and his charm in a blink.

"Two meetings in one day, huh?" he asked

Siena wondered why her throat had gone tight again. Still, she managed to speak. "Sorry about that. I was—"

Johnathan bent down and picked up her book. He eyed the title and the cover, and handed it over with another brilliant smile. "Distracted, I think. I can see why—the guy on that cover looks like he bathed himself in body oil, or something."

"They do say sex sells."

That smile of Johnathan's turned suggestive in a blink. "That it does."

"It's actually a book I've been waiting forever for," she admitted. "My birthday is today, and the shopkeeper remembered. It's my gift from him."

Johnathan chuckled. "A *gift*, huh?"

"He's old enough to be my grandfather."

"Well, happy birthday."

"Big, old twenty-five," she half-grumbled.

Johnathan scoffed. "*Old*, right. You're five years away from my thirty, and only when you get to there can you come talk to me about old."

"Thirty isn't old."

And he didn't look anything beyond twenty-six, *maybe*.

Johnathan shrugged. "It's all in how you feel, I guess."

Siena didn't believe in shit like fate or any of that kind of nonsense.

Not being a numbers girl like she was. She much preferred to see things in black and white. Reality. Written in stone, not a what-could-be kind of thing.

She wondered, however, what the odds were that she would randomly run in to Johnathan like this again. Twice. In one day.

Should she consider that a sign, or something?

Maybe she could try for a third time to see him, except without it being entirely random. More … planned.

The outspoken part of Siena's personality came forward before she could stop it with trivial things like nerves or anxiety.

"Hey, do you have somewhere—"

Johnathan's phone ringing loudly inside his pocket stopped Siena from asking him to dinner like she wanted. He pulled out the phone, and put it to his ear while he held up a finger for her to ask for a minute.

"Yeah, John here." A beat of silence passed, and then Johnathan said, "All right, man. I'm on my way."

Johnathan hung up the phone, gave Siena a wink, and shoved the device in his jacket.

"Business calls," he told her. "Try looking up when you walk, huh? Gotta be safe, *bella donna*. You don't know the kind of crazy you might run in to around here."

With a wave, John darted out into the street, and didn't give Siena another look.

She hadn't gotten to ask him out.

Maybe *that* was the sign.

Who knew?

• • •

Darren chewed loudly on an apple in the corner chair as Siena strolled into the club's office. You would think, given the kind of private work she did for her family, that they would allow her the privacy of her own office.

No way.

She almost always worked out of one of their offices.

"Late, aren't you?" Darren asked.

Siena shrugged as she dropped in the office chair, and turned the PC monitor the way she liked. "I'm here, aren't I?"

"Kev isn't happy."

Their oldest brother was never happy.

"Kev can chill," Siena said.

A couple of passwords, and one encrypted file later, and Siena had brought up the dirty books for the club. Next week, she would be at another office owned by her family to scrub out and cook those books, too.

It changed a lot.

Her bachelor's degree in accounting afforded her the knowledge of cooking and scrubbing books, but her respect for numbers kept her attention focused and interested. That was what mattered most.

She actually liked doing it.

The numbers in the excel charts were a comforting place for Siena. It was all about balances and checks. Numbers were straightforward, and didn't leave questions behind. Something either added up, or it didn't.

She liked that.

"Oh, so you finally fucking showed up, did you?"

Kev's voice—much like their father's—boomed. It could travel down hallways, and through walls. The men in her family didn't know how to have a quiet conversation if their lives depended on it.

Siena didn't look away from the computer screen as she brought up the accounts receivable and payable for the club. The proper books this time—not the ones she was about to make look proper.

"Got caught up in something," Siena said.

"Something like what?"

Shit.

She didn't want to mention the bookstore to her brothers. The two didn't have any respect or appreciation for things like books and escapism. They only respected and understood the life, Cosa Nostra, and their father.

She decided to deflect Kev's question with one of her own.

"So, I guess Johnathan Marcello is out of prison now, huh?" she asked.

Johnathan's prison sentence had been widely known across New York. It had been in the news, and even his sentencing had been publicized. It was one of the reasons she had called him infamous, though she thought it might be rude to point it out.

Siena peered over the PC screen.

Sure enough, Kev's brow had raised as he shot Darren a look. She mentally patted herself on the back.

"Did you know that?" Kev asked Darren.

"I didn't. How does she know it?"

Both Siena's brothers looked to her.

"I ran in to him on the bus," she said, shrugging.

She didn't mention the street, too.

"I guess we should let Dad know," Kev said.

Siena almost asked why.

She knew better.

They wouldn't answer.

CHAPTER THREE

TWO WEEKS AFTER beginning to look for a place of his own, and John finally had one. Well, he'd actually had it for a couple of days, but today was his move in day.

"All the money you have, and you rented a two-bedroom house in Queens," Andino said.

"Listen, not every fucker is like you, Andi. We don't all want to have the big mansion in Tuxedo Park."

"I don't have a mansion in Tuxedo Park."

"Yet," John shot back.

Andino chuckled. "Truth. You do have too much money to be living in a tiny house in Queens, though. Deny it."

"Money?" John scoffed. "I *had* money. Now I have investments, and a money manager who doesn't allow me very much control, man."

Andino shot John and look, but said nothing. He could still tell his cousin—and best friend—wanted to ask more questions.

"Go ahead," John muttered.

He unlocked the front door of the rental home while his cousin shoved his hands in his pockets. Andino shifted from foot to foot—maybe he was trying to figure out a way to phrase his question. John didn't know.

"Was that by choice, or …?"

John shrugged, and pushed the door open. "I mean, mostly. Do you know how much money I blew through during my last manic episode?"

"No."

"A little under three million."

Andino coughed hard, and looked like he couldn't breathe. "In a few months?"

"Yeah."

"That poor money."

John laughed loudly as they stepped into the house together. "It's one of my behaviors, that's all. Spending money. Hyper-sexuality. Bad decision after bad decision."

"The second one might not be such a bad thing."

"It is when you'll fuck anything that moves just to feel something, Andi. It's just another reckless behavior to add on top of the already reckless behaviors I seek out in an episode."

Andino blew out a breath, and then tossed his jacket to a bare corner. "Yeah, I know. I was just … kidding with you."

His cousin was just about the only person John allowed to kid with him about his bipolar disorder. Anyone else, and he was quick to point out he wasn't the fucking butt of anybody's jokes.

Andino meant no harm, though, and he was always down to help John. Or, keep him out of trouble, even. The two had been that way—ride or die—since they were kids.

"Anyway," John said, waving the moving guys in from the doorway, "now the money manager keeps me on track with everything regarding my trust fund from my biological grandfather. He earns me money, and gives me some to spend. I'm still working with a ten-thousand-dollar stipend every month, plus whatever I make working. He doesn't get that, you know."

"Yeah, it's not clean money, right? Wouldn't want somebody looking too deep in to how you made it, never mind the government getting easy access to documents that showed no taxes paid on it."

"Exactly."

John turned his back to the guys bringing the furniture and boxes in. Some had been in storage while he was in prison, and other things were brand new. Shit he had purchased over the last couple of weeks while he looked for a place.

"You said mostly, though," Andino pointed out.

"Huh?"

Adriano tipped his head to the side. "When I asked if it was by choice about the money manager, you said mostly."

"I recognized I had an issue that needed handling."

"But?"

"Dad threatened to file legal action against me if I didn't do it willingly," John admitted.

Andino flinched. "Ouch."

"Is what it is. So far, my disorder has never been brought into the public record. I don't want people in this life to know that I am bipolar."

"Like a target someone might see and use against you, huh?"

"Essentially. We're all fine and good pretending *mafiosi* are honorable made men, but the truth is a hell of a lot simpler, Andi."

Andino nodded. "We see a perceived weakness, and we exploit it."

"Yeah. Dad knows that, and if it gets him what he wants, he doesn't mind using the idea that my disorder will somehow get into a public record on me to make me do what he needs me to do. Filing legal action against me to take control of my assets or whatever else due to my failing to take care of it myself would absolutely do that."

"John, you know Lucian is only looking out for—"

"I know *why*," John interjected sharply. "That doesn't make it right."

Andino shoved his hands deep in his pockets again. "Point taken."

It was another reason why John held bitterness toward his father, sure, even if a part of him understood it had been for the best. The thing about Lucian Marcello and his only son was that a lot of the time, John was left feeling like his father was stripping the control of his life away from him.

Slowly.

One by one.

A thing at a time.

Or maybe his father didn't want to do that at all, and that was just John's misfiring emotions and brain working against each other again. Who fucking knew?

It didn't take long for the movers to get all the furniture and boxes inside the house. John simply directed them to drop everything in the middle of the large living room. He was so particular about his things and how it all needed to be placed that someone else doing it could send him into some kind of fit.

Anxiety.

Anger.

Sometimes both.

Sure, his meds helped a lot to keep him settled and allowed him a bit more breathing room to think before he spoke or reacted, but it wasn't a whole lot of space. Mostly just enough for him to recognize he might be making a bigger deal out of something than it actually was.

That didn't mean his brain accepted the conclusion, or that the problem still didn't feel *very* real to John.

It was hard to explain that to others. How could he explain something when sometimes, he didn't even know what he was feeling himself?

Andino knew, though. A byproduct of once trying to help John clean up his room as a teenager after his mother, Jordyn, had a fit about the mess.

His cousin looked over the boxes in the Queens house, but didn't touch a thing. He *did* ask.

"Anything you want me to help you with?"

John made a noise in the back of his throat, and scrubbed his hands together. A nervous tic that helped to give him an outlet for his simmering anxieties. "Maybe move some furniture once I know where I want to put it."

"I could unpack some stuff, and just not *put* it anywhere, too."

"No, don't do that."

Andino put a hand up. "All right."

There was something Andino was especially good at that John didn't mind letting his cousin do without looking over his shoulder the entire time.

"I filled the fridge and cupboards yesterday."

Andino smirked. "Still can't cook worth shit, can you?"

"I'm learning."

John tried not to sound defensive, and failed like a fucker. With a laugh and a clap to John's shoulder, Andino headed for the open concept kitchen. He still talked as he began pulling dishes from the cupboard, and then moved to another one where the food was.

"Right, right." Andino sighed loudly. "What is with all this organic shit, John? Haven't you heard of proper butter or sugar?"

"Every little thing helps to keep me at stable levels—diet, exercise, the money manager ... all of it."

"Ah."

John opted to change the topic. "How was Atlantic City?"

Andino kept his back turned to John. "Interesting. A nice break, anyway."

"Kind of surprised the boss let you head out for a couple of weeks when you had business here."

Andino stayed silent.

John didn't miss it.

"Something up?" John asked.

Slowly, Andino turned around at the island so that John could see his face. Like with so many other things that were affected by his disorder, eye contact was a big thing. For those he trusted, he preferred to see their face and look in their eyes when they delivered him any kind of news that he might perceive as bad.

It just *helped*.

John braced for the impact.

"Dante didn't have a choice but to let me take a break," Andino said.

"Shit, rub some of that magic on me because that man keeps riding my ass about everything."

"Don't you want to know why he didn't have a choice?"

"There's a reason?" John asked back, joking.

Andino laughed quietly. "Yeah, uh ... they want to move me up in *la famiglia*, John. The end goal is for me to take control after Dante is done."

Like a boss.

The boss.

A Cosa Nostra Don.

John took in the news, and let it process before he spoke. Not because he felt bad about it, or wondered why. He knew that was the best choice for the Marcello organization. *Andino* was the best choice, for more reasons than John could name.

Seems John would now have something to discuss with his father when he went to have dinner with his parents tomorrow. Their dinners were already stilted because John didn't have a lot to say.

"Okay," John said. "I don't understand what the problem is."

Andino blinked. "No?"

"No."

"A lot of us figured it would be you to do that, John."

Oh.

"Me, too," John said, chuckling, "a long time ago."

"I'm sorry, man."

John shook his head. "They're making the right choice, Andi."

Andino glanced down. "I didn't ask for this, John. I woke up being a very content Capo, and good at what I do. It's what I wanted to do, and they just shoved this at me. Like here you fucking go, so be thankful."

"You're the right choice. You already look out for this family like it's your first job, anyway."

"Family first," Andino said, nodding.

"God is a very close second."

So was the Marcello way.

• • •

"Johnathan."

At the sound of his mother's sweet voice, John's anxiety slipped away. It wouldn't last for long, he knew, but he enjoyed it while he could.

Bending down, he kissed Jordyn's smiling cheek. "Hey, Ma."

Jordyn's blue gaze took a silent inventory of her son. "You look well."

"I looked well when I was here a couple of weeks ago, too."

"Mmhmm, but you don't come over often enough for me to make sure you are always well, John."

"Ma," he said quietly.

Jordyn waved a hand as if to dismiss what she had said. "Never mind. It's just me thinking out loud."

John offered his mother a hand to help her up from the couch. He followed behind her as she headed for the kitchen. His mother's favorite room in the entire house. Despite all her efforts to teach him how to cook, John still sucked.

Jordyn checked the casserole in the oven as she said, "I didn't know if you were coming today or not, but I made you chicken and salad—all organic, John."

He smiled, and moved closer to wrap one arm around his mother's shoulders. He pulled her in for a quick hug because his mother always took care of him even when it was no longer her job to do so.

"Thanks, Ma."

Jordyn patted his cheek. "I know you have problems to work out with Lucian, but won't you come visit me more often? I've gone three years only seeing you occasionally, and it was always behind a Plexiglas window. The least you could do—"

"I will come visit you more often."

Her smile bloomed in to a brilliant sight. "That's my boy."

Thirty years old, and he was still a boy to his mother. He would blame it on the fact they were an Italian family, and the old saying about Italian mothers and their sons, but he couldn't. His mother's heritage sported maybe a twenty percent Italian bloodline—unlike his father's three quarter bloodline.

Still, Jordyn fit the bill perfectly.

"What are we talking about visits, now?" Lucian asked from the kitchen entryway.

Lucian Marcello was not a loud man, but he was a domineering man. He could easily silence people with a look, or make them uncomfortable with a single, soft spoken word. He rarely needed to use threats or violence to scare people, as a promise and a cold smile worked just as well.

Intimidating best described John's father.

Lucian didn't even have to try—he just was.

John nodded at his father, and then headed for the table. "Papa."

"I missed you when you came in," Lucian said.

"I was told not to flake on my mother, remember?"

One of those cool, calm smiles curved his father's mouth. "That you were."

Lucian crossed the kitchen, and dropped a kiss to his wife's forehead. He overlooked the food Jordyn was putting together, and then finally turned back to John.

"I heard Andino was helping to get your new place set up."

"He did."

"Do you think Queens is the best place when you do most of your work in the heart of Brooklyn, or over in Manhattan?"

Instantly, John's defenses started to raise. It wasn't even his father's fault, but their long history of John's choices being constantly overturned or undermined by his father made even the simplest of conversations difficult.

Mostly because John refused to open up another avenue where his father might step in and try to change or control something. Lucian hadn't even implied he thought one way or the other about where John chose to live—he only asked *a question*.

It didn't matter.

John's defenses worked their way up all the same. "I think I have a lot of people and connections in Queens, and some business there, too. It's close enough to Manhattan and Brooklyn. I'm not concerned, and you shouldn't be, either."

Lucian stilled, and eyed John like he didn't quite know how to reply to that. "I only wanted to know how you felt about it, son."

"I feel fine about it, Papa."

"Good. You're liking the house, then?"

John's defensive posture and tone lessened when he said, "It's all right. I grew up in bigger, but I just spent three years in an eight by eight cell, too."

Lucian chuckled. "Anything is better than a cell, right?"

"You could say that."

Jordyn gestured for Lucian to come taste what she held out on the spoon. Thankfully, it took Lucian's attention away from his son for the moment. John was grateful, as it allowed him to take a breath, and settle the rising irritation.

It wasn't his father's fault. Lucian hadn't pushed for information beyond what John had been willing to give. John was simply reactive to these kinds of things with his dad.

Taking his focus away from his father and mother, John realized then that someone else was missing from the table.

His littlest sister.

"Where's Lucia?"

Lucian passed Jordyn a look, but said nothing. John's mother quickly went back to putting together the dishes for supper.

John's youngest sister—the one sibling he was closest to for reasons stemming back to his childhood—still lived with their parents at her age. He tried to make time for her since getting out of prison, but shit kept coming up.

"The last time I saw her was last week after my car finally got shipped in," John said. "I took her out for a drive. She hasn't tried to get ahold of me since."

Which was entirely unusual for his little sister.

Lucian cleared his throat, and came to sit at the head of the table. A seat only reserved for him that no one else was ever allowed to sit in. John wasn't sure if that was something his father demanded, or a rule his mother made up.

It could have been both, knowing his parents.

"Lucia had to work late at the shelter today," Lucian said.

John raised a brow. "You don't sound sure."

"She's been … different lately."

All over again, John's instincts went into overdrive. If it wasn't anger, then it was anxiety. If not those, then concern or defensiveness. Sometimes he cycled so fast between them, or ran through the entire gamut of them all at once that it was hard to keep up.

"Different how?" he asked.

Lucian shrugged. "Don't worry about it, John. I think she's just made a friend, and while I don't approve of him, it will run its course soon enough."

Him.

"Who?"

Lucian sighed. "It doesn't—"

"It does to me. I look out for Lucia. She's the only one of my sisters that lets me look out for her. So, who is it?"

"Well, you would probably know him better than I do, but I've looked in to him. Renzo is his name."

John stilled in the chair. "Renzo Zulla?"

Lucian nodded. "That would be him."

Shit.

A foot solider for a crew John controlled as the Capo. Ren, the guy liked to be called. He grew up poor, and followed the footsteps of his father when it came to running the streets. The guy was nineteen, or maybe twenty.

"I don't know where she would have met him," Lucian said, sounding both irritated and confused at the same time.

"I do," John replied.

His mother looked to him, and so did his father.

"How?" Jordyn asked.

"Me," John said before scrubbing a hand over his face. "We took a drive, and I had some work to do. Ren was one of those things I had to handle. They didn't even talk, though. She never even got out of the car."

"That boy is trouble, John," Lucian said. "I already had one daughter get mixed up with a man that almost killed her, and I do not want another one falling into the same trap. I don't know this young man, but I know he did not grow up in a very good situation. That typically means he wasn't brought up to be a decent man. Hell, maybe he doesn't even know how to be one. I don't know, and I don't care. I just don't want my daughter involved with him."

John didn't need to be told.

Renzo was a street kid that would soon be looking at a prison sentence, or he'd simply serve more time on the streets. So was the way of their life—or rather, Ren's life.

Lucia was not a part of that world.

"I'll have a chat with him," John said.

Lucian cocked a brow. "Do you think you should?"

John didn't even let his defensiveness come out to play this time. "I think if you approach Renzo, he'll laugh in your face. He knows me, though. It's not the same."

"All right."

That was that.

• • •

John thought this part of Brooklyn was a little upper crust for Renzo's taste, but this was apparently where the kid was supposed to be today. Well, calling Ren a kid was a little disrespectful considering the guy's age, but whatever.

Pulling his new Mercedes over into one of the only parking spots available on the block, John turned off the engine. He excited the car, and strolled into the people walking on the sidewalk.

John checked over his phone again—details he had gotten from a friend of a friend about what Renzo's usual schedule was like through the week. It had taken him a couple of days, but John now had sufficient enough information to believe Renzo was in this area of Brooklyn because of his seventeen-year-old sister.

Apparently, the girl attended a private school for the arts in these parts, and Renzo came to visit her every few days. Today was supposed to be one of those days.

John had no idea how Renzo, or his delinquent parents, were apparently paying for a private school for the girl. He also didn't care, as that wasn't any of his business. He simply wanted to let the guy know to stay the hell away from his sister, and nothing else.

Across the street, a familiar sight caught John's eye. His walk slowed for a split second as he did a double take of the woman coming out of an old bookstore.

John didn't think he would see her again after the bus incident, not to mention running in to her right here almost two weeks ago.

Their families just didn't mingle.

Siena.

The woman had lost the jeans, blouse, and messenger bag from the first time they met. Today, she wore a knee-length black dress, suede ankle books, and carried a leather Gucci bag. She seemed caught up in the paperback she held—that was the same as before.

John had shit to do.

A guy to threaten.

A million other things he needed to take care of except Siena Calabrese. The bad blood between their respective mafia organizations should have been enough to keep him on that side of the street. Hell, her grandfather had been the man who killed his biological great-grandfather and the man's family decades and decades ago. That *should* have been enough to keep John away.

He was crossing the busy street before he even knew what he was doing. He flipped the middle finger to a car that was forced to stop to let him jaywalk.

Siena still had her head stuck down in the book when John came up in front of her.

"I thought I told you to watch where you were walking around these parts, *donna*."

Her head popped up, and those cerulean eyes of hers widened. She didn't even try to hide the shock of seeing him again.

"John," Siena murmured.

Now that he was right in front of her, he was able to get an even better look at the body-hugging dress she wore, and the heels that made her legs look fucking fantastic. His gaze traveled over her curves before settling back on her face once more.

"That's me," he said, grinning.

A pretty pink colored her cheeks when she returned his smile. "Any reason you're hanging around this part of Brooklyn again?"

"Business."

Siena raised a brow. "That so?"

John stuffed his hands in his pockets. "That's my story."

"Well, I'm heading to my brother's club for work. I'm late, so I have to go."

No, he couldn't just let her go this time. He was pretty sure the last time they had run in to each other like this, she had meant to ask him out. A phone call hadn't let her finish the sentence. John had to go right after, and he figured it was what it was.

Fate had different plans, it seemed.

"Can I walk you?" he asked.

"I don't know, *can* you?"

Just like that, his job to talk with Renzo was forgotten.

Someone far more beautiful and interesting had all of his attention now.

John chuckled. "May I walk you?"

Siena's smile softened. "You know what, yeah. Sure, John."

He moved into step with her as she headed down the road. Before she could shove the book she had been reading in her bag, he grabbed it out of her hand.

All over again, her cheeks lit up with that pretty pink.

John kind of liked it.

Another bare-chested man looked up at him from the cover, although this time, the guy did have a dress shirt opened, and he was working on tying a tie.

John cocked a brow. "Who knots their tie while their shirt is still open, anyway?"

"Oh, my God. Give me that back." Siena snatched the book out of his hand, and gave him a little glare. "Don't make fun of my books."

"I definitely wasn't. I was just saying that makes no sense."

"Mmhmm. Sure."

"The first full-length paperback I ever read was one of my mother's romances, actually. She was a huge fan."

Siena grinned. "Really?"

"Yeah, I mean, I was grounded, and couldn't do anything. She left it sitting around, so I picked it up and started reading. Took me a week or so to get through it—I was nine or something."

"She never noticed?"

John shrugged. "Yeah, I think she did, but it kept me quiet and out of her hair. You know?"

Siena's laughter sounded like wind chimes. John couldn't help but stare at her while she did it. Her delicate features lit up and natural pouty lips curved with happiness. She was quite a sight like that, he thought. Carefree and beautiful.

The heat that shot through his gut was such a foreign feeling that he didn't recognize it at first. It had been so long since he actually felt attraction and lust together. The past three years had been spent dealing with far too many other things that had very little to do with women, dating, or sex.

It took him by surprise.

"I know you're heading to your brother's place for work," John said, "but do you want to grab coffee or something later?"

Siena's steps hesitated, and the two stopped altogether on the sidewalk. "I—"

John's phone rang.

Just like the last time.

Again.

Fuck.

"Sorry," he told her.

Siena shrugged, and looked away. He didn't miss the flash of disappointment in her gaze, though.

John answered the phone with a sharp, "What?"

"Mr. Marcello, Dr. Goodane would like to confirm your appointment in two hours."

Shit.

John checked his watch, and realized he had forgotten one very important thing today. His therapist. It was one of the many requirements of his parole, not that he minded. A good therapist kept him on track with his bipolar disorder, anyway.

He couldn't refuse. The doctor would have to report a missed appointment to his parole officer. Then, that asshole would get on his ass, too.

"Yeah, I'll be there."

He would just have to leave *right now*.

John hung up the phone, and turned to Siena. Even though he had to go, he was still determined to get her number, and meet up sometime. Three random run-ins had to be a sign of something, right?

"So—"

Siena held up a hand, and stopped John from saying more. "Hey, it's okay. Maybe we'll have another one of these meetings, John."

She didn't give him a chance to say anything before she headed down the street. John was stuck staring after her.

Fuck his whole life.

• • •

John tried to brush off the pissy mood as he headed into the therapist's office. Amelia—a forty-year-old married mother with two teenaged sons whose pictures littered the walls—already sat waiting for him in the chair.

He took the couch across from her.

Twice a week, he had these appointments.

Mostly, he didn't mind.

Today, he did mind.

"John," she greeted.

"Amelia."

Down to business first, he knew.

It was just how she worked.

Amelia looked over the papers in the file. "How's the change in the dose of the Lithium working?"

"The first few days were a bad fog."

"We figured that, though, right?"

John shrugged. "It's still pretty thick most days. The medication fog, I mean."

"It's only been a couple of weeks since we changed the dose, right?"

"Something like that."

Amelia scratched something down to the paper. "I need you to give it some time to readjust, John. Lowering the dose could have bad consequences."

Sometimes, the meds were just … too much. A hazy fog descended over his brain, and took over everything. A single missed pill, or the wrong dose, could send him into a manic spiral within days.

"Yeah, I know," John finally said.

Not that he liked it.

"Every person managing their bipolar disorder is different," Amelia said. "You have to allow the medication time to settle with you, and your disorder."

"I'm aware. Except I was just fine for three years in prison taking only the Lithium. On your suggestion, I've added more medications to that, and all it's done is put me in a fog. I can't exactly be productive when my mind is like looking through frosted glass."

He'd been dealing with this and medications and everything else related to this disorder since he had been diagnosed as an older teen.

It never ended.

"You also deal with depression and anxiety, and the new med change should help with that. We discussed this. It's why we chose the med change."

She said *we*.

Truth was, she decided that.

John went along with it for now. Based on the way the new med regime left him feeling on a daily basis, he couldn't say how long it would last. Sure, some bipolar people needed more than just one med to manage their disorder—he wasn't sure he was one of those people based on his past experience. His therapist had a different opinion, but then again, she had only been treating him since his release, and not since his diagnosis.

Some therapists worked that way—they made decisions on medications, and the patients went along with it until they found the combination that worked. He preferred telling Amelia what worked best for him, and having her work that way.

So far, that's not how this whole thing had gone down.

Amelia rested back in her chair, and said, "For some people, bipolar is just one part of their life. A background thought that they manage with medication and whatever else. So today, I would like to talk about what being bipolar is—and means—to you, John."

Great.

He chuckled dryly, and toyed with the Rolex on his wrist. "For me, bipolar makes up a great portion of who I am. A lot of my relationships had been forged or broken because of this disorder. How I eat is determined by which foods might hinder or help my mood swings. It controls the fact that the first thing I do in the morning is take several pills because I won't remember if they're not the first thing I go to. What else do you want to know?"

"What's it like for you day to day?"

"Depends on where I am in a cycle," he replied.

"And where are you right now?"

"Low."

She raised a brow. "Low as in a depression, or ...?"

"No, just fine. There's low, and then there's low. I only get really low after the mania breaks. I mean, the depression is always there warring back and forth, but it never gets dangerous for me until after a manic episode."

"And how does that usually feel for you—depression *after* mania, I mean?"

"The way depression usually feels. Add in suicidal thoughts manifesting, and you've got depression after a manic break for me."

Amelia didn't seem to miss the bite in John's tone if her narrowed eyes were any indication. "You're not typically this snappy, Johnathan. Is something different? How are you feeling today?"

"At the moment, kind of pissed off."

"Why is that?"

"Your secretary interrupted me when I was trying to set up a date with somebody."

Amelia coughed, and hid her small smile by looking away. "Like a woman, or a business thing?"

"What do you think?"

The therapist sighed.

John knew what she was going to say before she even spoke.

"As good as it may be on the surface that you're trying to get back to a normal routine, you have to remember that you're still getting assimilated outside of confinement, John. I have to remind you that dating or sex or anything emotionally intense like those things could be detrimental to your success outside of prison while you're still attempting to adapt to these sudden changes. You have a history of hyper-sexuality, for one. Given how delicate the balance is while we work on med changes right now, I wouldn't toy too much with that behavior."

He knew she was right.

His disorder could be fickle—and predictable—in that way. Changes in his life, especially big ones, could easily tip the scales and lead him toward another manic cycle.

"I'll keep it in mind," he told her.

"Please do."

It was the best he could do.

Siena was still in the back of his mind, and she didn't seem to be going away anytime soon.

CHAPTER FOUR

SIENA CHECKED the calendar on her phone again—something she did upwards of twenty times a day. Like all the things she had put in to-do slots would suddenly change or disappear. Everything was still there, including the fact she was supposed to be at Kev's restaurant over an hour ago to look over some changes he wanted made to his books.

Also, it was the end of August.

How in the hell did two weeks slip by without her noticing?

She was losing it.

That, or she was too busy to have a freaking life.

Siena headed inside Kev's restaurant, and went to the back offices. She didn't even stop to say hello to her friend that was waiting tables. She didn't have the time.

The restaurant was full, though. The scrape of utensils against plates, and the conversations echoed behind her as she slipped into the back hallway.

Funny.

She worked here at least once or twice a month, but she had never actually eaten at the place. No, her whole life just revolved around which business she needed to be at from one day to the next in order to keep her brothers and father happy.

Siena tried to shrug off the irritation as she stepped up to the closed office door. Normally, she would have knocked if a door was closed. Her brothers demanded that she did for privacy. Not today, however.

She was too busy, and lost in her thoughts.

Siena opened the office door, and headed inside. She was still looking down at the calendar on her phone when someone cleared their throat.

Her head popped up.

Kev and Darren were both staring at her.

So was another guy.

She recognized Andino Marcello instantly. Of course, she only knew *of* the man, and very little else. He usually came to have meetings with one or both of her brothers every couple of months for Cosa Nostra business.

Something about crews, or streets.

Siena didn't really know.

She wasn't supposed to.

"Oh," she said, taking a small step back. "Sorry about that."

Kev cocked a brow at her. "You don't know how to knock today, or what?"

"I'm late."

Darren scowled. "Again."

"How about you two do even half of the stuff I have to do, and then tell me how well you're able to manage your fucking time."

That quieted her brothers.

Siena mentally patted herself on the back.

"I'll just wait outside until you're done," she said.

Kev sighed, and stood from the chair. "No, it's fine. We were going to continue our discussion over a meal, anyway. Better for you to get to work while you're actually here. And don't even think about taking off before the changes are made to the books, Siena."

She resisted the urge to roll her eyes, or tell her brother off. She only opted not to because Andino was there, and it wouldn't lead to anything good for her in the end. One of her brothers would tell their father that she had disrespected them in front of a man from another organization, and she would never hear the goddamn end of it.

All of these rules suffocated her.

It never ended.

Siena moved to the side of the doorway as her brothers moved past her to leave the office. Andino followed behind them. He gave her a tight smile, but nothing else.

She wasn't sure why, but her mouth decided to open up and ask something she had no business knowing. Andino was a Marcello, after all. He would have to know Johnathan. Cousins, or something.

It had been two weeks since she last saw Johnathan on the busy Brooklyn street. She had been so busy that when he got another phone call, she didn't mind letting him rush off even it was the second time he left her hanging.

Sort of ...

"How's John, Andino?" Siena asked.

The man's steps halted instantly.

So did her brothers' in the hallway.

"Pardon?" Andino asked.

"Johnathan. He's like a cousin of yours, right?"

Andino nodded. "He is, yeah."

"How is he?"

"Busy," Andino said, chuckling. "I didn't know you knew him."

She could plainly see the way he probed for information without outright asking her, but she didn't mind indulging him. If only because she was hoping to get a little bit of her own information, too.

"We've run in to each other a couple of times, I guess. Talked a bit."

Andino stuffed his hands in his pockets, and glanced at her brothers who had come closer to them again. Despite how the Marcello man was built, like a linebacker ready to tackle someone, he seemed uncomfortable discussing his family.

Or maybe it was just because *her* family was there. The Marcello and the Calabrese families never did mingle beyond business.

Bad blood.

That shit didn't wash out.

"The last time we talked, he had to run off," Siena said, shrugging. "I just wanted to make sure he was okay."

Andino cleared his throat, and smiled again. "He's good, Siena. Thanks for asking."

"Siena, get to work, huh?" Kev clapped Andino on the shoulder, and directed him past Siena. "And mind your damn business, *donna.*"

She heard her brother's warning loud and clear, and chose for now, to heed it.

What else could she do?

Once all the men had disappeared down the hallway, Siena headed into the office. She closed the door behind her, and locked it seeing as how she didn't need or want her brothers interrupting her.

She was a good thirty minutes in to reworking accounts for the restaurant's books, and the numbers were already starting to bleed together. A knock on the office door made her pop her head up from the PC screen for the first time.

Thankful for the break it would take to get up and unlock the door, Siena shook her wrists and cracked her neck as she stood. She figured it would be one of her brothers on the other side of the door, but it wasn't.

Andino Marcello stood there.

Hands shoved in his pockets.

A cocked eyebrow.

Smile gone.

The politeness he had shown her earlier seemed to be entirely gone. His warm gaze now felt cold as he looked her over.

Siena's gaze darted over his shoulder to check for her brothers. Neither Kev, nor Darren stood there with Andino.

"They're busy—having a smoke in the back," Andino said, flashing a smirk. "I don't smoke. At least, not with them."

Siena wasn't sure why exactly, but the way he sought her out like this did not feel friendly at all.

"What can I do for you, Andino?" she asked.

"Step inside," he said.

When she didn't move as quickly as he wanted her to, Andino simply put a hand to Siena's shoulder, and moved her inside the office. He kicked the door closed behind him, and completely ignored her indignant shout.

Siena hit his hand from her shoulder, and glared at him. "Who in the hell do you think you are?"

"What do you want with my cousin?"

She blinked. "What?"

"Is it your brothers—your father, maybe? Did they put you up to engaging with John, or what?"

Siena shook her head, so confused that it wasn't even funny. "We sat across from each other on the bus, and then randomly ran in to each other on the street a couple of times outside the bookstore where I get my books."

Andino sucked air through his teeth. "That all?"

"What the fuck is it any of your business?"

He moved closer—just an inch.

It was enough to make Siena take a step back.

"It's my business because I look out for John. I've had his back since we were kids. He doesn't have very many people thinking about his interests, so I make sure to be one of them. Got it?"

Siena swallowed the lump that had formed in her throat. "Okay, I got it."

"What else was there?"

"Nothing. We had a walk, chatted a bit, and he asked me to go for coffee once, but we didn't. Seems like he's always running off and leaving me hanging, you know?"

Andino simply stared at her for a long while before he finally said, "And no one has said anything to you about John, or the Marcellos?"

"No." Siena's gaze narrowed as she added, "You heard my brothers— I ask anything, and I get told to mind my fucking business. I just wanted to make sure John was doing okay. Friends *can* ask after friends."

"You don't know my cousin from a fucking hole in the ground, girl. How can you be his friend?"

"Maybe I would like to be," she shot back.

Andino tipped his chin up, and continued eyeing her in that intense way of his. It made her want to move back again, or fidget. Something.

"He keeps running off, you said?" Andino asked.

Siena shrugged. "Kind of. I don't think he means to. I've never even gotten his number, or whatever."

"Maybe he didn't want to give it to you, then. Ever consider that?"

Ouch.

She ignored that jibe.

"I did *only* want to check up on him," she said. "I didn't mean any harm."

Andino cleared his throat, and took a step back. It was enough to let the office feel like the large space it was when his imposing presence wasn't taking up a lot of her fucking air. Christ, the man was something else.

And for Siena?

That was not a good thing.

"How about I help you out?" Andino asked.

"How?"

The man grinned. "John works out of a club every other weekend. For specific people, it's just easier to find him there than to make him run for them. Not a lot of people know that he's been using that spot to do his business occasionally. His next weekend working at the club should be in a couple of weeks, if you're curious."

"And what does that mean for me?"

"You show up—only you, girl—and maybe you'll get more than five minutes with him."

"Just me."

"I don't trust your family. No Marcello does."

Siena pursed her lips in an effort to hide her frown. "Not even me?"

"Not while you still have that last name, anyway."

It was not as easy to let that insult roll off her shoulders, but she tried.

"Which club?" she asked.

Andino smiled, and this time, it was warm.

• • •

Siena was fifty pages into her new novel about a mercenary hero and heroine thrown together by circumstance when a knock on her apartment door interrupted her. She had all she could do not to glare at the door from across the living room.

The few minutes she was allowed to sit down and relax, and someone had to come over. It wasn't like she had a lot of friends or anything, and her brothers barely wanted anything to do with her unless it related to work somehow.

"The door is unlocked," she called out.

Siena went back to her book.

However, she eyed her father as he slipped in her apartment. Matteo practically swallowed the space with his large stature. His dark gaze looked over the place, and then skipped to where his daughter sat with a book in her hands.

"Don't you lock your door?" he asked.

"Why would I?"

"Because it's safer, Siena."

"Safer for whom?" She smiled sweetly. "Pretty sure if someone wanted me out of here for whatever reason, they would just break it down, Dad."

Matteo clicked his tongue at her. One of his many signs of annoyance or disappointment. "This is what you do with your free time—read?"

"Reading is good for the brain."

She didn't bother to add how reading also helped to shut off her brain when she spent eight or more hours a day looking at numbers, and falsifying them. Being a bookkeeper and accountant was only made harder by the fact that every book she opened, she had to scrub it clean, and cook it up.

It added more work and time.

Matteo came closer, and seemed to be peering at the cover. "There's a half-naked man on the cover. What is that garbage?"

"It's not garbage. It's a romance."

"Mmhmm."

"He's a mercenary."

"That so?"

"Apparently. What do you want, Dad?"

Might as well get right to it, she thought. For the three years she had lived in this apartment, she could count on one hand the amount of times her father had come to visit her. Typically, her mother came over a couple of times a month, but Matteo never joined her.

Besides, Siena spent enough time with her father through the week when she worked. Him and her brothers.

She didn't need more time with him.

"I can't visit my daughter?" he asked, taking a seat on the couch beside her.

"You don't typically make an effort to, no."

Matteo chuckled, and the force rocked them both on the couch. "Perhaps I'm making an effort to do just that, Siena. Your mother is always telling me how there's more to you than the numbers in your head."

She side-eyed her father, and doubted every single word he spoke.

She still kept quiet.

Matteo continued talking, anyway. "Besides, you *are* my daughter. My only—"

Siena couldn't keep quiet at that statement. "You have three daughters with Joy Kennedy."

The reddening of her father's cheeks almost made her grin. She held it back, but still took great satisfaction at the sight.

"Yes, well, I meant my only legitimate daughter," Matteo grumbled.

"I'm sure Ma appreciated that when she found out about the other ones."

"We're not talking about that right now, Siena."

No, they never did.

Another rule to add to the pile.

Nothing was discussed that her father didn't approve. That absolutely included his mistress, and the children she birthed him.

"As I was saying," Matteo muttered heavily, giving her a pointed look, "you are my daughter. I don't think I need a reason to check in with you every once in a while. Do I?"

Siena was desperately trying to focus on the words in her book, and not whatever information her father had come here to pry out of her. That's the only reason she figured he was there. Her lack of focus on the book made it difficult to ignore Matteo.

Besides, if she pissed him off, he would just make the next couple of weeks a living hell for her when it came to work.

He was not very sly in that way.

"I guess so," she finally said.

Matteo smiled, and patted a beefy hand to her knee. "Good. How about you go make me a coffee?"

Great.

Bookkeeper, and a server.

Perfect.

Siena tossed her book aside with a soft sigh, and stood from the couch. Her father followed behind as she headed for the kitchen. With the electric kettle turned on, she kept her back turned to her father as she pulled out instant coffee, sugar, and a mug from the cupboard. At least this way, she figured her father might get the hint that she was not up for conversation.

Apparently not …

"I wondered if maybe you would be out tonight," he said behind her.

Siena stiffened. "Why would I be out?"

"You're twenty-five. Surely you have friends, and you like to do things. Don't most girls your age?"

"Haven't you told me for basically my whole life that idle hands and bad behavior would only shame you and the family?"

Matteo chuckled darkly. "That I did."

"I don't go out very much, Dad."

Mostly true.

"No friends, either?"

"A couple."

"What about men?"

A knot of tension tightened around Siena's spine. She tried not to show how uncomfortable the question made her as she turned around to face her father.

"Like dating?" she asked.

Matteo nodded. "Exactly that. Are you seeing someone?"

"Would it matter if I was?"

"I should think it would be my business if you were," he replied.

"Yet, I'm not."

"At all?" he pressed.

Siena's gaze narrowed. "Where is this coming from, Dad?"

Because it all screamed strange and odd to her. It wasn't like her father to care much about her personal life as long as she kept it quiet, and private. As long as nothing she did brought shame to her family, then he never spoke a word about it.

After all, he wanted a compliant, easily controlled daughter. Much like how he preferred his wife, too.

Matteo waved a large hand. "Your brothers mentioned maybe you were dating, and I thought I should ask."

What?

When would her brothers—

Siena's thoughts slammed together with a heavy realization. All she did was ask about one single man in front of her brothers, and the first thing they did was run to her father with the information.

Like a bunch of assholes.

She was, however, planning on seeking Johnathan Marcello out in a week at the club he apparently worked out of every other weekend. She even made sure to clear things off her schedule so that nothing would be taking her away.

Siena was not telling her father that, though.

Andino had been clear.

Her family was not welcome.

"I'm not seeing anyone," she told her father. "At all."

"Do let me know if that changes," Matteo said, grinning.

With that, her father moved away from the small island, and headed for the door. As though he were completely finished with their conversation. And now had better things to do that did not include being there with her.

"What about your coffee?" Siena asked.

Matteo looked over his shoulder as he pulled open the door. "I'm not really in the mood to stay and chat longer."

Yeah, she hadn't thought so.

He had only come to pry information out of her.

But why?

Why?

Siena filed the strange encounter away in the back of her mind, and decided it was probably nothing.

For now, anyway.

• • •

Despite the name of the club, Heavy Metal had very little to do with scream-o music or hard rock. Siena figured that out the second she stepped inside the joint. The reflective lights and metallic accents left shimmering colors cascading over her body-con red dress, and the matching four-inch stilettos on her feet.

The bouncer at the front of the club had only nodded at her when she mentioned being there to see a Marcello, even though she hadn't technically been told to do that by Andino.

Whatever.

It got her through the door.

Siena kept a firm grip on the red clutch in her hand as she weaved in and out of the moving people. The flickering lights and bass pounding through the hardwood floors made for quite an experience.

She wasn't really a partier.

Clubs weren't her thing.

She did kind of like this, though.

Siena found herself moving toward the bar while her gaze scanned the crowd for a familiar face …

For John.

The bartender came down her way, and tossed a rag over his shoulder. With a warm smile, he asked, "What can I get for you, pretty girl?"

Siena smiled. "Something light."

"I can mix you up something virgin, but it'll look like the real thing if you want really light."

"Sure, do that."

It was a couple of minutes before the guy came back with her drink. As she paid for it, Siena thought to ask, "Do you know where Johnathan is by chance?"

The bartender cocked a brow. "Marcello?"

"There's only one, right?"

"That there is. He's usually upstairs in the VIP, or working out of an office. Either way, you won't find him on the floor."

"Thanks."

"Just tell the guys guarding the entrance that John asked for you, and they'll let you through."

Siena laughed. "Even if he doesn't know I'm here?"

"Only one way to find out." The bartender winked, adding, "And I bet

he won't say no to your pretty face."
Well, then …

CHAPTER FIVE

ANDINO PASSED John a subtle nod as he handed his cousin a glass of what would look like vodka to anyone else watching. Around the table tucked in the back section of the VIP area of the club, the two were working out a deal with a local gang leader who had been encroaching on their territories.

Capos had to talk a lot to make shit work, especially on the streets. Business could not always be done through bloodshed. It drew too much attention, and left them wide open for retribution. A good Capo could get anything done that needed handling with a few words, and a drink.

Or, that's how John had learned the business.

The gang leader—Maverick—took the second glass Andino had been holding with a nod, and thanks. Maverick held the glass up to John, and he did the same with his own, clinking the two together.

A peace offering.

After three years of lockup, it felt damn good to get back into business. Being a Capo—even if he did have other Capos looking over his fucking shoulder—was what he did best.

"Pleasure doing business with you, Johnathan," Maverick said.

John tipped his glass up for a drink, and smirked. "And you."

The two men sipped their drinks, although John's was nothing more than water. He didn't drink—or usually—as it wasn't good to mix alcohol with his meds.

Only a select few people knew that, though.

Andino was one of them.

John quickly finished his water, and set the glass to the table. Maverick followed along, and finished his own drink as well.

"So that's settled then," Johnathan said.

Maverick stood from the table. "Seems so. You'll supply, and I'll buy from only you."

"Keep that agreement, and you won't need to see us again."

"We wouldn't be as nice the second time," Andino added.

The gang leader gave a single nod in response, held up two fingers, and gestured at his men waiting a few tables over. With a quick goodbye between the three men, Maverick headed for the exit with his three men flanking him from the sides and behind.

John and Andino's two enforcers came closer damn near instantly. Their empty glasses on the table, and the one Maverick left behind, were picked up by the enforcers, and removed.

"Thanks," John said to Andino.

His cousin grinned. "For what, man? You handled that on your own. I don't know what the hell Dante is worried about with you. I wasn't even needed here tonight."

John chuckled. "Tell him that."

"I will."

He didn't doubt his cousin.

"I meant, thanks for the water," John said.

Andino shrugged a single shoulder, and shoved his hands in his pockets. "I've always got your back, John. Even when you don't know it."

John gave Andino a look. "Not really your job, though."

"Still going to do it."

"What about when you don't have the time anymore, huh?"

Andino's gaze narrowed. "Like fucking when?"

"How about when you're the boss, and have a whole organization to manage? You don't need to be worrying about me when that happens, Andi."

"Yeah, sure, but—"

"No buts. You work on you—make sure you are where you need to be in this organization, Andino. I'll handle me."

Andino scoffed, but clapped John hard on the shoulder at the same time. The two stood at the same six-foot-three height, yet Andino had a good thirty pounds of muscle on John's lean form. Still, he had never felt like the lesser when it came to his cousin. He appreciated Andino for that more than anything else.

"Man, even when I am looking out for me, I am still going to be looking out for you," Andino said, shrugging. "I don't know how to do anything different. Not after everything."

John knew Andino was telling the truth.

He wished he knew how to tell his cousin that it would be okay, one way or the other. It wouldn't matter. Not to his cousin.

Andino was going to do him, and that meant looking out for anybody he gave a shit about.

John included.

"Speaking of looking out for you," Andino said quieter.

John glanced at his cousin. "Pardon?"

"I ran in to somebody—looks like she listened to me."

"What are you talking about?"

Andino pointed over Johnathan's shoulder. He turned to see the sight of Siena Calabrese being escorted across the VIP floor by one of Johnathan's enforcers. The man stayed close to her side, like if she moved out of step, he was ready to grab her.

John hadn't expected to see her.

Especially not *here*.

"I figured that was fucked—finished," John said, more to himself than anyone else.

Andino cocked a brow. "What—her? I ran in to her when I had to handle some business with the Calabrese brothers. I hate them fuckers."

"Yeah, but no. I meant, I kind of ducked out on her. What did you do?"

A sly smile and another clap on John's shoulder accompanied Andino's next words. "She asked about you when I ran in to her. Kind of figured you must have made … an impression."

John cleared his throat. "Not really supposed to be dating."

Or fucking.

Or *anything*.

His therapist made that clear at every appointment. He was supposed to give it time, and work on getting himself straightened out and on the up before he worried about anything else. For good reason …

Relationships, women, and sex were intense things for John. When he mixed all three together, it could be one hell of a hurricane for him.

A good hurricane.

Damn, so good.

It could be a bad one, too.

"Who said anything about *dating*?" Andino asked like the word tasted bad in his mouth. "Have some fun, John. That's all."

It wasn't that simple.

John actually had an interest in Siena Calabrese. Her and those sweet smiles, the romance novels she always seemed to have, and her soft-spoken demeanor. It was only a little bit about her, but he liked it.

There was a lot about her he didn't know but wanted to, as well.

The two quieted as the enforcer finally approached with Siena at his side. She flashed John a blinding smile. He was so caught up in the way she looked at him, that he barely noticed the fact she was wearing a dress that showed off all her curves, and heels that made her legs look … fan-fucking-tastic.

Painted red lips.

Hair in curls.

Blue eyes lined in kohl.

All club and ready to dance.

She was not the same woman he had met on the street, and yet she was exactly that person, too.

"Siena," the enforcer said, jerking a thumb in her direction, "said she was told to come see you here tonight, Skip."

Siena glanced at Andino, and then back to John.

John waved a hand at the enforcer to make him scatter. The man went back to his post without a word.

Andino cleared his throat, and picked his jacket off the back of the chair. "John, I will see you … tomorrow, or something. I have business to do."

Sure you do.

John didn't really mind.

"Nice to see you again, Siena," Andino added as he passed her by. "Thanks for following directions."

"And you," she said quietly.

Then, they were alone.

Not entirely alone, as the VIP area still had a few other people partying, but no one was paying them any mind. For a long time, Siena and John simply stared at one another. He broke the silence first.

"I can't decide if you are out of your element, or not," he said.

She flashed him a smile.

Sexy and pretty in a blink.

How in the hell did she manage that?

"This is a little new for me—a club, I mean," she said.

John grinned. "That so?"

"Yep."

His gaze traveled up from her heels to her delicate features. He didn't hide his staring, and she didn't act like it bothered her.

John liked that *a lot.*

"That dress says differently—like you might know a bit more about this kind of place than you let on," he said.

Siena winked. "Guess you'll have to find out."

He laughed, loud and hard.

It had been too long since he laughed like that.

Way too long.

"I do owe you a coffee," he said.

"Coffee in a club?"

"I don't drink."

A beer once in a blue moon, but even that wasn't usual.

She didn't even blink.

She didn't ask a thing.

Instead, Siena said, "I know a place down the block, if you want to go?"

John's hand on her lower back led them both out. He left his anxiety about the rest at the door.

• • •

"Here," John said.

His fingers circled around Siena's small wrist to stop her from walking further. The cool September air had mixed in with the nighttime breeze, and made him think the thin sleeves of her tight dress were not enough to keep her warm.

"What—"

He already slipped his suit jacket off, and tossed it around her shoulders before she could protest, or say anything. He fixed the collar a bit, and the tips of his fingers grazed her collarbones peeking out.

John didn't miss the shiver that raced through Siena at the touch. He didn't think it was the cool breeze that time.

Her blue gaze stayed locked on him, even after he let her go. She didn't move to start walking down the sidewalk again, either.

"You didn't have to do that," she whispered.

John chuckled. "Sure I did, *bella*." He glanced down at the heels on her feet. "Let me know if your feet get tired because I don't mind helping you out there, either."

"And just how would you do that?"

"Carry you."

Siena stilled on the spot, and peeked up at him through long, dark lashes. "You're kidding, aren't you?"

"No."

Not in the least.

"Oh," she said softly.

"I don't mind."

She sighed. "You know, your cousin is kind of scary."

"Who, Andino?" John let out a laugh. "He's a fucking teddy bear."

"If by teddy bear, you mean a teddy bear built like a linebacker with the attitude of somebody ready to take you out, then sure."

John barely held back his smirk. "Really, he's harmless."

"Not if he thinks someone is trying to mess with you."

John sobered instantly. "Yeah, he doesn't play there. What did he say to you?"

Siena shrugged under his jacket. "Basically demanded to know what I wanted with you."

"Because ...?"

"I asked about you?"

He liked how she posed that as a question.

"You don't seem sure," he said, giving her a look.

"That's all I did. Like I said, kind of scary."

John shifted from foot to foot, and glanced down the quiet sidewalk. "And what do you want with me, huh?"

"Not really sure."

When he looked back at her, she was still staring at him. Not like she was looking for something in his eyes, or anything. No, she was just there … with him.

Present.

Curious.

It was a strange feeling for John.

And definitely not something he was used to.

"Are you really interested in coffee?" John asked.

Siena shook her head. "Not really, no."

"So, I can assume you came looking for me tonight because you're interested in something else."

"You can definitely assume that, John."

Well, then …

He didn't get the chance to reply because Siena pushed up on her tiptoes, and kissed him. It took him all of three seconds to snap out of the shock, and act. He did just that by wrapping an arm around her back, and grabbing her jaw. He pulled her closer, felt her soft lips grin against his, and just like that …

John felt alive again.

Kind of like when he met her gaze that first time on the bus.

When she blushed …

Siena's lips parted at his tongue teasing against the seam, and he got his first taste of her. A heady sweetness that reminded him of cherries and vanilla. Wicked and pure.

John would have happily stayed like that with her on the sidewalk, until he remembered where exactly they were. Siena's tongue peeked out to touch her bottom lip as he pulled away.

Her lips curved sweetly, while her blue eyes flashed with something that spoke of sex and sin. It was such a juxtaposition. A contrast that took him by surprise each time she did it.

John's thumb stroked her cheek. "So what did make you come find me, then?"

"I thought … why not do something different?" Siena asked. "Besides, how many more times do we have to run in to each other before we get a chance to actually finish a conversation? Kind of leaves a person wanting more, doesn't it?"

"It can."

"Like I said, I'm just doing something different. Giving us another option, if you want to put it that way. If you don't run off tonight, maybe we'll actually be able to have one of those conversations, John."

He didn't think she meant *just* talking. That wasn't a bad thing. Not at all.

"Oh?"

"Mmhmm." She gave him a look. "You seem unsure, John."

"It's been a long time for me—for something like this, I mean. Maybe I'm a bit rusty."

"About three years or so, huh?"

"How did you know that?"

"Infamous, remember?"

John nodded, and let out a dry laugh. "Yeah, that."

"I don't do this often, either," she admitted.

"No?"

"Nope."

John wet his lips. "I live in Queens."

Siena smiled. "I live five blocks away."

"Do you feel better with your place?"

"I would, actually."

John's hand rested just above the curve of Siena's ass as they began walking back in the direction they had come. He would be needing his Mercedes, now. Siena tucked tightly into his side the whole way.

• • •

"You're not second-guessing being here, are you?"

Siena's soft question drew his attention away from the window overlooking the street below. Her Brooklyn apartment was about as big as he expected it to be, given the area. Clean, though, and meticulous in organization.

He liked that.

John found Siena sipping on a glass of water just a few feet away in the space between the open kitchen and living room. She had discarded his jacket, and her lips were back to their unpainted pink.

Compliments of his kiss.

She started it.

He didn't want to stop.

Siena's fingertips edged along the hem of her short dress, and his gaze followed the path. A flash of creamy, shapely thighs, and his heart raced all over again.

His dick got hard, too.

Fuck, it had been *way too long.*

"Definitely not second-guessing anything," he told her.

Siena grinned, and hooked a finger at him. John took her silent gesture for what it seemed like, and came closer until he could take the glass from her hand. He set it aside on a small table beside the couch.

"I need a little help," she told him.

"With what, *bella mia?*"

Siena tipped her head to the side. "Getting this off."

John laughed a husky sound, and nodded once. He didn't mind helping her out with that at all.

It wasn't just her mouth that tasted like sweetness and sin, he learned. It was her jaw, too. The curve of her shoulder as he dragged her dress down. The spot where her spine met the back of her neck, and the dimples right above the swell of her ass. Skin so fucking soft, he couldn't stop touching her. Hair like curled silk when he drove his fingers in it.

A mouth meant to be put to use.

Sucking him.

Kissing him.

Begging him.

Siena's soft breaths echoed in John's ear as his lips ghosted over her jawline again. In just a couple of quick minutes, he had her standing in nothing but pink lace. In that same time, his mouth and hands had touched damn near every inch of her.

There was still so much more he wanted to find, too.

Explore …

Taste …

Darkening blue eyes met John's gaze, and Siena's bottom lip quivered when he tipped her head up to stare straight down at her. All it took was that one look—a silent, needy stare—that broke the haze for John.

Three years dry didn't make a difference then.

All he felt was need. A deep thrumming hunger that *burned*. A want so strong, it made his fucking bones ached.

Just because of the way she looked at him.

"Tell me you know how beautiful you are, Siena."

She blinked, but her lack of words said what she wouldn't.

"That's a shame," John murmured. "You are by far the most beautiful thing I have ever seen."

Another one of her sexy, sly smiles curved her lips. "Smooth talker."

"I don't do *smooth*."

"No?"

"Was never really my thing," he admitted. "I don't ever say things I don't mean, and sometimes that's the damn problem with me."

Siena swallowed hard. "Good to know."

"You have to tell me what you want next. It's only you calling the shots, sweetheart."

"My bedroom is the last door down the hall, John."

Good enough.

"Is there a condom in there?"

Because fuck him for not having one.

"A brand new box of six," she said, shrugging her naked shoulders. "Like a just-in-case, except just in case never actually happened."

He'd make sure the box was empty before morning came. Time to make up for, and all that.

John kissed Siena hard—harder than before, and yanked her to him with crushing force. She only sighed a happy sound, and parted those sweet lips of hers to silently ask for more. He didn't stop kissing her, or touching her, until they hit the bedroom floor.

Her hands worked far faster than his had to get rid of his clothes. They fell to the floor, forgotten, as her fingertips traced the hard lines of his naked abdominal muscles. With each touch, his nerves reacted. That wild feeling grew—the need he tried to shut off like it was a faucet of running water turned on, and cascading down.

A rush of feeling.

John just tipped his head back, and let her touch. He needed to let her explore. It was only when those teasing hands of hers slipped beneath his boxer-briefs that he look back down at her. Her fingers circled his hard dick—tightening and stroking, soft, yet fast.

"Christ," he grunted through clenched teeth.

"I bet it'll feel way better when I'm on my back, and you're inside me," she whispered.

Fuck.

"Yes to all of that."

Hell fucking yes.

Siena let him go just long enough to dig through the nightstand. Soon, she had a foil packet in her grasp, before she was tearing it open. He was the one to shove his boxer-briefs down and step out of them, but she rolled the latex down his cock.

John pinched her chin between his forefinger and thumb, and tipped her head back. Soft strokes of her hand circled up and down his length as he kissed her one more time, and then pushed her back to the bed. He climbed between her thighs, and hovered over her.

A kiss to her smirking lips.

Then her trembling chin.

Down over her throat.

Between the valley of her breasts still covered in pink lace.

The lower he went, the more she shivered. Those little breaths of hers picked up when his tongue struck out just below her navel.

"What other sounds do you make, *donna?*" he asked.

"Guess you're going to find out, John."

He grinned against her skin.

Yeah, he liked this woman a lot.

More than he probably should, considering her last name and all.

John's teeth nipped into her hip, and then he bit into the waistband of her panties. Siena let out a little squeak when he let the panties snap back against her skin. Just as fast, he bit into them again, and started pulling them down. Once they hit the floor, and all he could see was her bare, pink sex as she widened her legs, any desire he had to wait to prolong this was useless.

He couldn't do it.

She flashed her pussy at him, all wet and waiting, and he was done for.

John was back between Siena's opened thighs before she had blinked. Her hand guided him home, and he took her with one hard thrust. There was no hesitation to the way her pussy took him all the way in.

A wet, warm heaven.

Soaking him.

Hugging him damn tight.

She became like morphine to him, then. A shot of a drug he was addicted to, and hadn't gotten a good dose of in far too long. He was the fucking fiend in need of what she was supplying.

Those little breaths of hers turned in to gasps when he pulled back, and thrust in all over again. Those gasps turned in to the neediest moans when his hand slipped between their bodies to toy with her clit as he fucked her.

Siena's head fell back, giving him access to her throat, but it also let him see what he was doing to her. The way pleasure wrote heavily in her eyes, and in the shape of her lips when his name fell from her mouth.

So beautiful.

He hadn't lied.

She was perfect.

Her song when she came out high and broken with only his name. "*John, John, John.*"

She was like an ocean, he thought.

Like his mind sometimes was—large, wide, deep, and dangerous. Something he could get lost in, and something amazing to see. Frightening, too, but also too alluring to stay away from.

She could be the ocean.

He didn't mind drowning.

• • •

John listened for any sounds coming from Siena's bedroom as he dug inside the suit jacket he had discarded the night before. She was sleeping soundly, but he still took great effort not to make much noise while he searched for his pill case.

Just in case he wasn't home in the morning, he liked to bring along a smaller case that took care of his morning meds. Lithium, an anticonvulsant, and Zoloft. The final pill he set out on the counter was a mood stabilizer to keep the Zoloft in check with the rest of the pills. Sometimes one pill needed another pill to counteract the emotional or mental side effects it could have by mixing one with another.

Depending on the state of his current cycle, John's meds needed to be changed accordingly. He had become accustomed to knowing which meds he needed depending on where he was in his disorder. Any antidepressants during spells of depression meant no mood stabilizers, and no Lithium as they severely worsened and darkened his moods and thoughts to dangerous levels.

His new mix of meds—compliments of the therapist he had been seeing since his release—however, continued to leave him in a fog that he couldn't escape from.

Sometimes, it was a delicate balance. A balance that could easily be upset by things like a change in dose, or a new pill. Other times, it was an emotional upset that just couldn't be contained for whatever reason. Just like that, his balance would be tipped in a bad direction, and it only went downhill from there.

John had learned over the years not to fear that downhill slide. He could go months without having any kind of episode, be it manic, depression, or a mix of the two. He'd gone years without experiencing one once, but eventually, it would happen. Another manic cycle would start, and the mania festered until it got worse and worse.

It could be days.

It could stretch on for a couple of weeks.

Months.

And then the mania broke, and all John was left with was a blinding, crippling depression that coated his mind with blackness and dark thoughts. A depression that took all the euphoria-like feelings from the mania, and exhausted him emotionally and physically.

Still, he didn't fear the cycle.

He couldn't.

Not when it was just who he was.

Those four little pills he set out on Siena's counter—ones he took every morning—were just one of the many things he did to keep his disorder balanced. Despite his reservations about the new med regime, he opted to give it a fair try like the therapist wanted him to. There was still so much more to managing his disorder, too.

Medication. Diet. Exercise. Therapy.

Everyday.

Over and over.

Yet, he felt shame.

People heard bipolar and thought *crazy*. They thought, *highs and lows*. No one realized how much bipolar could vary between person to person. Or they looked at him like he was unstable, and might freak out any minute. The stigma around his disorder, and mental health in general, left him feeling very alone.

No one understood.

He didn't know how to explain it.

He couldn't be just Johnathan Marcello to somebody once they knew his little secret—he then became Johnathan who was bipolar.

That was every reason why he made sure to get up when it was still early enough for the sun to be down. Then, he wouldn't have to explain to a woman he had just spent the night with—but fuck, actually *liked*, too— why the first thing he had to do was slam back a cocktail of medications.

He couldn't be just John to Siena then.

He would have to be John and his bipolar.

It was selfish, sure.

Part of his therapy was being honest, and open about his disorder. Especially when it came to people he got involved with on an emotional level. Explaining his disorder and opening up to them was supposed to be healthy, and erase the stigma.

He often felt like it did the complete opposite.

Grabbing a glass out of the open shelf above the sink, John half-filled it with water. He scooped the pills up all at once, and tossed them back. A mouthful of water, and the pills were down. Some of them left a bitter taste behind if he let them linger too long on his tongue, so he just downed the bastards as fast as he could.

Breakfast, he told himself, looking around.

Food was also needed for some of the meds. They didn't mess with his stomach as much when he chased the pills with a meal, or even toast.

John didn't think Siena would mind waking up to breakfast, considering she had asked him to stay. Breakfast was one of the only damn things he could cook particularly well, too. It was a win-win all the way around the board.

He was still searching through the cupboards to find the things he needed to make pancakes when his cell phone rang.

Shit.

John damn near leaped over the table to grab his cell phone, and answer the call. It was still too early to be waking somebody else up because of his nonsense.

He put the phone to his ear with a, "Yeah, John here."

"Son, where are you?"

John stiffened at his father's voice, and the question. "What do you need?"

"Nice deflection, but I didn't miss it."

"I'm out."

"It's five in the damn morning."

John tried to keep his tone low and calm while he spoke. "I'm aware of what time it is, Dad. What do you need?"

"Somebody went over to your place this morning to grab you, but you weren't there. I need you to come to Amityville now."

"To your place, or the boss's?"

"Dante's."

Something was wrong. Nobody got called to the boss's home at this early in the morning unless something had happened.

"Dad—"

"I'll explain it when you get here," Lucian said. "I think it would be better to do face to face, all things considered."

Hesitation and concern slipped down John's ramrod-straight spine. He didn't like what he was hearing, or how defensive it made him feel. Like he couldn't be trusted or something with whatever his father had to say.

It wouldn't be the first time Lucian withheld things from John simply because he thought it was the better option. Sometimes, he understood why his father did it. Either way, every time it left him feeling the same thing.

Like his father didn't believe in him.

As though Lucian thought John was too unstable.

Again, John … who was bipolar.

That fucking circle was vicious.

"Just tell me what's going on," John said. "I'm kind of in the middle of something …" *To say the least.* "And I don't want to skip out unless it's important.

"You know that if one of us calls you and says something, it is important, Johnathan."

In the background, John heard his uncle, and boss, say, "Lucian, you need to trust your son. Explain to him what's going on because he asked."

Silently, John thanked Dante for stepping in like that. His boss didn't need to do that, but sometimes little things went a long fucking way.

"Lucia is gone," Lucian murmured.

John turned into a statue on the spot.

Cold.

Hard.

Unmoving.

"What?" he hissed.

"She took off last night—I thought maybe me and a few men could go out after them and bring her back before morning, but I misjudged how capable that young man is."

"Renzo," John said.

Just to be sure ...

"Yes," Lucian replied. "So, I need you to come here so we can—"

"I'm not going there at all."

In an instant, John's mind was made up, and his choices were done. He had gotten the chance to warn Renzo not to mess with his little sister, but the young man had just smirked at John, and walked away.

The Lucia and Renzo mess had been on-going for a good month now. His sister knew her parents didn't approve of the young man, but she didn't seem to want to back off. After John had privately approached Renzo, his sister practically cut off all contact with him, too.

She was supposed to be starting college in California for the second semester soon. She was smart girl—the good girl.

What in the hell was going on?

Fury slipped through John's veins.

"She's eighteen, though," Lucian put in, "and that makes things difficult."

"Not for me," John said. "I'll find her, and she'll be returned home."

And him.

John would find Renzo, and fix that issue, too.

Lucia was twelve years younger than John, but she was still the only sibling he had that actually gave a shit about him. His other two sisters barely spoke to him, let alone looked at him when they had to share a space.

Years of his disorder manifesting into outbursts, vicious words, broken walls, and spewed hate had ruined those relationships. He didn't blame Cella or Liliana a bit for how they felt regarding him.

But Lucia?

Lucia was not the same.

"John, you don't have to—"

"Yes, I absolutely do," John interjected, stopping his father from saying anything more. "Lucia trusts me more than anybody, and I know Renzo, his streets, and his people. I will find them. I will call you when I do."

John hung up the phone without another word. He quickly set the glass he used in the sink, and wiped down the counter.

Just like that, his mind had shifted.

He had a new task.

Things he had to do or wanted to do were shoved out to let the most important problem at the moment take over. That was just how his brain worked.

He shrugged on his jacket over his still-unbuttoned dress shirt as he stepped in the doorway of Siena's bedroom. She was still sleeping, and quite soundly.

He should have woke her up.

He should have said goodbye.

He didn't leave his phone number because he figured he would be back that night, or shit, at the most, a couple of days. An explanation later, and everything would be fine. Siena would understand what had happened.

After the night they had, surely she would know he hadn't just left her high and dry.

He should have left a note.

He should have … done a lot of things differently.

Problem was, his mind simply didn't work that way. It jumped from thing to thing—this to that—and he either got back to it, or he didn't. Siena was the same; she couldn't be any different.

John didn't realize, or even consider, that the next almost three weeks of his life would be spent chasing after his runaway sister, and her delinquent boyfriend.

A couple of days, he could have explained.

Three weeks?

John knew better.

He fucked that up.

He should have said goodbye.

Hindsight was always twenty-twenty.

CHAPTER SIX

SIENA KNEW SHE was alone before she even opened her eyes. Maybe because each time she had woken up the night before, Johnathan had been holding her. Or even, pulling her closer, and into him.

Now, nothing held her.

And she was cold because of it.

She was so accustomed to waking up in an empty bed that the feeling should have been comforting. She didn't mind being alone, usually. It was mostly okay.

On this morning … it wasn't.

Not at all.

Sure enough, when she opened her eyes and glanced over, she found the space Johnathan had occupied was now nothing but mussed sheets and a forgotten pillow. A pillow with an indent where his head had rested while he slept. For a long while, she just stared at the space, and did nothing. She didn't know what to do.

She wanted to give him the benefit of the doubt, sure, but a small piece of her knew better despite the hope in her heart.

Maybe he hadn't run off again.

Without an explanation.

For a third damn time.

The sheets still felt warm when she reached over and ran her palm over them. As though maybe he had only gotten up recently, and his heat still remained on the cotton. Another whisper of hope to bury into her heart, but would likely be ripped away all too soon.

She was a realist.

She dealt in black and white.

Still, a part of her held on.

A part of her hoped.

Johnathan's spicy scent still clung to the blankets … and her. The smell of sex still lingered in the room, too. The feeling of his kiss still lingered on her mouth, and down her body where he'd spent far too much time kissing every single inch of her. As though she was the most beautiful thing to have ever graced his presence, and he needed to show her just how much.

It had definitely happened.

They had happened.

Except where was he?

She sat up straight in the bed, and used the bedsheet to cover her from the chest down. Not that there was anyone around to see her nakedness. Not a sound echoed from outside her bedroom.

Like she needed another fucking reminder.

Something akin to sadness stabbed in her chest when she looked for the clothes Johnathan had shed the night before. Her bedroom floor now only held what remained of her club dress, and the lace panties he had taken off with his teeth. Nothing of his were anywhere to be seen.

Fuck.

The contented thrum echoing through her veins—the kind of satisfaction one could only get from great sex and a hard sleep—should have been enough for Siena. It should have kept the anger and sadness at bay about having to wake up alone.

Still, she felt those things.

Still, she wanted to give him a chance.

Maybe he was still here.

Maybe he was somewhere in the apartment.

Siena got out of the bed, and snagged an over-sized sweater hanging off the dresser. One of her favorites for the colder months. She slipped it over her head, and sunk her arms in the sleeves. Folding her arms over her chest, the coldness slipping over her skin ebbed a bit as the sweater gave her a different kind of homey warmth. She needed everything she could get at the moment.

She didn't even bother to grab a clean pair of panties as she stepped over her crumpled dress, and forgotten things.

The sweater covered her ass, and that was enough for her to be satisfied. At least for the moment.

"John?" Siena called out.

Nothing and no one answered her back.

The apartment was still empty, although colder than it usually was when she spent time in it alone as she typically did. John was nowhere to be found.

All over again, Siena felt those stabs of anger and sadness.

A heavy sensation settled in her gut.

She'd thought, surely, their conversations and connection was not only felt by her. So why was she alone?

Why was he gone?

He hadn't left a note.

Nothing with his number.

No way to contact him unless she chose to seek him out again. Siena wasn't interested in that, not this time.

She found him once.

She would not be doing it again.

This was on him.

Siena Calabrese was not the kind of woman who continued chasing after a man who clearly did not want to be caught. She was not the type.

Who fucking knew if Johnathan was even worth the trouble?

Not her.

And he definitely wasn't worth the trouble when he pulled shit like this.

Her sadness swelled.

The anger grew flames.

Three strikes and you're out, John.

Siena went back to bed.

• • •

October ...

• • •

November ...

• • •

It was only the month of December that time actually began to slow for Siena. Or rather, the week of Christmas. Everyone just ... relaxed.

Finally.

It was just too bad that slowing down meant she had to spend more time with her family. It was the price she paid for less work.

Of course, it also reminded her of just how lonely she was considering all she had was the family that didn't feel very close at all.

She grabbed the rope of fir garland Coraline held out for her, and hung it the way her mother liked along the banister.

"Kind of late getting some of this up, aren't you?" Siena asked.

Coraline waved it off. "I didn't have much help."

Siena frowned. "You could have called me over, Ma."

"You're very busy, Siena."

That was true, too.

"Still ..."

Coraline flashed her daughter with a wide, brilliant smile. It was her mother's best defense, and one of her few distractions. Anything could be made better, or ignored entirely, with a single beautiful smile.

"You're here now, and the Christmas party will be lovely because of it," her mother said.

"Sure, it will."

Siena seriously doubted her mother's annual Christmas party would be any better or worse despite her presence, but she didn't argue the point. Whatever kept her mother happy and pleased, or so their father liked to say.

Usually a nice fur coat or diamond was enough to keep Coraline happy.

Or a good party.

"What did you get your father for Christmas?" Coraline asked.

Siena worked on weaving another fir garland through the banister. "A custom-made watch from the jeweler he likes."

"Is it ready?"

"I have to pick it up in a couple of days," she said.

"Cutting it close, Siena."

Like she needed to be told.

Christmas was only five days away now. The jeweler was cutting it terribly close.

"And your brothers?" her mother asked.

Siena gave her mother a look.

Coraline laughed as though she knew without needing to be told. "Money, then?"

"Money," Siena echoed.

It was the only thing her brothers loved more than their father, after all.

"Oh, you did that wrong … Here, give it to me." Coraline took the rope of garland, and shooed Siena up a couple of steps with a single wave of her hand. "It has to wrap around the top like this, Siena."

"Yes, Ma."

She wasn't even paying attention.

Everything she had already done, her mother would redo, anyway.

So was her life …

"So, have you been seeing anyone lately?" her mother asked.

Siena instantly said, "No."

She didn't consider mentioning Johnathan. She hadn't spoken to him since that night two months ago when they slept together. He didn't leave her with a way to contact him, and she left the rest up to him.

The whole three strikes thing, after all. He hadn't contacted her again, and he didn't try to seek her out.

Siena figured that spoke for itself.

Despite the way it hurt at first—rejection always hurt—the pain ebbed. She threw herself into work, and forgot the darkly grinning man with his lost hazel gaze.

She clearly hadn't been anything to him.

Why would she let him be something to her?

If only shit was that easy.

It never was.

"Shame," Coraline said. "You're going to be a lonely woman for the rest of your life at the rate you're going, Siena."

"Ma."

"I'm just saying. Why don't you go check on your father and brothers for me?"

"For what?"

"See if they would like a drink," her mother suggested.

"They can get their own drinks, Ma."

Coraline shot her a look. "Not in this house, Siena."

Great.

"Sure, Ma."

Men were the kings.

Women were meant to serve them.

Or, that's what her mother liked to believe.

Siena didn't wait on her brothers and father outside of this house, but if it gave her a chance to get away from her mother for a minute, she would do it. At least it gave her an excuse not to see every single one of her decorations redone.

The party was still a couple of hours away yet. She wouldn't be able to blend into the people until the house was full, and her parents stopped looking for her.

Same with her brothers.

"Nothing, you're sure?" she heard her father say down the hallway.

Siena headed to the kitchen where Matteo was discussing something with her brothers at the table. Like always, Matteo sat at the head of the table while her brothers sat on the right and left sides.

None of them paid her much attention other than a look.

Her father did make sure to say, "Make us coffees, Siena."

Like she had come in there to do anything else.

"Well?" Matteo asked. "Nothing?"

"Nope, nothing," Kev replied.

"And the one was definitely …" Matteo trailed off, and then said, "You know what I mean?"

"Yeah," Kev said. "It was definitely that."

Siena stayed out of their conversation as she made coffee just the way the three liked. A little bit more milk for her father, an extra sugar for her oldest brother, and all black for Darren. The three continued talking like she wasn't even there as she stirred the coffees.

"Maybe it's not a matter of not wanting to, but being unable," Darren said. "You know, the logistics or shit."

"Unlikely," Kev replied. "Just considering how it was, man. Think about it."

Darren made a noise under his breath. "True."

"Can we not safely say we have passed the point of perhaps something being in the way? Perhaps it's more like Kev thinks, and it's done. We missed our chance to see something come of it."

Business.

It was always business in their house with the men. They never took a break, and didn't care who was around to listen.

Business was always the first discussion to have.

She wasn't surprised considering the Christmas party happening that night. A lot of her father's men would be there to celebrate. Matteo always got his plans set up before the men gathered, so he didn't look like a boss out of the loop.

Siena paid attention far more than her father and brothers thought she did.

Someday, it might save her life.

"So maybe something happened," Matteo added, and then grunted under his breath. "Well, shit. The better question is, can it be fixed?"

"You could … tip the odds to your favor again," Kev suggested.

"How should I do that?"

"There's a million ways, specifically one that would mean bringing the main goal close, you know what I mean?"

"This has always been at arm's length," her father explained, "and that's never changed. I don't think this would change that, either."

"It might not make a difference at all," Darren said.

"He's right," Kev agreed, "when you consider something preferred is right there to be taken, then anything is possible."

Silence echoed for a few moments as she walked her father and brothers their coffee. First, serving her father, the head of the house, and then going back for her brothers' mugs, too. None of them thanked her except for her father.

Matteo touched her wrist with his beefy hand—a gentle stroke that surprised her. "You're my good girl, huh?"

Today was not the day to piss off her father. For one, because she didn't want to listen to his nonsense. And for two, because it would seriously displease her mother.

"Yeah, Dad," she said with a smile.

He liked smiles.

They were the best distraction.

She thanked her mother for that lesson.

Matteo waved her off. "Go help your mother."

Of course.

Her father went right back to his conversation with his sons, and she was already forgotten. Shame, really.

Despite how festive their home was, how beautiful their family looked, they were really so far apart at the end of the day. People who spent a great deal of time together, but barely liked each other at all.

Even at Christmas time.

It was a lonely way to be.

A lonesome life to live.

Maybe that was why she had gotten so strangely attached to the infamous Johnathan Marcello without barely any effort at all. She had been lonely, and he was easy. Or ... close enough to latch onto.

Two months later, and he still seeped into her thoughts like a fucking weed that kept on growing. And why? Because of nothing at all.

She didn't have any other reason, after all. Her stubbornness reared its head again, and she gave in to the instinct as it kicked her in the heart. She was going to hold true to the three strikes, and Johnathan was out of her life thing.

Even if a big part of her still wondered ... *what if?*

What could that have been?

Siena was never going to find out now.

"Give me some time. This will be good for us; we need this." Matteo laughed, not even giving his sons a chance to reply. "For tonight, though, we enjoy ourselves. Merry Christmas, boys."

Siena was already heading out of the kitchen while their laughter echoed behind her. Soon, the house would be full of that sound, and clinking wine glasses, and Christmas music.

The place would still be as cold as hell in the morning.

It always was.

CHAPTER SEVEN

"SO HEY, DO you want to talk to me today, or what?" John asked, leaning in the entryway to the living room of his parents' home.

Lucia didn't even look away from the flickering TV. "No."

Her tone came out flat, dry, and dead.

Ouch.

"I tried to call you while you were in California." John cleared his throat, and then added, "Every couple of weeks, actually."

"Maybe my phone doesn't work there."

"I think it does, Lucia."

"Then maybe that's a sign, John."

Damn.

She was not going to make this easy on him. His kid sister was pissed off at him, and maybe rightfully so. He had been the one to track her down months ago, and bring her home kicking and screaming the whole way.

Business picked up a lot after that, and John was given more responsibility. His boss, and uncle, seemed to think he could handle it, considering everything. Between his therapy once a week, sometimes more, the parole officer he had to keep up with, the public service hours he did every week, and business … John had no time to do anything.

He could barely breathe.

Lucia was home again, though, so he was trying to make time for her. He wanted to fix this rift he made months ago, but she wasn't having it.

Not at all.

"You've been back from California for a couple of weeks, kiddo. I thought—"

Her gaze turned on him—hateful and rage-filled in a blink. Eighteen, young-dumb, and angry. Those were the things he found in his youngest sister's eyes when she stared at him. It was not something John was used to with Lucia.

She was beautiful like their mother, sure.

She was also dark, vicious, and stubborn like their father.

"Don't ever fucking call me that again, John," Lucia hissed.

His spine stiffened. "What—kiddo? I've always called you that."

"Not anymore."

Her words stabbed at his guilt, and made it worse. Maybe he deserved it, after what he did.

"How's California?" he tried asking. "You've been there for a couple of months now."

Still, she ignored him. Her hazel eyes, ones so like his own, were hard and cold.

Lucia was the spitfire of their family. Young blood, and still learning the ropes of this thing they called life. She should have been out there having fun, but in a way, John had taken all that away from her when he dragged her home.

"You could at least talk to me, Lucy."

He used the nickname she hated just to get a rise out of her. She disliked Lucy even more than kiddo. Her response shocked him further.

"California is hot," she said.

"Yeah, I bet," he murmured.

"I start classes during the second semester. Next month after I go back."

"You're all settled in, though?"

"Guess so."

Everything about the conversation felt wrong and bad. Had this been one of his other sisters—Liliana or Cella—John wouldn't have thought anything of the cold demeanor and flat responses. Instead, it was Lucia.

His baby sister.

The kid he looked after since she was born, and he was twelve.

"You were supposed to be my best friend, John," Lucia whispered.

Angry eyes turned on him again, but now, they were filled with tears. She let one escape, and it made a track line down her cheek. With a quick hand, she wiped the tear away, and let out a harsh breath.

"You shouldn't have run off like that," he replied.

Lucia's cheek twitched—a sure sign she was clenching her jaw for all she was worth. Hiding that anger behind a stone facade and calm words.

Just like their father.

She wore her namesake well.

"I was hoping you might let me apologize, and we could spend some time together while you're visiting," John said. "But even at Christmas, you ignored me."

"Perhaps you should take a fucking hint, then."

"*Lucia.*"

He didn't get anything from that—not a damn thing. She didn't even flinch at his rough tone.

John tried a different direction once more. "What made you get mixed up with a guy like Renzo, anyway? Didn't I tell you not to mess with boys like that?"

Her laughter stung when it escaped her smirking lips. She turned on the couch to face him completely.

John should have took that as a warning, maybe.

"Like *him*?" she asked. "John, you and every other man in our family are no better than him. Except what? We've got money, and you guys wear nice suits and drive expensive cars. So, you've got a last name that gives you respect, and a family legacy that affords you privilege."

Lucia shook her head, never backing down for a minute as she continued with, "And guys like him? They come from the streets, and hustle every day of their lives just to survive. Did you know he was paying for his sister's private schooling? Nobody else paid for it. He was trying to let her *be* something when they came from nothing. Where do you think that left her? Or his little brother—his parents fucked off a couple years ago. Where does that leave the boy? Don't worry, I'm sure his sister—who can't go to school anymore—took him, or better yet, maybe a nice foster family picked him up."

John blinked, unsure and wary.

The contempt in Lucia's words were coated with bitterness.

He didn't know what to say.

"Fuck you with your guys like him shit," she snapped. "So, you've got money and a suit, but that's all you've fucking got, too."

Who was this girl staring at him like she hated his guts, and everything he stood for?

This wasn't the Lucia who fawned over expensive cars, and liked diamonds on her birthday. This wasn't his sister who was the quiet, perfect Marcello *principessa*.

No, this girl was entirely different.

"You come from the same privilege I do," John said quietly.

"Except I can own it now. Can you?"

John didn't know how to answer that. "I'm sorry, Lucy. Really, I am. I didn't think that it was all going to lead to him being put away for—"

"Shut up," Lucia spat. "I bet Daddy had that planned, and you knew about it, too."

"Dad didn't plan anything. I just came after you to bring you home. The rest was circumstance, and shit."

Lucia turned away from him, refusing to even grace him with her attention again. It burned, but John took it. Seemed he had managed to ruin the last good relationship he had with someone in his immediate family.

This time it wasn't even because of his bipolar.

Funny.

"Why don't we talk about you, John?" Lucia asked dryly.

Nope.

John didn't talk about him.

His defenses always flew up at the idea.

People probed, and it felt like needles swimming in his bloodstream.

"No, I'm good," he said folding his arms over his chest.

Without even looking at him, Lucia said, "Then we have nothing else to say here. Daddy and the rest of them are upstairs."

The rest of them.

He didn't miss the contempt in that, either.

John left Lucia to her thoughts and anger, though.

What else could he do?

"So that's it for us, then?" John asked. "You're going to go back to California in a couple of weeks, and you won't even bother with me at all while you're here? Nothing at all?"

"Don't take it personally, John. It's all of them, not just you."

Well, then …

• • •

John walked in the home office of his father to find there were more men sitting around the room than he expected. John's father, and Giovanni and Dante, his uncles. Andino, too, sat on the edge of the desk. A place Andino shouldn't be sitting considering Dante—the boss—was behind it.

It was sometimes strange and difficult to grow up in the world of Cosa Nostra. Made men with an entire family dynamic that was governed and controlled by the rules of the mafia sometimes created complexities that no one could understand.

John's father had never been able to be just his father, after all, not when he had also been an underboss. The same went with his uncles—Gio and Dante. They, too, had always held positions of power.

Family was family.

Cosa Nostra colored them up.

And now …

John gave Andino a nod, and a grin. "Don't you look comfortable, just like a spoiled little underboss should."

Chuckles passed around the room.

Had it been anyone else, John never would have disrespected the new underboss of the family with that kind of a joke. However, this was Andino. It wouldn't be normal for the two of them not to trade some kind of barbs with one another.

It was expected, really.

Andino was still kind of new to the position. A whole change that had come about over the last couple of months. Nobody was kidding around when they decided to move him up.

John still felt it was the right choice.

"Careful, I'm allowed to make *mistakes* since I'm so new and all," Andino threw back, grinning himself. "I would hate for you to be one of those mistakes, John."

"You could try."

The chuckles turned in to laughter, then.

For a moment, it was nice.

It never lasted long.

Not in Cosa Nostra.

Lucian looked to his son. "Did you talk to your sister?"

John scoffed. "Do you mean, did I let her rage at me? Because if so, the answer is yes."

Silence saturated the room, thick and heavy. It left a bitter taste behind in John's mouth, but it was what it was. It seemed like he wasn't the only one on the bad end of Lucia's moods since she had come home for a break from California.

"It's almost better when she ignores you, isn't it?" Lucian smiled sadly. "Never thought I would see the day."

"We all make choices we sometimes regret," Dante said from behind the desk. "And so, we have to live with those."

The boss of their family would probably understand that lesson better than anyone, considering the hell he had gone through with his own daughter recently. No family was perfect, John had come to learn. Not behind closed doors.

Those lessons were the hardest.

They hurt the very most.

"I don't regret it," Lucian said, "but I wish she wasn't so angry."

"More like ... full of contempt, I think," John said quietly.

Nods passed between the men, and then it was right back to business as usual. Family only got so much time in before the mafia had to come out and play again.

So was their life.

Mostly, John didn't mind.

As long as they all had Lucia to worry about, they would not be getting on his ass for a while. It was a shitty thing for Lucia, sure, but silver linings were still quite silver.

"Lucian, are you staying or going for this?" Dante asked. "You're not required to being that you've unofficially stepped down, and Andino is here. The option is open, though."

Even in another man's house, sitting at that man's desk, the boss still owned the room. He directed the men, and where their conversation had to go.

Lucian passed John a look, and then went back to his brother. "I think I'll step out, actually."

Dante waved a hand as if to say, *go.*

John was surprised at that turn of events. Decades as a made man—and as the family's underboss beneath his brother—and Lucian just seemed … done with it all. Ready to move on.

"Find me after you're done here, son," Lucian said, clapping Johnathan on the shoulder as he passed him by. "Got it?"

"Yeah, sure."

For what, though, he didn't know.

Once the office door was closed, John gave his attention to his two uncles, and Andino. For the most part, Giovanni sat in the corner and worked on lighting his cigar. As the consigliere to the boss, it wasn't as though Gio really had to handle the men all that much. He was middle man for Dante in a grander sense.

John liked his uncle, though. Gio was the fun one, so to speak.

"How's the new crew going?" Dante asked.

"It's good," John replied.

"Just good?"

"Andino's crew might as well be a bunch of fucking saints, compared to some of them."

Andino chuckled darkly. "That's because I put the fear of God in to them."

Gio looked over the tip of his burning red cigar. "Not his crew, anymore. It's yours now, John."

John passed a look between his uncle, and then to his boss. "I was told this was temporary."

Dante smirked a little. "I wanted to make sure you could handle it again, John. It's been months since you were released from prison—you've done everything I asked you to do."

He had.

No messes.

No nonsense.

Business kept clean.

Attention low.

Dante's demands had been clear. John had even taken extra care with his disorder, and managing it because he didn't want to disgrace his family when they welcomed him home after everything he had done.

"It's not my crew, though," John said, gesturing at Andino. "It's his."

"The whole underboss gig keeps me busy," Andino replied.

Yeah, he bet.

"Or spoiled," John muttered.

Andino smirked, and flipped John the middle finger.

Dante continued talking like the interaction hadn't even happened. "I told you that the babysitting was only temporary, too. It's time to get back to being a proper Capo, Johnathan. It's what you're best at, *nipote*."

"It is," he agreed, chuckling.

Dante jerked a thumb in Andino's direction. "So, he's got a few dealings between crews of other families. Some schemes that get run on other territories, and things like that."

"A warehouse is shared on schemes that run between families to make it easier and keep the peace," Andino added. "You'll need to handle meeting up with the Capo of that crew. It's like a once a month thing or something."

"Who?"

"Darren Calabrese," Andino said.

John stiffened, but hid it.

Andino passed him a subtle look. "You okay with that?"

The question was loaded.

John shrugged. "Sure, don't see why not."

"Our history with the Calabrese family makes certain things tricky," Dante added.

"History—like their grandfather killing my great-grandfather, you mean?" John asked.

Giovanni coughed.

Dante cleared his throat. "Yeah, exactly that history."

"To be fair, Carl Calabrese is dead now," Andino said.

"That kind of shit doesn't wash out, Andi," John murmured. "They killed my family—even if Lucian was already adopted into the Marcello family—to take over, and nothing else. They wanted the seat, so they did what they had to do. My biological great-grandfather doesn't even have a proper grave. We don't know what they did with him.

"Bad blood like that doesn't wash out," John finished sharply.

"No, but we do put the stains aside for the sake of business," Dante said. "But we never fucking forget they're a bunch of snakes, John. There's a difference."

John didn't entirely like that, but it was what it was.

Siena Calabrese was a whole other issue.

She certainly wasn't like her brothers, and that made all the difference to him. However, he hadn't seen her in months. He meant to check in on her once he returned from finding his sister, but one thing after another thing kept coming up.

A new crew.

More business.

Family.

A cousin nearly getting killed in Cancun.

John wasn't even overstating it. He bet none of that shit would make a difference to Siena because like a prick, he had bailed on her.

Women took offense to that.

"Well?" Dante asked.

John looked to his boss. "I can handle the fucking Calabrese."

Andino snorted from his perch on the desk. "You can start by not calling them the *fucking* Calabrese, John."

Yeah, he would try.

No promises.

Johnathan found his father sitting in the small library downstairs. Lucian sipped from a neat whiskey while he flipped through a newspaper. He looked laidback, and entirely relaxed. Like the man who never stopped moving had finally taken a break.

It was an unusual sight.

"You wanted me to come find you?" John asked.

Lucian looked over the edge of the newspaper. "Seems the stock market is up two points."

John's brow furrowed. "All right."

"And some action movie is breaking box office records."

"Okay."

"Stop looking at me like my head is growing bigger, John."

He wet his lips. "We don't usually do this kind of small talk, Dad. That's all."

"Never really got the chance, did we? Cosa Nostra was always getting in the way, and putting up barriers that kept us apart. I couldn't only worry about my son—and the problems he constantly faced—when Cosa Nostra made me stay at arm's length."

John blinked.

Lucian waved at the chair beside his. "Come sit, and talk."

"I—"

"John, please come sit with me."

"All right," he said, his voice feeling like an echo.

He joined his father, and Lucian passed over a section of the newspaper.

"We're going to start doing this. You and me, I mean."

John stared at the paper. "So, doing nothing?"

"Not nothing. Being *normal*, John. Have I ever told you how proud I am of you, my boy?"

He had to think about it.

"Sure you have, Dad."

"Things I thought you wouldn't be able to do or handle because of the bipolar, you've done all of it and more. You still are. Expect me to tell you how proud I am more often now, John."

"Did you ever think that I liked the way we were?"

"Did you?" his father asked. "Like it, I mean."

No.

"I've done a lot of shit, Dad," John settled on saying, "to everybody—you included. Said a lot of things, you know. I burn bridges, but I don't usually fix them."

"And here we still sit, John."

• • •

"Darren," John greeted.

The Calabrese Capo shoved his frame off the barstool, and stuck out a hand for John to take. He did and shook Darren's hand, but made sure to keep a tighter grip than he normally would.

John had to do these meets and work with the Calabrese brother—or both, who knew, since the two stuck together a lot—but that didn't mean he was going to bow down to either of the fuckers. He didn't trust them with an inch.

"John, it's good to see you," Darren said with a smile.

John wished it felt welcoming.

It didn't.

"Care for a drink?" Darren asked, waving at the bar.

John used one of his old excuses to pass that offer up. "I don't drink during work time."

"You Marcellos are always so stiff with your rules."

"It's what makes us the best."

Darren's gaze flashed with something unknown, and John took that as a point to his favor. "Yes, well, sit. We can discuss how Andino and I have managed to have parts of our crews working together, and whatever else."

"He filled me in on some of the details."

"But not all, huh?"

John shrugged, and took a seat on an open barstool. "Better to jump right into it, I think."

"Sure."

John waved for the bartender, and asked for a water. Once he had the glass in front of him, he used it as a distraction to keep his attention focused rather than looking at Darren Calabrese. The longer he was near one of the Calabrese men, the more his old bitterness and rage grew.

It had never really gone away.

Not since he learned the truth about why their two families didn't have a lot to do with each other. He had been, oh, thirteen or so at the time when his father finally told him everything.

John thought he was a Marcello through and through.

Their blood ran through his veins.

The truth was dirtier—his father, the product of an affair with a *goomah*, had been the son of a murdered man. His biological grandfather, Johnathan Grovatti. And his great-grandfather, the former boss of one of New York's most powerful crime families, had been taken out because of greed, and nothing more.

By a bunch of Calabrese bastards.

John was still a Marcello, sure. In thought and mind, in body and spirit, he was every inch a fucking Marcello man. He spoke like them, lived like them, and *was* them.

But he knew now that he also had Grovatti blood keeping him alive. A whole family that had been wiped out without a thought or care.

So was the way of their life.

Or it was supposed to be.

That kind of shit was hard to let go.

So, when Darren spoke about a friendship between them, and good business, it made John's fucking skin crawl. It took every ounce of effort he had, all of his control, not to reach over and choke the life out of the cocksucker.

"What do you think, John?" Darren asked. "Is the deal up to spec with you?"

John had barely been listening.

He just wanted this first meeting over with.

Andino thought the next one would be easier, and so on. Well, John had a whole week to get used to the idea of working with someone from the Calabrese family, and he was still just as disgusted as he had been.

"Actually, it kind of seems like the Calabrese side of things might be getting a longer end of the stick," John said, "if you know what I mean."

Darren chuckled. "Come on, now. It's our warehouse, and most of our streets. Sure, the crew on the Marcello side does a lot of the work with the delivery and distribution of the shit, but—"

"I take it this deal was something to keep your business relevant," John interjected, cocking a brow before he took a sip of his water. "Am I right?"

"More money is always a good thing."

"Those streets—Dante handed them over to your family in a deal a few years ago at the Commission meeting, right?"

Darren nodded tightly. "Yeah, and we were owed them, considering the mess that went down between the guys."

"Except they're hard streets to work because your people don't have shit there. It was all built up by Andino's guys. I know because I used to work those streets with my cousin before I got locked up."

"Your point, John?"

John flashed a cocky grin. "Nothing, really. Just making it clear why it's like that. Even if the territory seems like it's yours, it's nothing without a Marcello crew backing it."

Darren sucked in a deep breath.

John smirked inwardly.

It was never good to make problems with someone whom you needed to do business with for the unforeseeable future. However, in this case, John absolutely wanted it clear that between him and Darren, he would always be the fucker coming out on top.

It was what it was.

That was just what Marcellos did.

"Good talk," John said, standing from the stool. "I'll be around the warehouse to chat with the guys, if you want to drop by. I'll leave my number with the girl at the front so you can, uh, give me a call when we have to do this nonsense again, Darren."

John stuffed his hands in the pockets of his slacks, and headed for the exit of the business. He didn't make it halfway across the floor before a much larger and more important Calabrese man stepped in his path.

Matteo.

The boss.

And … Siena's father.

"Well, well, if it isn't Johnathan Marcello," Matteo boomed.

Damn, the man was loud.

John gave a laugh, and tried not to let it show his irritation. He shook the boss's hand because fuck him, even if the boss was one he despised, he couldn't be rude. It was not the Cosa Nostra way.

Made men did not shun bosses.

"I heard through the grapevine that you're taking over Andino's business now that he's … stepping up, shall we say," Matteo said.

The man was as wide as a table.

Tall as a fucking tree.

Rings adorned all of his fingers.

His wealth, and his status?

It came from the blood running through John.

"Guess so," John said.

"Funny," Matteo murmured, "I always thought *you* were the second generation of the Marcello boys that would be stepping up, John. What happened to that, huh?"

The man reached out and patted John's cheek.

Inwardly, his blood boiled.

The touch was affectionate, and even … friendly. Like a family member might do.

John hated it, but managed to stay calm on the outside. "I don't think anybody thought anything about who was going where in the family, and I like where I am."

Matteo nodded. "Mmhmm, I bet, John."

"Is what it is, boss."

That word burned his tongue.

He said it anyway.

"Well, to have good vibes between our families, and this new arrangement with you and Darren, I think you should come over and have dinner."

John stilled. "I beg your pardon?"

"Dinner," Matteo repeated. "At my home with my family. It's the proper thing to do. Deals are best made over good food, John."

Not in the Marcello family.

Business was not had at the dinner table. Still, the rules his life were governed by banged around in his head.

Never shun a boss. Never, John. Even if he is not your boss.

John swallowed his pride, and the disgust weighing heavily on his tongue. Now, it just weighed down his stomach. "Sure, dinner. You let me know when, boss."

Matteo clapped John on the shoulder, and then moved on.

It was a strange encounter for more reasons than one, but mostly because John knew bosses didn't have their hands directly in the pot of business. They oversaw a lot, and directed people as to the business. They didn't, however, step right in.

It was almost like Matteo had been waiting for him.

John glanced at the beefy, tall Calabrese Don as he headed for the bar of the restaurant. Then, he turned back to leave the place.

He needed to get out of there.

The sight of someone far more beautiful coming in through the doors stopped him straight up. She was lost in the tablet she held in one hand, and the earbuds in her ears. Her hair was a bit longer, and darker like she might have gotten it tinted a bit. The knee-length dress and ankle-high boots she wore were far more conservative than the clothes he had taken off her that night.

Fuck.

He could still kind of taste the salt of her skin on the back of his tongue when he looked at her. He could hear those pretty little sounds she made in bed when she was underneath him, and begging for more.

Like music, really.

John slipped up because sex was supposed to be a no-go until his therapist gave the okay, but damn, Siena had been worth that. He was still a little bit tripped up on her considering he still hadn't found any female worth looking at since the day he saw her on the bus.

Fuck his life for being like this.

And then, Siena looked up—sea-blue gaze and still perfect.

John stared back.

CHAPTER EIGHT

"JOHNATHAN."

Siena didn't miss how John subtly winced when she used his full name with a tone as sharp as glass.

Good.

He'd slept with her, and then fucked off like a coward before she could even wake up the next morning. All she got after that from him was nothing but radio silence. For three whole months. Who did that kind of thing to people?

This man, apparently.

She had done well trying to let go of that anger and hurt over the last while, but fuck him because now it was bubbling up all over again. At just the sight of him, looking so damn good in a fitted suit and a half grin, she was pissed. Like he didn't have a care in the world. All tall, dark, and handsome without even trying.

He probably didn't even know what he had done to her, and how much it stung. Maybe she was just one of many.

Siena resolved herself never to let it happen again. She attempted to move past Johnathan, but he stood too close to a table on one side, and people were eating at another table on his right. She had to slide in beside him, which only made her rub against him. His familiar spicy scent—like sex, man, and deliciousness—filled her lungs with one breath.

Fuck.

"Siena, wait," Johnathan said.

His hand came up to touch her shoulder. She stiffened; instantly frozen in place like a statue by his gentle fingertips sliding along the line of her shoulder. His touch grazed the exposed patch of skin where the neckline of her dress was open, and a shiver raced over her flesh.

Fuck.

Again.

Siena looked up at him, and all she saw was dark hazel staring back. "What?"

Her one word came out a hell of a lot quieter than she intended it to. She wished it had been that same sharp tone she first greeted him with.

No, instead he got her breathy and confused question.

Jesus Christ.

"Do you have a minute?" Johnathan asked.

Siena hardened her jaw, and schooled her features. "Not particularly."

And not for you.

"After work, then? I assume that's what you're doing."

He assumed right, but that didn't mean she was giving in. Or that she was going to make time for him.

"I'm kind of busy," she told him.

Johnathan nodded once. "Yeah, me, too."

"I bet."

He winced again.

Her sharp tone had found itself again.

Siena could see her father sitting at the bar with her brother. She was stuck between wondering why her father was even at the restaurant—he rarely showed up when she worked at one of her brother's places—and the fact that both men were very obviously staring. They made no effort to hide it.

Matteo and Darren had their gazes glued on Siena and Johnathan like they had found the most interesting show, and couldn't tear their eyes away.

It was unsettling.

She went back to Johnathan.

"Listen, Johnathan," she said, falling back to his full name, "I really am busy, and I have to get to work if I plan on getting out of here before dark."

Johnathan didn't look like he wanted to move at all. In fact, the two of them stayed locked in a staring contest, and his fingertips grazed her throat momentarily before he dropped his hand altogether. She thought there was something new to be seen in his eyes—usually she found a lost, wild glint there. Now, she saw something else.

A silent request, maybe.

A demand, possibly.

Siena didn't know.

She had learned through three months of silence that she really couldn't afford to find out much about Johnathan at all. Not when things like her feelings were in play, and he didn't seem to mind hurting them.

A weak woman she was not.

He would not make her one.

Still, Johnathan didn't move. He didn't say anything, either, but she could see he wanted to. He was holding back—maybe for himself, or for her. She didn't know, and she didn't really care, either.

"Excuse me," she said.

It came out like a whisper this time.

Soft, unsure, and barely there at all.

Johnathan still heard it because he finally stepped aside a little more to let her pass. Behind her, she heard him say, "I'm sure I'll see you around, Siena."

Doubtful.

She didn't answer him back, though.

She didn't even look over her shoulder.

Siena made a left before the bar to head for the back offices. Books to scrub and cook, after all. Her work never ended, and her life only seemed to revolve around what business her father or brothers needed her to do next.

Matteo calling her name stopped her. "Come sit with me, Siena."

She glanced at her father, and then at Darren who pushed off the stool behind him. The two men shared a quiet word as she made her way over. Darren left their father's side just as Siena came to stand beside Matteo.

"Pinot Noir—the dark red," Matteo told the man behind the bar. He looked to her. "That's the one you like, isn't it?"

"Usually," Siena said. "Not when I'm working, though."

It was not good to mix alcohol and numbers. Especially not when those numbers were fraudulent, but had to look better than real when the IRS looked at them.

Matteo laughed. "Oh, take a break once in a while, Siena. It's good for the soul. You can't work all the time."

What?

She only worked as much as she did because that's all they wanted her to do. They didn't give her any choice.

Siena said none of that, and instead, took the glass of red wine when the bartender offered it. She took one small sip, but kept her nose down in the glass as she swallowed. It gave her the chance to smell the wine, and ignore her father at the same time.

Heady fruits and the sting of alcohol filled her lungs, and coated her tongue. She wasn't a big drinker to begin with, but wine was the only thing she could stand to imbibe when she had to.

Red wine, specifically.

"Siena," Matteo murmured.

Damn.

"Yeah, Dad?"

She looked at him, but he was staring back across the restaurant. At the same exact spot where she had been standing with Johnathan only moments before. He was no longer there, or inside the restaurant at all, it seemed.

Thank God for small miracles.

Her heart was already a mess.

"Do you care to tell me what that was about between you and Johnathan Marcello?" Matteo asked.

"Not particularly."

"I'm sorry." Matteo chuckled. "I posed that question like you had a choice—you don't, Siena. Start talking."

"It's nothing, Dad."

"Is, or *was* nothing?"

"Both," she returned, and then took a much larger drink of wine. "There's nothing to tell. We met up a couple of times randomly on the street around where I get my books, and once on the city bus."

"And that's all?" Matteo pressed.

No.

She was not about to tell him that she slept with Johnathan. He was her father, not a fucking friend. The only reason she got away with occasionally having a boyfriend was because Matteo needed to keep Siena happy to a certain extent.

He needed her work with numbers. He needed her bookkeeping skills, and her understanding of how to cook his fucking books. A little bit of freedom in this life could go a long damn way.

Or so she had learned …

"Yeah, that's all," she said, shrugging.

"He looked very uncomfortable when you wouldn't indulge his conversation," her father added after a moment.

"Perhaps that was because I didn't want to talk to him, Dad."

Siena knew that wasn't the right thing to say, but she hadn't been able to hold it back. Maybe if she got that out of the way, her father would back down on whatever he was trying to get at.

Unlikely.

"You know how I expect you to act around other men in this life, Siena. You're to treat them with the respect you give me, or your brothers. Should you run in to Johnathan again, I expect you to be your pleasant, sweet self. The good girl I know you can be, huh?"

Her father cupped her cheek, and patted it gently. A wave of bitter irritation swelled at the action.

She shoved it deep down.

What else could she do?

"I'll try, Dad," she said, offering nothing else.

Matteo smiled. "There is no trying. Not in this circumstance."

"All right."

The words felt like glass in her mouth.

Matteo chuckled deeply. "Oh, and we're having a dinner next week. I expect you to be there."

Even better ...

• • •

"Dad made this seem like it was supposed to be a big dinner," Siena said as she eyed the placements on the table. There were only six. Just enough for her parents, brothers, her, and one other person. "This isn't a big dinner at all, Ma."

Coraline rolled her eyes. "I think he means it's supposed to be an *important* dinner—a big deal, if you will."

"Why?"

Her mother didn't answer, but Siena's attention was distracted by her father and brothers roaring through the dining room. Their laughter carried through the space, and then followed them into the hall. The laughter echoed back, and muffled as the men headed into another room.

Siena turned back to her mother. "Again, why is this a big deal?"

And why the hell did she have to be there for it?

Coraline finished placing the cloth napkins on top of the plates, and gave Siena a look that scolded her. The kind of look she used to give her as a child when Siena was being too loud or whatever else.

"You know how this works—you're not new to this life, Siena," her mother said. "You don't get to ask questions. You follow the rules, and nothing else. Now, go find something to do, and get out of my hair."

Yep.

Just like a child.

Frankly, Siena didn't mind this time. It gave her the chance to get away from her mother who just kept redoing every little thing that Siena set out on the table, anyway.

She headed for the back of the house, and slipped in the sunroom. The space was fully enclosed, but had large windows that overlooked the backyard, and a door to exit out of should someone want to go outside. It was heated in the winter, and the potted plants in all the corners and on shelves gave the space an earthy smell.

Next to her old bedroom, this had been her most favorite space in the Calabrese family home. Barely anyone used the sunroom, except her mother to water the plants twice a week. Siena was almost always guaranteed some form of privacy here.

She sunk in one of the wicker chairs, and overlooked the brownstone's small, fenced in backyard. A recent storm had dropped a good half of a foot of snow on top of what little bit they already had. Now, covered in a heavy fresh sheet of pristine, sparkling white snow, it looked peaceful.

And cold.

Christmas was over now that it was a week into January, and all the decorations that usually warmed the place had long been taken down. The tree was gone, like everything else. Her mother had never liked to leave anything up for longer than she had to when it came to the holidays.

It was a good thing her mother hadn't been to her apartment in well over a month. Siena still hadn't taken her Christmas decorations down—what little bit she put out. Even the small five-foot-high fake tree was still lit up with the gold star twinkling on top in her living room.

Coraline would be aghast.

Maybe that's *why* Siena kept it up.

Who knew?

Siena wasn't sure how long she stayed hidden in the sunroom. Long enough that she wondered if maybe she had missed the dinner altogether, and someone forgot she was even there. It was unlikely, but she could still hope.

Her hope was for nothing.

"There you are," came a voice from the doorway.

Siena found her oldest brother standing there. Kev looked her over, and then peered around the room.

"You weren't playing with the plants or something, right?" he asked. "Dad won't be happy if you mess your dress, or whatever."

Siena scowled. "First, I'm twenty-five, not a toddler. Try to speak to me like an adult, and I'll remember not to use big words for you when I respond. Second, what do you want?"

"Time for dinner."

She waved a hand. "Yeah, I'll be right behind you."

"Siena, you could try to be pleasant tonight."

"No, what I could have done tonight, Kev, was stay at home on my couch under a blanket and watched the newest episode of my favorite show. Instead, I am here. Dressed and prettied up to show off Dad's beautiful family for whoever he's putting this show on for."

"And we're so awful, right?"

He flashed her a grin.

She smiled right back.

"Something like that," Siena said.

Kev sobered momentarily. "Seriously, what's up with you?"

"I don't know. Nothing in particular at the moment."

"But still something. I know how women work. You all say nothing is wrong, but in reality, you're stewing in some kind of shit inside your crazy heads."

And that, everybody, is one of many reasons why Kev can't keep a woman.

Siena didn't say that out loud.

But it didn't make it any less true.

"You going to tell me what's wrong, or what?" he asked. "Because I don't have all day, and they're waiting for us at the table."

She shrugged. "Don't you ever get tired of putting on airs for Dad and his people?"

Kev cocked a brow. "Siena, I am one of his people."

Yeah, shit.

She hadn't thought of that, but she should have. Her brothers never understood why she didn't enjoy being the child of a mafia boss the same way they did. Kev and Darren were revered as sons and made men, while she was the toss-away girl.

This conversation was going nowhere.

And fast.

Standing from the chair, Siena brushed down her skirt. "All right, let's get this over with."

"Smile," Kev said as she left the sunroom.

Siena flipped her brother off over her shoulder instead. *How's that for a smile?*

It only took a minute or two for them to get back to the dining room. Siena heard his voice echoing out from the space before she even stood in the entryway.

"Whiskey is fine," he said.

His voice came out dark and rich.

Like honey.

Fuck.

Siena's gaze drifted to where Johnathan Marcello stood beside her father and Darren at the small wet bar against the far wall. His stare found hers as Matteo passed him a three-fingered glass of whiskey.

He doesn't even drink.

Or, that's what he told her.

Siena was stuck between staring at Johnathan in his black on black suit, and wondering why in the hell nobody had thought to tell her he was the guest tonight. She felt tricked somehow, but she didn't know why.

After all, her father and brothers didn't actually *know* she had history with Johnathan. Or ... what one might consider to be a history.

Nonetheless, it was sure to be an awkward fucking dinner.

Johnathan still hadn't taken his gaze off Siena. Kev passed her in the doorway, however, and that allowed her to break the staring contest for a moment.

She took the chance to grab her chair at the table, and sit down. Fixing the napkin over her lap, she ignored the conversation happening between the men of her family and Johnathan. Soon, her mother was coming out of the kitchen with dishes in hand. She thought to help her mom, but Coraline was quick to tell her to stay put.

It was only once the table was full and wine had been poured that the men finally joined Siena and her mother at the table. Like always, Matteo sat at the head of the table, while her mother sat on the end. Darren sat beside Siena, while Johnathan sat directly across from her, and Kev sat at his left.

Every single time she looked up after grace had been said, he was right there. Looking at her. Talking to someone else, but passing her glances. Never calling her out directly for conversation, but still managing to get someone else to pull her in to it every once in a while.

Before Siena knew it, half of her plate was gone, and she had downed three glasses of a white wine that tasted like rotten grapes and old vodka.

The buzz was just enough to keep her from letting the growing butterflies in her stomach take over completely. Barely …

"Siena," her father said, "have we ever told you that Johnathan is connected to our family's history?"

She peeked up from her plate, and her gaze darted between a suddenly frozen Johnathan, and her grinning father.

Something in Johnathan's stiff as hell posture told her he was very uncomfortable. He picked up that whiskey glass he had barely touched, and tipped it up to his lips. Still, when he sat the glass back down to the table, the liquid level was still at the same spot.

He hadn't sipped on even a drop.

"No," she finally said quietly.

Matteo's grin grew wider. "His great-grandfather was once the boss of the Calabrese—"

"Grovatti," Johnathan interjected with a dull tone. "Then, it was called the *Grovatti* family."

"My mistake, John. You're right, but it's been our family for so long now that it's easy to forget."

Johnathan's grip on the steak knife in his hand tightened until his knuckles whitened. Siena again glanced between her seemingly oblivious father, and a very irritated Johnathan.

What was happening?

"Nonetheless," Matteo said, "Siena, your grandfather Carl took over after Johnathan's great-grandfather passed on. And that is how this organization came to be."

The silence that passed over the table felt thick with something Siena didn't really understand. Haughtiness from one side, she thought, and pain from the man across from her.

Johnathan hid it well, but for some reason, she could see it.

In his eyes.

There, he was hurting.

Siena downed what was left of her fourth glass of wine because she didn't know what the hell else to do. The bitter, sour flavor stuck to her teeth and tongue, but it was better than talking.

Awkward was not a good enough word for this dinner.

"I never did understand why Johnathan Grovatti's bastard son changed names after his father was killed," Darren said from beside her. "Lucian, I mean."

Johnathan's gaze darkened with a barely hidden hate as he looked at Darren. "My *father* was adopted by Antony and Cecelia Marcello. That's why he took their surname."

"Even if he was birthed by a *goomah*, he was still a Grovatti."

Johnathan flashed a smile—cold and sharp in a blink. "We certainly are, and don't you forget it, either."

• • •

Siena hid in the sunroom the very second she was able to get away from the dinner table without earning herself a glare from her father. No one seemed to notice when she left, thankfully.

She toyed with the velvety leaves on one of the corner plants as she ran over the things that had been said at the dinner.

It still felt like a set up.

She still couldn't prove that it was.

"The information that your father neglected to mention was that your grandfather killed my great-grandfather."

Siena stiffened at Johnathan's voice, and then stood straight up. She spun on her heels, and found him leaning in the doorway of the sunroom.

"How did you know I was back here?" she asked.

He shrugged, and swirled the still-full glass of whiskey in his hand. "I skipped out on them by saying I had to use the bathroom. Apparently there's none on the bottom floor of this brownstone, so I'm going to pretend like I got lost."

Siena swallowed hard. "But you came looking for me."

Johnathan flashed a warm smile, and his hazel eyes drifted over her, unashamed. "Yep."

She refused to let this man in again. She would not let her walls down for him after the stunt he pulled on her.

Siena brought her cold demeanor out to play again. "Did I not make myself clear at the restaurant, or what?"

Johnathan looked down at the glass of whiskey, and then stretched his arm out to dump the contents in a potted plant on a shelf. "Shame to waste liquor and all, but I don't drink even for a boss."

"You could have refused."

His gaze cut back to her. "Made men cannot *refuse* any boss. I would not be here tonight, if I could."

Oh.

She heard what he didn't say.

"Was that the truth?" she dared to ask. "About my grandfather and your great-grandfather?"

Johnathan's lips curled at the edge—a sneer that roughened his handsome face, and gave her the answer before he even spoke it out loud. "Every bit of it, yeah."

"Huh."

"That's what you have to say?"

"What would you want me to say?" she countered.

Johnathan tipped his head back, and that intense gaze of his stabbed in to her with reckless intent. Like he had caught something he really liked in his sights, and he was ready to snatch it up.

It just happened to be her in his line of vision.

Fuck.

"I don't expect anything from you, Siena Calabrese," Johnathan said. "But I *hoped* you might let me say a few things."

"Like what?"

She knew better than to ask.

She wished she could take it back instantly.

The words were still out there.

Johnathan's throat bobbed as his tongue peeked out to wet his lips. "What happened a few months ago, for starters."

"Nope," she said.

Just like that, she was done.

Siena moved to push past him in the doorway and head back to where her family was, but Johnathan grabbed her wrist, and yanked her back. "Wait a damn minute, *donna.*"

In a blink, she was spun around and facing him. Dark hazel, and sharp lines clouded her vision. The hardness of his body fit perfectly against the softness of hers.

All she could see was him.

All she could smell was him.

It was bad, intoxicating, and addicting all at the same time.

"Just ... wait a minute," he murmured softer.

"You don't *deserve* even a second," she replied, trying to level her tone.

"Maybe not, but will you give me one?"

"Why, so we can fuck again, and you can run off one more time? You didn't even leave me a note, or your number. I don't know if you expected me to chase you like this was some kind of game, John, but I don't run after any man. Ever."

He didn't even blink.

He barely moved.

She yanked her wrist out of his grasp, and took a step back. "So, no, I don't really want to hear anything you have to say."

Siena turned her back to Johnathan, and then quickly disappeared down the hallway. She grabbed her coat and bag from the hallway closet, and then headed for the dining room. Only one of her brothers was still there, and he was pouring yet another drink, it seemed.

Darren, that was.

"Let Dad know I'm leaving," Siena said as she dug through the bag for her keys. "I have work to do early tomorrow."

Darren snatched the keys out of her hands the second she pulled them from the purse. "Hell no. You've been drinking. You can't drive."

Siena glared at her brother, but didn't try to get the keys back. He towered over her, and she wasn't going to jump for the fucking things like a child. "Then call me a cab, or get Kev to drive me home. He barely drank anything at all."

"We're not your fucking chauffeurs, Siena."

Ouch.

Because she remembered more than one occasion when she had taken them home after dinners due to drinking.

The bastards.

"Listen, Dad mentioned you should probably stay the night anyway since you're supposed to be working with him tomorrow at the new dealership or something. You can just follow him in the morning since you don't know where it is."

Siena's irritation grew tendrils inside her heart and squeezed tight enough to kill her. "I want to go home."

Darren shrugged. "Too bad, I guess you're staying."

CHAPTER NINE

JOHN HEADED after Siena, determined to get her to talk to him for more than five seconds. She disappeared into the dining room, and the Calabrese boss's oldest son stepped out of what appeared to be the living room at the same time.

"Here, let me take that."

John handed over the empty glass of whiskey he was still holding. "Thanks."

"You're not leaving yet, are you?" Kev asked.

John's gaze drifted toward the dining room, but went quickly back to Kev. "No, not yet."

But soon.

John wasn't about to tell Kev Calabrese that being in the brownstone was a special kind of hell for him. A constant battle between showing respect for the boss of the Calabrese Cosa Nostra, or defending the honor of a dead man.

"My father asked me to let you know he'll be waiting in his office to chat a little more," Kev said. "He thought you might have gotten lost or something."

John forced himself not to look toward the dining room again. Kev didn't mention having seen John following after Siena, and he wasn't about to make it obvious. He didn't know what the woman's family was like regarding her, men, and dating.

She didn't need trouble.

Not because of him, anyway.

"The office is on the third floor," Kev said gesturing at the stairwell. "Last door on the left—he usually leaves it open for us."

John nodded, saying only, "*Grazie.*"

Silently adding, *for fucking nothing.*

The very last thing John wanted to do was sit down with Matteo for longer than he already had. The dinner had been more than enough. Even still, he climbed the flights of stairs, and glanced over the family portraits hanging on white walls because the rules of their life happened to be a hell of a lot clearer than his wants at the moment.

Never shun a boss.

A boss is a boss is a boss, John.

He now understood—in a way—why the Marcellos tended to keep their distance where the Calabrese family was concerned. Friendships made from situations like these only led to men who did not actually like one another, but rather, made nice for the sake of appearances.

But when no one was watching ...

That's when a man really had to worry.

John stood in the open doorway of the Calabrese Don's office, and tried to keep his posture as least defensive as he could. His arms stayed down at his side, and not folded over his chest. He kept his face expressionless, instead of the scowl he wanted to present.

Respect was not always easy to give.

"Johnathan," Matteo said with a wide smile.

Too wide.

John didn't move an inch. "Kev said you wanted to chat a bit more. In private, I take it."

Matteo nodded. "You guessed correctly. Come, have a seat."

The man waved at the chairs directly across from his large, cherry oak desk. Behind him, an entire wall was filled with old leather-bound books that lined the shelves. A skyline painting of New York hung on one wall, while a portrait of Carl Calabrese rested on another wall.

All over again, John fought to hide his discomfort.

It was getting harder to do.

John rested into one of the two leather chairs. His fingers clasped around the curved edges of the armrests, and he waited.

For what, he didn't know.

But *something* ...

Matteo gestured at a glass crystal filled with golden liquid. "Bourbon?"

John shook his head. "The whiskey was enough, if you wouldn't mind? I have to drive home."

Of course, he had to pose it like a question to Matteo. As though the man would get to decide whether or not John was done drinking for the night. He couldn't outright refuse the boss, so he had to try a different approach.

Matteo shrugged his large shoulders, and leaned back in the chair he dwarfed with his stature. "Yes, we wouldn't need you getting in trouble, all things considered."

John's jaw tightened. "Considering what, exactly?"

"Well, you've only been out of prison for what ... a couple of months?"

"Five at the end of December, actually."

Matteo pointed a finger at John, and wagged it. "Ah, see. And I bet you're still on some kind of parole conditions, aren't you?"

John stayed quiet.

The boss didn't seem to mind. "Mmm, I bet you are. If I remember correctly, your sentence was a five-year term. Yes, but you came out at, what, three years or so served before release?"

That time, Matteo did look to John for him to speak.

"Yes," John settled on saying.

Seeming satisfied with that line of questioning, Matteo came forward a bit to rest his beefy arms along the edge of the desk. He tipped his head to the side, and regarded John for a long moment before he spoke again.

And when he did speak, he completely changed directions.

"I heard some interesting information the other day, Johnathan," he said.

John cocked a brow. "What was that, boss?"

"Your cousin—Andino—has moved up in the Marcello family. An underboss, they told me. We didn't get the chance to properly speak about it at the restaurant. I'm expecting a meet with Dante and his new right hand soon, and it'll all be official then."

Typically, Cosa Nostra families didn't talk specifics about their respective organizations. It just wasn't good business practice. Despite the fact they all took the same oath, each family kept their secrets safely guarded.

For good reason …

Matteo didn't seem to need John's confirmation, however. "I did find it a little strange though, all things considered."

The man seemed to like that phrase a lot.

John didn't like it at all.

"Considering what?" John asked.

This all felt like one big circle. Matteo talked about what he wanted, and he led John exactly where he also wanted him to go in the conversation. It might have appeared like an open conversation from the outside looking in, but it definitely wasn't.

Matteo drummed his jeweled covered fingers to the desk. "Oh, come on, John. I'm sure you know that the Three Families in New York are always keeping up with the politics of the family next to them. It keeps us all in the loop."

"Sure, I guess."

John wasn't one-hundred percent sure why Matteo was doubling-down on this topic about his family, but he didn't like it. At the moment, there wasn't much more he could do other than sit there and listen to it.

Respect, and all.

"I think we all assumed it would be you moving up in the family when it came time—as I mentioned at the restaurant. You are the oldest, and your father is a very well respected made man. The longtime underboss to Dante Marcello—one of the most feared bosses in North America. And your other uncle—Giovanni—acting as a consigliere. That was the kind of structure and influence you grew up in. It just made sense for it to be you."

John didn't blink. "Andino grew up with those same people, and those same influences."

"So he did, I suppose." Matteo sighed, and looked to his left out the window at the dark sky. "But it's still a little odd that you haven't been given more control, John. A shame really. I don't think your potential is being put to work at its fullest. Not by a long shot."

"Maybe not, but it is what it is," John returned.

Matteo's lips curved at the corner. "So it seems, doesn't it?"

John chose not to answer that time.

• • •

John had his back turned to the entrance hallway as he shrugged on his jacket. He didn't see Siena coming for him until she had grabbed his jacket, and yanked him into the mudroom with her. She slammed the door shut behind them as he righted himself.

"What the *hell*, woman?" John asked.

Siena folded her arms over her chest, and refused to look him in the eye. "*Why*, John? Why couldn't you have just woke me up that morning? Knocked on my fucking forehead or something to make me wake up and say you had to run. You didn't even try to contact me after, and then out of the blue, you're here again like it's fine. It's not fine!"

John's brow lifted. "Are you usually this back and forth with your emotions? It's a little concerning, Siena."

She glared.

He shrugged.

"I thought …" She pressed her lips tightly together, as though she was refusing to say whatever had come to her mind.

"What?"

"That maybe you weren't like every other guy that tries to get me in bed, John. It turned out that you were exactly like every other guy."

John did stand a little bit straighter at that comment. "First, I was interested in you—still am. Second, shit came up, and I had to bolt. After that day, more things kept coming up that I had to deal with. I wasn't supposed to be getting romantically involved with somebody anyway, and I figured after I left you without fuck all the first time, you probably didn't want to see me again."

"You were right about that."

Her posture screamed defensive.

Her eyes shouted pain.

She was still lying.

"I don't want to be somebody's plaything," she told him quietly.

John nodded. "I don't want somebody to fuck with my emotions. So hey, I won't treat you like a toy, and you try not to give me whiplash with this kind of nonsense. It's a two-way street."

Siena still wouldn't meet his eyes when she said, "I don't know what to feel."

"Welcome to my world."

He felt like that all the time.

Either he had too many feelings.

Or he had none at all.

There was no in between.

Siena's tongue peeked out to wet her lips. "I *want* to give you a chance to apologize."

John barely hid back his smile as he inched closer to her. "Oh?"

"A little."

"So do that, *donna*."

She peeked up at him through dark lashes. "Something tells me you're kind of a risk, though."

"That instinct is correct."

"Maybe, but are you a risk worth taking, John?" she asked.

Well, that he didn't have the answer to.

"I'm sorry I took off," he murmured.

They stood toe-to-toe, now. He moved his pinky outward, and stroked the side of her hand with it, that's how close they were. If he leaned down just a bit, his kiss could graze her forehead.

John wouldn't do any of that unless Siena wanted him to. However, that didn't mean that he didn't want to do it. Because he did. A whole lot.

There was something about this woman that had kept her on his mind for months. Sometimes, she wasn't always the focus because he dealt with one thing at a time when it came to his brain. She was always there, though, buzzing and poking. Occasionally, thoughts of her would come back to the forefront to tease him.

She was right.

He was a risk.

But so was she.

A woman like her with a family like she had—not to mention the shit he dealt with being bipolar and how it fucked with his relationships—was a *huge* risk for John.

A mess he didn't need.

A problem he might not be able to fix.

Something bad.

Siena tipped her head back, and stared up at him. "Say it again."

"Hmm, what?"

"How sorry you are."

"Will it make it better?" he asked.

Siena grinned. "Probably not entirely, but it'll get us there."

"I *am* interested in more than sex, Siena."

"And if I asked you to take me home tonight ..."

John smirked. "I would not say no."

He might be sorry, but he was also very much a fucking man. She was all woman. Every single part of him knew it, too.

"So maybe we could do that?" she asked quietly.

John cupped her jaw and neck with his palm, and felt the way her heart raced under his touch. Or maybe it was her nerves from approaching him like this after everything. That risk she had mentioned.

"How about this," he murmured, "I will take you to *my* place, and if something comes up, you are more than welcome to stay until I get back. Because really, shit always comes up for me first thing in the morning. So hey, it'll be up to you if you want to take off on me as payback for what I did to you."

Siena nipped on her bottom lip. "Yeah?"

"Yep."

"I'm supposed to be somewhere for work around eleven, or so."

"I can take you there," he promised, "and cabs do go to where I live."

She laughed.

John waited ...

He'd been waiting months for this, after all.

He could wait a few more seconds.

"Do you have good coffee?"

John chuckled, and bent down to press a quick kiss to her grinning mouth. He let his thumb drag over her lips as he pulled away. "The best coffee, actually."

"Okay, your apology is accepted."

"Thought so."

"For now," she added.

John could deal with that.

• • •

Typically, when John woke up to the sound of his phone dinging, it automatically put him in a shitty mood. He didn't mind so much when he rolled over to grab the chiming device that morning because he was fucking *satisfied.*

Not at all tired.

Feeling damn good.

Yeah, satisfied.

He rolled to his back, and peered at the screen of his phone while he rubbed his palm down his naked chest. His hand rested just above where the sheet covered his semi-erection, and he scrolled through the text message update.

From the pharmacy, it seemed.

Prescriptions for Johnathan Marcello are ready to be picked up at—

John tossed the phone aside, already done with the message. He knew he had to go pick up his new dose of meds. He tried the higher dosage of Lithium with the mixture of antianxiety and mood stabilizer meds that the therapist wanted him to use.

His mind felt like a fog from it all.

The therapist had suggested she lower the dose of the Lithium. John hadn't bothered to tell her, but he had already started to half the Lithium every day, anyway. It was the only way he could break his mind out of the medicated fog it created.

He'd grab the prescriptions, but he still had a good three weeks' worth of his old meds before he had to worry about it. Then he would have to play the new pill game with the therapist while she tested yet another dose on him.

John didn't even need to roll over in the bed to know that the other side was empty. He'd felt the loss of Siena the moment she crawled out of bed about an hour ago, and had only gone back to sleep when he heard the shower turn on from the connecting bathroom.

He rested his arm behind his head as a makeshift pillow, and listened. Something metal clanged downstairs—a pot, likely.

Unlike him, Siena didn't seem to be a flight risk. She would have had every right to bolt on him even if she had promised to still be there in the morning after she dragged him into the bedroom.

He took that as a battle won.

Fucking that woman was like taking a five-mile run first thing in the morning. It woke him up out of the stupor that was his everyday life, and left him out of breath. She worked him good, made his muscles ache by the end of it all, but still feeling like another go 'round was a likely possibility.

A louder clang echoed from downstairs, and was followed by a loud cuss. John decided it was time to get up before Siena fucking hurt herself, or something. He pulled on a pair of sleep pants to cover his lower half, but nothing was hiding the half-mast of his dick pushing against the cotton.

Fuck it.

Soon enough, John was leaning in the entryway of the kitchen, and he watched as Siena balanced on a chair while she tried to pull a mixing bowl off the highest shelf in the pantry cupboard. Her wet hair hung in rivulets down her back, and he could see just a peek of her bare ass beneath the dress shirt she had thrown on.

His shirt.

It looked far better on her.

He didn't even mind.

Those bare legs of hers—all soft lines, and sweet curves—looked damn good as she tried to balance on one foot and stretch to reach the bowl high above her head. He was so caught up in staring at her that he didn't even mind she had seemed to tear his cupboards apart.

Anyone else, and John's odd tendencies about his place and things being just how he wanted them might have come out to play in a not so nice way.

But this was her.

And he didn't mind so much with her.

"Need some help?" he asked.

She must not have heard him coming downstairs because the shriek she let out damn near burst his eardrums. Not to mention, her body swayed on the chair, and she missed her step when she set her foot back down.

John bolted forward, and barely managed to catch Siena before she hit either the chair, the floor, or fucking *both*. Her brown hair created a curtain over her face, and she blew out a hard breath. A couple of strands puffed forward before Siena used a hand to push the hair back.

He'd caught her just a few inches from the floor. Lucky, really.

"Make some noise," she told him, glowering. "I almost killed myself."

"Thank you, John," he mocked, "for not letting that happen."

Siena pursed her lips. "And that, too!"

"Mmhmm."

She grabbed his jaw with one hand, pulled him in close, and gave him a kiss that made his dick go from half-mast to all the way hard. *Damn*. All it took was her teasing little tongue flicking against his lips, and then the promise of a taste of her, and there he was … ready to go again.

"I was trying to make breakfast," she whispered against his grinning lips.

"You needed the biggest bowl to do that?"

"Pancakes are messy, okay."

John nodded. "Sure."

"I kind of tore some cupboards apart looking for things."

"As long as you put it all back, I don't care."

Siena winked. "Deal. Will you get me the bowl?"

"You bet."

He straightened up, and put Siena to her bare feet. He didn't even need the damn chair that she had been trying to use to kill herself and get the bowl. All he had to do was lean up and grab the stupid thing out of the cupboard.

John easily snatched the bowl without trouble, and handed it to a scowling Siena. "Oh, don't look like that, now."

"It's not fun being short. Do you know how much it sucks to need a stool to reach anything? Nothing is made for my height."

"You're not … *short*. I mean, not for a woman. You're average."

Siena's mouth popped open, and then she took that bowl and smacked him in the arm with it. "Don't you call me average!"

John laughed, and rubbed his arm at the same time. Shit, that hurt. Her glare was also funny which only made him laugh harder. It felt strange and good. He couldn't remember a time when he had a morning like this. If he ever had one …

Siena pouted. "Don't laugh at me, too! That's doubly insulting, John."

Her downcast gaze was the only thing to sober him up. Instantly, he was reaching out to grab hold of Siena, and drag her to him. She softened against his chest, and tipped her head back to stare up at him. Those pretty pink lips of hers kissed the underside of his unshaved jaw.

"You're not an average woman," he murmured, kissing the top of her head. "You're beautiful and amazing, and you come in a slightly smaller package when it comes to height."

Her palm tapped against his chest jokingly.

"You're forgiven."

"Good." He dropped another kiss to her head. "Now, someone owes me breakfast. So, get on that, would you?"

John let Siena go, and smacked her ass as she passed him by. The cute little glare she shot over her shoulder at him only earned her a wink in response.

While Siena busied herself at the counter, John eyed the cupboard over the fridge. Nothing looked out of place on top of the fridge to say she had looked up there for anything. All his medications were kept safe, it seemed.

At least, for now.

If the two of them continued with whatever this was, John was going to have to bring up the topic of his disorder, and what it all meant. For him, and for her. It was the right thing to do, but the idea also left him with a heavy weight in his gut.

For more reasons than he cared to admit.

Would she bolt?

Would she look at him differently?

"Hey," Siena said from the island.

John glanced her way as her voice dragged him from his black mind.

"What, *bella?*"

"Do you have honey?"

"For what?"

"It's better than plain old corn syrup. You don't have *real* maple syrup."

"Aunt Jemima isn't maple syrup?" John asked.

Siena arched a brow. "Are you serious?"

"It says maple on the bottle."

"It says *flavored*. It's corn syrup with flavoring added."

Huh.

"I have honey."

She gave him a look. "*Real* honey?"

"Yes, real honey."

Siena winked. "Good."

John turned to the pantry, and pulled the honey in question from the shelf. Still unopened, the jar was filled to the rim with golden sweetness. He strolled over, and set it beside the bowl where Siena was already starting to fill it with dry ingredients.

She peeked over at him. "Do you want to help?"

"I think I like watching you more."

Her smile teased him. "That so?"

"Yeah, love."

"*La dolce vita,*" she said, grinning.

"The sweet life."

Siena nodded. "Every man likes to feel like a king in his home, doesn't he?"

John laughed a husky tune. "Some men certainly do."

"Are you one of those men?"

"I am right now."

Siena's floury hand patted his cheek, and left powder behind. "You're lucky I like you, Johnathan Marcello. I don't particularly care for spoiled men most of the time."

"Maybe you've been around the wrong kind of men, then."

Her blue eyes traveled over him once, and then twice.

"Most definitely."

John wasn't sure what did it for him—the way she was looking at him with those clear, honest eyes of hers, or the way her tone echoed with sin when it reached his ears. It could have been the way she looked in his shirt, too.

Whatever it was, it made the need for food come second to the need he felt for her.

John reached for Siena, and had her backside up on the counter before she even blinked. His mouth was on hers as his hands skimmed under the hem of the dress shirt covering her body. Soft, smooth skin met his warm palms while her tongue danced with his.

Something fell off the counter—the smaller bowl she had found, maybe. He didn't even care.

Her flour dusted hands left marks down his chest while her fingernails raked over the same spots. She widened her thighs as his hands slipped higher under the shirt, and found her pert tits. Hard nipples rolled under his thumbs, and then her teeth sunk into his bottom lip.

She promised.

She teased.

She gave.

She took.

Siena didn't have to say a thing, either. It was all in the way she touched him, how she kissed him, when she looked at him, and the way he felt from it all. The sensations clashed together like a wrecking ball coming through to tear down what little walls he had left for control, and there he was, pieces of a mess on the ground.

Her mess.

John yanked open the dress shirt to expose more of her body to him, and likely ruined three buttons in the process. Her skin heated and pebbled under his touch. She tipped her head back, and let him ghost kisses over her throat while his exploration went lower. The taste of her skin on his tongue was unlike anything else. He found one taste was not enough.

It never was.

Silky smooth, wet flesh met his fingertips between her thighs. Her little gasp when he stroked her sex with the pad of his thumb made him grin.

"So fucking responsive," he murmured against her throat.

Siena's throat bobbed with her hard swallow. "Something about you, John."

"That what it is?"

"Something," she echoed again.

He was more than happy to get her making more of those sounds. Nothing made him harder, or got him fucking hotter. Pulling back, he kissed her once hard.

"Don't move," he said.

"Promise I won't."

Siena stayed like a sexy little statue on the counter while John dug through the junk drawer on the other side of the island. Anything he had extra of, he just shoved it in there. Soon enough, he found what he needed.

A condom.

By the time he was back between the heaven of Siena's thighs, she seemed to have decided to take the lead. Her deft hands snuck beneath his sleep pants, and found his cock. The way her palm circled him, and stroked him even more awake was damn addicting. He handed over the foil packet when she reached for it.

Pants shoved down around his hips, and latex rolled onto his length, John figured he had waited long enough. He yanked Siena to the very edge of the counter when he first heard the phone ringing upstairs.

His cell phone.

The familiar tune—one he used for the boss—echoed in the back of his mind.

John ignored the call, and kissed Siena instead. The heat of her mouth tempted him while the wet slit of her cunt teased him. She rubbed the head of his cock along her pussy, and rocked her hips back and forth at the same time.

The phone call stopped ringing upstairs damn near to the second John flexed his hips forward. He found himself buried nine inches deep into Siena, and instantly without air. It all rushed from his lungs with the wave of relief that slid down his spine.

A heat like no other filled him.

A satisfaction like he'd never known slipped through him.

A want he had never known thundered inside him.

Her soft voice in his ear, and her fingernails dragging down his back urged him on. Every *please*, and *there, God, there* mixed in with her high and breathless cries. The prettiest music he had ever heard.

The phone started ringing again.

John was lost in something far better.

His fingertips dug into Siena's ass as he pulled her into every one of his thrusts. He could feel the tremor working its way through her legs when she tightened them around his hips. Her pussy squeezed him tight, and sucked him deeper.

It was in her eyes, though—a high, crazed look stared back at him.

He knew that stare.

It looked far better on her than it did on him.

Especially like this.

"Jesus Christ," she breathed.

John bit her jaw. "It's *John*, actually."

Siena's breathless laughter was interrupted by the clenching of her muscles. Her orgasm came on quick, and left her raking lines down his naked back.

John wasn't even close to being done.

• • •

"This better be fucking good," John grumbled when he walked in his uncle's office.

His steps faltered at the many men who waited inside the space. His uncles, father, and Andino. His gaze skipped to the most important man in the room because the boss was always the first one to be respected before anyone else—Dante.

"What's going on?" John asked.

Lucian spoke up first. "Have a seat, son."

John straightened his suit jacket. "Nah, I'm good. I kind of want to know why I'm here, though. I don't like to be interrupted, you know."

Those phone calls didn't stop coming until John forced himself away from Siena to answer one. His uncle said nothing except to get to the fucking mansion. Just like that—nothing else.

"Yeah, I bet," Giovanni muttered.

John gave his youngest uncle a look. "What the fuck does that mean?"

"John," Dante said, his tone thick with a warning. "Show some respect, huh?"

He checked his attitude, but not because he fucking wanted to.

"Yeah, all right." John gave the boss his attention. "I'm here—what's up?"

"You didn't think to tell any of us that you were going to be having dinner with the Calabrese boss and his family last night?" Dante asked.

"I was invited," John replied, shrugging. "Tell me how to refuse that without breaking the rules we live by, and I will do that next time."

"You still didn't tell anyone," his father said.

John didn't see why that mattered. "I didn't need to. It was a *dinner*."

"With the Calabrese *boss*. You know how the Marcellos feel about that family, John," Giovanni put in.

John's attention was still only on the boss. "I couldn't be disrespectful, and refuse. So, I went. It's over."

"You cannot trust a Calabrese," Dante murmured.

The familiar green eyes of his uncle bore into John. For some reason—not one he could pull forward right away—he didn't think Dante was only talking about Matteo and his sons.

"I don't trust the Calabrese boss, or his shithead sons," John countered. "I remember what they did to my father's family."

Lucian cleared his throat, but said nothing.

"Why didn't you answer my calls this morning?" Dante asked quietly. "You were fine with telling me you couldn't disrespect Matteo, and yet you made me call you ten times before you finally answered. What was so important this morning that you couldn't answer me, Johnathan?"

"I was busy."

His answer was not good enough.

He knew before he said it.

Dante nodded, and leaned back in the chair. "I know you took the

Calabrese girl home with you, John. See, I found out about the dinner invitation, and thought just in case, you should have someone follow behind. I don't trust snakes like those ones in Brooklyn, and in no way will I allow a man of mine to confer with them without some kind of backup."

John only heard one thing in all of that.

One thing that made him enraged.

One thing that burned him like betrayal.

"You fucking had someone *follow me?*" he asked, deathly still and dark in his heart.

"I—"

"Someone tailed me?"

"John," Andino said, pushing off the edge of the desk. "He thought it would be best considering how the Calabrese are sometimes."

John's vision blackened.

His lungs ached with every breath.

All over again, he was left feeling like he did when he was first released from prison. Like a fucking wild animal that nobody trusted. Like he couldn't do his damn job because someone always had to be looking over his shoulder.

"Because I can't look out for myself or be trusted, right?" John asked. "That's funny, *boss*, considering the Calabrese didn't make any effort to hide fuck all about their intentions when they invited me to dinner. Except my own family does exactly that instead of just fucking asking me. But they're the ones I have to watch out for, huh?"

John let out a bitter laugh.

"It's not a big deal," Dante said, "and it's not like you're making it out to be, John."

"Or is it exactly that, boss?" he asked. "Have you gotten someone to follow me before this time, too?"

No one answered.

John didn't need them to at that point.

"Why?" he asked.

At least, his family was honest.

Brutally so.

"Andi mentioned you had an interest in the Calabrese girl," Dante said.

John's gaze flew to his cousin—bitter and full of anger. "What, you ran to tattle on me like a fucking baby, or something?"

"No, I—"

"Screw you, Andino."

Andino stepped forward, but John pointed at his best friend to keep the new little underboss back a step. A silent warning that Andino knew all too well.

John's father, on the other hand, had never cared. Lucian came closer, and John's jaw clenched so hard his molars might have cracked.

"John, they cannot be trusted, and you know that," Lucian said. "Not the men, and certainly not one of their women. No matter who she is."

That probably stung the worst.

They didn't even know Siena.

It was just her last name that colored her bad.

Like his disorder left them assuming shit about him.

It was all the same.

"Fuck you all."

The three words slipped out of John's mouth easier than he expected them to, and he let them escape before he really thought it over.

Dante stood from his chair.

Lucian came one step closer.

Giovanni didn't move.

Andino just frowned.

John shook his head, and turned for the door. He was done with whatever this was. He was done with them for today.

"Yeah, fuck every single one of you."

CHAPTER TEN

JOHN'S PLACE was spotless ...

Siena kept that thought in mind as she finished up washing the last few dishes from the pancake mess she had made. A plate of pancakes sat on the cupboard, untouched and getting cooler by the minute.

She remembered the night before that Johnathan's bed had been perfectly made before they climbed in it, and messed it all up. Then, when he left this morning, he had taken five minutes to fix his bed again before he left the house.

For a bachelor who lived on his own, Siena expected Johnathan to be at least a little untidy. Like most men who lived alone were. A few clothes scattered somewhere. A floor that could use a sweep. Knickknacks or mismatched treasures spread out on shelves or tables.

Nothing.

Johnathan had none of those.

His place was meticulously clean. His floors were shiny enough that someone could probably eat off them. She noticed that morning even the clothes in his walk-in closet were carefully hung by color, and arranged by each type of item.

It was all a little OCD-like, in some ways. Except ... Siena knew Johnathan likely wasn't struggling with Obsessive Compulsive Disorder. She only leaned toward that impression because she noticed him, too.

He didn't say a word when she went through his kitchen, or made a mess. He didn't have any strange rituals or compulsions, so to speak, for her to take note of. He washed his hands before and after he ate, and when he went to the bathroom, but that was about it.

Was it possible he just managed the disorder through tidiness and organizing every little thing? Sure, but she really didn't think that was the case at all.

Siena was also quite aware that OCD could not be simplified in to strange habits and a compulsive need to do very specific things.

She really shouldn't be speculating at all.

It wasn't her place.

Those pancakes are going to be disgusting.

Siena scrubbed the massive bowl John had barely needed to reach for. She eyed the stack of three pancakes on the plate a couple of feet away.

She didn't know what to do with them because she didn't have the first clue when John was going to be back. The man had no plastic wrap in his house to put over food—she hadn't even found containers for leftovers.

Whether or not that was because John didn't eat leftovers, or perhaps it was something else entirely. Like the fact those containers always somehow magically lost their lids, made a mess in the cupboard, and were not at all very tidy despite how the commercials made them look.

Who knew?

Siena had also noticed in her search of the kitchen that Johnathan tended to favor healthy foods. Organic seemed to be a favorite of his, like the eggs in the fridge, and the honey she had used on her own pancakes. However, that corn syrup in the fridge was not healthy at all.

Seemed he made a few exceptions.

Like the Oreos in the pantry.

Siena smiled to herself as she rinsed off the bowl. For as fit as John was, she couldn't exactly imagine him binging on a package of cookies.

But what did she know?

Siena went about drying the dishes and putting them all away. She opted to leave the big bowl on the cupboard beside the pantry where she had found it.

The clock on the wall said it was only nine, which meant she still had a couple of hours before she needed to be at her father's dealership. It only really registered to her in that moment that her phone had been dark all night and morning.

No calls from Matteo.

No calls from her brothers.

None of them had even come downstairs when Johnathan left the night before, so she seriously doubted that they knew she had left with him. Except … her car was still at her parents' brownstone, so they must have suspected.

Yet, no calls.

No check-in to make sure she wouldn't be late today.

Nothing.

The cupboard over the fridge caught Siena's eye. It was the only cupboard she hadn't gotten the chance to check while she was prepping to cook earlier.

Maybe a container or something would be in there to store the food until John got back. Pulling a chair out from the table, she pulled it over and stepped up onto it. The half of a dozen cards and papers pinned to the fridge made her pause.

One in particular made her stop altogether.

Dr. Amelia Goodane, PhD and PsyD, the card read. It had an address and phone number printed on the plain, white card. Under the woman's name, it said, *Psychologist.*

The appointment printed on the card was for January eighth, at eight o'clock in the morning.

Today.

Siena glanced at the clock. Actually, an hour ago.

Had he blown off his appointment, or just forgot altogether?

Her gaze drifted back to the card as she took in the doctor's qualifications once more. John was in therapy—but for what?

Siena figured it didn't matter because it wasn't her damn business to begin with. Had he wanted her to know, then John would have brought it up.

Besides, it wasn't like they were a *thing.* They weren't anything where he owed her something, and certainly not an explanation about his personal business.

She put the card aside in her mind, and reached for the cupboards. Better to get the food put away, and deal with whatever else later *if* John decided it was something she needed to know about him.

The cupboard did not have containers or plastic wrap.

It didn't even have food.

Medication greeted her. Pill bottles with child safety orange caps stared back at her. She thought to close the door to the cupboard because this was—*again*—none of her business, but her gaze stiff drifted over the labels.

Johnathan Antony Marcello

His name was on every single one.

Lithium. Zoloft.

Another mood stabilizer.

Antidepressants.

Antianxiety meds.

It was a lot.

Some were obviously discarded meds, maybe ones he no longer used for whatever reason, considering the dates on the bottles and amount of pills still inside.

There were lots of rumors about the infamous Johnathan Marcello. Many of them passed Siena by because she only heard things from afar when made men gathered, and she happened to be around.

Some of them called John crazy. Some said he was just a little wild.

His arrest years ago that took him to prison had also led to lots of speculation about just what had gone down between John and his cousin in a restaurant. Apparently, some people that had been there said it was like

John had fallen into a mental break or something.

No one knew for sure.

Siena had heard those rumors.

All of them.

She didn't entertain whispered gossip and stories. Not when it came from the mouths of men who would only say something behind someone's back, and never to their face.

And that was enough for her.

Siena instantly slammed the cupboard doors, and stepped down from the chair. She did it without thinking, and never having touched one of the bottles.

A huge part of her felt like she had just betrayed Johnathan in some way, even though she couldn't pinpoint exactly what it was. She hadn't been snooping, and in fact, didn't even leave the kitchen the entire time he had been gone except to use the bathroom once.

And yet, she still felt wrong.

Like she had done something wrong to him.

The purr of a Mercedes pulling in the driveway outside made her forget about it.

At least now for …

• • •

"Ease up on the pedal a bit," Siena joked, "I'm not even late or anything."

John's white-knuckle grip on the steering wheel loosened ever so slightly. His gaze slipped to the clock on the dashboard, and the car slowed down subtly. "Yeah, sorry."

Something in the lilt of his tone caught her attention. Siena looked at him, but John's focus was only on the road ahead of him.

"Everything okay?" she asked.

John nodded. "Sure."

"Really?"

The bobbing of his throat as he swallowed hard did not escape her notice. Neither did the way his fingers tightened around the wheel again like he needed something to keep hanging onto. All of it felt wrong to her.

She just didn't know why.

"Did something happen?" Siena asked.

John chuckled. "Oh, something is always happening, *dolcezza*. Don't worry about it."

"You can tell me anything, if you want—"

"It's fine," he interjected quietly.

Siena let it drop.

What choice did she have at the moment?

"You sure we're going to make it to the dealership in enough time?" he asked.

Siena settled in the passenger seat. He had already taken her to her apartment to change, and freshen up. "We have lots of time."

She didn't bother to mention she might be a little late. Thirty minutes, or so.

The phone in her purse was still silent, though. No calls or texts from her father or brothers. It was like—for once—they didn't care at all that she was late.

Any other time, and her phone wouldn't stop until she walked through the front door of whatever business she was supposed to be working in.

John cleared his throat, and said, "So, I never thought to ask before …"

"Hmm, what?"

"You do their books, huh?"

Siena smiled a little. "Something like that."

"What's what mean?"

"Someone does the main books for the businesses, sure."

John nodded. "Let me guess, you go in and clean 'em up."

"Something like that," she echoed.

His hazel eyes drifted to her, and then slowly looked her over. It was enough to make Siena heat up under the jeans, blouse, and tweed coat she had thrown on at her place. John wasn't even ashamed of his staring when he smirked, and then went back to staring at the road.

"I wouldn't have taken you for an accountant," he admitted.

"No?"

"Maybe a school teacher, or nurse. Something like that."

Siena snorted. "I like numbers, actually. I like *facts*. Things that add up, or work in the end. It's just how my brain tries to see everything, I guess."

"Yeah, I get that."

"My dad noticed that my grades in high school for math and sciences were high. I was taking college prep courses for those areas. Numbers make sense to me, if you get what I'm trying to say."

John laughed under his breath. "Numbers make sense to me, too. You know, when I can add more zeroes behind the first number."

Siena grinned. "I bet."

"Yeah, but keep going with your story."

"He had me doing books for some of the little businesses he owns when I was a senior in high school. He pushed me toward accounting degrees and whatnot after I graduated. I would have went in to something with math or science as a focus, anyway, but …"

John glanced over at her. "Does it feel like you didn't get a choice?"

"Sometimes," she admitted.

"So, you're the one who handles the Calabrese numbers, huh?"

Siena wet her lips. "Not supposed to talk about business, John."

His eyes glinted with amusement. "How good can you scrub and cook a book, Siena?"

Well …

"I haven't found a dollar amount yet that I can't hide, John."

He whistled low.

"Damn, *donna*."

Siena laughed right along with John. A second later, he reached over to find her thigh with his palm. He squeezed her inner thigh overtop her jeans, and shot her a wink. Then, just as quickly, his hand slid in with hers. Silently, he intertwined their fingers together, and held on tight.

John brought her hand up, leaned over, and pressed three light kisses across her knuckles. He didn't say a thing while he did it, but he didn't really need to, either.

It was such a small action.

A little bit of affection.

She didn't know what to make of it, but she liked it.

"What are we doing?" she asked him.

John didn't even think about it before answering. "I mean, whatever you want to do, Siena."

"Are we … doing something now?"

"Like what, Siena? Right now, I'm driving you to work."

"No, I mean, you and me, John."

He cleared his throat, and shifted a bit in the driver's seat. "Depends on if you're still angry with me about taking off on you and shit."

"Blackmail, huh?"

John didn't even try to hide his grin. "I have to make you forget about that somehow, don't I?"

"I'm not … mad," she said. "I might bring it up, but I'm not mad."

His laughter came out thick and husky.

A melody of sin.

"I see," John said.

"Anyway, I just … want to know. If we are doing something, or whatever. So, I know from the jump what's going on here. I don't like games, John."

"We can be doing something," he murmured, his gaze drifting from the road to her, and then back again. "You might want to let me take you out properly or something, but that's up to you."

She hummed under her breath, very much liking the idea he proposed. "I will hold you to that."

"Noted. But you should know, I'm a terribly jealous fucker, and I

117

don't like to share."

"Me, either."

John's lips curved sinfully at the edges. "Got it, love."

"You can't blow me off without an explanation ever again," she warned.

"I can't make promises, but I'll always be back."

Siena took that offer in, and said, "Okay."

"Sometimes, I'm not very easy to deal with," John said, keeping his gaze firmly on the road and anywhere but on her. "It's just a part of who I am, Siena. I don't mean to make shit difficult, but it happens, regardless."

She thought about the things she found that morning.

Even though she hadn't meant to …

He was trying to tell her something without giving it all away.

"Okay," she said again.

John finally looked over at her. "Just okay, huh?"

Siena shrugged. "I never really liked easy—I like things that make sense. Like romance novels with a happily ever after, or numbers that need to add up in a book. You, too."

His dark, low chuckles rumbled in the car. Unbothered, grinning, and looking like he didn't have a fucking care in the world, Siena thought John was the most beautiful man she had ever seen in her life. All over again, at the sight of him like that, she was stuck silent.

"Not sure I always make sense," John admitted after a moment.

Siena thought differently.

"Everything makes sense when you look at all the details."

John nodded. "Maybe you're right."

There was no maybe.

On that, Siena knew she was right.

All too soon, John was pulling the Mercedes over along the side of the road. An unfamiliar dealership awaited her—luckily, she had been able to pull up the address of the place from her emails.

"This the place?" he asked.

"Yeah, this is the place."

John gave her a crooked grin. "Give them my apologies for making you late, and you know, whatever else."

"Not really worried about it, John."

He gave her no warning before he leaned over in the seat, and kissed her. A hard, bruising kiss that took her breath away, and had her heart racing out of control. Every stroke of his lips against hers, and his tongue darting into her mouth to dance with hers, felt more and more familiar.

His hand cupped her cheek, and his thumb stroked her skin.

Siena smiled as John pulled away. "You still haven't even asked for my number."

"I do know where you live, Siena."

"Still …"

John smiled widely, showing off white teeth and sex appeal in a blink. "Give me your damn phone, *bella*."

• • •

Siena's week crawled by at the usual slow pace she had become accustomed to. One day was spent dealing with her father, and the next, Darren. She jumped between businesses from day to day finishing up last minute details before the taxes would have to be filed for each and every one.

It was mid-January, after all. The deadline for filing was looming. Technically, it was her busiest time of year. Most of the work was left up to her.

Normally, Siena didn't mind because it wasn't like she had much of a life to begin with. Except when she was supposed to be focusing on cooking the books and making numbers work, her mind was on something else entirely.

Or rather … someone else.

John.

Sitting in the office of her oldest brother's favorite restaurant, Siena's gaze drifted between the three-inch high pile of documents she had just finished printing out, and the business accounts she had pulled up on the screen. While she electronically filed everything, she kept a physical backup just in case.

She still had things left to do.

Shit to go over.

Her finger hovered on the mousepad of the laptop. On the screen, the cursor rested on top of the web browser. She didn't use the work computers for personal business. Not that she couldn't, it was just the way she kept work and everything else separate.

Still, she clicked on the browser.

The office door was open, but the sounds of the restaurant filtering down the hall told her no one was coming. Kev had stepped out a while ago saying something about being hungry.

Siena still kept one eye on the door, and one eye on the Google search bar as she started typing in keywords.

Something had stuck with her for the whole week. Something just wouldn't let go of her mind. It kept going back there even when she tried to force it out for good.

She kept telling herself that it wasn't her business. The medications she had found in John's place was his thing to deal with, and he would tell her if

119

he wanted to.

And yet … she wanted to know.

Siena typed in *Lithium*, and hit the enter button. The first thing to come up was the metal element, but she scrolled down past that, and clicked on the medical information. She already kind of knew what the drug was used to treat—mostly being that it was a psychiatric medication. Clicking on the link that directed to a medical page dedicated to the drug, she found a list of disorders that Lithium was specifically targeted to.

She clicked on the back button, and came to the Google page again. This time, she added *psychotherapy and Lithium* into the search bar, and then hit the enter button. The first thing to come up on the page was some article on the correlation of the medication lithium being best used in conjunction with therapy.

The following pages that came up in the search continued to use the same disorder again and again in the preview texts.

Bipolar.

Major Depressive Disorder.

Mania.

Siena clicked on a link, and read down through the information. Just as fast, she went back and clicked on another. And then another.

Back on the search bar, she added in new keywords—other meds she remembered from the cupboard. All over again, the information seemed to lead straight to a cocktail that suggested Bipolar.

A huge part of her wanted to close the browser down because none of this was supplied by Johnathan. He had not told her these things, and she didn't even know for sure if this was what he was dealing with behind closed doors.

Another part of her wanted to … understand.

If this was a part of his life, and something he was managing privately, she wanted to know more about it.

So, she went back to the search bar again. She typed in, *Bipolar*, and hit enter. She read through signs and symptoms, and how it was managed. Information came up on things like mania, cycles, and the depression that so often trailed those dealing with the disorder.

She found accounts from people who explained what their mania had been like for years before it was finally properly diagnosed. Not to mention, the things they had done to those around them during the spells, and the way their lives had been upended in the struggle for help.

Some of it was frightening.

Some of it was uplifting.

A lot of it was hopeful.

A bipolar diagnosis for a lot of people seemed to be a relief. An actual confirmation that yes, they did feel things differently, and see the world and themselves in a different way. They processed emotional events or feelings at a different pace, and most of the time, at a far greater intensity. It didn't mean they were crazy, but rather, had to use different treatments and methods to manage the aspects of bipolar that negatively impacted them.

Siena just kept reading. She kept looking for more information, and a better understanding. She was a good thirty minutes into reading before voices directly outside the office finally made her blink away from the screen.

"So he's fine with letting all of that go on, then?" Kev asked.

"Guess so," Darren replied. "It's that opening he's been looking for, you know what I mean?"

"Yeah, it just might be."

Siena moved to click the exit button from the browser just as her two brothers walked in the office. She just got the browser closed as Kev rounded the desk, and jerked his thumb for her to move out of his chair.

His gaze darted to the accounts on the screen that had replaced the browser. Siena gave a silent sigh of relief that the browser closed in time. She didn't know how she would even begin explaining something like that to Kev.

"Move your ass," Kev said.

"I still have work to finish up, Kev," Siena told him.

Her brother shrugged like he didn't give a damn. "Take a break, or something."

Siena's brow furrowed. "Since when do you want me to take breaks?"

"Yeah, well, Dad reminded me to keep you fed," Kev grumbled as he began closing out the accounts on the screen. "There's a plate waiting for you in the kitchen, and somebody stopped by to see you, I guess."

"Who?"

"Just go find out. You've got an hour at the most, and then you need to get back to work."

She gave her brother a dirty look before leaving the office. There was a plate waiting for her, but the waiter simply directed her out onto the floor, but not before grabbing a second plate to carry.

It was John waiting for her.

He sat at a private table away from the rest of the diners. Blocked off by a partial wall, he stared out the window until Siena came to sit with him. The sexy grin he flashed had her pulse picking up. He looked damn good with his dark hair slicked back, a well-fitted suit tight to his fit form, and that goddamn smile.

Standing from the table, John allowed the waiter to sit the plates down, and then the man scattered. John reached for Siena, and pulled her in for a quick kiss. For the most part, all they had gotten to do over the week was text back and forth. She was too busy with work and everything else to go out, or stay over. He seemed okay with it, though.

"Sit, and eat with me," he murmured against her lips.

"This is why you texted me this morning to ask where I was going to be?"

"All you do is work, *donna.*"

He kind of wasn't lying.

"So, is this …" Siena waved at the food, and then between them, "… like a date?"

John chuckled, and his smirk deepened. "Exactly that, yeah."

"And what comes after said date, Johnathan?"

"Whatever you want, Siena."

She laughed, and wagged a finger at him. "Smooth. Leaving the details up to me."

"Hey, I got over here today, didn't I?"

He did.

It meant the world to her.

Had someone asked her what she would like for a date, anything that didn't include being within five miles of her family would have been at the top of the list. Johnathan managed to keep her within thirty feet of her family, and she didn't mind at all.

All she saw was him.

John first.

Everything came second.

"How was your week?" John asked.

"Good."

"Anything come up?"

Siena could have asked or said a lot of things at that moment. The thing she knew, or the stuff she suspected. Yet, she didn't ask or say a thing. Not about any of it, and not because she didn't want to know, either.

John was John.

She saw him first.

Everything else was second.

CHAPTER ELEVEN

"COME ON, LUCIA," John muttered. "Pick up the damn phone."

He drummed his fingers to the leather-wrapped steering wheel, and glared at the form leaning against a car just ahead of his. At the moment, he had something else to focus on other than the fact Andino was following him around.

Like his goddamn sister, and the fact she wouldn't answer his calls. None of them. He'd called repeatedly since she went back to California, but he got nothing back. Not even a *fuck you* text.

It was driving him crazy.

John wanted to fix shit with Lucia, but he couldn't do that when she wouldn't even let him speak to her. Apparently, his sister was not messing around when she had told him after Christmas that she planned to have nothing to do with the rest of them.

Fuck.

"Call me, Lucia," John barked into the message when the phone beeped.

He shoved the phone in his pocket, and got out of the car. Staring at the warehouse across the road, he tried to relax a bit before he had to do business. He didn't need to go in there already in a bad mood.

"What, you're going to act like I'm not fucking standing right here or something?"

"That's exactly what I plan on doing, Andino."

To make his point clear, John slammed the door of his Mercedes shut, and crossed the street without as much as a wave at Andino. Grumbling something under his breath, Andino pushed off his own car, and headed after John.

"Wait a second, man."

"I have fuck all to say to you."

"Listen, I came all the way down to this part of the city to talk to you today, John. The least you could do is fucking listen to me for five minutes."

"No, the least I could do is what I am doing. Ignoring you, and not beat you into the ground for the shit you pulled on me."

"Hey—"

"And how the fuck did you know I was going to be here today, anyway?" John asked.

He never turned around.

Andino's footsteps kept following behind.

"Kev and Darren Calabrese do the same shit every month. Today is the day the crews get together with the Capos, and everything gets worked out for the next couple of weeks. I figured since you kept letting my calls go to voicemail, I might as well come here."

"Maybe you should have taken that as a goddamn *hint*."

And left him the hell alone.

John wasn't asking for a whole lot.

A little over a week after the men of his family cornered him—or that's how it felt—and John was still not over it. In fact, he felt worse about it than he had that morning.

They didn't trust him.

Not to get shit done.

Not to make the right choices.

Nothing.

To put the icing on that cake, they had to try and dictate his fucking romantic life like it was any of their goddamn business. It wasn't. He wouldn't allow them to think it was, either. That shit was never going to be on the table for them to meddle in.

Ever.

"Are you going to slow down and talk to me?" Andino asked.

"My legs are still moving. A lot like your dumbass mouth. Take the hint."

"Come on, let me explain, John."

The warehouse where he had to meet up with the Calabrese brothers was all but twenty feet away. If he picked up his pace, he could be inside and working in a few minutes. Andino's little show would be over and done with.

John couldn't do that.

Andino's words hit a damn nerve.

Spinning on his heel, John took one huge step forward, and came toe-to-toe with Andino. His cousin had a good thirty pounds of muscle on him, but they stood damn near eye level with one another. It wouldn't be the first time the two of them went to blows over something.

He wasn't scared of Andino.

Andino wasn't frightened of him.

It was a bad combination.

"Say that again," John urged, his tone dipping low.

"What, that you should let me fucking explain what happened?"

"Yeah, man. Go on, tell me how you sold out my personal business to our fathers and Dante like you had any business doing so in the first place. Tell me how you not only put Siena in my path by inviting her to a club, but then went behind my back and told them I was involved with her, too. That's fucking shady, Andino."

John hit his cousin in the chest with a closed fist. Not hard, but firm enough that it made his point loud and clear. "Fucking. Shady."

"Get your hand off my body before I break it."

"You could try."

Andino's jaw clenched, and his green eyes darkened with anger.
Good.

He should be angry. Just like John was.

"It doesn't feel really fucking great when your family does shitty things to you, huh?" John asked.

"I didn't do what you think I did, John!"

John pushed his fist against Andino's chest again. "Fuck you. Thanks for the lesson, man. I needed it."

"What—"

"This conversation is over, Andi."

With that, John turned around and headed in the direction of the warehouse's entrance. Andino should have left it alone, but like the stubborn shit he was, he came after John. His cousin grabbed the back of his jacket, and pulled.

"John, you're going to talk to me!"

John spun around once more, and didn't even think about his next actions. He shoved Andino hard enough to send his cousin stumbling back.

Andino righted himself, and glared at John. He made a move like he was going to come forward at John, but didn't in the end. The two of them were left standing with ridged postures waiting for the other one to make a move.

"That's what you want to do?" Andino asked.

"No, man," John said, "but I will if you don't fuck off. I warned you, so figure it out before you force my hand here."

"I just want to explain."

"Your actions told me more than enough, Andino."

"John, we're Marcellos. The only people we have to trust in this life is each other. So fuck off with your mood, and give me a chance to tell you how this really went down. Give me that respect—don't you at least owe me that after everything?"

They'd been friends since Andino was born. His cousin always had his back, no matter what. Andino saved John from himself more times than he could count.

This still left a bad taste in John's mouth.

"When you were selling me out to Dante about Siena, did you think to mention that chick you're fucking behind everybody's backs?" John asked.

Andino stiffened, and his gaze hardened. "Excuse me?"

"Haven—right? That's her name. You think I don't know about her?" John smirked and nodded, saying, "Yeah, I heard you were seeing somebody they didn't approve of given your new position and all. Unlike you, I didn't go digging in your business, or mention that you were still running around with her despite the fact you're putting on a good show for them."

"You don't know anything about that, or her, John."

"I know enough to make it hurt." John pointed a finger at his cousin. "When, or *if*, I am ready to speak to you, then I will do that. Not one fucking second before. Get that through your thick skull, Andino. I decide when to see you, not the other way around."

"All right," Andino said.

"Good."

"One other thing, though."

John had all he could do not to punch Andino right in the throat. "What now?"

"You're ignoring your therapist appointments. Why?"

All over, John felt like someone had dumped ice cold water on him. "I beg your goddamn pardon?"

"You heard what I said."

"How in the fuck do you even know that?"

Andino glanced away, and shrugged. "I got a friend in with your parole officer. You miss an appointment, and the therapist has to report it. You miss three, and the parole officer has to write you up on it. What, are you trying to get your parole revoked, so you can go back in? Is that what it is?"

Again, someone was checking on his business. Again, someone was trying to stick their fucking nose where it didn't belong regarding John.

Again, he was shown how little faith they had in him.

"You know you have to go to those appointments, and not just for parole, either," Andino said. "I'm only trying to look out for—"

"Look out for yourself, and keep me out of it. You make me tell you that again, Andino, and we're going to have another incident like we did years ago. Only this time, I'll fucking finish it for good."

John didn't wait for his cousin to reply. He turned fast, and headed for the warehouse. This time, Andino didn't follow behind.

Inside the large building, John found the Calabrese brothers were already waiting for him. None of the crews from either organization had arrived yet, but he expected that. They showed up early to figure out any last minute details in private.

Kev and Darren Calabrese both sat on a table side by side in the middle of the warehouse.

"You two got nothing to do, or what?" John asked.

Kev shoved off the table with a chuckle. "Waiting on you, man."

"Sure, sure."

Darren ticked his chin up at John, asking, "Was that Andino I saw out there?"

John hesitated, and wondered just how much the Calabrese brothers had seen of his conversation with Andino. "Maybe. What about it?"

"Curious," Darren said.

"Curiosity kills men," John replied.

He headed for the corner where a white van had been parked. Inside the van would be some of the shit that needed to be dispersed between the foot soldiers of the three men's crews. Maybe if he got his hands busy with work, he could focus on other shit.

"Is that a thing for you, or something?" Kev asked.

John climbed in the back of the van, and wanted nothing more than to just get this work done. He had energy to burn. He was sleeping erratically, and very little when he did actually close his eyes.

"Is what a thing?" John asked.

He tore open boxes, and pulled out wrapped bricks of drugs. Weed, cocaine, meth, and more. A lot of pharmaceuticals. All hidden and packed in paper hay.

"Them babysitting you," Kev said, leaning into the back of the van. "Sending someone to check in on your business, and making sure everything is on the up. What, you can't handle your own shit, or something?"

All of John's irritations and misgivings about his family and how they treated him were being reflected in Kev's statements. A man who didn't know John, the shit he dealt with on a daily basis because of his disorder, or how that made his family treat him differently.

Yet, they could see it.

Kev saw how John was the weak link to the Marcellos.

Or, that's how it felt.

"I handle my shit," John said.

"Yeah, but do they really let you?"

"Or do they just make it seem like they're letting you?" Darren asked, leaning in beside his brother.

John shot the two men a look, and hated how unease and distrust burrowed into his nerves even more. Not for these men—he didn't give a fuck about the Calabrese idiots. No, for his own blood; for his own family.

The things they were doing made him unsteady. In his heart, and in his life. It made for shitty days, and bad moods.

It screwed up his mind.

It messed with his emotions.

It fucked him up.

"I handle myself just fine," John said.

He wanted to get Kev and Darren off the topic of him and his family.

"Yeah, I mean," Kev said, "that's obvious, John."

"Except not to your people, I guess," Darren added. "Do you get what I'm saying, Marcello?"

Did he?

That was the million-dollar question.

• • •

"Johnathan?"

John cursed under his breath at the sound of his mother calling out for him. Still, he kept his attention focused on his tasks. Things he wanted to get done—it kept piling up, but he just worked through it, regardless.

The cupboards were stacked high with everything inside of them. Bowls he had placed by size. Glass and silverware that he wanted to change from one cupboard to another. The food from the pantry that needed to be reorganized because why in the hell had there been boxes with cans? And on the same fucking *shelf.*

It drove him nuts.

Nonsense.

He'd already ran through his office upstairs, took a five-mile run that morning, and reorganized his collection of movies and music from alphabetical to most liked through the most disliked.

And it was only …

John shot a look at the clock.

Ten in the morning.

It probably helped that he had enough energy to burn that sleep wasn't even a bother at the moment. An hour felt like three, and two hours of sleep felt like a whole night's worth.

His thoughts were scattered and erratic. Something he hated because he preferred a calm mind to one full of chaos. Unless he was focusing his attention on doing something—cleaning, working out, or working—then he couldn't get his thoughts to chill.

Siena, too.

His thoughts calmed when he put his focus on her.

"John, what are you doing?"

He found his mother standing in the kitchen entryway. Jordyn Marcello looked over the mess John had made with a carefully guarded eye, and a relaxed posture. John knew that look from his mother—it meant she was concerned about him.

"What does it look like?" John asked, wiping down the inside of another cupboard. "Cleaning and fixing shit."

"Is this all you've done today?" his mother asked.

"No, but it's the last thing I'm doing in this house today."

Jordyn took a couple of steps into the kitchen, and continued her perusal of the items scattered everywhere. She didn't reach out to touch anything, which John appreciated. He didn't want to fucking bark at his mother, but he didn't want her bothering things, either.

"You don't have to work today?" Jordyn asked.

Her tone came out calm and smooth. He recognized that, too. His mother only used that tone when she was trying to get something out of him, or needed to relax him.

John's defensive walls shot up—he didn't know what his mother was pulling. "I work, Ma."

Jordyn gave him a smile. "I meant, you didn't have anywhere to be *today*?"

"Yeah, later."

John offered nothing else, and Jordyn didn't press for more. Instead, she stood there rubbing her hands together while her gaze drifted between him and the mess.

He didn't have to be anywhere until after lunch. He had some drop-offs to make for business—people needed their drugs to sell, after all.

John didn't trust anybody to handle substance. He had to be the one to pass it off, and that way, he knew nobody was stealing from him.

"It smelled very clean in the hallway," Jordyn noted.

"So?"

Was it a problem that cleaning helped him to focus?

That keeping busy was a *must*?

That moving let him fucking breathe?

Jordyn just stared at her son. "When did you get up this morning, John?"

"What?"

"Just curious. The sunrise was nice," she added with a little shrug. "I wondered if you might have seen it, too."

Nothing on his mother's face spoke to the fact she might be lying to him. Her soft smile felt like safety and his childhood. Her familiar presence was calming in some ways.

At the same time, John was wary.

He didn't know why. He couldn't put his finger on exactly what it was.

Still, he hesitated in giving his mother the truth. Being wary was enough to add to his already growing paranoia about why his mother was even there in the first place.

The very second John felt any kind of paranoia that was it for him. He didn't indulge any other questions or conversation from anybody.

Not even his own mother.

"Well?" Jordyn asked quietly. "Did you see the sunrise, my boy?"

"Yeah, I saw it," John said.

Because he had been up since one after a two-hour nap that felt like ten hours of solid sleep. How in the hell else would he find the time to rearrange his whole house and clean it from floor to ceiling?

"John—"

"I'm kind of busy, Ma."

He looked over in just enough time to see Jordyn frown, but also hide it. She took one deep breath, and then glanced out the large kitchen window that overlooked the front of the Queen's house.

"Your father mentioned something to me, and I just wanted to check in on you." Jordyn took a couple of steps closer to where John was working at the counter. "Do you know when was the last time you came to visit me?"

"Yeah, you worry, I know."

"Johnathan."

He heard her call for him, but he was just lost in other things. The erratic, spinning thoughts in his mind. The shit he had to get done. The way he felt like he had suddenly been turned on high-speed for no reason at all.

"They're only looking out for your best interests, John," his mother said.

She had said more, but he only caught the last part of her sentence. It was enough to send a hot burst of anger shooting through his bloodstream.

Mostly because he knew exactly what she was talking about without even asking. His father, uncles, and Andino.

Watching him like he couldn't be trusted.

Acting like he didn't know how to do his fucking job.

Like he couldn't handle his shit.

"Fuck them," John uttered.

He picked up Dante's calls because he couldn't ignore the boss. Their conversations consisted of Dante asking a question, and John answering with yes or no. It never went deeper than that, though his uncle tried.

Anyone else, though?

His father, Andino, or even his uncle, Gio?

John ignored all of them.

"Maybe if you actually sat down and heard them out," his mother tried to suggest.

"What I want to hear is them saying they're going to stay the fuck out of my business, and let me handle my own shit, Ma. Nothing else. Pass the message along if you think they actually give a damn."

Because he didn't think they cared.

His whole life had been this nonsense.

"John—"

The cell phone on the island rang out with a familiar tune. John had gotten to the point where he added specific ringtones to certain people. That way, he knew who was calling without even having to look at the phone.

Jordyn made a move to grab the call, but John spoke up first.

"Leave it, Ma," he said. "It's just Andino."

Still, his mother glanced at the phone, but she didn't actually touch it. "Looks like he's called you ten times this morning."

"Came over last night, too," John said, "and I showed him how he could leave just as fast as he came."

Andino's visit damn near ended in the two of them going to blows—again. Like Andino promised a couple of days earlier, he came to check in on John. He should have just stayed away a while longer, and gave John some damn space.

John was still pissed at his cousin for spilling his personal business like it was public fucking consumption. Andino kept trying to say that hadn't been the case. The fucking proof was right there in black and white.

What more needed to be said?

He needed one thing from his cousin—something he gave to Andino without question.

Loyalty.

Nothing more, nothing less.

Being like John was, with the way his life sometimes spiraled out of control, he needed just one fucking person on his side no matter what. Andino was supposed to be that person, but it turned out, he was just like everybody else.

Loyalty was not promised.

John didn't have time for that, either.

"Come on, now," Jordyn said, "Andino is your best friend, and you won't even listen to him?"

"There's nothing to listen to, Ma. Now if you don't mind—"

The phone chimed again, but this time, with a new ringtone. Instantly, John pushed away from the counter, spun around, and grabbed the device before his mother could even look at the screen. He picked up the call, and put his back to Jordyn.

"Hey," John said.

"Hey, you," Siena replied on the other end.

Just like that, his day was better.

Just like that, he had something else to focus on.

"So, I am getting off early today because I finished up the details for this file, and it is getting sent off in like … five minutes," Siena said.

"That so, babe?"

"Mmhmm."

"What's that mean for me?"

She worked too goddamn much.

He sometimes wanted to hide her away.

Life was a bitch like that.

"It means," Siena drawled, "that if you come pick me up, we could go see that action movie you mentioned was showing this afternoon. I mean, if you want to."

Hell yeah, he wanted to.

John didn't even think about it. He knew he had work, and places to be, but whatever. Siena and her time was already scant, and he could get back to business another day.

All that shit would still be there.

"Where you at?" he asked.

Siena rattled off an address.

"I'll be there in forty, love."

"See you."

John hung up the phone, and spun around to see his mother was watching him with curious, but guarded eyes.

"Got a date?" she asked.

John smirked, and pointed at the entryway. "I'm headed out, Ma. So, you can look around or whatever, but I won't be here. I'm sure Dad and the rest of them might like an update on the Calabrese situation—or, the Calabrese woman, because fuck them, they can't even use her name. Let them know I'm still good with what I'm doing, including her."

Jordyn cleared her throat, and glanced away. John simply headed out of the kitchen, and didn't bother looking over his shoulder to say goodbye.

He had fuck all left to say.

• • •

John brushed stray snowflakes from his leather jacket, and glanced up just in time to see Siena strolling out of the restaurant. Her grin bloomed into a full-blown smile at the sight of him waiting for her. He couldn't stop his gaze from wandering over her—it was strange how every time he looked at her was like the first time.

He kept finding new things to admire.

The way her eyes darkened when she peeked at him. How her lips curved just before she kissed him. How her hips swayed when she walked.

The wool dress she wore did little to hide the curves of her body. The knee-high leather boots she had on covered her legs up to where the wool dress ended just above her knees. Today, she'd left her hair loose in soft waves, and she wore just enough makeup to color her cheeks and lips, but not much more.

John liked her anyway he could have her.

It didn't matter to him.

The girl was damn gorgeous.

"Don't you look nice," she said, coming closer.

He pushed off the car with a grin, and reached for her. Catching her hand with his, he pulled her in close enough to rest his hand at her lower back, and drop a kiss to her smiling, pink lips.

"Shouldn't I tell you how good you look?" he murmured against her mouth.

Siena winked. "Sure, but you do look good."

"I'm not even in a suit today."

"Maybe that's why I think you look … different."

John cocked a brow, and pulled back a little from Siena. "Different?"

"I don't know …" She looked him over, and brushed her hand along the cut line of his jaw. "Something about you is different lately. You're … laughing more, and whatever else."

"That sounds normal to me."

Siena hummed. "I didn't say it was a bad thing. Just different."

"You think?"

"Yeah."

"And you're sure that's not a bad thing?"

"Never," she promised him. "Did you end up getting some sleep last night?"

"Very little. I'm fine—wide awake, *bella*."

He tickled a hand up her side, making her giggle.

"I can see that." Siena gave him a look, and said, "And playful, too. Where's that coming from?"

"I can't be playful with you?"

"You can. You usually aren't, though. Serious to a fault. A bit intense."

"Give it a little bit, and I'll go that direction, too."

Siena laughed. "No doubt. But, you're sure that everything is good with you?"

"Yeah. So, my mood is little up."

Siena lifted a brow. "Just your mood?"

John's throat tightened with her suggestion. "Give me some time today, and we'll see what else gets popping up."

"I didn't mean it like that," she said, her cheeks reddening.

"I bet you did."

"Mmhmm. What were you doing when I called, anyway? Work again?"

"No, cleaning."

Siena's smile faded a bit. "Your house is spotless, John."

He shrugged. "Gotta do something to keep my attention focused."

"You could focus on me."

John laughed, dark and husky. His hand skimmed up her back, and tangled in the ends of Siena's hair. He tugged gently, and leaned in to capture her mouth with another one of his kisses. A hotter, and harder kiss. One that left his lungs aching with the need to breathe, and made her pupils blow wide while she stared back at him.

He pulled away.

But not because he wanted to.

"Trust me," he said, "the only thing I plan on doing for the rest of today is focusing entirely on you, Siena. Whatever you want to do, and wherever you want to go. That's what we're going to do, love."

Her smile softened and sweetened. "Yeah?"

"Yeah."

"You are a little different today. Something, anyway."

John chuckled. "I have no idea what you're talking about, *donna*."

She winked, but gestured between her eyes, and his. "Just know, I've got my eyes on you. Don't you try anything cute on me."

"Hey, as long as somebody's watching out for me. That's all that matters."

Lately, he trusted her way more than anybody else in his life. The funny thing was that he knew her for a fraction of the time he knew all of them.

Still, something told him …

Something inside said she was gold.

Precious.

Pure.

Priceless.

That couldn't be ignored.

John didn't know what exactly to make of it, or what it would mean for him. He would figure out all of that later.

Now wasn't the time.

CHAPTER TWELVE

SIENA GRINNED when John dragged her closer, and engulfed her in his embrace. He rested his chin on the top of her head, while she buried her face against his chest. The busy theater ceased to exist for the moment. The long line they had been waiting in for thirty minutes just to grab snacks for a movie that had started ten minutes ago no longer mattered.

John's lips skimmed the top of her head when he said, "We could always pick a different movie, love."

"You wanted to see this one, though."

"What's the damn point if you miss the first twenty minutes of it?"

"We've only missed the first ten," she pointed out.

John's grip tightened on her, and his fingertips tickled up her sides. "Yeah, but by the time we actually get in there, it'll be twenty."

Probably.

Siena didn't care.

"The first bit of a movie is always an info dump and backstory, anyway," she said, tilting her head back to peer up at him. "It's like we'll go in and know nothing, and have zero preconceived notions."

John chuckled under his breath. "That's quite a way to sell a movie. Buy expensive tickets for something we're just going to drop you in the middle of, but trust me, it'll be good."

Siena poked him gently in the chest with the tip of her finger. She felt his muscles tighten and jump under the touch. "Maybe you just don't have a big enough imagination, John."

"Maybe not."

He was only half in their conversation at that point. She knew it by the way his eyes drifted over to something behind her, as though he had to keep a close watch on it for whatever reason. He had been doing that a lot lately.

John never outright ignored her when it happened, but she could tell he wasn't entirely present, either. Siena didn't know what to make of it.

Or a few other things …

There was something different about his eyes lately—the hazel was darker, and his gaze seemed sharper. Like the way he didn't let anything that moved around them go unnoticed. He was always looking from one thing, to another. Watching one person, and then the next that passed them by.

"Hey," Siena whispered.

John's gaze was back on her in a blink. "Hey."

"I'm here, you know."

She said the words quietly, and offered them softly. She didn't want him to take it as anything other than a quest to bring him back to her for a second or two.

"I know where you are," John murmured. His words made her heart pick up speed by a few beats. "I always know where you are, Siena."

"Oh?"

"If I don't know where you are, it's like some kind of itch under my skin that I can't scratch."

Siena's brow furrowed. "That sounds unpleasant."

John shrugged. "So be it."

She heard what he didn't say.

He didn't mind it. Maybe a part of him preferred it.

"Because it's me?" she asked.

John's slow smile curved those lips of his in the sexiest way. "Yeah, *donna*, because it's you."

"So, even when I tell you I'm here …"

"I'm already there," he said, winking.

"Hard to tell sometimes with the way your attention flips all over the place."

John lifted a hand and tapped a single finger to his temple. "No matter what, there's one part of this that will be—" He twirled that same finger over her head. "—always focused on that. Even if it seems like I'm not."

The heavy warmth that spread through Siena's veins at John's words was both comforting, and terrifying. A lot of things were like that with him—he barely had to try, and it felt like he was drawing her in, and warning her at the same time.

Maybe that should have been a sign.

She still didn't care.

Wordlessly, John dropped a kiss to the very tip of her nose, and then another one to her mouth. She felt his hands splay wide to her sides, and squeeze gently. All over again, the busy movie theater ceased to exist.

He was looking at her.

He was touching her.

Nothing else mattered.

Of course, as the saying went, nothing gold could stay.

John's phone rang not a second later, making his attention on Siena break as he pulled the device out of his pocket. He checked the screen, and then offered her a shrug.

"Have to take it, *bella*," he said. "You good for a minute?"

"Sure. What do you want me to get you?"

John scoffed as he looked over the long line. "You'll still be waiting by the time I get back."

Probably.

He gave her a quick kiss, and then put the phone to his ear as he stepped out of the line. She kept an eye on him until his back disappeared around corner a few steps away.

Mostly, Siena tried not to worry about John as much as she could. It was made difficult by the fact she noticed the changes he refused to acknowledge when she asked about them.

Like his attention.

His lack of sleep.

His ups, and his downs—moments that came, literally, in a moment. Then, gone in the next.

Yet, those things were offset by the fact he was also highly productive. Upbeat, and constantly on some kind of move. He never stopped doing something.

Siena didn't know what to think. She worried that asking the wrong questions—ones that zeroed in on the medications she had found, and the disorder she suspected he lived with—might push him away.

No part of her wanted to allow that.

Except she knew … the longer she kept what she had stumbled upon hidden from John, the more likely it was that he would feel betrayed or something worse.

She didn't want that, either.

"The line is moving."

Siena came out of her thoughts with a shake of her head to see that, yes, the line was moving. She gave the blond-haired, green-eyed guy a smile, and thanks. He winked back, which made his group of friends grin.

They all looked like they had walked out of a frat house.

No thanks.

Siena turned her back to them, and looked up at the signs overhead advertising junk food, and drinks. The guy's voice in her ear made her realize how close he had come when she turned around. Just a little bit too late.

"They make this crazy mix of popcorn, chocolate chips, and small marshmallows. They drizzle salted caramel and milk chocolate all over it. It's awesome. You want to try it?"

Siena turned slightly to give the guy a look, and make him back off. Thankfully, he did take a step back. He was probably harmless, but she also wasn't interested in finding out.

"No, thanks."

The guy shrugged. "Shame. You looked kind of lonely standing there all by yourself."

Siena didn't know if the guy and his group of friends had been standing behind her and John minutes ago, so she took him at his word. "I'm fine, really."

"If you're sure …?"

"She's sure."

Johnathan's rough reply coming from her right made Siena stiffen. She couldn't remember a time when she had ever heard him sound like that.

Angry and cold.

Seemed he had come back from his phone call without her even noticing. She turned to face him, and slipped a hand in with his. Instantly, he pulled her in close, and rested one of his arms around the back of her neck.

The comfort came back.

Just like that.

"Sorry," the guy said.

John didn't even reply. He only grunted unintelligibly back.

"You good?" he asked her quietly.

His words murmured into her hair.

"I am now."

"Good, love."

John moved them subtly so that her back was facing the group of guys, while at the same time, he could watch them. Never once did his arm release her from the tight hold around the back of her neck and shoulders. Siena didn't even mind. She tipped her head back to stare up at him. The sharp line of his jaw showed a tic, and his gaze wasn't on her.

"Everything good—with the call, I mean?"

John didn't look down. "Yeah, babe. It's good."

"Fucking shame, man. Lucked out on that ass. Almost had it."

The ruckus of laughter from the group of frat boys, not to mention the one guy's words, had John stiffening.

"I hope you're not fucking talking about this girl," he said over her head.

Siena's heart leaped into her throat. She pressed her hands into his hard stomach to try and get his attention on her, and not on those fools. "Hey, it's fine, John."

Nope.

He didn't even look away from them at all.

"And what if I was?" the guy from earlier asked. "Chill, man, she's with you."

"Say something about her again, and see what I'll do."

"John," Siena murmured.

He wasn't hearing her at all. His blazing gaze was locked on a group of idiots, and yet, his hold on her hadn't loosened a bit.

"She isn't worth it, anyway," the guy said with a laugh.

It kind of sounded like he meant it to be dismissive. A way to back away from John's threats, and yet still keep some kind of pride with his friends.

Siena knew it was a mistake before he even finished talking.

She felt it in John's body.

Saw it in his eyes.

Heard it in the clench of his teeth.

"Don't," she whispered.

Siena barely got the chance to blink, and she was on the other side of John. She spun around in just enough time to see his fist crash into the face of the guy who had been talking to her. One single punch, and the man was down.

One of his friends moved forward.

John hit him, too.

Somebody's face was bleeding.

Somebody else wasn't moving.

Shit.

She was pretty sure John wasn't supposed to be getting in trouble while on parole. And yet, he didn't seem to think about that at all as his fists rained down, and another guy jumped into the mix.

It was like his judgement was gone, right alongside his inhibitions. Did he even realize that getting caught up in an assault charge would probably revoke his probation? Did he *think* about that at all?

Siena didn't know.

"John!"

He didn't hear her the first time, so she moved in to physically put her hands on him, and see if that would help. She grabbed the back of his jacket, and swore she could feel the way his muscles coiled tighter.

"John, that's enough!"

He spun around fast, and damn near knocked Siena off her feet. His gaze landed on hers—wild and pissed—but he relaxed. Not a lot, but just enough to take a fucking look around.

At the security coming closer.

At the girl behind the counter on the phone.

At the cameras up above.

"Shit," he hissed, "we have to get out of here."

Yeah, she figured.

• • •

"Siena," John murmured from behind her.

She ignored him as she unlocked the door to her apartment. Sure, she wanted to talk. Oh, she had *a lot* of things to say to him.

Just not right now.

"I'm sorry, Siena."

Finally, the goddamn door unlocked, and she pushed it wide open. Siena stepped into her place, and threw her bag aside. She couldn't get her coat off fast enough, but once she did it too was tossed aside.

Turning around, she found John was still waiting outside in the hallway.

"What are you *doing*?" she asked.

"I'm not sure."

"You're not sure?"

Her tone came out as a harsh hiss. John winced a bit, but still he didn't move an inch.

"I'm not sure if you want me to come in," he said.

Siena shook her head. "Well, I sure as fuck don't want you standing out there. I don't think my neighbors care to hear us talk, John."

"All right."

Taking careful steps, he came into her place. Yet, he didn't remove his shoes, jacket, and he didn't move beyond the entryway once the door was closed behind him. She wasn't sure if that was because he meant to leave, or perhaps he thought she was going to make him go.

Honestly, she didn't know what she wanted to do.

"They were just idiots making stupid comments," she said.

"Maybe," he replied.

He didn't sound like he believed it.

"What would happen if tomorrow someone knocked on your door because one of them decided to press charges against you, John?"

He stuffed his hands deep in his pockets, and glanced beyond her. "I suppose—"

"It would be a violation of your probation. I don't even need you to tell me the details of your probation to know that! Why would you do something like that?"

"A person can't let shit like that slide, Siena."

"Yes, you *can*!"

"Fine, then I can't let it slide."

Siena let out a harsh sigh, because at that point, she didn't know what else to do. His responses to hers were so flippant. Words he tossed out with an indifferent tone, as though it didn't make a difference to what had happened at all.

"You have to use a bit of judgement, John," she told him.

John's laugh came out dark and bitter. "Right, okay. I should let some fucking idiot come up on my girl, and then when he insults her, I should just use judgement to decide whether or not he needs his face fucking broken in. All right, sure."

For a long while, Siena simply gaped at John like a fool who suddenly forgot how to speak. Mostly, because she didn't know what in the hell to say to him.

John shrugged. "I get it, Siena, I crossed a line."

"No, I just ..."

She couldn't figure out what she needed to say to make him understand. The words stuck to her throat like tar.

John came closer, and tipped his hands over like he was offering them to her. It took her all of a breath to reach back. Palms pressed tightly together, and fingers woven, he tugged her to his chest. He pressed his mouth against the top of her head, and held her tight. Neither one of them spoke, but she didn't have much to say, anyway.

Just like that, her anxiety simmered down to low, and she tried to let go of the rest. Because this—with him—was better.

"Maybe it scared me a little," she whispered.

John used a single hand to brush a few stray strands of her hair out of her face when she tilted her head back to look at him. "I'm sorry for that."

Siena frowned. "But not for the rest?"

"Shit like that can't slide, babe."

"It has to when it means worse things for you."

John's lips curved into a semi-sneer. "I'm not really concerned about shit happening to me, Siena."

"Well, what about me, then? Aren't you worried about what it does to me, or how I would feel if you were taken away?"

He hesitated, and his grip on her tightened. She didn't need him to reply, not when she felt it in the way he stiffened all over. Still, he gave her the *right* answer. In a way.

"I hadn't considered it," John said, "or thought about it like that."

It was something. She only needed something to make sense of the rest. Something worth it, anyway.

John was worth it.

"Think about it *now*," she urged.

John dropped a soft kiss to her forehead. "Yeah, I get it."

"Okay."

"I'm sorry."

"I know, John."

He cleared his throat, and asked, "Do you, uh, want me to go? I ruined the movie, and all."

"No, I want you to stay."

Amusement lit up his gaze. "That so?"

"Yeah. Besides, we can find something to watch here. And you can make me popcorn. I may even have chocolate for you to drizzle on it."

"I guess that sounded good to you, huh?"

"You guessed right. So, is that a deal, or what?"

"Deal," John said with a chuckle.

It was only later, once the sky had darkened, and they were halfway through a movie that both of them had already seen a few times over that Siena noticed something ...

John was still keeping his distance. He sat across the couch from her, even though he had stretched his arm across the back, and played with the strands of her hair. He kept his gaze glued on a movie he clearly wasn't that interested in. His responses to things she asked or said were quiet, and short.

Like he was pulling away, maybe.

Is that what he does to others, too? She wondered, *is that how he protects himself ... or them?*

Siena didn't like that at all.

"Hey," she said.

John looked over at her. "Hmm?"

She moved fast, then. Crossing the space between them, and climbing into his lap. She grabbed his face, and dipped down for a kiss as his hands landed to her waist and grabbed tight.

"You're too far away," she whispered against his lips. "I don't like that."

John's nose skimmed hers when he replied, "Sometimes, that's just easier."

"Don't pull away, John."

Something unknown warred in his eyes. She was seeing that from him more and more lately, and sometimes, she could hear it in his voice. She didn't know what it was, or how to fix it.

Then again, maybe it wasn't something that could be fixed. Or rather, it was something that didn't need to be fixed.

It was just another part of him.

"Siena—"

"Don't," she interjected. "It's okay, John."

"Is it?"

"It is. I told you it was. I'll never say something if I don't mean it."

His lips curved into one of her favorite grins. "Yeah, I got that. I'm never going to be able to let something like that go, though. Somebody insulting you, or fucking with you. I can't—they're lucky a beating is all they got from me. I can't change that, love."

"You could be more careful."

It was the best she had.

John just laughed. "Yeah, something like that."

She could still hear a lilt in his tone that suggested he still felt like he had to put up a wall between them. Keep the distance a bit.

Siena couldn't have that.

Not now.

Her next kiss came down hard on his lips. Demanding and wanting from him, and taking more when his lips parted to let her in. The squeeze of his hands against her side only urged her on. Like a shot of heat and lust straight to her veins, she only wanted more.

Always more.

She knew then that she had him caught—his focus and attention was all on her. His needs would tangle with hers, and lead them down a better path.

It took no time at all for their clothes to be removed, and discarded. His fingertips drifted over her cheeks, and down her throat while she climbed back into his lap. The foil packet he'd pulled from his pants before taking them off was passed over, and she tore it open.

John's mouth traveled a hot pathway under her chin, and down her throat. Her fingers shook while she slid cool, slick latex down his hardened length. He lifted her easily by grabbing onto her hips. She had his cock heavy in her hand, and hard between her thighs in the next breath.

Nothing was better than that first thrust. The way he filled her full, and took her completely. It was addictive—how he stretched her, and the way she soaked him.

Every single time.

It was always the same.

It was still so different.

Filled full of him, and feeling the way her sex clenched tighter as his hips flexed upward, Siena let out a happy little sigh.

"Love that," she whispered.

John's hand left her hip, so he could ghost his fingertips over her trembling lips. "What do you need, love?"

"*You.*"

His grin colored with sin.

His gaze only reflected her.

John pinched Siena's chin between his forefinger and thumb to draw her closer. Their lips grazed while he pressed his forehead to hers. Her hair made a curtain around them. It blocked out the rest of the world, like it didn't even exist in the first fucking place.

Just them.

Right there.

In that moment.

Together.

She only rode him when he asked for it, and came down harder on his cock when he pulled her into him. Every stroke of his length inside her brought her a little bit closer to the edge. It made the high already filling her mind that much better.

"Who's my sweet girl, huh?" John asked in a murmur. "You're all mine, aren't you?"

His husky, rough words slipped over her skin.

Like a silken promise with sharp edges.

It wouldn't hurt, though.

She knew that.

Pleasure snaked through her body, and assured bliss was soon to come. Every drag of her fingernails over John's broad shoulders only made his muscles twitch against her touch. The way her name rolled off his lips in a groan was beautiful.

"Are you mine?" he asked again.

"All yours, John."

At least, until he didn't want her to be.

And even then, she thought …

She would still be his.

• • •

Siena rubbed at her sleepy eyes with the back of her hand. She was unsure if the sight in front of her was real, or she was still stuck in a dream.

She blinked.

Nope.

John was still there, doing exactly what she thought he was doing. For another minute, Siena said nothing, and simply watched John as he placed books back on the shelf. One by one, with careful hands, he arranged each book and pulled the spines out to the edge of the shelf.

"John?"

"Hmm?"

He didn't even sound surprised that she was awake, and watching him. He didn't turn around to see her watching him from the hallway, either.

"What are you doing with my books?"

"Fixing them," he said.

Siena tipped her head to the side, and squinted. "Why?"

"Because they were a mess."

"But they're my books, John."

He shrugged. "Figured it gave me something to do."

"And that was what, exactly?"

144

John glanced at her over his shoulder, and then gestured to different shelves as he spoke. "I organized them by author—I take it the more you have by the same author, the more you like them."

Siena nodded. "I mean, yeah."

"So, your favorites are at the top, in alphabetical order." John gestured at the shelves down below. "And the rest are organized in alphabetical order."

"You know readers discover new authors who are favorites, but they only have one or two books, right?"

John gave her a look, and pointed at the third shelf. "Any books that seemed like you had thumbed through them a lot, or the spines seemed worn from being cracked open a few times, are here."

She didn't have any rhyme or reason to her bookshelves, and she wasn't really overly particular about what to do with them. It wasn't that it bothered her for John to reorganize something in her place.

Not at all.

It was something else entirely.

"When did you get up, John?"

"Two, or something. I took a run, too."

She looked down the hallway where a small window overlooked the cold, white outside. "Outside?"

"Where else?"

"It's almost the end of January."

And it was *cold*.

"I needed a run."

He said it so flippantly. His attention was already back on the books.

"And you're not tired at all?" she pressed.

"Nope."

He hadn't looked tired, either.

She remembered things about bipolar disorder that she had found on the web. Sure, she didn't think that it should be taken as gospel, but it was still concerning.

"Do you have to run over to your place this morning, or anything?" she asked.

John spun around to give her a smile. "Nope. I'm all yours today."

"Not for anything, John?"

Like his meds.

John gave her an odd look. "No."

"You didn't want to sleep, or what?"

"I had things on my mind."

"Like what?"

Slowly, John turned to face her. "Just ... some things."

Siena didn't want to push, or pry. She didn't want to do or say something that might offend him, or worse, make him throw up those walls of his. "You can tell me or talk to me about anything, John. You know that, right?"

"I figured that last night, yeah."

"Is there something you want to talk about?"

She hugged the blanket she had brought from the bed closer around her shoulders. It smelled like him, and her. It grounded her for whatever he might say next. She needed that.

John's easy smile drifted away, and so did his gaze. "There's something, yeah. I didn't know when or how to bring it up. I kind of have to, though. And if you want to tell me to go after, then I get it. Don't feel like—"

Siena held up a hand. "Can I just … preface this with something?"

She had to be honest.

Especially if he was.

"All right," John murmured. "What?"

"Let me say first that it was accidental, and I wasn't snooping. I don't do that kind of thing to people because I don't want them doing it to me. I stumbled on it by accident, and different things that I had heard made me look up some things."

John's jaw tightened. "Heard about me?"

"People say things, and sometimes I overhear them. That's not what's important, though."

"Might be."

"Not right now, John."

His posture had stiffened, and he turned slightly like he wanted to put a barrier there between them.

"I was looking for something to put away the food I made at your place, and I found meds above the fridge. I didn't touch them, and I didn't go through them. I saw what a couple of them were, but that was it."

"Wait, you—"

"No," Siena said fast. "I didn't go through anything. I wasn't looking through your shit, or prying. I found them on accident."

"No, I meant, wait and go back. So, you found my meds and didn't think to mention it to me?"

"They're yours, John."

He blinked. "What?"

"The medication—whatever it's for. That's all your business, not mine. It's personal, okay. So, I figured if you wanted to tell me, or if you needed to then you would. It wasn't my place to get in your business, and demand answers."

John cleared his throat, but he still wouldn't meet her gaze. "And you, uh, said you looked some shit up?"

"It doesn't matter. This is about you, and if you want to tell me something you think I should know, then go ahead and do that. Do it because *you* want to do it, and because you feel like I should know. Don't do it because you feel like you owe me something. Not for what I found, or what you think I might know, or—"

"I was diagnosed with Bipolar I when I was seventeen."

Siena thought hearing him say those words might make her suspicions all too real, but if anything, she was just ... proud of him.

"Do you tell people that often?"

John shook his head. "No."

"Why not?"

"Because of the way people look at me after—you can see it in their eyes. *Crazy*. You know, my family doesn't even use that word to me. Crazy, I mean. It's been pretty much banned in the context of saying it to me like it's a slur, or whatever."

"Yeah, I get that. I mean, before someone would have said bipolar and I would have thought, *high and low*. You know what I mean? Up and down constantly. I didn't really know much about it at all."

"Rapid cycling," John said.

Siena's brow dipped. "Pardon?"

"When someone goes from high emotions to low emotions like it's a roller coaster on a regular basis, it's called rapid cycling. It's actually more common in women than men. I mean, I have high and low moments, but I don't rapid cycle, and I fall more in spells of one or the other."

"Like a long bout of being high."

"Or a long bout of being low," he said, nodding. "Yeah, like that. My first episode came when I was thirteen. I never went into full blown mania back then, but the shit I did was sketchy. I was all over the place, and it was ... a bad time for my family."

"Probably would be. You would have been, what, just going into puberty?"

"Just after, yeah," he confirmed quietly. "I went back and forth from what they call a hypomania to depression, and then back again. A cycle, but for a long spell with each, and not a quick up and down. Nobody thought something was wrong up in here."

He pointed to his head, and shrugged, adding, "Everybody just thought I was difficult, and a little too wild for my own good. It always felt like I was bulletproof. Nothing was ever going to hurt me, and I could do anything I wanted. And then it would change—I would be shattered glass. Broken with sharp edges, and cutting everyone who came too close."

"That's what it feels like?"

John laughed darkly, but sobered quickly. "No, only sometimes. Bipolar feels like ... everything all at once. It doesn't give me time to process one thing before something else decides to wreck me. Mania is all of that, but times ten or more."

"I'm sure that word scares people, right?"

"Mania?"

She nodded.

John scratched at the underside of his jaw. "It's a good word for it, though. Manic—because that's what it's like. You just go, and go. The more you do, the better you feel. Sometimes my mania manifested physically. Things like fighting or sex. Sometimes it focuses on the shit around me. People I don't trust, or my work. It's a lot. It's everything. It's—"

"I get it," she interjected softly.

He frowned. "Then when the mania breaks, the cycle hits its peak before it goes way low."

"Depression?"

"Yeah." John sighed, and dragged a hand through his hair. "But I never went into full blown mania until I was seventeen. I disappeared for three weeks, and showed up in an ER. I had no idea how I got there, and I had so many different drugs in my system that I could have been a pharmacy. It was bad."

"But that's when you finally got diagnosed?"

"Around then, yeah. I found out after that there was someone else in my family history with the same disorder, so it showed a genetic link, too."

"Who was that?"

"She would have been my biological grandmother—my father's real mother. I'm named after my dad's father, actually. Johnathan Grovatti. Lina was my father's real mother. She was Johnathan's mistress, though, so a lot of stuff about her was destroyed after she was killed. It took some digging by my father to find the information on her."

"I'm sorry."

John smiled. "Don't be. I was in the height of mania when I went at my cousin three years ago—the whole shit that got me put away."

Siena's brow furrowed. "But if you were sick, then—"

"People can't know," John interrupted firmly. "Not in this life. Something like bipolar just makes me a fucking target, or worse, a stain on my family. So, I chose to go to prison instead of getting my disorder put on public record for anybody to know about."

Why wouldn't he look at her while he talked?

It bothered Siena in a way she couldn't explain.

"John."

He still kept staring at anything but her.

"John, look at me," Siena pressed.

He did.

She found pain there.

And fear.

"I don't want you to leave," she said.

John swallowed hard. "I would understand if—"

"I don't *ever* want you to leave. Not because of this. Okay?"

He didn't answer.

She didn't back down.

"Okay, John?"

Finally, he said, "Yeah, okay."

Siena moved closer until she could reach out and touch him. First, it was just her fingertips gliding up his taut arm. His muscles felt like fucking rocks under her touch. Then, she went higher to stroke the cut line of his jaw. Those hazel eyes of his never left her face, but his wariness remained.

"It's not an all the time thing," he said. "I've gone years without an episode as long as I keep up on my meds, and everything else. Don't think that—"

"You owe me *nothing*," she said, wanting to stop him from going further if he didn't want to. "Not anything, John. Not an explanation, nothing."

"It's a lot to take in, though. I know that."

"No, it's *you*. It's just another part of who you are, and nothing else. Don't be ashamed, John. Not with me."

John's gaze drifted over her face, and he gave her a little smile. "You're something else, Siena Calabrese."

"I'm pretty boring, actually."

"That's impossible. You can't be boring when you're amazing."

"Keep sweet talking me, John."

His grin deepened. "So, that's it, then? I thought this conversation would end far differently than it did."

A part of her heart broke for him.

How many people stigmatized something he had no control over? How many had hurt him with ignorant words, and ignorant minds?

She would not be one of them.

Ever.

"Thank you for trusting me," Siena said.

John stroked his thumb over her cheekbone. "You might be the only person I do trust right now, *donna*."

"I promise you always can."

"I might need a reminder. Just a warning."

Siena nodded. "Okay."

CHAPTER THIRTEEN

THE BLONDE, tattooed woman to open the front door of Andino's brownstone was not who John expected to see. Tall and willowy, her smile came off soft and welcoming. John had only met the woman in passing a handful of times. None of them had been very deep meetings, and Andino didn't actively welcome his family around the girl.

"Johnathan, right?" she asked.

John could see why this woman would have caught his cousin's attention. She had a pretty face, and by all accounts the first impression was a unique one. She could certainly draw attention to herself. It was whether or not that attention was good that could be the problem for Andino, given his ... status in *la famiglia*.

John nodded. "It is. And you're Haven."

"I am." The blue-eyed woman glanced at the woman standing beside John. "He didn't say you were going to bring someone with you."

Siena stayed close to John's side even when Haven stuck out a hand to shake. She did offer her own hand, though. "Nice to meet you. I'm Siena. You're Andino's wife?"

John stiffened.

Haven gave a bitter laugh, and waved a hand. "No, see, I'm not appropriate enough to be a wife, Siena. I'm just ... something."

"Ouch," Siena murmured.

Still, she didn't bat an eye.

Haven smirked. "It's a work in progress."

Okay.

That was enough of that.

"Come in," Haven said, stepping back from the door and widening it further. "John, Andino is upstairs in his office."

"I'll be okay down here," Siena told him.

John hadn't even thought to leave her downstairs. "You sure, love?"

Siena shrugged, and smiled. "Yeah, I'm sure."

He dropped a quick kiss to her mouth, and left her standing in the hallway with Haven. Upstairs, he found Andino's office door open.

John stepped up to the doorway, and rapped on the doorjamb with two knuckles. Andino didn't even look up from his paperwork.

"You finally came around to see me, huh?" Andino asked.

"You finally decided to pull the underboss card and make me come see you," John replied dryly.

Andino glanced up with an indifferent gaze, and a posture that screamed *what's it to you?* His cousin had always been a complex person. Much like John, but without the mental illness to add to his different issues.

"Had you given me a choice, I still would have come over eventually," John said.

He was trying to forgive Andino, after all. Actually talking to his cousin would factor in there at some point.

"When would that have been?" Andino asked.

"Eventually."

"I sped it up, John. One of the perks of being the family underboss—nobody gets to ignore my ass."

John chuckled. "Yeah, lucky you."

Andino's amusement faded fast. "Well, the luck is debatable. Sit, John."

"I would rather stand."

"Why, are you going to fuck off if I say something you don't like?"

John tried to let that statement brush off his shoulders, but it was damn hard. "I see Haven is downstairs. Siena is chatting with her."

Andino's gaze narrowed. "You brought her here?"

"I was with her when you called. I promised to spend the day with her since all I do is work my fucking ass off. I owe her time every once and a while, don't I?"

"Sure, John, but you know how they feel about—"

"I imagine, the same way *they* feel about Haven, no?"

Andino tensed, and his broad shoulders stiffened. "Point taken."

"Yet, she's here, I noticed."

"You sound like a broken record."

"Give me something to give a shit about, cousin. It's been weeks, and all I've wanted to do is break your face. So yeah, give me something right now."

Andino glanced up, and cleared his throat. "Maybe I'm taking a page out of your playbook."

"Which is what?"

"Doing what I want."

John laughed. "That's not going to be an easy road."

Andino smirked. "No, definitely not. I didn't want to pull the underboss card to get you here, John. Honestly. I know you think I'm a fucking jackass right now, but I was fine with letting you come to me when you were ready."

"That so?"

"You felt like I crossed a line, and I get that."

John bristled. "You *did* cross a fucking line, man."

"They already had somebody watching you, John. I was approached because Dante had a guy trailing you, and he thought I might know something."

Instantly, John found the closest chair, and sat his ass down. He felt like that was going to be needed for whatever Andino might tell him next.

Andino leaned back in his chair, and steepled his fingers. "So yeah, Dante and your father came to me asking about the Calabrese, and whatever else. I thought if I tried to explain that Siena was really just a random encounter you had then they would leave it alone."

Anger simmered in John's gut.

Hot, heavy, and poisoned.

Somehow, he hid it.

"You didn't think to give me a fucking heads up that they were trailing me like that?" John asked. "And why the fuck can't they just *trust me?*"

Andino shook his head. "I get the intentions were good, or that's how Dante meant for it to be, but I warned him then that he was crossing a line with you. That kind of shit messes with your head."

John looked away.

Fuck yeah, it messed with him.

"I should have let you know, John," Andino said. "I'm sorry that I didn't."

John glanced back at his cousin. "They're never going to feel like I can handle this business without somebody babysitting my every move. It puts me on edge like nothing else. I fucking hate it, Andi."

"It won't be like that forever, John."

"Really?" John scoffed. "I've gone years without a major episode. I do everything they want me to do, and they still pulled this kind of shit on me."

Andino nodded. "I know, but it won't be forever, John. Trust me on that. I'll fucking make sure of it, man."

Now, he kind of felt bad for threatening his cousin.

Andino was good like that, though.

He knew John.

"Anyway," Andino said, hitting the desk with his palms, "the reason I had to pull the underboss card is because now, I am the one babysitting you."

Instantly, John's defenses were back in a blink. "Excuse me?"

"The boss wants me to keep an eye on you. Seems you're dodging your father, the boss, and even my dad."

"You know what they did," John said.

Andino waved a hand. "Doesn't matter, John."

"It does fucking matter."

"How's work?"

Just like that, Andino changed the subject.

John's irritation settled for the moment. "Work is work. I've got my crew handled. Money is coming in just fine. All the Calabrese work is going fine, as it should."

"Good," Andino said.

Confusion fluttered through John, and he eyed his cousin curiously. "That's it? *Good.*"

"Yeah, why?"

"You're not going to push and question me on every fucking aspect of everything I do?"

"Nope," Andino said. "If you say shit is on the up and up with you, then that's what it is, John."

He didn't know how to take that statement. No one ever simply took John at his word, and left it.

Then again, this *was* Andino.

His best friend.

Something clicked in John's head. "I see what you did there."

Andino smiled. "Did you?"

"I'm bipolar, but not crazy or stupid."

"I would never call you those things, anyway."

"I know."

"And I'm not going to treat you like the rest of the men in this family do a lot of the time," Andino said, giving his cousin a look. "I just want to make sure you're handling whatever you need to handle. Probation, work, and therapy. Anything else—who you're fucking, or the rest of that—is none of my goddamn business."

John cleared his throat. "You sure on that?"

Andino pointed to the ceiling, but kept his gaze on John. "As sure as the sky is blue, man."

"I still don't like it."

"Give them something, and they'll back off."

"But not about her," John countered. "Not on Siena, Andi. They won't back off a bit."

"You're really messed up on this woman, huh?"

John smirked. "How's that Haven thing working out for you?"

Andino returned his grin. "Yeah, I get it, John."

"But yeah," he added quieter, "I am, Andi."

"I guess nothing else matters, then."

No.

Not at all.

This entire meeting had not gone the way John expected it to at all. It wasn't a bad thing, but he had come here prepared for a war with Andino.

His cousin made peace.

Funny how that worked.

• • •

"You missed two appointments, and rescheduled three others," Amelia said.

John kept checking his watch because the goddamn time was not passing fast enough for him. "Busy, that's all."

The therapist tapped the tip of her pen against the pad of paper. It drew John's attention back to her for the moment. "Part of your probation involves therapy, Johnathan. Once a week, or more if I say it's needed."

"My probation says I need to attend therapy," he countered, "not that it needs to be with *you*."

And he wasn't entirely sure how he felt about his current therapist. She had a habit of fucking with his meds—leading him to screw with his own meds to counteract the way it messed with him physically and emotionally.

He felt like her test subject a lot of the time, and that didn't make for a good patient and doctor relationship. Regardless of how often he spoke up to say the new med regime she wanted to try wasn't working, or whatever else was the case, she consistently pushed him to continue on with it.

Like it would change.

Like the fog would lift.

Like it was *helping*.

None of it helped.

Ever.

He had done just fine using only Lithium and therapy while in prison, and then adding an antidepressant or antianxiety with a mood stabilizer when he needed it. His doctor, while in lockup, had allowed John to only use the medications needed to treat him at whatever point in his cycle he was currently at.

It worked.

He liked it that way.

Too many medications made him feel like he was constantly in a bubble. It wore him down, and made him tired. Too many medications mixed together reacted badly with his brain chemistry, and he knew it.

This bitch thought he needed all of them at once, or a change of dose when one didn't work to her satisfaction. He wasn't sure if she thought that he didn't understand his disorder, or if she believed she had a better handle on it. Whatever it was, John didn't like the way she handled his medication, therapy, or otherwise.

"Have you found someone else for your weekly therapy?" Amelia asked. "I would be more than happy to send your file over."

John kept his expression blank. He only needed to get through this goddamn appointment to satisfy his probation office, after all. Nothing more.

"Not yet," he settled on saying.

But he would look.

Soon.

"You seem distracted," she said quietly.

John's gaze darted between her, and the watch on his wrist. "Things to do today, that's all."

"Like what?"

"Work."

"Anything else?"

"People to see."

Siena.

His mother.

"You're awfully jittery, too. Bouncing your knee. That's new." The two of them stared at one another until the therapist moved on with, "What are your plans after you leave here today?"

John gave the woman a look, curious at where she was trying to go with this line of questioning. Usually, she tried to focus on how the meds were working for him—or not, typically—and his history, or his family.

"I have to be on one side of New York this morning, and on the other side tonight," John replied.

"Is that an everyday thing for you lately?"

John shrugged. "Can be. More often than not, it is."

"You must be exhausted."

"Not really."

"You're getting enough sleep, then?" Amelia asked.

"Enough."

"Like a few hours?"

"A couple," John said.

The therapist scratched something down on her pad with the pen, and said, "And you are keeping up with your medications, right?"

John lied, then. "Every single day."

He halved her dose of Lithium, and when that hadn't worked to stop the fog in his head, he got rid of the other three medications she put him on. She wouldn't agree to stop prescribing the anxiety and depression meds when he wasn't even battling those to begin with.

Sure, he made it look like he was taking the pills, but he didn't. He filled the prescriptions every month like he was supposed to. He didn't actually take them, though.

"*All* of them?" she pressed. "Did the fog you mention lift?"

John shrugged. "Not particularly."

He didn't offer more. Not even when Amelia stared at him like she was waiting for him to continue explaining.

"Do you find the meds helped with the anxiety and depression that took you up and down from day to day?"

Yes.

Mixed with two mood stabilizers and an anticonvulsant, they also made him feel like he couldn't think a coherent thought on a bad day.

"They did their job," he said instead.

"Are you getting a lot done?" the therapist asked after a moment. "Work wise, and whatever else."

"Always," John returned.

She continued on that line of questioning for whatever reason. She focused in on the things he did daily, and how he was spending his time. She asked him different questions about his family, and how they seemed lately. Not that he had much to tell her for that side of things.

John knew she was pressing for something—maybe trying to gage something with him—but he couldn't put his finger on it.

Whatever.

He let her dig.

Soon enough, his time was up.

"Do not reschedule your appointment for next week, Johnathan," his therapist said from behind him as he left her office. "Or I will report you for a third time to your parole officer."

Well … *shit.*

• • •

"Ma!" John called out.

The front door of his parents' Amityville home slammed closed under his hand. The female murmurings coming from down the hall quieted damn near instantly.

"In the kitchen, Johnathan," he heard his mother say back.

He kicked off his shoes, and shrugged off his jacket. Setting the items aside, he headed for the kitchen where the smells were already wafting from. Something sweet, with a hint of cinnamon. His mother could cook—goddamn, could she cook. His childhood had been filled with memories of things his mother made for him to eat.

Especially in more difficult times of his life, he could bring forth strong memories of Jordyn's sweets and other things she made just for him.

It was a way she had gotten him to talk, or whatever else.

John found his mother sitting with his second youngest sister at the kitchen table. In her arms, Cella rocked a bundled-up baby. Swaddled in pink, this was the first time John had actually gotten a glimpse at his two-month-old niece.

She had not even been christened, yet.

"Ma," John greeted, crossing the space to drop a kiss on Jordyn's cheek.

"How was your day?"

"It was good."

"Say hello to baby Tiffany," Jordyn said, waving at the baby.

John passed Cella a look, but his sister only shrugged. The two didn't even speak as he leaned over to tug the blanket aside with one finger. The sleeping newborn barely stirred at her uncle. Her cream skin, and long eyelashes were a sweet sight. One tiny fist had grabbed tightly to her swaddling blanket.

"She looks like you, Cella," John said. "She's beautiful. Congrats."

His sister smiled faintly. "Thanks, John."

Jordyn's gaze drifted between the two—her smile saying one thing, and her eyes saying another. He knew it hurt his mother that her oldest daughters were not welcoming to their brother. John knew that was never going to change. He had said too much and done too much in the midst of episodes where Cella and Liliana were concerned. Their issues ran too deep, and wounds like those never healed properly.

"I thought you were coming over a little later," Jordyn said.

He heard the question his mother didn't ask out loud. She wanted him to be there when his father was also at the house.

John had different plans.

The men of his family were no longer going to be messing in his business or life. Not if he could help it.

"Some stuff came up, Ma," John said, taking a seat at the other end of the table. A couple of chairs away from his sister, Cella finally looked like she relaxed a bit. Usually, his guilt would compound at the idea that being near his sibling caused her anxiety, but he simply brushed it off. What was done, was done. "I don't think Dad will mind."

"Your father was looking forward to having dinner with you tonight, John."

John shrugged. "If he wants information, Ma, he's got all sorts of ways to get it when it comes to me."

Jordyn outright frowned at that. "What are you talking about?"

"Ask Dad."

He wasn't going to hurt his mother like that.

Jordyn sighed, and reached over to stroke the top of the newborn baby girl's head as she spoke again. "Well, what came up, then? Because I was looking forward to having you come over tonight to eat, too."

"I'm here."

He would *always* make time for his mother. Sure, he had alienated himself away from his family over the years. He put up walls, and made the distance grow as time went by. His mother *never* factored in to that. Ever. He would figure a way around anything that put up a roadblock when it came to his mom. Simply because he loved her enough to do it.

Jordyn had constantly loved him, after all.

Through everything.

No matter how awful he could be.

She loved him.

"I know you're here, John," Jordyn said as she stood from her chair, and headed for the stove that started to beep. "I also like to have you here when everyone else is, too. You're always coming and going when it's just me, but there's more than just me in this family, my boy."

Jordyn turned around to point a finger at him. "And your father loves you, too."

"Sure, he does."

He also didn't trust John.

How could the two ever repair the burned bridges when something like that came into play? He didn't explain that to his mother because she wouldn't understand. She loved them both—Lucian and Johnathan. Their faults were not something she liked to look at for very long.

"I also didn't forget that you avoided my question about what came up," his mother said.

Cella smiled at that, and looked down at her daughter. "She never misses a click."

"Tell me about it," John muttered. Then, louder for his mother, "I promised to take Siena to a new restaurant and bar in Manhattan, actually. I forgot that the opening was tonight."

He didn't forget anything usually, but it was happening lately. Little things—unimportant things. He figured as long as it didn't bleed over into business, it wouldn't matter.

Jordyn hesitated as she pulled a cake pan from the oven. "You forgot?"

"Yeah. She reminded me this morning."

His mother waffled in her gaze before she finally settled on asking, "Was she with you this morning?"

"Usually is."

He didn't offer more.

His mother let out a quiet sound, but said nothing else.

"Is that a cinnamon bunt cake?" he asked.

Jordyn gave him a smile. "It is—your favorite."

"I might be able to squeeze in some more time before I have to leave, then."

She laughed.

"So, you're still seeing her?" his mother asked as she worked at the counter. "The Calabrese girl, I mean."

"Please don't start with that, Ma. Don't be like the rest of them."

"Them?" Jordyn met his gaze from across the room. "For one, that's your family. Not *them*. For two, it's not the family that I worry about, John. It's *you*."

"I'm fine."

Cella cleared her throat.

John just ignored his sister, and kept his attention on his mother. "Really, I am."

"A relationship could possibly—"

"There's nothing to say, Ma," he interrupted sharply. "Not about me and her."

Jordyn nodded. "Sure. But what does she really know about you, John? Does she know everything? Have you been honest with her?"

John bristled at that comment. "If you're asking whether or not I told her about my disorder, then yes. I did."

His mother brushed her hands together. "All right. I just wanted to make sure. You should maybe bring her over for dinner on Sunday. Church, too. I assume she's Catholic."

John gave his mother an odd look.

What in the hell was she on?

"Do you think it's a good idea for me to bring a Calabrese to church and Sunday dinner with our family after I was told to stay away from her by Dad, and the rest of them?"

Jordyn shrugged. "You won't know unless you try."

She had a point ...

• • •

"John!" Matteo Calabrese's voice echoed across the quiet restaurant. The heavy-set boss sat on a stool, and had what looked to be a glass of whiskey in his hand. "My boy, come over here."

John did his best not to bristle at the *my boy* thing. Matteo was always respectful, and John was dating the man's daughter, so to speak.

"Are you here for my girl?" Matteo asked as John came closer.

"I promised her dinner."

"Not here, I hope." The man gave him a look. "You can't call it a proper date when it's the same place she works."

"Not here," John said.

Matteo waved at the stool. "Sit, John."

He didn't have a reason to refuse, so John sat.

"I never get to sit and chat with you," Matteo said, grinning widely. "You're always running with my daughter, or working with my boys. You should stop and say hello once in a while. We're all friends, right?"

Friends.

Right.

If by friends, he meant two men who came from a long history of bad blood, then sure.

"Friends," John forced himself to say.

"Oh, I saw that father of yours the other day. Asked about you since I hadn't seen you in a while."

John stiffened. "That so?"

"He didn't have much to say about you. Kind of a shame, really."

John tried not to let that admittance sting him on the inside, but it kind of did. Seemed his father couldn't muster up a good word about John, unsurprisingly.

"Here, have a drink," Matteo said, waving at the bartender down the way.

Soon, two fingers of whiskey were sitting in front of John. He didn't have a reason to refuse, and he couldn't say no to a boss, anyway. So, he stared at the drink while Matteo nursed his and overlooked the patrons.

Before he thought much about it—he didn't really think at all—John picked up the whiskey, and tossed it back. The glass clinked to the bar when he sat it back down.

"Another," Matteo called, waving a finger between John and the glass.

He threw back three glasses of whiskey before he finally found Siena in the back of the restaurant working. She peeked up at him from the computer with a wide smile. Bending down, he pressed a quick kiss to her sweet lips.

Siena hesitated when he pulled away. "Were you drinking?"

"A couple with your dad."

"But you don't drink, John."

"Don't worry about it, love." It was just a drink. Alcohol wasn't great with his meds, but he was already fucking with those anyway. He jerked a thumb toward the door. "Are you ready to head out of here, or what?"

"Almost."

Siena went about saving all the files, and turning the computer off. She packed up her bag, and rounded the desk to come and stand beside John.

"So hey," he said.

He slipped two fingers under her chin, and tipped her head back to make her look up at him. Those blue eyes of hers darkened with lust when he dropped a soft kiss to her mouth. Her tongue teased along his when her lips finally parted for him.

"Hey," she whispered when he pulled away.

"I was thinking ..."

"I thought you did that quite often." Siena winked. "Thinking, I mean."

"Cute. No, I meant about this weekend. How would you feel about coming to church with me, and then to a big Marcello dinner afterward? It's a regular thing."

"For them, or for you?"

John shrugged. "I don't go as often as I used to. You coming with me, *bella*, or not?"

Siena stood up on her tiptoes and kissed him again. "Definitely coming, John."

Something in the lilt of her tone sent a shot of lust straight through his bloodstream. John barely thought about what he was going to do next—his rationale entirely gone with a little smile and wink from her.

Lately, his grasp on good and bad decisions fell more to the reckless, stupid side of things. This would probably fall in that category as well.

John just couldn't find it in himself to care.

He was who he was.

Bulletproof.

Untouchable.

Invincible.

Especially with Siena.

He didn't care that her father was just twenty feet away. He didn't consider that this was a public place, or how disrespectful it might be to her family.

No, he just closed the door to the office, picked Siena up, and set her on the edge of the desk. She laughed breathlessly as he pushed her skirt up around her hips, and got down on his knees. The black cotton panties she wore slipped down her legs easily, and she widened her hips without even needing to be told.

She tasted like honey on his tongue.

A drug he wanted more of.

She muffled her cries with her hands. Every stroke of his tongue against her silken pussy, and hot little clit had her rocking into his mouth.

So perfect.

It was the recklessness of it all that got him off, next to the way Siena looked while he ate her out, of course. Still, the danger and craziness of it all made it that much fucking better. He couldn't deny the way the high slipped through his blood like a needle shot straight into his veins.

It was everything good and bad for John.

A part of him understood that—his life and actions lately were reflecting symptoms of his mania, and he knew it. From the lack of sleep, to the irresponsible decisions, and the wild behavior. The bigger problem was the part of him that recognized his spiral was quickly shut down, and shut out. Irrationality took control.

As quick as the understanding came …

It was gone again.

Forgotten.

He *felt* instead. He felt everything.

It was overwhelming.

It still felt like air, though. He just kept sucking it in.

No matter if it was poison.

Siena's cheeks were still blushed with a pretty pink when they left the office. John thought to say goodbye to Matteo as they left—for respect's sake—but the Calabrese boss was on the phone, and only eyed the couple as they left the business.

It was odd, but John figured it didn't matter.

He had what he wanted tucked into his side.

And she was still smiling.

CHAPTER FOURTEEN

SIENA WAS NOT panicking.

She was *not*.

It was church.

Sunday service.

Mass.

She did this every week with her own family. She attended services every single Sunday since she could remember. Her first communion was one of her fondest memories. Church and God were a *must* for her family.

It wasn't a big thing.

It shouldn't be a big deal.

So, why couldn't she just pick a damn dress?

Five church appropriate, Catholic service approved dresses rested across her bed. She had pulled out far more than five at first, but these were the ones she ended up with after discarding the others on the floor of her closet.

All had been spread out, so she could get a good look at them. She kept going from one to another, either finding something she didn't like about one, and then finding something she loved about the same piece.

They ranged in color—a white, off the shoulder number, another light green dress, one dark blue, a maroon red, and even a violet shade. All with designer names, respectable style, and modestly cut necks. Nothing too low, and nothing too short. All the skirts fell at her knees, or even an inch below.

And these dresses?

That was all before shoes. Shoes were a whole other kind of hell. Siena was not ready for that hell.

This was not hard choice on any other day. Usually, Siena just grabbed a dress, and tossed it on. She didn't buy something if she didn't love it right off the rack.

The thing was, this wasn't any other Sunday. Her family would not be attending with her, and she wouldn't be going to her familiar church.

No, this was about John's family.

Other than Andino Marcello, Siena didn't really know any of John's family. Some of them by face or name, sure, because of her own family or things she had seen on the news over the years. That didn't mean she knew them on a personal level.

Not who they were beyond the last name. Not what they thought of her. She didn't know anything about the Marcellos. Nothing at all.

It made her so anxious, she was damn near ready to puke. And wouldn't that just be fucking fantastic to add to her problems. She could go to service smelling like a vomit factory, and two steps away from spilling what was left of her breakfast on a pew, or something.

Maybe she was being a little dramatic, but Siena figured it was better for her to prepare for the worst. Then, she wouldn't be all that shocked or disappointed if that was exactly what happened to her.

Her luck, it would.

The ding of a text on her phone drew her attention away from the dresses on her bed. She grabbed the device, and swiped at the touchscreen. A message from John rolled across the screen, and made her anxiousness pick up a bit.

A lot.

What was wrong with her?

Be there in twenty, his message read.

Siena let out a low breath, and tossed the phone aside. She put her hands to her hips, and eyed the dresses once more. She didn't have a choice but to pick a damn dress and get ready right now—John was nearly there.

At least her hair and makeup were done. That was one less thing to worry about. You know, on top of the mountain of other things she was already worrying about.

Fuck her life.

The knock on her apartment door sent Siena's heart jumping in her throat. For a whole three seconds, she thought she had dazed out staring at the clothing, and lost time. Like that might have been John coming to pick her up, or something.

She quickly realized that wasn't the case when her mother's muffled voice carried through her apartment.

"Siena, I let myself in, darling."

Why was her mother here?

"In the bedroom, Ma," she called back.

Soon enough, Coraline was standing in the doorway of Siena's bedroom, and surveying the dresses on the bed. She acted like it was totally normal for her to be there, and not at all like she actually barely visited her daughter's apartment to begin with.

"Did you or Dad need something?" Siena asked.

"No," her mother replied. "I came to help you."

"For what?"

Coraline smiled widely, and gestured at the dresses. "To get ready for church, Siena."

Siena felt like she had swallowed a fly. "I know how to dress myself."

"Of course, you do."

So, why did it sound like her mother was patronizing her?

"It might not seem like a big deal to attend services with a family like the Marcellos, but I can promise you that it is," Coraline added.

She had not told her parents that she wouldn't be attending services with them that morning. She simply said something else had come up.

Sure, she had thought it was a little strange when her father didn't question her on it. Attending church was non-negotiable in their family, after all. She let it go and didn't press her father, thankful for one less argument.

"How did you know I was going to church with John this morning, Ma?"

Coraline stepped closer to the dresses, and looked them over. "At least you didn't pick anything black."

"Who wears black to church unless it's a funeral?"

"Siena, you would be surprised."

"I know black is a no, Ma."

"Good," her mother replied with a smile. "Also, the red one is a no. Catrina Marcello, the wife of the boss, prefers red. It's never respectable to show up in the same color as her, and since you never know if she's going to be wearing red or not, simply don't ever wear it at all."

Huh.

Siena blinked. "Ma."

"Yes?" Coraline moved to the white dress. "This one is nice—you have a pair of Valentinos that match the color, too."

"Ma, did John mention to Dad that he was taking me to church this weekend?"

"Siena, focus on the dresses. I know what time their Mass starts. You do not have time to be messing around with silly conversations."

Her mother was right.

Siena put her attention where it needed to be.

The white dress it was.

• • •

John looked good in anything. Of course, he did. But a well-fitted suit, on an early February morning, grinning like he didn't have a care in the world, and looking at Siena? She thought he looked the best like that.

He brought their connected hands up from his side. Tucking her hand into his elbow, she was brought even closer to him while they climbed the stairs to the entrance of the cathedral-style church.

The gathering people at the top of the stairs couldn't seem to drag their gawking eyes away from the two. It was a little disconcerting.

"Ignore them," John said like he could read her mind. "Marcellos always seem to draw attention when it comes to church. Half of the parishioners think we shouldn't be allowed to attend, considering who we are, and the other half just like a good soap opera."

Siena swallowed her nerves. "Huh."

Then, the people parted, and several men came down the steps. One, she recognized. Andino. The others, she thought she knew, but wasn't comfortable enough to say. They met them half way up the stairs.

"John," the man standing beside Andino greeted. "Good to see you this morning."

"Uncle Gio," John greeted.

The oldest man—his face weathered with age—smiled at them both. "You don't come to church nearly enough, Johnathan."

"I'll rectify that, Grandpapa."

Antony, Siena realized.

The oldest Marcello. A man she had only heard people whisper about, or spoken with great respect in their voices.

"Where's my mother and father?" John asked.

"Inside," Andino said.

John gave a little laugh under his breath, and his gaze darted somewhere higher on the stairs. At the people gathered, maybe. "What, he couldn't come out and greet me or something?"

"You didn't really give him a choice about this," Gio said, his gaze darting to Siena. "You simply said this would be happening, and he had to make a choice."

"So, his choice is to make me walk into church alone?"

"You're not alone," Andino jumped in. "We're all here."

"Yes, but my father *isn't*." John shook his head, adding, "And neither is Dante—the boss. So, not only did my father shun my choice, so has the family's head. Someone could have given me a little warning about that, couldn't they?"

Siena felt like she had missed something important. Like maybe the traditions and customs in the Marcello family were a lot deeper than anyone actually knew. Surface appearances seemed to be important, but it went far beyond that, too.

The hurt in John's gaze—though he hid it everywhere else—was evident to her. Something about this hurt him, and she didn't like that.

Not at all.

"It's like deja vu all over again," Antony murmured.

Everyone looked to the man. All of them wore masks of confusion. The older man simply chuckled at the attention turning on him.

"Oh, I get it," Gio said, grinning a bit.

"What is so fucking amusing about this?" John snapped.

All eyes flew back to him.

He was so up and down lately. One minute, he was light, carefree, and happy. The next, he snapped at somebody or at something.

Never at her, though.

"I just meant," Antony said calmly, "that there was a time once when your father stood on these steps with a woman whom he too made a choice about, and this same thing happened to him. He took my lack of presence out here to greet him as a sign of my disapproval, and rejection. It was neither of those—I was being cautious, and had something else to deal with."

"Does he?" John asked.

"Hmm?"

"Have something else to deal with, Grandpapa?"

Antony smiled slightly, and his gaze drifted in Siena's direction before going back to his grandson. "We all have things to deal with at the moment. It's a part of being a Marcello, John. You shouldn't forget that, regardless of other things in your head or heart."

Gio cleared his throat. "We're going inside. Do you want to walk in with us, or not?"

The three men waited.

John sneered. "Nah, I'm good."

That was that.

Andino gave John a nod as the older two Marcellos turned and headed back up the stairs. Gio kept a hand on Antony's arm as the two navigated the icy parts. Andino stayed behind them both, and a couple of paces back.

"What was that about?" Siena dared to ask.

John shook his head, and gave her a smile. "Nothing, *bella*. Don't worry about it."

She didn't think it was nothing.

"Do they not want me here?"

"It's not that."

"What is it, then?"

"Bad blood," John murmured. "It's always been that way, and it's probably not going to change."

"You mean—"

"You're a Calabrese. I'm a Marcello. The history between those two names in this city is enough to make any man in my family cautious."

"Cautious," she echoed.

"Yeah, love."

"About me."

John coughed, and squeezed her hand tucked into his elbow. "Like I said, don't fucking worry about it. We're doing us, not them."

"Yeah, but—"

"I did what I did, and here you are," John said, giving her a look with hazel eyes that stopped her words, heart, and breath for a split second. "Now, come on. God doesn't like people to be late to Mass. Or, that's what everyone told me growing up. Apparently, He fucking takes attendance like it makes a difference or something."

Siena laughed.

What else could she do?

• • •

"It's inviting them *in*," someone growled. "That's what this does, or at the very least, gives them the idea that's what we're doing."

"That's not necessarily—"

"The idea of it can be just as fucking dangerous, Lucian."

"Everyone knows that isn't his intention."

Andino's voice added reason to a conversation that only seemed to be growing louder the closer John and Siena came to the dining room of the large Marcello estate. A mansion that rested on six acres of land in Tuxedo Park, and belonged to his grandparents. Or, that's what he explained to her during Sunday service.

"The intention doesn't have to be known," the first man said again. "That's where the problem is, and we all know it. An idea is more than enough. I do not want even the suggestion that our home or lives are open to them. Not even her."

"Do you think *I* want them in my life, Dante?"

"He's your son, Lucian, so you tell me."

John's suddenly stiff posture straightened impossibly more at Siena's side. Yet, she kept holding his hand because for no particular reason, she thought it might ground him to her. His stress was obvious enough, and he didn't need more added on just because of her.

The two rounded the last corner of a long hallway, and came to stand in the entryway of a massive dining room. A chandelier the size of a small car hung from a vaulted ceiling overtop a table that was so big, it looked like it could fit three families in every seat.

Standing around the table, glaring at one another, or staring at the shiny oak top were several men. The same ones who greeted them outside the church, but also, the ones John had introduced her to after the services.

His uncles—Gio and Dante.

Gio's son, Andino.

His grandfather, Antony.

And his father, Lucian.

Another man sat in the corner nursing what looked to be a glass of bourbon. Siena did recognize him, although he hadn't been at the church, and he definitely wasn't a Marcello. He did come from a family like theirs, though.

Cross Donati.

Like the Marcellos, Cross's family occasionally did business at arm's length with Siena's brothers. That was the only reason why she recognized his face. That was about all she knew regarding him.

Her introductions to John's family after Sunday services had been, at best, tense and short. Even his aunts, cousins, and mother had made sure to keep the conversation to the point, and respectful.

Nothing they did made her feel out of place or unwelcome at the church. At the same time, she didn't particularly feel their friendliness or care, either. They would smile at her, but it was guarded. They shook her hand, but little else.

Still, she could tell …

She didn't need to be told.

Siena was not a stupid girl.

None of these people trusted her.

All because of her last name.

At the sight of the two of them standing in the entryway, the conversation between the Marcello men silenced damn near instantly.

John laughed darkly. "Now, isn't that the kind of conversation we reserve for a weekday, and not in the dining room where any-fucking-body can hear it?"

Dante—who Siena now knew was the man heading the Marcello family—gave John a look, and it clearly voiced his displeasure without him needing to. "I can discuss issues with my family wherever I want to, Johnathan. You are quite aware of that."

"Except when anybody else does it on a Sunday, you're quick to shut them up."

"This isn't business. This is family."

"John," Lucian said, taking a step closer to his son. "Maybe we should go upstairs, and have a chat for a minute before dinner is served."

John shook his head, and tipped his head in Siena's direction. "No, I have a guest, so I'm going to settle her in. It's what a gentleman does. We don't leave anyone out to the wolves, right?"

At that statement, Dante stiffened.

"You think we would—"

"I think nothing at the moment," John interjected.

"Don't interrupt me, Johnathan. I am your—"

"Son," Antony murmured, his voice cracking a bit, "let him take the girl in, and have her meet Cecelia."

Antony's old gaze turned on Siena. "She had to help at the church after services, and so she didn't get to meet you properly, young lady. She would really like to say hello."

"Thank you," Siena said.

At her soft reply, the defensive postures in the room lessened a bit. John seemed to take that as their cue to get the hell out of the room.

Once the dining room was behind them, the conversation started up again. Although this time, it was a little bit quieter.

"She's just a woman," Andino said. "Did you hear her talk? She heard you insulting her, and she still spoke like a little mouse. How in the hell is she going to do anything to us?"

"It's not her," Dante said sharply, "it's where she comes from."

"I'm sorry," John murmured.

Siena shrugged. "They're probably right."

Who the hell knew?

Cecelia Marcello—with her dark hair snaked with tendrils of white, and kind eyes—shooed anyone in her kitchen out with a single whistle. All she had to do was see John and Siena standing in the entryway, and she made everyone else leave.

Johnathan's mother gave her son a quick smile, and a pat to his cheek as she passed him by. Her gaze barely drifted over Siena at all.

The rest of them followed the same suit.

She wasn't even offended, now.

"Grandmamma," John said, grinning wide, "what are you cooking?"

"Everything," Cecelia said, just as happy. Her soft eyes turned on Siena. "And you must be this Siena I keep hearing about."

"Nothing bad, I hope," she joked.

Everything was bad, she knew.

Cecelia let out a quiet laugh, and waved a hand. "It's a little awkward right now, Siena, but those are only details. You have to give these Marcello men a little room to figure out their nonsense. But me, on the other hand, is another story."

Already, Siena liked this woman with her wise words and her kind offerings.

Cecelia gestured at the dough in front of her. "Do you cook?"

"Of course."

"Then, come cook. I talk best when I cook, Siena."

"Watch yourself, love," John warned her. "Cecelia is a well-known tyrant in the kitchen."

Cecelia didn't even deny it. "And yet, you all come back every Sunday for more."

• • •

Careful conversation flowed at the Marcello dinner table. Siena couldn't help but notice how everyone made a great effort not to discuss anything too personal or behind the scenes when it came to their family. If someone did accidentally say something of that nature, Dante Marcello's gaze would dart in Siena's direction, and the topic would change.

She tried not to be offended.

She didn't want to take it personally.

It still stung a little.

John kept one hand on her leg under the table while at the same time, discussing the upcoming opening of a new restaurant with Andino at his left.

Across the table, Lucian Marcello's gaze continued to drift between Siena, and his son. Lucian, maybe even more than Dante, was the most intimidating to Siena. Where the others were loud and talked, he was still and quiet. His presence felt imposing. His words—when he did speak— were careful and delivered with a flat tone.

She didn't know what to make of him at all.

"You work with your brothers and father, don't you?" Lucian asked.

John's fingers squeezed Siena's thigh at his father's question. She, too, was surprised Lucian had engaged her outright in conversation. He hadn't done that yet, except to say hello earlier. Very little else.

Siena answered quickly. "I do."

"Doing what?"

"I handle all the bookkeeping and accounting for them."

Lucian's brow raised at that statement. She wasn't sure if it was surprise, disbelief, or interest. He gave nothing away. Hell, it could have been all three.

"For *all* their businesses?" Lucian pressed.

The chatter at the table had all but stopped. All eyes were on their interaction. John had yet to step in and speak, but Siena was grateful he didn't.

"All of it," she replied.

Down at the other end of the table, Dante spoke up. "I don't think you understand what my brother means when he says all of it, Siena."

She passed a look down the way. "I do know what he means. And yes, all of it."

Criminal.

Legal.

She did it all.

Siena wasn't supposed to talk about those things outside of her immediate family, but she wanted that one thing to be clear. She didn't say things she didn't mean, and she understood exactly what these men were.

"Smart girl," said the redheaded woman beside Dante.

His wife.

Catrina.

And she was wearing red, just like Coraline said.

"And how does your father feel about ..." Lucian waved between Siena and John before saying, "This whole thing."

"Fine, I assume."

Lucian's lips curved a bit—not a complete smile, but not the expressionless, grim line he had been sporting. "You assume?"

"Matteo has no issues with speaking up about things he doesn't like," John said, finally coming into the conversation. "If he had a problem, he would let me know."

"You. Not her."

John stiffened in the chair. "That's what I said, Dad."

"That implies a friendliness, Johnathan."

Silence coated the room heavily again.

A second later, Antony said, "If everyone is finished eating, I think it's time we take this conversation upstairs."

"I agree," Dante said.

John looked to her—a silent question in his gaze. Siena patted his hand still squeezing her leg. "I'm fine."

"Now."

Their words were too quiet for anyone else to hear.

"I will be fine."

John nodded once. "All right, love."

Once all the men were gone from the table, the women started an entirely new conversation. Cecelia made every effort to bring Siena into the chats, and she appreciated it.

Down the table a couple of chairs, John's other cousin turned to Siena. Catherine, her name was. Beside her sat the only man who hadn't followed the rest—Cross.

"Are you really that good with numbers?" Catherine asked.

Siena laughed, and nodded. "Yeah, I'm really that good."

"I can make money."

"But you can't hide it, huh?"

Catherine smiled. "No, I can't hide it. I mean, someone does it for me, but it's always good to know more people."

Siena shrugged. "You know where to find me."

With that, Siena felt like she might have made another friend in the Marcello family.

Only another couple dozen to go …

It was good half an hour later before the Marcello women stood to clean the table. Without being asked, Siena got up to help. She and Catherine ended up handwashing dishes while the others cleaned up the dining room and kitchen.

Cross poked his head in the entryway where there was only a couple of plates left. "Hey, babe, you want to come look at something for me?"

Catherine dropped the dishrag. "You good?"

Siena nodded. "I can handle the rest of this."

"Thanks."

Shortly after Catherine left, Siena realized she was all alone in the kitchen. She didn't really mind. It allowed her quiet time to go over the events of the day.

She was lost in her own mind when someone else saddled up beside her at the sink. She didn't realize Johnathan's mother was standing there until Jordyn Marcello picked up one of the washed plates to dry them.

"I thought we should talk, Siena," the woman said. "And since this is the first time my son has left your side, now seems as good of a time as ever to do it."

Siena wasn't sure why … but that didn't sound good.

"What about?" Siena asked.

Jordyn set the dried plate aside. "My son. What else?"

"Considering you've barely spoken to me at all today, it's not a big surprise that I'm shocked."

The light laughter from Johnathan's mother was unexpected. Siena found herself smiling when Jordyn winked.

"I didn't mean to seem standoffish or cold, Siena."

Siena shrugged. "Yeah, well …"

"But I worry about my son. All the time, and every single day. He's thirty, so he doesn't let me have any say now. I still worry. I wonder, though, do you?"

"What?"

"Worry about him?"

CHAPTER FIFTEEN

"I THINK WE could have done this on any other day," Antony said as the Marcello men headed toward his office. "The no business on Sunday rule barely exists anymore, son."

"This isn't business, this is—"

"Family," Antony interrupted. "Except it falls in both categories, and you know how I feel about that, Dante."

"All right, Papa." Dante spun around on his heels in front of the two oak doors that led into the office. He pointed at his father, and then at Lucian, and Andino, too. "All three of you can stay outside for this. Gio can join me, but only because I think he's neutral."

John had no idea what his uncle meant, but Dante was the boss. He made the calls, not any of them. It was his choice to make.

"Dante," Lucian started to say.

"No, I don't want to hear it, brother."

"At least allow Andino in for Johnathan, then."

"No," Dante said simply. "He's another one that needs to learn a thing or two."

Andino's hard gaze settled on the wall, and his posture was stiff enough to be fucking ice. John saw all of those things, sure, but he didn't take them in properly for what they actually meant. At the moment, he was too pissed off to think about anything other than his own anger.

"It's *my* office," Antony said, his old voice sharpening with a warning.

Dante nodded. "And if this is going to be a problem, then I will move this discussion elsewhere. Speak now, or don't."

Antony said nothing.

Dante waved a single hand at John and Giovanni to follow him. John caught sight of his father shaking his head, and scowling just before the doors closed behind them—a sure sign of Lucian's disapproval.

Likely with John, all things considered.

Hadn't his statements at the table been enough to tell John that?

Inside the office, Dante headed for the desk. He stood behind it, but didn't take a seat in the large chair. "Choose some place to sit or stand, but do it fast."

Gio took a seat next to the window. John stayed standing in the middle of the room.

"I'm good," he said when the boss shot him a look.

"For now," Dante replied.

"What do you want, boss?"

Dante smirked, and looked up at the ceiling like he was sending out a silent prayer. "Where is this rudeness coming from, John?"

"I think after the little show downstairs, no one should expect me to be pleasant."

"And how about *your* show, huh?"

John straightened on the spot. "What show?"

"Bringing that woman to our church. Having her here for dinner with our family." Dante pointed a single finger at him, and then shook it with a laugh. "You didn't even consider for one second to call me and ask if that would be okay. No, you just did it. You know what kind of statement that is to bring a woman with you to church. We do not do that for just anyone, and—"

"She isn't just anyone to me," John replied.

In his chair, Gio cleared his throat. "That's a heavy statement to make, John. You've been seeing her for how long, now?"

"On and off after I was released—steady for a couple of months."

"That long?" Dante asked.

John shrugged. "Yeah, that long. But I guess we're going to pretend like you didn't already know that because you've had people watching me since I got out."

"John, that was my choice to do because of your history."

He didn't reply, simply scoffed with a nod. What the fuck else could he do? At every turn, someone else in his family had to remind him how little they actually trusted him. It stung like nothing ever had before.

"And I didn't know it was a steady thing," Dante countered. "It concerns me even more to know it, actually. Why any Calabrese woman would be crawling into bed with a Marcello man is concerning, all things considered about our families."

"Why, because she can't want me?" John asked. "Because it can't be just a me and her thing, it has to have something underhanded to go along with it, too?"

"Knowing them—"

John's thin control snapped.

It had been holding on by a thread.

"Jesus Christ," John exploded, "she is a fucking *woman!*"

Dante barely blinked at his rage. "A woman who apparently has a hand in the Calabrese business—albeit behind the scenes. Still, it would not be a stretch to think she is close to her father, or brothers. That perhaps her loyalty to them is far more than her loyalty to you, or even us."

John clenched his fists so hard that his fingernails bit into his skin, and broke the surface. It was better than punching his uncle like he wanted to do.

"That's what it comes down to—loyalty?" John asked.

"Her last name is Calabrese, Johnathan. She is their daughter—a woman from *their* family. How many times do I need to explain this to you before you understand it?"

Rage vibrated through John's bloodstream. A thick, beating thrum of hot anger that filled him up, and ate through his heart all the while. It had been a long damn time since he had gotten this angry, this fast.

Yet, he embraced it.

He wasn't scared of it.

Right then, he kind of needed it.

"You know nothing about Siena," John returned. "Nothing to make any kind of assumption that she is feeding them information, or fucking me over for them."

"Do *you* know?" Dante countered. "Would you know it if it were happening? Could you even see it happening?"

Damn.

The sharp slice of betrayal stabbed John in his chest. Over and over. Every single word his uncle said only cut worse.

"Because I must be entirely fucking incapable at anything like that," John said, his voice quieting. "Paranoid, sure. Unstable, yeah. So much so, that you don't even trust me to be a capable made man. So fuck it, she's got to be one of those things, too. That's what it is, right?"

Dante tipped his chin up. "I did not say that, John."

"You said enough, boss."

"Your bipolar has—"

"Everything to do with me," John interjected. "It is everything that is me, and you know it. Except you use my disorder as a crutch—something to hold me back, or justify your shit. That stops, now."

"John, he doesn't mean to do that," Gio said quietly. "None of us mean to do that, honestly."

He ignored his other uncle.

Dante ignored Gio, too. In fact, the boss switched topics entirely.

"You have handled the Calabrese side of the business since December, haven't you?" Dante asked. He didn't give Johnathan a chance to respond before saying, "And you see, I know Andino barely did a thing with them. He didn't meet them for dinners, and have private chats with the boss. He spent as little time as possible with Matteo's two sons, and kept them at arm's length at all times. But what do you do, John?"

Again, he didn't give him time to answer.

"You date his daughter," Dante said, letting out a bitter laugh. "You work hands on with the Calabrese brothers when you could easily delegate the jobs to men on the crew. You're seen coming and going at all hours from Calabrese businesses, and I know you've had private invitations from that family."

For Siena, John held back from saying.

He did a lot of that for her.

"So," Dante continued, leaning forward with his hands splayed on the desk, "perhaps, John, you can understand why I am wary of how close you are getting to that family. Our history with them is long, and tainted. They are snakes—they cannot be trusted. Except you seem to be doing exactly that."

His uncle knew nothing.

John felt like that was the story of his life, though. He could talk, talk, and talk more. He could explain that all of those were either situations he had been put in to, or something involving Siena, but it would do them no good.

Dante would not care.

Why?

John was a Marcello.

Siena was a Calabrese.

"You don't know who she gives her loyalty to," Dante said, "and you can't trust her with it, Johnathan."

"So says you," he replied.

He refused to say much else, though.

"Marcellos will do a lot of things, but getting into bed with a Calabrese isn't one of them. Or, it wasn't. You may think that she's a woman, and she's fucking harmless, but the rest of them are most certainly not, John."

Siena wouldn't hurt a fly. Shit, she probably *couldn't* hurt a fly when it came right down to it. She was pure and good and gold. Everything that John wanted.

Dante didn't seem to care.

"You're telling me that she isn't going home tonight to feed her father information about us, and our family?" Dante asked. "Do you really trust her that much? You know how the Calabrese are, Johnathan. Do you know how very different your world might have been had a Calabrese not ruined it?"

John's nerves prickled with irritation. "I bet you probably would not be sitting where you are had things been different, actually."

Dante's jaw stiffened.

Point made.

"Is it your loyalty that I have to be worried about, then?" Dante asked. "Not hers, but yours, John."

At that statement, Gio did stand from his chair. "Dante, come on."

John was over it. That one remark from his uncle had effectively ended the conversation for him altogether. Nothing else Dante said would make a difference to him, now.

"Nah, it's fine." John laughed, dark and hollow. "Fuck him."

"John!"

Dante's roar hit his back.

It didn't matter.

He was already gone from the office.

John headed down the hallway, bypassing his father, grandfather, and cousin. He didn't hear anyone following him, but he didn't care. All he wanted to do was find Siena, and get the fuck out of there. Do something else with just her .... Anything except being in this house, with these people.

"John, wait, son."

His father's words came just as he rounded the second floor's staircase. Lucian caught him by the back of his jacket, and yanked hard enough to spin him around.

"Look at me," his father said.

John found familiarity staring at him from his father's eyes. He also found a raised Marcello there, too. Not born, no, but *raised*.

"You're all the fucking same," John told his father. "Every single one of you."

"What are you talking about?"

"You know exactly what I mean."

Lucian looked upward in the direction they had come from. "Give Dante some time, John. Old habits die hard in this family and business— this is one memory for us that cannot be washed out in one run. You have to give it time."

"Like you give a shit. You couldn't have been clearer downstairs going on like you were with Siena at the table, Dad."

Lucian frowned. "I feel people out differently than my brothers do, that's all."

"Bullshit. Like I said, you're all the same."

"Don't you see—can't you see—I'm on your side, John? There's a reason he wouldn't let me in that office. Are you even listening to me right now?"

He didn't care. His perception of his father was colored heavily by his anger, distrust, and everything else that put distance between them.

Lucian said one thing, but John heard another.

It had always been this way.

Neither of them could fix it now.

• • •

"Where's Siena?"

Catherine looked up from the tablet her boyfriend was showing her. "What?"

"Siena. She's not with everybody else in the theater. Where is she?"

"Probably still in the kitchen," Cross said, lifting a brow. "That's where Catherine left her."

"Did anybody think to ask if she might like to join them, so she wouldn't be alone?"

Catherine frowned. "I was with her—we were washing dishes. She's really nice, John."

"Quiet," Cross added.

John tried to soften his defensive stance a bit, but it was hard after the shit show upstairs. "Yeah?"

Catherine—his favorite cousin next to Andino—nodded. "Yeah, I really like her."

"Even if she is a Calabrese?"

Cross scoffed. "That old bullshit again?"

Yeah, that old bullshit again.

John only shrugged.

"So, the kitchen?" he asked.

"The kitchen," Catherine said before going back to whatever Cross had been showing her.

John left the two of them behind as he navigated the halls and rooms of the mansion. He never understood why his grandparents didn't sell their large estate. It was far too big for them, yet they held strong and refused to let it go.

He had hoped that by the time he found Siena, his anger from earlier would have lessened. That wasn't the case at all—more than ever, he just wanted to get the fuck away from his family. Quick, fast, and in a hurry.

John crossed through the dining room to get to the kitchen, but the sound of his mother's voice carrying from the kitchen made him slow down.

"You have to understand what he's like in those times," he heard his mother say.

"He's told me," Siena replied.

"John saying one thing, and actually experiencing one of his episodes are not the same thing."

"No, I get that, I just meant—"

"In his mania, he can be reckless in everything from his choices, to his

179

behavior. He can blow through thousands of dollars in an hour, and the next day forget where the money went. We used to have boxes of things show up on the doorstep when he was a teenager because he would steal one of our credit cards, and order things online."

Jordyn let out a sigh, adding, "And relationships—romantic ones—can be difficult for him to navigate when physical attraction adds to his mania."

"I don't understand," Siena admitted.

John hated how quiet she sounded. Like the entire conversation had her backed in a corner, and she didn't how to fight her way out of it. He should have explained more to her, so that a conversation like this one didn't take her entirely by surprised.

It pissed him off, too.

How dare his mother do this? How dare she corner Siena and air out all of John's history like it was her right to do so?

It wasn't.

Siena could come to *him*.

Not anyone else.

The conversation in the kitchen continued with his mother saying, "Hyper-sexuality means physical expressions of attraction can often be confused for other things. And it only adds to his reckless behavior—like a high he chases. If he can't get high, he can do things that make him feel high. It's another way for him to self-medicate."

"He's not like that, though."

"Not *now*," his mother said sharply. "But I can see it—his father can see it. This is how it starts. Snappy conversations, and up and down moods. He seems productive. He bounces from one thing to another, and it looks like he's getting so much done.

"He rarely sleeps, and he focuses on the strangest things. This is how it starts, Siena. And I don't think you understand how it *ends*. It ends with the energetic him turning into a manic version of that—the snappiness and up and down changes into nastiness."

"He's not nasty—not to me," Siena said.

"Yet. Not *yet*. His sisters? They grew up fearing John, and his mood swings. He destroyed their things, and he would call them names. Threaten them, or worse. Now, they barely speak to him despite the fact those episodes were years ago. They can't let it go because it was awful for them. Apologies and ownership do not take away two decades worth of destruction that mania has caused in their lives.

"He becomes someone else," Jordyn continued. "A nasty version of himself that lashes out because he wants to hurt someone else. It's a dangerous game to play with him if you don't know what to look for, and if you don't understand what you're doing. And this is how it starts. All the signs point to where it's going, but you don't know that because you haven't lived an entire life with my son like we have."

"He's not like that right now," Siena said, repeating her earlier sentiment.

"*Now*," Jordyn echoed. "Are you helping him, or hurting him? Do you even understand the difference, Siena?"

"I—"

His mother didn't even give Siena a chance to reply.

"That's what I'm trying to explain to you. It's hard to tell with John because one thing he does may look like this to you—it may seem okay—but to him, it's something else entirely. It means something else entirely."

Silence answered Jordyn's statement.

John decided in that second that he had enough. This whole day had all been quite fucking enough for him.

He crossed the last few steps to the kitchen entryway, and instantly the two women inside noticed his presence. Siena looked as though she didn't know what to say. His mother only dropped her arms to her sides, and let out a soft sigh.

"Is this why you asked me to bring her to church and dinner, Ma?" John asked. "So you could corner her like this, and tell her all the reasons why I'm such a fuckup to you, and the rest of this family?"

"John, no," his mother said. "That's not what I was doing at all."

Her denials meant less than shit. He knew what he heard her saying to Siena, and he wasn't fucking stupid.

He looked to Siena. "Are you ready to leave?"

She nodded once. "If you are, sure."

"Let's go."

Siena darted for him, and discarded a dishcloth on the edge of the counter as she passed it by. "Sure, John."

"John, wait," his mother said.

John let Siena pass to exit out of the room before he turned and pointed at his mother. "Out of everyone, Ma, I trusted you the most. I didn't think you would do something like this to me."

"John, I was only trying to help." Jordyn stepped forward, but he took one giant step back. Siena had already passed through the dining room, and was gone. "I don't even think you realize it, but a lot of your behavior lately suggests you're slipping into another manic phase. I only wanted to warn her, so that she would understand and know how to help."

"You've got a strange fucking way of helping."

"You're not listening. That tells me I'm right, John. Listen to me."

"I am fine!"

"Are you?"

"Go to hell, Ma."

"John!"

Her shout echoed at his back. He found Siena at the front of the mansion. He helped her to slip on her coat.

"John, she meant no harm," Siena murmured. "She wasn't saying any of that to hurt you, I swear."

"It doesn't matter. They're all the same."

Siena frowned up at him. "What?"

"This whole family. They're all the fucking same. They talk about loyalty, but they don't know what it means."

"John."

Her whisper made him look down at her. Siena kept searching his gaze like she was trying to find something. He didn't know what.

"They love you, John."

Do they?

It was hard to tell when he was like this.

• • •

Siena laughed as John pulled her up the steps of a brownstone that was only a few blocks away from Fifth Avenue.

"What are we doing here?"

"Taking a look inside."

Siena peered up at the black brick of the home. "Who lives here?"

John flipped open a keypad, and punched in the numbers to make the door unlock. "A friend, but he's out of town. He's trying to sell the place, and let me know the code to get in, so I could check it out."

The door pushed open under John's hand, and he reached back to grab Siena, and pull her inside with him. He shut the door behind them, and Siena's laughter filled up the front hallway of the brownstone.

"Wait, shouldn't the realtor be here, then?" she asked.

John shrugged. "Who cares?"

"Because it's a break and entering charge, John!"

He only chuckled, and pulled her into his side. There, he could kiss her temple, and so he did just that.

She relaxed at the kiss. "At least you're in a better mood than you were earlier."

"Yeah, well, getting away from my family has its benefits."

Siena frowned, but didn't say more. John slipped his hand in with hers, and pulled her along. The first place he headed was for the stairs.

"I thought we were looking around?" she asked.

The two climbed the stairs to the second level, and then up to the third.

"Actually, there's only one part of this place I'm interested in," John said as they reached the top floor. It was an open concept space for what seemed to be an office on one side, and an artist's studio on the other side. "Look up, babe."

Siena did, and froze on the spot. "Holy shit."

John grinned as he looked upward, too. The entire ceiling was actually inverted for an indoor pool that had been built into the roof. The pool was surrounded by heated frosted glass walls that provided privacy from the neighbors. It didn't matter that it was February because it would feel like August inside the pool's walls.

"Let's go try it out," John said.

Siena followed behind him at a slower pace as they climbed the stairs leading to the roof. "Are we really allowed to be in here?"

"Who's going to tell, *bella*?"

She gave him a look. "Well, someone might."

"Have some fun with me."

"Kind of reckless, John."

"Not even close to being reckless, Siena."

She didn't respond except to tug on his hand again. John simply tugged back, and pulled her the rest of the way up the stairs. When he opened the door to the roof where the entire pool was closed in, he got the first whiff of chlorine.

"Are you seriously considering buying this place?" she asked.

John tugged his shirt off, and then kicked off his socks, shoes, and pants. "Maybe. Do you like it?"

"I like your place in Queens, too."

"That's a rental."

"I know, I just—"

"It's temporary," he added.

Siena gave him a look. "I like this, too, John."

"How could you not, babe?"

Her grin made him wink when he shoved down his boxer-briefs.

And then he dove in the pool a second later. The heated pool felt like a giant bathtub as he cut through the water, and then came back up for air. It was only about twenty feet long and ten feet wide. There was no deep or shallow end as it was eight feet deep all the way across except for a small portion on the other side that seemed to go from a couple of feet deep into a slope until it met the eight-foot limit.

John sucked in air the second he broke the top of the water. Shaking his head, water droplets flew all over the place that had been clinging to his hair. He found Siena watching him from the edge of the pool in that way of hers.

Like she couldn't stop.

Or she couldn't get enough.

He loved it.

"Are you getting in, or what?"

"Maybe," she said.

"Maybe?"

"Mmhmm."

John grinned, and waded closer to her. "Get in, Siena."

"I'm actually not a good swimmer."

He cocked a brow. "Seriously?"

"Yeah, kind of."

"*Donna*, everybody can float."

Siena gave him another one of those looks. "Yeah, but—"

John reached up out of the water, grabbed her wrist, and yanked hard. Siena fell in the water with a shriek, coat, shoes, white dress and all. He kept his hands on her waist as he pulled her high, and let her break the surface.

"Oh, my God," she growled at him, smacking his bare chest. "You ruined my coat!"

John kissed her lips, kept one arm around her back, and dragged the sopping wet coat off her arms. He tossed it aside to the side of the pool. "And I'll buy you a new one."

Siena sucked in a sharp breath. Her white, off the shoulder dress was almost entirely see-through now. Her wet hair stuck to her face. The caramel locks were darker when wet. John brushed them out of her eyes.

"I can't believe you did that," she said.

John smiled. "You have to be a little risky with me, Siena."

"I told you I wasn't a good swimmer, John."

"You're doing okay."

"Because you're holding onto me!"

"I always will," he returned easily. "You know that, don't you?"

Her anger melted away instantly. "Yeah, I do."

"Good."

Carefully, John moved them to the other side of the pool where it had that shallow slope for a good five feet. Siena rolled over to her back, and let the water lap around her while John sat beside her.

"I'm sorry about my mom," he said after a moment.

"Don't be. She really wasn't trying to hurt you, or scare me off, John."

"Doesn't seem that way."

"I wouldn't ever lie to you."

He looked down at her. "I know."

And yet, he still had the tendrils of distrust and betrayal where his family was concerned. It was disconcerting. Like his heart was being tugged in two different directions. A familiar war that fought back and forth with his thoughts and emotions.

Overwhelming, really.

"I am worried about you, though," she whispered.

John glanced down at her, and saw the truth in her gaze. He didn't want her to worry at all. Not about him. He had his shit handled.

Didn't he?

In a blink, he had rolled himself from his backside, to be hovering over Siena. She looked up at him through thick lashes, and gave him one of those sweet grins. He couldn't help himself but to lean down and catch her teasing little mouth in a kiss.

Against her lips, he murmured, "With you, I am always fine."

"Are you?"

Sea-blue eyes searched his gaze again.

"All the time, I feel like I'm drowning." John dragged a finger down Siena's parted lips and over the column of her throat. "Drowning in too much of everything. Responsibilities. Emotions. Reactions. People. Business. It never stops. Like I'm on my back in water, and it's getting higher by the second."

Kind of like her right then.

"But it doesn't feel that way with you," John admitted. "Or if it does, it's a good feeling."

"It's good to drown?"

"To drown in you, sure."

She reached for him, then, pulling him close again for a kiss that was harder, and deeper. Her tongue snaked into his mouth, and battled with his. Her hands slid down his naked, wet chest, and then her fingers slipped lower. His breath caught hard in his throat when her hands circled around his cock.

One stroke, then two.

Three, then four.

He was hard as hell in her palms, and she just kept stroking him awake even more.

"Fuck," he grunted against her mouth. "You're going to make me want something else, love."

"Please."

That was all she said.

Please.

His heart raced with want. His blood thickened with need.

He ran his hands down her sides, and grabbed a handful of her ass to grind her lower half in to him. She widened her legs even more, and hooked her heels at his lower back.

"Fuck, my pants are on the other side," he said, dragging himself away from her mouth.

His unspoken words clung heavily in the air. They didn't fuck without condoms. It was never a question as John always used them.

"I have the shot, John," Siena said, stroking a finger down his lips. "I

185

get it on time, and I'm not with anybody else."

His gaze cut back to her. "I sure fucking hope not."

Her eyes lowered.

He realized his mistake instantly.

"Me, either, huh?"

Siena nodded, and her lips curved at the edge. "Good to know. It's fine, though. Just me and you, John."

Yeah, him and her.

The way it should be.

The way he needed it to be.

John worked fast after that to drag Siena's white cotton panties down over her legs, and toss them aside. Like the rest of her, the panties were soaked. He fit himself between her thighs, and let her pull him close as his cock slid through the lips of her sex.

Her back came up out of the water in an arch when he thrust in. Every single fucking inch of her took him in, and hugged him tight.

She was wet, sure, but her pussy was something else. Warmer than the water, and wrapping all around him. A deep ache settled in his chest as he tried to stay still for a second—long enough to feel her, and just *be*. Without something between them. All bare, and feeling everything because of it.

Just like that, he was inside her, and everything was right again.

He was alive again.

Breathing again.

Siena's fingernails made red lines down his back when he drew out, and slammed right back in. Her white dress slid up under his hands, exposing more skin for him to kiss, and taste.

He liked her throat the best.

How sounds crawled from it when his tempo picked up. How her muscles and tendons strained when he fucked her harder. How her pulse raced when his teeth cut into her skin and left a mark behind.

He liked those marks.

It meant she was his

"Oh, my God, John."

Her words were a light whisper in his hear.

Perfect and full of sin.

Blissed and high.

Fucking her did that to him, too.

Made him so goddamn high.

She came the first time with his name falling from her tongue. He flipped them over to get her on top for round two. He only let her ride him long enough to get that second orgasm, and then he was done for.

Nothing had ever felt better than coming inside her. He doubted anything would feel that good again.

CHAPTER SIXTEEN

"YEAH, MATTEO here."

"Hey, Dad, it's me."

"Siena?" her dad asked.

"Yeah, would you mind if I took today off, and didn't come in to the restaurant?"

Matteo hummed a sound. "Well, you're supposed to be at the restaurant for noon, aren't you?"

"Yeah, I am," Siena said.

"Then, what's the problem here?" her father asked.

"Nothing's wrong. I just wanted a day off."

"It's a busy month, Siena. For both sides of business, if you get what I mean."

She did know what he meant, and her father was right. They were still in February. The tax deadline was coming up to have everything filed. While most of the businesses' books were closed for the previous tax year, there were still a couple left. Not to mention, the illegal side of business picked up in the new year, and that forced more work on her to scrub and cook books. Her books were ace, though.

It wasn't that she was concerned about. She really did just need a day off.

"I work all the time, Dad," Siena said. "I rarely ask for time off. Sometimes I'm working seven days a week. The least you could do is give me one day when I ask for it. And I don't ask for it very often."

"No, you don't."

"Exactly," Siena said.

"What were you planning to do today, then?" her father asked.

"I was going to spend the day with John."

"John." Her father didn't even sound surprised, simply interested. "And how is he lately?"

"He's … fine."

"Fine?"

"Yeah."

Matteo made a noise under his breath. "Your brothers mentioned that he seemed a little off last week. Not his normal self, or something of that sort."

"Off?" Siena asked.

"Yes, *off.*" Matteo chuckled, adding "All men in our business get a little off sometimes. It's not unusual. They simply mentioned that he didn't seem up to par."

"He's fine with me. I haven't noticed anything."

Or rather, nothing that she was going to tell her father.

"Well, maybe that was just Darren and Kev."

Siena placated her father's assumption, but inside, she knew differently. After talking to John's mother a few days earlier, she was more observant of him. She noticed things that she might otherwise have overlooked. She paid closer attention to his behaviors, and the things he did when he thought she wasn't looking.

Sometimes, it was worrying.

What was more concerning to her was the fact that other people were starting to notice. Clearly, people were noticing. John's family. Her brothers, if this conversation with her father was any indication.

Siena was sure John would not want people like her father or brothers knowing anything was wrong, if something was.

"Nothing's wrong with John, Dad," Siena said. "He's a little tired lately. Like me, he works too much."

"Sure," Matteo replied. "Men like us always work too much."

Siena wished she believed her father. Something in his tone—a lilt she didn't recognize right away—felt like he was placating her. Matteo wasn't very good at hiding those things. Or most times, he didn't even try.

He was the kind of man who believed women should be seen, but not heard. Especially the women in his life. He would never expect Siena to ask him anything, or to call him out on his lies. She had not been raised to do that, but right then, it took every ounce of her willpower not to do it.

The only reason she didn't do it was for John. She didn't want her father thinking something was wrong. Or rather, that she knew something was, as he said, off with John.

The Marcellos didn't trust the Calabrese family. Unfortunately, that also included her. There was nothing Siena could do about that, except stay loyal to the one person that mattered the most to her. *John.*

Regardless of how John's family felt, Siena was going to take care of John. That meant watching his back and looking out for him. He needed somebody on his side, and she was that person. They didn't have to believe it—or like it—for it to be true.

As for her father ... well, there had to be a reason why the Marcellos didn't trust the Calabrese. Knowing her family like she did, she didn't need to question *why*. They had done enough things over the years that Siena had seen from afar to know that they would do anything to get wherever they wanted to be.

And her father?

Her brothers?

They had always wanted to be on top.

Had they done anything to John? No. At least, not that Siena had seen. Nothing that she could point to and say, yes, this was directly related to harming John, or his family.

She had seen nothing like that.

She knew nothing like that.

Yet.

Because with the men of her family, it was hard to tell what they might do next if given the opportunity. She didn't trust them, and she definitely didn't like her father digging for things about John.

Siena asked, "Is it okay if I take a day?"

"I guess so," Matteo said.

"Great, thanks."

"And do let John know he can come to me anytime, if he needs something."

"Yeah, I'll let him know."

Except she wouldn't.

Not at all.

Siena hung up the phone, and set the device aside. On the countertop, the screen blanked out. She continued to stare at it long after the phone call was over. Something just wasn't sitting right with her. Not about her father, and not about John.

She was brought back to the things she had been noticing about John. Things she had overlooked before because the changes had come on slowly, and she felt maybe they were normal for him, considering. She didn't have experience with bipolar.

Only John.

Siena knew the truth was clearer than she wanted to admit. She was close to John. *Very* close. Her perception of him was tainted by her feelings. She was willing to turn cheek to certain things because she cared, and she didn't want to upset him.

She was worried she might not be able to do that anymore. Not if it meant his health—mental or otherwise—well-being, and safety was on the line.

There was no doubt in her mind that John was not aware of the changes he was exhibiting. If he knew, wouldn't he ask for help? Wouldn't he do something about it?

She thought so.

Siena didn't snoop. She wasn't the type, and she didn't want to betray anyone's trust by doing so.

Especially not John.

But at the moment, John had headed out for a jog because apparently he needed to run even though it was February. He was grabbing them breakfast on the way back, or so he said.

What that meant to Siena, however, was that she had a few minutes alone inside John's place. She could either confirm or deny some of her suspicions about his current state.

It made her sick to think about it.

It hurt her heart to consider it.

Yet, she knew she didn't have a choice. If John was in the midst of a hypomanic episode, or working towards a full-blown mania, then it would only hurt him to continue to ignore it.

She couldn't ignore it.

She had to know.

Jordyn's words had been playing on repeat every day since the dinner.

He seems fine, she had said. *He seems productive. He'll work and work. He'll deny if you ask because he really doesn't think anything is wrong. Sometimes he can recognize his problem, and sometimes he can't. It's a roll of the dice.*

For whatever reason, Jordyn had felt like she needed to tell Siena those things. A part of her was grateful because it gave her a better sense of what was really going on with John, and maybe how to help. A smaller part of her had been stuck in a constant state of worry since that night.

Because …

What would it mean if John was approaching a full blown manic episode? What would it mean if he was already there? How could she help him, then?

Siena didn't know, so right then, she opted to push those thoughts aside. She would deal with it later.

Walking through the small two-level Queens home that John kept meticulously clean, Siena took things in again with a new eye. No dirt could be seen, and nothing was out of place. The bookcases and shelves showcasing the movies in the living room were organized by what seemed to be his favorites. The black shelves didn't have even one speck of dust. She was pretty sure she could eat off the floor, not that she would try.

Every room downstairs was the same. Clean, organized, and looking almost like a showcase. Not as though someone lived there, but as if it was ready for a buyer to come in and have a look around.

Cold, in a way. A lot of John's personality was not actually on display in his home. Sure, he had things he liked here and there. Artwork, knickknacks, and different things. But little else. Nothing to say he had just spent a good eight hours walking around in his own home, and once again, cleaning it from top to bottom.

Eight hours, Siena knew, because yet again, John had not slept. Every time she spent the night at his place, or he at hers, she would wake up to find John roaming the halls. He might be scrolling through his phone, or watching TV. Sometimes he would be cleaning something, or staring out the window at nothing.

When she asked, he assured her that he wasn't tired. Nothing he did belied that fact. He was full of energy, he kept going constantly, and he never missed a click. There was no sign of exhaustion in his eyes. He never even yawned.

So no, she didn't think he was tired. At least, not physically.

Mentally, though?

Mentally he had to be exhausted.

And maybe that was the problem. Maybe his mind just wouldn't stop. Maybe he couldn't sleep because his mind wouldn't slow down enough to allow his body to rest.

She was upstairs looking through the meticulously organized closet when she heard the doorbell ring downstairs. Quickly, she made her way down to the main floor, and didn't bother to check the front door before she swung it open.

On the other side, a delivery man waited. He had a whole moving dolly full of boxes. Big ones, and small ones.

Siena did a quick count.

Fifteen boxes in all.

"Sign for these, ma'am," the man said.

He held out a tablet and pen for her to write on.

"Are you sure these are for the right address?" Siena asked.

"Definitely for this address," the man said. "I've been delivering here every day for the last week."

Siena stilled. "Every single day?"

"That's what I said, ain't it?"

Siena signed for the goods, then allowed the delivery man to roll the dolly in, and set the boxes of things in the hallway. She didn't even bother to say goodbye to the man as he left the house, and closed the door behind him.

She was too busy staring at the pile of boxes. This was the first time all week that she had spent the night at John's house. She had been busy with work ever since the dinner with his family the week before.

Siena didn't even think about it as she stared at those boxes. She didn't consider that it might be a betrayal of John's trust. She had promised him she wouldn't overstep his personal boundaries, but this was worrying to her.

His mother had mentioned one specific thing that really stood out. One of his behaviors when he was dealing with mania was spending money. A lot of money. Sometimes, he didn't even remember that he had spent it. The things he bought didn't have to be needed, wanted, or otherwise.

It just had to be things.

In the kitchen, Siena pulled out a chair from the table, and dragged it to the fridge. Climbing up, she opened the cupboard doors overtop the fridge. There, she found his medications. By the looks of it, more medications than what he had the last time she accidentally stumbled upon them.

But this wasn't like the last time.

Siena actually pulled out the medications from the cupboard. She looked them over. She read the prescription dates when they had been filled, and for some, she even opened up the bottles and counted the pills. One bottle had been filled a month ago, and according to how many pills had been prescribed, it should have been empty.

Yet, it was still half full.

Lithium, the prescription read.

Another prescription of Lithium she pulled from the cupboard had been filled the week before. And yet, it had not even been opened.

And another med that had just been filled was also not opened. Several, actually.

Siena knew it for sure then.

John was in trouble.

• • •

Siena was waiting by the door when John finally came up the walkway. His one-hour run, and the promise to bring home breakfast, had turned in to three hours. It was already closing in on noon. She tried not to be worried, but she was way past that point now.

She opened the door before he could even reach for it. His wide smile at the sight of her standing there said he didn't see a thing wrong. Not with her, or with himself.

Siena knew that was half of the problem. At least for John.

"What happened to getting breakfast?" she asked.

John laughed. "Shit, I forgot."

"Forgot?"

"Yeah, I got caught up with something else."

"And what was that?"

John shrugged. "Saw somebody I recognize from way back. Before I knew it, we had been talking for a fucking hour."

She stepped back, and he walked into the house. He barely even passed a glance at the mountain of boxes sitting in the hallway. It was like they weren't a surprise to him, but he wasn't interested in them, either.

"John, these came this morning," she said.

He waved a hand, and nodded. "Yeah okay."

"When did you order them?"

"Not sure."

Siena frowned. "Well, what's in them?"

"Shit, I imagine."

And just like that, John was gone from her view and inside the kitchen. The boxes were forgotten, and he had moved on to something new.

Siena tried to work up the nerve to bring up his medications as she headed for the kitchen. Inside, she found him pulling out a glass, and filling it up with cold water. She had been up with him since six that morning. Because of that, she knew he hadn't taken his medications. He took them at breakfast.

With food.

Always.

He hadn't done that this morning. She wondered when the last time was that he had taken his meds, or even had an appointment with his therapist.

In sweatpants, a sweater, and with a wool cap pulled down over the top of his head, he didn't look like the cold weather outside had affected him at all. Like maybe he didn't feel it.

"John—"

Siena's question was interrupted by knock at the front door. She looked out the kitchen window, but couldn't see who it was from there. John dropped a kiss to her cheek as he passed her by, and left to answer the door.

Siena slipped into the hallway just as John pulled open the front door.

A man Siena didn't recognize stood waiting with a folder in his hands. The color of blood, the folder stood out brightly against the black outfit the man wore, and the white of the snow falling down around him.

"Kent," John said. "What are you doing here this morning?"

Kent handed over the file. "Somebody ran this to me today, and let me know I needed to get it to you as soon as possible."

John took the file, and tapped it against his palm. "Thanks, man."

The man nodded. "No problem, John."

Kent turned on the stoop, and left without another word. John closed the door, and faced Siena.

"Who was that?" she asked.

"An enforcer," John said, still looking at the file in his hands. "One that works for a Marcello Capo on the other side of the city."

"He came all the way over here to give you a file?"

"That's his job. He does what he's told, not what he wants to do."

John opened the file as he slid past Siena in the hall. It took all of two seconds for his easy-going posture to change. He went from unbothered and calm, to as stiff as a board just like that.

"John?"

He was silent. His back stayed turned to her. She couldn't see his eyes, or judge from the expression on his face what was wrong.

So quiet.

Deathly so.

"What the fuck?"

That was all he said.

Siena was frozen to the spot. "What is it?"

"I … don't know. I mean, I do—fuck."

His outburst sent a sharp stab of cold dread piercing into her heart. The file went flying from John's hand, and crashed into a wall in the next second. Papers scattered everywhere. In the next breath, he grabbed the small table that held knickknacks and a decorative glass bowl, and overturned it with just a flick of his wrist.

Glass shattered all over the floor. John's curses reverberated through the house.

Siena was still frozen in place.

She didn't know what to do. Move, or stay right where she was. A fear settled deep in her gut. Not a fear of John, but of the unknown. Because she realized in that moment that she didn't know how to help him.

"John," Siena said, "are you—"

"Why would they fucking send me that?" John's fist crashed through the wall, crumbling plaster. He didn't even flinch. She didn't think he felt the pain. Turning fast, he faced her with wild eyes and teeth bared. "Like they think I don't already know what your family did to mine? Like I need a fucking reminder everyday now, or something?"

Siena didn't understand what he was talking about. She didn't understand what had set this off.

"John—"

No matter what, this was still John to her. *Her* John. Even angry, confused, and irrational. He was still her John. She saw his outburst, and faced it head-on.

"Tell me what's wrong," she said.

"Fuck."

One last curse, and one more thrown item to the floor, and John turned his back. As fast as he was in front of her, he was gone. She heard his footsteps echo as he headed up the stairs.

Yet, she was still frozen in place.

It took far too long for Siena to move again. Instead of going after

John, she moved to the papers on the floor. She picked up one, and then another. Newspaper clippings, and items of a similar nature stared back at her. Her gaze drifted over the words, and the pictures attached.

Old newspapers. Old news.

It was still as clear as day.

The intention was obvious.

Marco Grovatti, one of the headlines read, *killed in his home.*

Another one … another headline… *Johnathan Grovatti, son of murdered mob boss, attends father's funeral with wife.*

Young Calabrese Capo suspected of murdering former boss.

Carl Calabrese takes over Grovatti family.

Over and over again.

Headline after headline.

Newspaper clipping after newspaper clipping. All sent to John. Apparently, by his own family, if she had understood him correctly.

All that bad blood between their families was suddenly staring Siena right in the face. She didn't know what to do. Go upstairs to John, or stay stuck in her fear?

She knew one thing for sure, though.

John still needed help.

• • •

"Andino."

Andino turned from the man he was currently going over paperwork with, and his gaze found Siena standing just a few feet away. The restaurant bustled with patrons, and employees. It was closing in on dinner time, and the place seemed filled to the brim.

"Siena?"

She brushed her sweaty palms off on her tweed coat. Her heart raced. At that moment, her nerves were out of control. She felt like she was going to puke. Every single part of her screamed that this was wrong, and bad. She shouldn't be here. She shouldn't be doing this.

Not to John.

But she had to.

"How did you find me?" Andino asked.

Siena took a deep breath. "I heard John mention something on the phone to someone. He said he might come see you later. He mentioned this restaurant."

"John hasn't been here. Not today."

"He probably forgot. He's been doing that a lot lately."

Andino frowned. "What, forgetting things?"

"That's one."

He cleared his throat, and nodded once to the man at his side. "Give us a few minutes. Find a table, and I'll come see you when I'm done."

Then, to Siena, he said, "Let's go to my office."

Siena didn't say anything, simply followed behind Andino. He strolled through a busy kitchen, and bypassed the bustling employees. Once inside the office, he closed the door behind them. He didn't take a seat at the big desk, but he offered a chair to Siena.

She shook her head. "I just … kind of feel better standing right now."

"All right."

"I think John needs help."

In a blink, Andino shoulders dropped. It was a subtle action, and someone else might not have even seen it. His face gave away nothing. There, he was still cold, and emotionless.

"Help how?" Andino asked.

"Today, he got something. This morning, I mean. A file, I guess. He said it was from—or the guy was from your family. An enforcer." Siena hoped her rambling made sense because she had been dealing with more than enough, and this was just one more thing to add to her pile at the moment. "He threw the file, and had a fit. Broke things, and then he left. I've been trying to call him. He's not taking his meds."

"Slow the hell down," Andino said. "One thing at a time."

Siena was shaking. Her fingers trembled, and her shoulders felt heavy. She stuffed her hands in the pockets of her coat, trying to hide her nerves. Anxiety was most definitely not her best friend.

Not in this circumstance.

"I think John's manic," she said.

Andino sucked in a sharp breath. "Manic."

"Yeah."

"What makes you think that?"

"Why are you so calm right now?" Siena asked. "Doesn't knowing that he's manic bother you?"

Andino cocked an eyebrow. "This is how I am, and how I need to be. Now, what makes you think that?"

"Things he's doing. Things he's done. Today. Yesterday. Everything."

"And you said he's not taking his meds?"

Siena shrugged. "No, I don't think so."

"I don't deal with maybes when it comes to John."

"Definitely not taking his meds the way he should be," she said.

"And this file that was delivered to him," Andino said. "What was in it?"

"Things about his great-grandfather. The one that was murdered by my grandfather."

Andino folded his arms over his chest. "And you're sure it was delivered by a Marcello man?"

"An enforcer. That's what John said."

"Why come to me?"

All over again, Siena's nerves made themselves known. She wanted to be anywhere but there. She couldn't betray John, and yet here she was, doing exactly that. She no longer had a choice.

"They might take him away from me," she said.

Andino quieted for a long time. He simply stared at her, and said nothing. It only made Siena's nerves worse, but she figured in that moment, the truth was better than lying. She knew how much John cared about Andino, and how much he trusted him. Whenever John spoke about his cousin, it was with great respect and a genuine fondness. Something she had never heard John use when he talked about anyone else. Except for maybe his mother.

"His mother told me things at the dinner on Sunday," Siena said, "about his mania. Things that he does, and how to recognize it. She explained the way he acts, and what might cause it."

"Which can sometimes be the smallest of things," Andino added.

Siena nodded. "Yeah, but it made me stop, and pay attention. Things I was overlooking before, or whatever else. Maybe this is partly my fault, and I don't want them—they already don't like me—to blame me for this, and take him from me. Would they do that? I don't know, and I don't want to risk it."

"And so you came to me."

"Yes."

"You said he left?"

"In a fit," she confirmed. "He was really upset, and he wouldn't even talk. I don't know where he went, and he won't answer my calls."

Andino let out a harsh sigh. "Well, the most important thing to do is find him, get him calm, and then get him settled enough to actually talk."

"I don't know how to do that," Siena said.

"It's not an easy thing to do with John, and you kind of learn how to do it over time. You came to me, Siena, and that's the best you can do. That was the right thing to do."

"Is it?"

"Sure. Why would you think differently?"

"Because it feels like I betrayed him."

"Trust me," Andino said, "when this all blows over, the last thing John will ever think you did is betray him. It's quite clear where your loyalty is, woman."

What did that even mean?

CHAPTER SEVENTEEN

"JOHN!"

John heard his cousin's shout from behind him, but continued walking. His mind was entirely focused on one thing, and one thing only. He was just a few steps away from getting some answers. Or at least, something that would get him closer to finding out who exactly in his family had sent him that file.

Days later, and he was still looking for answers.

He'd been on the move for hours. Too many—he lost count. His phone wouldn't stop ringing in his pocket. Buzzing and buzzing, and only irritating him more. He ignored it every time it rang.

He only knew it was the next day because the sun was out, and nightfall had already left him behind. Not that he spent it sleeping because he didn't. He hadn't even gone back home after he left.

Not once.

"John," Andino called again, "wait up."

Once again, John ignored his cousin. He grabbed the handle on the pool hall's front door, and swung it wide open. The smell of liquor, and walls that spent years being coated in smoke from cigarettes and cigars smacked him in the face. Nobody could smoke in the place now, of course, but that smell just didn't wash out. Sometimes, it couldn't even be painted out.

"Jesus, John," Andino growled, "what the hell is wrong with you?"

His cousin was right behind him, but John's eyes were scanning the crowd. Men playing pool at the tables, and gathered patrons at the bar paying for drinks. It was only a little past noon, and already, it looked like quite a few of them were drunk.

Good, this would make things a lot easier for John.

Andino's hand clapped John on the shoulder, but he brushed the touch off. He heard his cousin saying his name, and trying to talk to him, but he just had other things on his mind. Other shit to do.

Other fuckers to take care of.

Quickly, John found the fucker he was looking for. A short, chubby twenty something year old at the farthest pool table across the hall. Drake was his name. Or something like that. A foot soldier in a crew belonging to the same Capo of the enforcer who had delivered the file to John the day before.

"John, will you talk to me for a goddamn second?"

"In a minute, Andino," John said.

He didn't think to ask his cousin how he had found him, or why he was looking for him. Those were details, and at the moment, they were not the details John needed to know.

John headed across the pool hall, his strides long and heavy. He recognized a face or two, and a couple even called out his name with a wave. A greeting he otherwise would have returned, but at the moment, he just didn't give a fuck. He was not here for them, and he had no interest in speaking to them. They would not help his cause.

Drake didn't see him coming. He was too busy bent over the pool table, aiming for his next shot. A winning shot, if he had made it. The five hundred dollars sitting on the edge of the pool table told John that the guy wanted to make that shot.

The guy didn't get to take the shot.

John grabbed Drake by the back of his shirt, and yanked hard. In one swift motion, John flipped the guy over, and smashed his back into the next pool table. Drake let out a shout, one filled with pain, but John only smiled at the sound.

A couple of the guy's friends stepped forward, but Andino moved in fast. He always had John's back. Ride or die, no matter what. His cousin was there, doing what he needed to do. Even if he didn't know why John was doing what he was doing.

"Hey, Drake," John said smiling coldly. "Looks like you and me need to have a fucking chat."

Drake's brown eyes widened, and words stumbled from his mouth. "About what?"

John chuckled. "Guess you're going to find out, cocksucker."

Uncaring about the people watching or those closing in around him, John kept a firm hold on Drake as he dragged him across the pool hall. Someone from behind the bar, a face John didn't recognize, stepped out like he was going to help the guy. John just pointed a single finger at the man.

"Fucking try it," John dared.

The guy held up his hands in surrender, and it only made John laugh. His face was recognizable. He'd been here before, but not to do this. Nonetheless, they knew who the fuck he was, and what he could do. They knew his last name, and what it meant in this city.

Nobody wanted to get fucking messed up with that mess.

Nobody wanted to get messed up with the Marcellos.

Soon, John had Drake out of the pool hall. The cold February air whipped around them. John didn't feel anything at all. Seemed he couldn't feel anything, lately. When he did feel something, it was just a mess. He couldn't process it. It was too much, and he didn't want to deal with it.

Drake didn't fight too much as John dragged him behind the pool hall. A dirty alleyway filled with dumpsters, and moldy cardboard boxes. It stunk like death. It looked like some animals had been chewing on shit, and digging through garbage.

Rats, likely.

New York was filled with rats in more ways than one.

John tossed Drake to the ground, uncaring that the guy landed in filth and wetness. Standing over him, John bent down to make sure Drake got a good look at his eyes. He needed to look somebody right in the face when he wanted to know if they were lying to him or not.

"Who the fuck gave you the file?" John asked.

Drake blinked rapidly. "The-the—"

"The file, you stupid fuck. Who gave it to you?"

"I-I can't remember."

John let out of scoff and rolled his eyes out words. "You can't fucking remember something that happened within the past couple of days? You can't remember who put a giant red file in your goddamn hand? Maybe if I cut your fucking hand off, it'll jog your damn memories, asshole. How about that?"

"Well, I …"

The guy started to scramble back on the ground. His hands dragged through the wetness, and his clothes were now covered in the dirt and filth. He looked like he wanted to be anywhere but there. Like he needed to get the fuck away from John, and fast.

He was right. His instincts were on point. He did need to get away from John, but it was too fucking late.

"Who gave you the file?" John asked again. "One last time to tell me who gave it to you, and told you to give it to Kent."

Drake stumbled over his words again, trying to come up with some fucking excuse. He mumbled a name. Tim, or some other generic bullshit. There were a million fucking Tims in the city.

"Tim who?" John asked.

"Tim-Tim-Tim …"

Fuck this shit.

John pulled out the gun hidden inside his jacket, took a step forward, and beat Drake in the head with it. Once, and then twice. Again and again until the man's face was a bloody fucking mess. The rage that swelled through John was addictive. Finally, an emotion he understood, and one that was not so overwhelming because he knew exactly what to do with it.

John blinked, and in the next second, Drake was dead on the ground. His face was smashed in, and bloody. No breath left his lips.

"Jesus Christ, John."

He'd forgotten about his cousin. Andino hadn't forgotten about him, it seemed.

John stepped back, and straightened. In a flash, Andino had taken John's gun out of his hand and kept it out of reach. John took another step back, and then another. Andino kept looking at him in that way of his.

"John," Andino said, "look at me."

He did, but he didn't like the sight looking back at him.

"What the hell are you doing?" Andino asked. "Coming here like that, making a fucking public scene, and dragging him out of there where anybody could see you do it, John? And now somebody's going to come back here, and find his dead body. Guess who they're going to call. Guess who's going to take the rap for it, John. *You.* Where's your judgement—you didn't know this was a bad idea?"

John blinked, and his fists curled in tight balls at his sides. "I'm trying to get some fucking information."

"About the file?"

"How did you know about the file?"

Andino glanced away. "Not important, but is that what it is?"

"It is fucking important. Was it *you?*"

Disbelief stared John right in the face.

"Do you seriously think it was me?" Andino asked.

No.

Still …

"Somebody from our family sent me that file. They want me to know—they think I forgot what the Calabrese did to my family."

"John, listen to yourself."

This was all bad.

All of it.

His brain raced, and his heart thundered.

"John, where are you going?"

He didn't answer his cousin. He was already at the mouth of the alleyway, and stepping out onto the street when Andino yelled for him again.

Behind him, he could hear Andino making a call.

"Yeah, I got a mess that needs cleaned." Andino rattled off an address. "No, don't let the boss know and don't tell my father, either. This is for me. Let's keep it on the low."

John was already gone.

• • •

John slipped through a restaurant that shouldn't be familiar to him because of who owned it, and yet it still was. He visited the business a couple of times a week just to spend time with Siena, but before her, he wouldn't have stepped foot near the place.

She was already waiting for him at a table. Standing, too. He could see concern in her eyes, but he didn't know why.

She outstretched her arms to him, and he took the embrace. Dropping one kiss to her forehead, and then a second faster one to her lips. Her sweet little smile made his grin grow.

"You didn't answer my calls," she said.

John shrugged. "Busy."

"For three days?"

He didn't like where this line of questioning was going, so his best defense was to simply ignore it. Apparently, she had been one of the people who kept blowing up his phone non-stop.

"Everything's fine," he told her.

"I didn't ask," Siena said.

John gave her a look, and then took a seat at the table. "You going to sit, or what?"

Siena did take a seat at the table, but she still had that look in her eyes. She was searching for something in him, but he didn't know what to tell her. He didn't know what the fuck she was looking for.

"I thought we were going to that show last night," she said. "An early Valentine's gift."

Shit.

"I forgot," John said.

He tried to wave it off, but he could tell she didn't want to let it go. He knew what talking would do. Talking would only lead to a fight. The last thing he wanted to do was fight with Siena.

Not now.

Not ever.

"I'll make it up to you," he promised.

Siena frowned. "And how are you going to do that?"

"Give me a little bit to figure it out."

"Maybe we don't have a little bit."

John heard her, but he was already waving to the waiter.

"Our usual," he called out.

The waiter nodded, and headed for the kitchen.

"John," Siena said. "Are you listening to me?"

"Yeah, I'm listening."

"Then, where have you been?"

"Working."

"Did you see your cousin?"

With one simple question, John's attention was entirely focused on Siena again. "What do you mean, see my cousin?"

"Andino."

John tipped his head to the side. "Did you talk to Andino?"

Siena's gaze darted away. "We ran in to each other."

Lies.

He saw her lies.

This woman never lied.

Not to him.

"Try that again," he told her. "This time, though, with the truth."

Siena swallowed hard. "I was worried about you."

That was all John needed to hear. In a second, his desire to have food, and even be near this woman was gone just like that. Andino had been following John around since he found him at the pool hall. Talking about John's frame of mind and shit he had no business discussing. Things John wasn't willing to talk about with anybody other than his useless fucking therapist.

"John, wait," Siena said, standing from the table.

No, he was done.

At least for now.

"I'll call you," he told her.

Siena sucked in a sharp breath. "John, I'm sorry."

Fuck that.

His back was to her in the next breath, and then he was gone. He never walked out of that restaurant so fast before. Unfortunately, the man he ran in to outside the business made his blood boil just as badly.

Matteo Calabrese.

"John," Matteo said. "I didn't expect to see you here. Siena again?"

"Actually, I was just leaving."

"Well, wait a second now. I hear the Marcellos are having a Valentine's party for the family."

John hesitated. "Are they? I wouldn't know."

Matteo nodded with a chuckle. "Guess you're not invited then, huh?"

The two men stared at each other as the busy street moved around them. Matteo, a Calabrese man who John both despised and distrusted with every fiber of his being. And John, the one Marcello who always seemed to be on the outside looking in when it came to his family.

Something Matteo always like to point out. Or maybe it was just something that the man recognized, when everyone else seem to want to ignore it.

"You know where I am, John," Matteo said, "if you ever need somebody to talk to. You know I'm always around."

Why did that feel like a hand to help him up as much as it did a threat?

• • •

The Marcellos were known for their parties. All through the year, the family threw events for nearly every holiday. Everyone in the organization was welcome to attend. It was always an open invitation. Made men, the wives, and their kids. John had become accustomed to these kinds of parties over the years.

Yet, as he strolled through the old Marcello mansion, passing by people he knew, and even his own family, he had never felt more out of place. Like mannequins smiling, waving, and talking to him as if they knew each other, like they were old friends.

Except, like mannequins, they seemed plastic. Realistic to look at, and yet still fake.

In the crowd he picked out his grandparents. Old in their features, yet animated and young in their cheer as they chatted with guests. In the corner, he found Andino drinking something dark red from a wine glass.

He didn't know if his cousin had seen him. John's attention was elsewhere.

Like always, the top men of the Marcello organization gathered in the same spot for these parties. The main room where they could see and talk to everyone, and also be the center of attention.

This party didn't look like it was anything different.

John cut through the people, and headed for the one man he needed to speak to. His father.

Lucian saw him coming, and stepped away from his brothers. "John."

"You didn't think to invite me?"

"You didn't think to answer your phone?"

John shoved his hands in his pockets, and stared hard at his father. The differences between them in that moment were a bright contrast, and easy to pick out. Lucian, in his fitted suit. John, in jeans and a hoodie.

"Have you been talking to Andino, or something?" John asked.

His father frowned. "Why would I talk to Andino?"

Did his father not know? Did none of them know what he had done to a man just a couple of days before in a back alleyway?

"I don't know if it was you, or Dante, or who the fuck it was," John said, "but I don't need any of you sending me shit like you did last week."

"What are you talking about?"

"Don't play fucking games with me, Dad."

Lucian took a step toward his son. "John, are you all right?"

John bristled at the question. "Is that all any of you ever think about with me? If I'm okay, if I can handle myself, if my shit is taken care of? I am fucking *fine*, Dad."

The level of John's tone drew attention. His uncles looked his way, and some of the guests. He saw his mother break away from his aunts, and come their way. John had no interest in talking with her, either.

"I only came here to make one fucking thing clear," John said.

Lucian held a hand up high when Dante stepped closer, as though he were going to step in on the conversation. It kept the Marcello boss from coming any nearer to them. Although, it wasn't like John gave a fuck either way.

"And what's that, son?" Lucian asked.

John smirked. "Remember, it's not my loyalty in this family that ever needs to be in question."

With that peace said, John turned on his heel and headed back into the crowd. People parted, letting him pass through. Their murmurs reached his ears, but he didn't really hear what they were saying.

His point had been made.

People would talk.

John was not to be fucked with.

Not by his family.

Not by anyone.

• • •

The grogginess in John's mind was so heavy that he struggled to stay awake as he peeled open his eyes. He wondered how long he had been asleep while he stretched his arms high above his head. He rubbed his palms against his face. The thickness of his facial stubble said it had been far too long since he had a shave.

He stared up at the familiar ceiling, but confusion filled his mind. He knew instantly where he was. It was as comforting as it was concerning.

He struggled to remember the events of the night before. A party for his family. He went, and made a scene. On his way out, he tossed back a couple of drinks. The frantic pace of his mind grew and sped up until he could barely take anything in at all.

Still, he pushed through the clashing and crashing thoughts to dig for more information as to how he got here. He left the Marcello mansion, and that was the last thing John could remember.

He struggled to bring back more memories. His chest burned like he had been drinking hard liquor all night long. The taste in his mouth said he likely had been doing exactly that. A deep pounding headache in his temples only confirmed it further.

But even drunk, or hungover, John wasn't one to lose his memories. He was not one to forget.

Yet, the space in his head was only a giant black hole filled with nothing, and giving him nothing when he tried to pull something from it.

"John?"

Her soft voice in the bed comforted him, and also made him stiffen. He looked over in the bed to see her staring at him with soft, familiar blue eyes.

"Siena," he murmured.

Her hand reached out. A tentative touch stroked his cheek, and woke him up further.

"How are you feeling?" she asked.

"The same way I did yesterday."

Out of control.

Bulletproof.

Confused.

Pissed off.

Too fast.

Too slow.

Not right at all.

"When did I get here?" he asked.

Siena's brow furrowed, and she stroked his cheek again with her fingertips. "Showed up here around twelve."

"And you just let me in?"

"I couldn't just keep you out."

Something wasn't right with him. Everything was wrong with him. He knew it now more than ever.

"John—"

Siena's words were cut off by his ringing cell phone. The last thing John wanted to do was answer that phone, but he had been ignoring it for so long, and putting off too many things. Waking up with no memory and feeling like he was meant one thing.

He crashed.

Hard.

Now, he was scattered in broken pieces and wondering how he had gotten here to begin with.

Picking up the phone John put it to his ear and said, "Yeah, John here."

"What did you do?"

John rubbed at his eyes. "Andino?"

"The warehouse, John. Did you do it?"

John didn't know what in the hell his cousin was talking about. "What warehouse?"

"The Calabrese warehouse. The one your crew uses with them. It burned to the ground last night, John. Guess who is blaming you for it?"

John hung up the phone, and stared up at the ceiling. The deadweight settled in his stomach, and a burning dread drove into his heart.

Yet, his mind raced.

Up and down.

Unstoppable.

He shouldn't have hung up the phone. He should have said he didn't do it.

Problem was, John didn't know if that was the truth.

CHAPTER EIGHTEEN

JOHN SHOVED his legs into his pants. "You're sure I got here around twelve last night?"

Siena crawled out of the bed. "Yeah, around then."

She kept the sheet clutched to her chest. It wasn't like she was trying to hide her body from him, or anything. Most of the night before had been spent with them in bed together. He arrived at her place looking like he was out of his mind, and without a thing to say.

He didn't want to talk. He only wanted to fuck.

Siena hadn't been able to turn him away. As much as it killed her to see John like that, and to let him use her like that, she let him in. She had already let him into her heart, her bed, and into her life.

What difference would last night make?

None at all.

Fact was, Siena was selfish. She wanted John. She didn't care about the rest—those were details that they could handle at another time. She needed him close, and she wanted him with her. No matter his frame of mind, she just wanted him.

So, when he showed up at her door, she didn't ask questions. She didn't press him for information, or ask him where he had been. She didn't demand to know why he hadn't answered her phone calls or reply to any of her texts. He was there, and that was all that mattered.

"Did I smell like smoke?" he asked.

Siena frowned. "Smoke?"

"That's what I said!"

Siena straighten on the spot, and clutched the sheet tighter in her fist. "You don't need to yell at me, John."

"I didn't yell."

"You don't even hear yourself right now, do you?"

John hesitated when he grabbed his shirt. Instead of putting it on, he stared over at her. The two of them stood like that, staring at each other for a long while before one of them finally spoke and broke the silence.

"Have you seen your therapist?" Siena asked.

John's throat bobbed with a swallow. "Monday, maybe. Or Tuesday."

"You're not sure?"

"One of those days."

Siena nodded once. "When you *did* actually see her, have you told her that you haven't been taking your meds?"

John tensed all over. In a blink, Siena could see how his entire demeanor changed at her simple question. She doubted anyone had outright asked him that lately, if at all. Had he even been around anyone who would dare to ask him that question?

"Have you told her?"

"I've been taking my meds," John said.

"Have you?" Siena asked. "I've seen your meds, John. I counted the pills. They don't add up to the prescription and fill date."

His jaw hardened as his lips pulled back into a sneer. He turned on her with that look, and she knew something nasty was about to leave his mouth. A defense mechanism, maybe. Or it could have even been his mania still manifesting in a verbal form.

Siena really didn't know.

She couldn't let this go.

"Before you speak," she told him, "think very carefully about what you want to say to me. Consider if I am asking these things to hurt you, or because I care, John."

His posture softened.

As did his expression.

Siena took that as a good sign.

"My meds aren't important right now," John eventually said. "What I need to know is what happened last night."

"You showed up here."

"Nothing else? I didn't say anything? I didn't tell you anything?"

"No, all you really wanted to do was fuck, actually."

John shook his head, and pulled the shirt on. "I need to know what happened last night."

"I can't tell you."

"Then what fucking use are you?"

Siena sucked in a hard breath. His words stabbed at her skin, and cut out her heart. He might as well have just punched her in the chest, and ripped her heart out from between her rib cage. It would have hurt just the same.

"I'm sorry," John quickly said. "I didn't mean that."

And yet, even when he apologized, he was still getting dressed. He didn't look at her, or see how badly his words had hurt when they made their impact.

He didn't know at all.

His impulse control, judgement, and empathy was gone out the window.

Entirely.

"I know."

And she did know.

But it still hurt.

It still worried her.

Then, John's words came out in a ramble. A mess of thoughts and feelings that Siena could only stand there and listen to, but not do much else. It was more than he had said to her in a long while.

Too long, really.

She thought it was probably the most honest thing he had said in a long while, too.

"The bitch kept messing with my meds," he said. "First it was I needed to try this, and then try that. Up this dose, and then lower that dose. If it wasn't one thing, it was another. All the meds put me in this goddamn fog that I couldn't get out of. I would be sleeping twelve hours a day, and I could barely think when I was awake. I told her—I told her again, and then I would tell her *again*, but all she would do was tell me to give it time. Like I had to let the fucking meds do what they had to do, and let them settle. She wasn't even fucking giving them time to settle."

John scrubbed a hand down his face. "She didn't seem to want to fucking listen to me when I said the one was enough. The Lithium worked for me for the last three years when I was in lockup. She kept saying this wasn't lock up. I felt like her fucking lab rat."

Siena came a little bit closer to him, being careful and mindful in her steps. She didn't reach out, or try to touch him despite how much she wanted to. And oh, how she wanted to.

Her heart ached for her to touch him.

Her fingers itched to feel him.

All of her wanted all of him.

Even like this.

"Back when I went after my sister, I was without my meds for a little while," he continued, shaking his head with a bitter laugh. "It's strange how your own head fucks with you—makes you think you're okay without the meds because you feel better for a split second. I got back after going after Lucia, and I wasn't in a fog. So, I started dropping the cocktail of meds the bitch kept feeding me."

"John," she said, "please let me help you. I love you. You know that, don't you? You have to know I love you."

John's hazel gaze drifted to her. "Do you?"

"You think that I can't?"

"I think that maybe you shouldn't."

"I do."

John reached for her then, and his arms wrapped around her. He dragged her close. There, in his embrace, she was happy again. They were fine again.

It would only last a moment.

It would never last forever.

It *couldn't*.

"I love you," he murmured against her forehead.

That was enough for Siena.

That was all she needed.

It made everything else worth it.

• • •

John kept Siena close to his side as they headed in a restaurant that looked to be in the midst of renovations. She didn't recognize the business, and since she was always aware of when her father or brothers bought a new business, she knew this one didn't belong to the Calabrese.

"Neutral grounds," John said, as though he could read her mind. "This belongs to a Donati man. They agreed to allow the Marcello and Calabrese families to gather here for this meeting. That way, no one is stepping on anyone else's toes here, so to speak."

Siena nodded. "Makes sense."

Inside the restaurant, she found more people than she expected waiting. She recognized almost all of them. Men from her father's family, and several people from John's side.

At the head of the room, her father and Dante Marcello stood toe-to-toe. The two men looked as though they were ready to brawl. She took that as a bad fucking sign.

At Siena and John's presence, the two men finally looked away from one another. She wasn't sure that she particularly like their attention on them, either.

"John, move to anywhere except where you currently are," Dante said.

John didn't move an inch. "No, I don't think I will."

Matteo look at Siena. "I've called you five times this morning."

Her gaze drifted between her father, and her brothers standing with the other men of the Calabrese family. She could feel their judgment, and their silent opinions searing into her skin. She didn't need to hear them say it, not when she could feel it.

"Busy," she said.

Matteo coughed as his gaze cut to John. "I bet."

"Why would you bring a woman here?" Dante asked.

"I brought her here because she asked to come."

Siena's fingers tighten around John's. She no longer wanted to let him go. Something felt like a thorn pricking at her heart. Her worst fear was that someone would take John away from her—because of this, or something else.

It didn't matter, because the end result would be the same.

John would not be with her.

Siena had barely finished getting dressed earlier when John's phone started to ring again. This time, it was not Andino calling him, but his uncle. *I'm eating*, was all he said.

He was to be there—at the meeting.

No matter what.

That was the order.

Siena didn't even think about what it would mean if she went with him to the meeting. She only knew that she wanted to go. John agreed, and so here she was.

"He burned down my warehouse," Matteo said, his gaze darting back to Dante. "You will answer for that, or he will. I do not care which one it is."

"You don't know for sure that—"

Matteo took one more step forward, the threat blazing in his eyes. "Who the fuck else would have done it, Marcello, *you*? One of your men, perhaps? Did you order it because you felt I was too close? You never did like it when the Calabrese get close to your men. Did you finally have enough?"

Dante's jaw hardened, but his face gave away nothing. Not an emotion, nothing at all.

"There's a reason why the Marcellos and the Calabrese don't mix business," Dante said. "And you know very well what that reason is, Matteo."

"And yet," Matteo said, "you had no problem with my daughter and your nephew."

"I had every problem with it."

Matteo sneered, and his eyes drifted to John once more. "Who's to say he didn't do it? Everyone in your family knows the man is unstable. Hell, anyone who spends time with him knows it."

John's stiffened beside Siena. She held tighter to him when she felt his muscles tense as though he was about to spring forward. His body felt like a winding coil about to come undone.

"John," she whispered too low for anyone else to hear, "it's okay."

It was like he didn't hear her at all.

"Say that again," John uttered.

Matteo gaze stayed firmly on John when he said, "It's no secret that you're crazy, John. The way you go on sometimes, and the shit you do … this isn't a surprise. What is a surprise is how long your family was able to keep it quiet."

Siena couldn't keep her hold on John after that statement. He ripped away from her side like a bullet shooting from a gun. He was a foot away from her father before someone was quick enough to step in and grab him.

Actually, several people.

And just like that, a meeting that had a possibility to be peaceful and calm was now chaos and violence.

"Say that again!"

John's words echoed above the shouting men.

Only a laugh answered him back.

Held back by his cousin, father, and uncle, they were barely keeping ahold of John. Matteo gave another one of his sneers. A signature look for her father. Something he always gave to someone when he felt above them, and he wanted them to know they were beneath him.

She was not surprised to see him use it on John.

"I think this meeting is done," Dante said.

Matteo turned away, and waved a hand to his men. "It was done before it ever began, Dante. We both know that. We're leaving."

Siena moved toward John, but she didn't make it far.

Kev grabbed her arm forcefully enough to leave bruises behind, and dragged her with him. Her protests, and her shouts to be left alone, went unheard. All she saw was the burning hazel of John's eyes before the restaurant door slammed closed.

• • •

Siena's heart felt as heavy as her feet. As though cement had been poured in both, and were now weighing her down.

She glanced back at the enforcer who stood with his arms crossed at the car. He kept an eye on her—a threatening eye—as she stood on the sidewalk. Her new best friend, as her father like to say.

She couldn't go anywhere without the enforcer either driving her, or following her.

Today was no exception.

The enforcer was just one new change in her life since the week before. Her father had also taken her cell phone away, and refused to provide her with a new one. The freedom she had been given with living away from home was suddenly ripped from her grasp. She had been relocated to her parents' home without any explanation.

Her days now consisted of waking up, working wherever her father told her she had to work, and going home to her parents' brownstone.

She didn't know where John was, and had not spoken to him in days. She didn't even know if he was okay.

"Are you going in?" the enforcer asked from behind her.

Siena gritted her teeth, and forced herself to be polite. There was no need to make the man run back to her father, and report bad behavior. All that would make for was another long night with Matteo raging on.

She didn't need that.

Nobody needed that.

She was struggling between keeping her father happy, and needing to know something—anything—about John.

"Well?"

Siena looked back at the enforcer. "Yeah, I'm going in."

"I'll be here waiting when you get out."

Unfortunately, Siena didn't doubt it.

She headed into the business, and was thankful that today, the restaurant wasn't as busy as it usually was. Instead of heading right for the back to an office to work, she went to the bar first. The blonde acting as the bartender for the day gave her a smile.

"Want a drink?"

Siena laughed. "A whole bottle would be great."

"Not sure I can do that."

"How about something to make this day worth it?"

"One of those, huh?"

Siena scoffed—the girl had no idea. "One of those."

The girl nodded. "Yeah, I got something for that."

Less than a minute later, the bartender slid three fingers worth of whiskey across the bar in a lowball glass. Siena eyed the drink, but didn't pick it up. She really wasn't a big drinker, but she also really needed something to get through the damn day.

"You don't like whiskey?"

"Not particularly."

"Throw it back fast, and hold your breath."

Siena did just that, but the whiskey still burned, and her chest felt like it was on fire when she sucked in a hard breath. At the same time, a deep warmth spread through her blood and body. It was enough to feel like she might make it a couple more hours today without a breakdown.

Anything to get through the damn day.

Siena pushed the glass back to the bartender. "Did you see my brothers come in yet?"

The woman nodded once. "Yeah, both of them. They're in the back."

Great.

Not wanting to waste any more time lest Darren or Kev get on the phone to her father, Siena headed for the back of the restaurant. She still walked a bit slower than normal to get that extra minute or two, so she didn't have to be in the presence of one of her brothers. What a sad mess her life had become.

She heard the voices of her brothers filtering down the hall the closer she came to the office. Kev first, and then Darren.

"The Marcellos are in a fit," Kev said.

"It worked, though," Darren replied. "Shame we couldn't get John to turn on them like Dad first wanted."

"Can only do so much. Move onto Plan B, when Plan A doesn't work out the way you want it to. Dad couldn't get John in close enough, so he pushed him on a little bit with the file. Still didn't get enough out of that, so we made it worse by burning the warehouse. See what all that did for us?"

"We're going to have to be careful for a little while," Darren said. "On the streets, I mean. I got word it's going to be all out war once we finish this off."

"Who would have thought the Marcello family gave that much of a shit about a fuck up like Johnathan Marcello?" Kev laughed. "As if being fucking crazy isn't enough of a disgrace for his family with the bipolar, now they're going to back him in this mess, too."

"You don't know that. You're assuming they'll back him here, but maybe this could be a last straw type of deal for them," Darren said. "How long has he been like this—how many messes have they cleaned up for him over the years? John's crazy. It didn't take very much for us to make it worse for him. I don't think he can count on his family as much this time around."

Kev's laughter came out louder the second time around. "Let's hope that's the motherfucking truth. Either way, they're all going down."

Siena couldn't stop her footsteps if she tried. Her heart filled with rage and hate as she stepped in the office doorway. Both brothers looked her way, but neither of them seemed very surprised to see her standing there.

"You're late," Kev said.

Story of her fucking life.

"I'm always late," she said. "It's nothing new."

"Yeah, well, you've got work to do," Darren said. "So get to it."

She had other shit to do now, too.

"How fucking dare you?"

Darren's gaze narrowed.

Kev's eyebrow raised. "Excuse me?"

Siena didn't bat a lash. "You heard what I said, and I heard exactly what you were just saying, too."

"Heard that did you?" Kev asked, waving a hand at her as if to flick her away from him. "Listen, Siena, you know enough about this business to know the Marcello family and the Calabrese family can't mix. The fact that

Dad let you go on as long as he did with John should have been a hint that something was up."

Should it have?

She didn't think it should.

"How did you know?" she asked. "About John's disorder, I mean."

Darren smirked. "We had our suspicions. Rumors travel far and wide in this business, you know."

"And you forgot about this little thing called browsing history," Kev added.

Siena's heart stopped for a split second. She knew exactly what her brother was talking about without even asking for him to explain. The one time she had searched for information about her suspicions regarding Johnathan, she had used a computer in one of Kev's offices. Sure, she had closed the browser in time, but she should have known better than to trust her brother.

Privacy was an illusion for Siena. She wasn't actually granted any at all when it came to the men of her family. She should not have assumed otherwise. Look what happened.

Marcellos were right.

The Calabrese family was full of snakes.

And she was looking at two of them.

"Don't worry," Kev said, "this will all be over soon. Dad will get what he wants, and we can all move on. This has been a long time in the making, Siena, and you won't be the one to ruin it."

"And what does that mean?" she asked.

Kev shrugged from his position behind the desk, saying, "Well, the Marcellos are two seconds away from starting a war with the Calabrese. A war Dad thinks he can win. They just need a little shove."

"Might as well start with John," Darren added.

Siena's soul slipped from her body. She swore it did. Nothing had ever felt quite so painful before.

"You're a Calabrese, Siena," Kev said. "You should really start acting like it."

CHAPTER NINETEEN

"AMELIA WILL see you now," the receptionist said.

John stood from the chair, and his father followed suit. The receptionist's gaze widened when the two headed for the office door.

"I'm sorry," she said, "but only John can attend his appointment unless the doctor has otherwise stated for the session."

"No," Lucian said, "I will be seeing her, too."

"I can't allow—"

"It doesn't matter what you can't allow," Lucian interjected fast. "It matters what will happen regardless of what you say."

John was only half listening. A part of him was there, and present. Another part of him was somewhere else entirely.

He followed behind his father as Lucian entered the office, feeling like a child again. It reminded him of all those times when as a young boy and teenager he had visited office after office, doctor after doctor, therapist after therapist with his parents. Each one offered something different as an explanation. He had been diagnosed as ADHD, and then ADD, and even by one, as on the autism spectrum. It was difficult knowing that none of those really fit, either.

His parents had never done that to harm him, or anything of the sort. In fact, it had been the exact opposite. They took him to person after person, desperately trying to help John when he was a child. They needed answers, not for them, but for him.

And eventually, they got those answers.

Bipolar.

He wasn't sure if that was the answer his parents had wanted, however.

Now, here they were again. John was thirty, a grown ass man, and his father was attending yet another appointment. To be fair, Lucian only came after he went through John's home, and found the massive pile of medications prescribed by Amelia, and then overheard as his son tried to deflect yet another scheduled appointment with the therapist.

John should have had this shit handled. Neither one of his parents should be involved. He didn't know which emotion to deal with first.

The guilt.

Or the irritation.

The way the two battled against each other was a poison to John's mind. It was hard to know that his anger was irrational when his mind came up with too many different reasons to justify it. The reasons didn't have to be good ones, of course, just *reasons*. It was even more difficult to deal with the guilt when the anger was an easier emotion to feed.

Yet, the two warred.

On and on it went.

Distracting him.

Sucking him in.

Taking him away.

"Johnathan."

At the sound of his therapist's voice, John realize that he was actually sitting in her office. Just like that, once more, he lost seconds. More moments gone from his day that he couldn't explain.

Time erased.

"How long have you known my son was manic?" Lucian asked.

"I'm sorry," Amelia said, "but I can't speak about my patient—"

"This is my son," Lucian interrupted. "And at the moment, what he needs right now the most, is the proper help. And I need to know if that is you, or if you are unintentionally hurting him."

"Hurting him?" The therapist stood from her chair, and discarded the clipboard and pen in her hand to the seat. "I've been treating John since he was released from prison. Yes, I have noticed that he was possibly entering a hypomanic stage, but—"

"But nothing," Lucian said. "At that point, the discussion ends. At the point you understood, or at the very least suspected that he was hypomanic, your job was to stabilize him. Nothing more."

"I—"

"Stabilize him," Lucian echoed again. "Not feed him more medications, or allow the hypomania to worsen into full blown mania by ignoring it."

"I did not ignore—"

Finally, John snapped out of his daze. He wasn't sure what did it—his father being his voice when he had suddenly stop learning how to be that for himself after all these years, or the therapist who was blatantly lying. John had tried to tell her for months on end what was happening with him in too many different ways to count.

"I said over and over again," John muttered, "that it was too many medications. I didn't need them. I need less, not more. I went through intensive therapy learning how to manage my anxiety and depression because I can't mix those medications with extra mood stabilizers. Putting them on top of medications I already take only puts me in a fog."

"Yes, but John—"

"But *nothing*," John said, sick, tired, and entirely over this whole charade. "I'm telling you right now what I need. I've dealt with this disorder. I've went through medication after medication. Not you. *Me*."

Lucian looked to John, and frowned. "He is his only voice—you are supposed to be the advocate for that voice, but you weren't. And for what? To suit your beliefs? Because you believed he didn't have a grasp on his disorder? What was it?"

Amelia didn't reply.

Lucian didn't back down.

"He came out of prison *stable*," Lucian stressed. "The most stable he has been in years."

"It's normal for those with bipolar to need medication changes!"

Finally, his therapist was able to get out one full sentence without being interrupted. Still, it was the wrong thing to say.

"But did he need it?" Lucian asked.

Amelia tipped her chin up. "I felt so, yes. I felt he could better manage other aspects made more present because of his disorder in this way. Like the depression, and the anxiety. Medication can help with all of that."

"Yet, he managed fine without extra meds before."

John glanced up at the clock. He was acutely aware of the ticking sound it made. For some reason, it felt like it was ticking inside his body. Something was counting down inside him, but he didn't know what it was.

"I stopped taking the other meds, and halved the Lithium to every other day just so I could think again," John said.

All eyes in the room turned on him.

Not for long, though.

Lucian turned back on the therapist in a blink. "You will hand over his files to whichever doctor's office contacts you for them. If you so much as breathe a word in his parole officer's direction that he is no longer having appointments here before we can find someone new, I will ruin you."

Amelia straightened on the spot. "Excuse me?"

"Have you ever seen a building this size burn?" Lucian asked. "I've seen them come down in twenty minutes or less. Oh, and your husband is an interesting man. He's thinking about running for the mayor next year, isn't he? I would hate for something to change that."

John's gaze drifted between the conversation happening in front of him, and the clock on the wall. The damn thing was still counting down.

But to what?

"And if you hand in your license to practice," Lucian said, "even fucking better."

• • •

"It's like a fucking pharmacy in here."

John heard his cousin, but he was too busy looking at the clock on the wall of his parents' kitchen. That tick-tick-ticking was still counting down inside of him. A count down that had not yet reached the end. A count down that he did not know what exactly was counting down.

He counted the numbers on the clock once, and then twice. He watched the second hand tick-tick-tick its way through another minute, and then two more.

Time was passing.

Time was moving.

John felt suspended.

Unmoved.

Frozen.

It was only when Andino sat at the other side of the table did John finally look at his cousin. How many days had it been since he last saw Andino? A few, maybe. Or could have been only one.

John had no clue.

Andino said nothing, simply stared at John for a long while. He didn't press John to talk.

For that, he was grateful. At the moment, he didn't know exactly what he would say anyway.

He remembered that over the last several months, Andino had been the one who stepped in time and time again to try and help John. He did so at the risk of himself, and without asking for anything in return.

Even after everything that happened between Andino and John years ago, his cousin was still one of the only people John could count on. No matter what.

And how had he repaid his cousin for that kind of loyalty?

John pushed Andino away. He dropped the ball, and left Andino holding it. His cousin had cleaned up his messes over and over.

The guilt growing inside John's chest only compounded at those thoughts. It darkened his mind, and grew like tendrils inside of him to clench around his heart and squeeze tight. Those brief moments of lucidity and clear thoughts were quickly interrupted by something else entirely.

It was easy then for words like *worthless* and *useless* to whisper through his mind. Those black, dark thoughts should have been a clue to John as to what he was now edging towards, but like everything else in his life, it was difficult to recognize.

Spread out on the table were all the medications that had been prescribed to John over the last several months. He hadn't realized just how many medications it actually was until his father dumped them out on the table.

It damn near filled the whole thing.

Three different mood stabilizers. Antidepressants. Antianxiety meds. A different dosage of Lithium for every month that he had been seeing Amelia.

Andino was right.

It did look like a pharmacy.

"What is all this?" Andino asked.

He gestured at the bottles of pills.

John shrugged. "My meds."

Andino's eyes widened at the admittance, but otherwise he gave nothing away as to how he felt. "You take all of them?"

"No, maybe one or if it's going badly—a lot of shit happening, you know what I mean?—then I might add another just to settle it out."

"Then why is there so many?"

"Somebody thought I was a guinea pig."

Andino nodded. "Well, as long as it's settled now."

"Something like that."

John could see that Andino wanted to ask more. He probably wasn't satisfied with the lack of responses, or John's unwillingness to talk.

It wasn't exactly purposeful. It wasn't like John meant to be so quiet, or off-putting. At the moment, he simply had nothing else to say. He had other things to think about. He had memories that continued to stick to the back this mind like tar.

Impossible to get off or shake, and burning him over and over again. It wouldn't let him go, and instead, taunted him with the reality he had not been able to see before.

Memories of those he trusted, and those he distrusted, had muddled together overtime. He had mistook his paranoia and his raging emotions, and directed them in the wrong place because of his own bias. He had assumed wrongly about those who had never given him a reason to think that way.

It was a strange conclusion to come to.

Yet, he knew that no one around him would hear him if he tried to explain. It was hard to hear John when he was manic. The rational side of him was often lost to the irrational. In violent outbursts, and rambling admissions.

Who could make sense of that?

He understood.

He didn't blame those around him. It wasn't their fault. They could only deal with what was presented in front of them because they didn't know what was hiding underneath.

"You know now," Andino said, "don't you?"

John looked up at his cousin. "Know what?"

"That you can't trust any of them."

"Not all."

Andino shook his head. "John, the Calabrese family has done nothing but try to ruin you, and the Marcellos. You see that now, don't you? We're damn near in an all-out war with them on the streets right now. This is exactly what they wanted from us. Matteo might as well have just fucking admitted it."

"Not all," John said again.

His cousin's frustration grew, and with it, John's irritation spiked up as well. It was another by-product of being in the state that he was. Conversations were not easy, and communication was made harder.

He could talk and talk and talk for days like this, but it would still lead them in the same goddamn circle. That's just how it was.

John knew it, and it made him less willing to speak in the first place. Besides, he had said his piece. He said what he meant, and he meant what he said.

He couldn't help if Andino did not—or could not—understand John's compromise.

He didn't blame any of them, though. None of them understood what it was like to be him.

John couldn't explain it.

No matter how hard he tried.

• • •

Mania for John was a vicious bitch. It manifested in so many different forms that it was sometimes hard to keep track. One day he could be highly productive, and laughing because he was almost high with the way he felt. The world seemed to move so fast around him on those days. The next day, he could be so low that the only thing he felt was right was lashing out at anyone he could reach.

It was violent.

It was mean.

It was nasty.

He knew after it was all said and done, and the dust cleared, that for those around him, his mania could be terrifying.

It was every reason why Cella and Liliana no longer made any effort to have a relationship with John. They had been some of the first people to experience the way his mania manifested in horrible ways. Like a tornado, he had ripped through their lives when they should have been doing anything but trying to hide from their older brother.

Instead of having happy memories of years that should have been good, they were tainted and colored dark. Too many moments of peace when John had been stable, and then bouts of chaos when his mania came out to play.

His sisters never spoke as adults about how their brother's episodes had affected them when they were younger; they simply kept a distance. They didn't allow him into their lives beyond the shallow surface, and they didn't intrude on his life, either.

It also taught others in John's family that when the mania darkened, it was better to step away unless they could handle what it might throw at them.

"John, listen—"

"I'm not taking those fucking pills!"

Lucian shot his wife a look from the side. Jordyn wrung her hands together from the kitchen's entryway, however, she didn't step in more than she already had. Her worry was as clear as day, but so was her fear.

Of what might come next.

Of what John might do next.

Of what her son might say next.

This was not the first time.

It would not be the last time.

It could never be the last time. John's brain was wired this way. He was who he was, and eventually, he always came back to this manic stage.

It would break, sure.

He would have moments of peace, yes. A long spread of time when he was right and good again. He always came back to this, eventually. It was the one thing he could bank on in his life.

"Jordyn, go."

Lucian's order drifted over deaf ears. John's mother didn't move an inch. Unlike a lot of the women in his life, his mother was one who was unafraid of him in his mania a good portion of the time. She always faced it head-on, but with soothing words and a comforting touch.

He heard her. He felt her.

It just didn't help.

"I want to go home," John snarled at his father.

Lucian didn't blink in the face of his son's rage. "You can't."

"I've been here long enough!"

"You've been here a day."

John felt like someone had punched him in the throat.

A day.

That was all.

A single day felt like weeks to John. Time was bleeding together, and he was missing it. Time was running out to fix the things he had somehow missed, and he was letting it.

"I'm not taking those pills," he repeated.

Lucian frowned. "They could help stabilize you a little more until we get you in with someone else."

No, they wouldn't.

They would make his mania worse now.

Lithium had to be stopped when other antipsychotics were introduced. Otherwise, more meds needed to be added to the regime to balance out the counter effects of the mix. That only led John into the fog that had gotten him into this mess in the first place.

No, he wasn't doing that again.

"If you won't take meds, then I need you to stay," his father said. "I can't let you—"

"Because you don't get it," John hurled at his father. "You don't give a shit what it will do, or how it will change what's going on in my head right now."

He couldn't forget.

He couldn't afford to forget anything right now.

"John, you have to let us take care—"

"I don't have to do fucking anything!"

Lucian stepped forward at John's rage, but all he saw was a threat coming at him. One that was meant to hold him back, and stop him from finishing what had started decades and decades before.

They would lock him in.

They would hold him back.

He needed to do this.

They wouldn't understand.

The second Lucian grabbed ahold of John, he snapped. What control he had over himself was gone. It had already been holding on by a thin thread as it was. He shoved his father hard, and didn't even feel the slightest flicker of guilt when Lucian slammed into the kitchen island.

He heard his mother's gasp, and his father's curse.

Still, he knew what he had to do.

The clock was still ticking.

Tick. Tick. Tick.

Counting down …

John grabbed his jacket from the back of the chair before he darted past his mother in the entryway. Her shout echoed from behind him. His father's footsteps reverberated down the hall.

Lucian wasn't fast enough. He had never been able to catch John once his son made the choice to run.

John snatched the keys from the glass bowl on the table near the front door. Keys for a black Mercedes SUV belonging to his father. It wouldn't be the first time John had stolen one of his father's cars.

"John!"

The front door slammed behind him. He didn't even feel the cold wind as it wrapped around him. Inside, he was a fire burning out of control.

A raging devastation ready to ruin.

John was already pulling out of the driveway by the time his father had come out of the house. In the rearview mirror, he saw Lucian toss his hands up high. Exhaustion and wariness stared back in his father's eyes.

He knew that look well.

This could be a tiring state.

John was tiring.

The lights of the highway bled together. Like a scene from a fast-moving movie, it felt just as surreal.

John pulled the phone from his pocket, and turned the device on for the first time in he didn't know how long.

Too long.

He dialed a number. One he would have never called otherwise.

The man answered cheerfully. Like he had everything to be happy about.

"You said I could talk," John said into the phone. "Whenever, right?"

CHAPTER TWENTY

SIENA'S GAZE drifted between the screen in front of her, and Kev sitting across the desk. Something on her brother's phone had become extremely interesting to him, but she didn't know what exactly it was.

Still, she couldn't ignore how heavy her stomach felt. Like a dead weight had come along to sit down and make itself at home. Nothing she did was getting rid of the dreadful feeling.

Her gaze darted to the landline on the corner of the desk. More than once since she had arrived at the restaurant, she had considered trying to make a call. Yet, every time she attempted to do just that, her efforts were thwarted by one of her brothers coming in the office.

Even when Darren had left for a couple of hours earlier, and Kev stepped out for a smoke, the enforcer came inside to sit with Siena while she worked.

For some reason, they were keeping a very close eye on her.

She couldn't breathe loudly without one of them looking at her.

What were they planning?

What was going on?

Nothing good, she suspected.

"What are you doing?" her brother asked.

Siena looked at Kev again. "Working."

"Then, why are you sitting there doing nothing?"

Jesus Christ.

She couldn't even be still without one of them suspecting something was up.

She knew it then …

Something was definitely about to happen.

Siena just wished she knew what it was.

"Do you want to stare at a computer screen for hours on end, and sit in this uncomfortable chair without barely moving at all? I can't take a minute to stretch my fingers and blink?"

Kev cocked a brow. "As long as that's all you do."

Asshole.

Siena kept her thoughts inside her head, but barely. If only she could get a couple of minutes alone, then she might be able to send out a call from the landline.

Something to warn John that her brothers and father were planning an attack on him. One that would push his family in to a war with the Calabrese.

Who else would tell them?

Kev stayed sitting in the chair across from Siena's desk. He wasn't moving an inch. The longer she stared at her brother, silently willing him to even get up and use the damn bathroom while Darren had stepped out, the more pissed off she became.

Siena's mouth opened to tell her brother off just for existing. Darren slid into the office, and stopped her from saying anything. The grin he sported was downright smug.

If not altogether evil.

"Well?" Kev asked.

Darren nodded. "Yeah, it's happening."

"How do you know?"

"Dad got a call. By tomorrow, this city is not going to know what hit it."

Kev returned his brother's grin. "About damn time."

"The Calabrese have waited a long time for this day."

Siena tried to remain calm as she listened to the conversation between her brothers. She didn't let a single emotion crack through her calm facade. If Kev or Darren thought Siena was planning something, or was even a little too interested in their conversation, she had no doubt they would lock her in even more than they already had.

At the moment, it was a risk she was not willing to take.

Sure, they didn't mention any names, and were careful about details. It didn't matter. It was enough for her to figure out something bad was going to happen.

Something between the Marcello and Calabrese families.

Something that probably involved John.

And she just couldn't allow that to happen.

"Does he want us to head over there just in case?" Kev asked.

Darren shrugged, and dropped into the chair beside his older brother. "No, he's sure he can handle it alone. He did mention something else, though."

"What's that?"

"I guess you-know-who is sounding even more unstable today."

Two pairs of blue eyes drifted in Siena's direction. Her gaze was firmly stuck on the computer screen in front of her, but she still saw her brothers' passing glance out of the corner of her eye.

That confirmed it.

Without any doubt.

They were talking about John.

They were planning something.

Tonight.

Siena's fingers drifted over the keys on the keyboard. Random letters and numbers appeared in the tables, but didn't actually make any sense. She only wanted her brothers to think she was working, after all.

The two continued talking, albeit quieter than before. It was hard for Siena to discern their conversation, so she opted to continue typing.

Not for long, though.

When she thought Kev and Darren were too distracted in their conversation, she took the risk of standing from her chair.

Neither one of her brothers missed it.

"Where the fuck are you going?" Kev asked.

Siena didn't hesitate. "To the bathroom. I have to change my tam—"

At just the suggestion she was on her period—she hadn't had a period since starting the shot two years ago—both of her brothers looked like she had smacked them in the face with a shovel.

Had it been any other time, she might have laughed.

"Go, then."

Darren scowled. "But hurry up and finish here, Siena. We have other shit to do tonight."

For the first time all day, Siena was out of her brothers' sights. The bathroom was at the very end of the hallway. There was a men's and women's, but no private bathroom for the employees.

The restaurant had closed about an hour ago, and Siena was grateful. She pushed a hand against the bathroom door as she passed it by to make it sound like she had gone in.

She didn't go inside, though. Instead, she went further out onto the restaurant's main floor. At first, she considered just leaving the restaurant while she had the chance. The enforcer still sitting in the car outside the place told her that wouldn't be a very good idea.

Siena let out a hard breath. Her gaze darted over the room, and then to the kitchen.

The phone in there, maybe.

It was worth a shot.

As long as she got a call out, then the rest didn't matter. She would deal with whatever came her way from her brothers.

She only needed to make a single goddamn call.

Siena darted for the kitchen. The landline hanging on the wall was a godsend. She picked it up, and dialed the only Marcello phone number she knew.

John's.

It rang and rang.

Her heart grew heavy.

Seconds passed.

The call went to voicemail.

Siena cursed, and tried again.

More ringing.

More nothing.

The sickness in her stomach damn near climbed up her throat, and threatened to spill out onto the floor. She tried one last time, but again, she got no response.

Siena didn't know if that was because John refused to take a call from her, or if he couldn't. The very thought of that almost made her puke, too.

She hung up the phone with a little more force than she meant to.

Think. You're not stupid, so figure this out.

Her thoughts taunted her.

The dark kitchen stared back at her. The chef made sure to clean his space thoroughly before leaving for the night. Hanging above the stainless-steel counter was a row of frying pans, skillets, and more. A deep-dish frying pan caught her eye.

Siena hesitated.

She was not violent.

She did not do this kind of thing.

But for John?

Rules did not apply.

She grabbed the deep-dish pan, and gave it a second look when she realized how substantially heavy it was in her palm. Really, she didn't have the time to second guess which pan to use. She headed out of the kitchen, and tried to keep her footsteps light as she crossed the main floor again. She had only rounded the corner nearing the hallway when she heard her brothers talking again.

"I don't know what this is," Darren said.

"These aren't even numbers. It's just a damn mess. Go get her."

"Yeah, all right."

Siena quickly darted into the women's bathroom. Holding that pan back as far as she could over her shoulder, she waited for the bathroom door to open.

When it did swing inward, she closed her eyes and let the pan go.

The sound it made when it cracked against Darren's forehead was sickening. It nearly matched the way his body slumped forward, and fell head first into the tiled floor.

"Darren?" Kev called.

The bathroom door wouldn't shut completely. Darren's body—he was knocked out entirely—was in the way.

Siena stepped over her brother, not sure if she should be happy that he was still breathing, and moved into the hallway. She took a couple of steps until she was just outside the office.

Kev appeared in the doorway.

She swung the pan again. Kev wasn't like Darren. She had to hit him twice before he stayed down. She didn't bother to check if he was still breathing, too.

Siena made sure to grab both of their cell phones, and cut the wires to the landlines before she left the restaurant from the back exit.

How much of a head start did she have?

That was the million-dollar question.

Siena had too much riding on it to lose.

• • •

The taxi driver glared when Siena tossed a handful of bills over his shoulder to pay for the ride. She wasn't even sure if it was enough money to pay the man. She didn't particularly care at the moment, either.

"Don't leave yet," she said. "I may need you again."

His shout echoed at her back when she jumped out of the back of the car, and to the sidewalk. She took the stairs leading into the entrance of a familiar restaurant two at a time.

Andino Marcello's restaurant.

The place looked like it was closed. The business hours hung from a sign on the door, taunting her further. Not one single light was turned on inside, and she could see the tables had been cleared. The chairs were all upturned on the tops of the tables, too. The front door was locked when she tried to pull it open.

Shit.

She yanked and yanked on the door until a sob broke through her chest.

Fuck.

Why did it have to be like this?

Why couldn't one single thing go right for her tonight?

"Siena?"

Siena turned fast on her heels to face a blonde she recognized. Haven. The woman climbed the restaurant steps quickly until she was just a foot away.

Salvation stared Siena in the face.

"What are you doing here?" Haven asked.

"Where is Andino?"

She didn't have time for small talk.

She didn't have time to explain.

"He was here working in the office," Haven said. "But he got called out a while ago."

"Where is he *now*?"

Haven glanced away. "Why?"

Siena could tell just by the look in Haven's eyes that the woman didn't want to give up any information about Andino. Maybe she had been told not to, or something.

It really didn't matter in that moment.

"Let me guess, you're not supposed to trust me either, right?"

"Well—"

"I don't have time for this," Siena hissed, heading back down the stairs. "John is in trouble."

"John?"

Haven's quiet question made Siena's footsteps falter. She hesitated, and glanced over her shoulder.

"Yeah, John."

"Andino is a couple of blocks away. I guess John's father called. He took off."

"John did?" Siena asked.

Haven nodded. "Yeah. Earlier."

Oh, God, no.

Siena didn't have time to go somewhere else yet again. She couldn't chase people all over the city in hopes that she would finally find someone who would actually listen to her, believe what she said, and help.

Her brothers had said it. Tonight was the night.

They didn't say John's name, but what they had said had been more than enough to make Siena believe that's who they meant.

Which meant he was probably heading to her father's place now.

Siena turned back on Haven. "Please, tell them John is at my father's home."

Haven swallowed hard. "Why would I do that?"

"Because if you don't, Andino will never forgive you when they finally get John's body back from my family."

The blonde stilled in place like a statue with a gaze full of ice.

Siena was already heading back down the stairs. "I can't chase them. I have to help John instead."

Behind her, Haven called out, "Don't make me regret this, okay?"

Siena laughed.

The only thing she regretted at the moment was being born a Calabrese.

• • •

Siena didn't recognize the black Mercedes SUV that had been left running on the side of the road in front of her parents' brownstone. The taxi driver pulled away from the curb, still pissed that this time, she had all but thrown a handful of credit cards at the back of his head.

Her mother's car was not parked in the driveway beside Matteo's tan-colored Suburban. She wasn't surprised about that. Her father often sent her mother away for the night when he planned to do business inside the brownstone.

Coraline never questioned Matteo.

She never refused him.

The perfect little mob wife.

Siena found the brownstone was unlocked. She opened the door with a careful hand, not wanting to make more noise than was necessary.

She had no idea what she might walk in to. She didn't know what to expect just beyond the front door.

Surprisingly, she found the foyer and front hallway empty and dark. Her father's boots and coat rested in their usual spot, while her mother's belongings were missing. Further proving her belief that Coraline was not home at all.

Even the kitchen and living room were dark and lifeless. The counters were spotless, and nothing was out of place. It almost made her wonder if her mother had been home at all as it didn't look like someone had even cooked supper.

Siena didn't go to the back of the house on the bottom floor because she didn't hear anything coming from that direction. Nothing was really back there, anyway, and her father always had his meetings in his office upstairs.

Would he kill Johnathan in his home?

Would he risk doing something like that where his wife might come home and see?

A memory stood out to Siena. One deep in the recesses of her mind from when she was just a child. A loud noise had woken her from bed one night when she was barely five, and scared her to death because of the moaning that followed.

The next morning, she remembered watching her mother cover a reddish-brown stain on the living room carpet with another decorative carpet. Before the day was out, the carpet had been ripped up and replaced with hardwood flooring. Any carpets in the home had been replaced as to not have a similar incident occur.

No one ever spoke about it.

No one ever explained what happened.

Siena figured she knew.

And it answered her own question.

Yes, her father would kill here.

No, he would not care.

Siena was on the second floor of the brownstone when she first heard their voices echoing from one floor higher.

Her father.

And John.

"Of course, you can trust me," her father said. "I wanted you to understand, Johnathan, how they see you. Like the dirty little secret they have to hide. I didn't hide it. Doesn't that say you can trust me?"

John's answering words made her heart miss a beat. "More than them?"

"Far more than them, Johnathan."

No, he couldn't.

He couldn't trust Matteo at all.

Siena picked up the pace, and took the last stairwell two steps at a time. She was sure her footsteps would be heard, but that was exactly what she wanted.

Maybe …

God, maybe, Matteo would not kill in front of her. Maybe her presence would be the one and only saving grace for John.

She didn't know.

But she had to try.

More conversation drifted down from the office, giving Siena a bit of hope that she still had a few seconds left to spare. Siena ran from the top of the stairs, and down the hall when her father's voice rang out first.

"Loyalty is hard to come by in this life. You need to take it from those who have always proven they're willing to give it to you."

"Every Marcello knows loyalty doesn't come from a Calabrese," Johnathan replied. "You forgot that even though I bleed Grovatti blood, I've always been a Marcello man."

Bang.

The gunshot was so loud that Siena flinched. The scream caught in her throat as she rounded the doorway to her father's office.

She thought for sure …

Every part of her believed …

A gun fell from John's hand.

Her father bled out as his body slumped over the desk. Blood trickled in a thick stream from the circular wound in his forehead.

John looked over his shoulder.

Siena stared back, unafraid.

"I'm not sorry."

Didn't he know?

"You don't ever have to be, John."

He never had to apologize to her.

Not for himself.

• • •

Siena stayed close to John in the bed. His features were relaxed, telling her that he had finally slipped into a deep sleep.

She had never seen him so out of it before.

It had only been those brief few seconds in her father's office when he had seemed lucid and understood what was happening around him. And then as easily as his mind was clear and right, he was lost again to some place she couldn't bring him back from.

It had only been his father and cousin's arrival minutes later that saved John from doing something else he might have regretted later.

Siena made only one demand.

Take him to his own home. Let him wake up in his bed. Somewhere he would recognize instantly. A place that was comforting and familiar to him. He would have chosen his own home, she knew.

Lucian had agreed to bend to that one demand. He didn't give her much else, though.

"You know," came a voice from the doorway, "it isn't usually this exciting with John."

She found John's father standing there watching her. She didn't care how she looked resting beside John while he slept, and stroking his face.

This is where she wanted to be.

So, she didn't move.

"Oh?" she asked.

Lucian chuckled dryly. "No, these episodes have become less and less frequent over the years, and not nearly as severe as they once were. Maybe that's why when they do happen, they take us all by surprise."

"When was the last severe one?"

She thought she knew the answer.

But she wanted to be sure, too.

"Over three years ago." Lucian leaned against the doorjamb, adding, "And before that, four years. Sure, he's gone into a hypomanic stage—the hyperactivity, lots of energy, and highly productive—but recognized what was happening and got it under control before it worsened. I think this was a mixture of a lot of things for John. Too many changes in his life at once, and trying to push through it regardless.

"One part of it, anyway," Lucian continued. "His family plays a big role. Maybe more than some of us want to admit."

"How so?"

She felt like these were important things for her to know. Her only goal after this was to be the one thing—the one person—whom John could depend on, no matter what. No one would ever hurt him or do to him again what had been done to him this time.

She would make sure of it.

"He often says we smother him, or make him feel as though he can't take care of himself," Lucian said, shrugging his broad shoulders. "We do things that seem as though we're taking away his control, or managing his life for him. We know he can handle it—he's been on his own since he was eighteen. Still, we're always waiting for that next episode, and I think he knows that, too. And so, he pushes away from us, and stays on the outskirts of our lives where we can't come close enough to touch his. We have things to change, too."

Siena nodded. "I can understand that."

"Does that … bother you?"

"That this sort of thing is a possibility?" she asked back.

Lucian shrugged.

"No, it doesn't bother me."

John's father stared at her for a long while before he nodded, and then pushed away from the door. "I have to make some calls, Siena. We're downstairs if you need us."

Alone with John again, Siena settled back into the bed. She tucked her body in closer to his, and wished sleep would take her under, too.

Reality kept her wide awake.

What was going to happen now?

How would things change for them now?

Siena didn't know how long she had been lost to her thoughts before another form darkened the doorway. This time, it was Andino.

"Siena."

She glanced his way. "What?"

"Someone is here for you."

She straightened in the bed. "Who?"

"I assume he's one of your father's men. Or, was. Either way, he says Kev has sent for you."

Andino's dry, flat replies bothered Siena in a way she couldn't explain. Her heart thudded hard in her throat.

"Understand," Andino said, "that we don't have a choice but to hand you back over to them right now."

Her eyes prickled with tears.

"But why?"

Andino stared hard at the floor. "We're unprotected at the moment. We thought about John, but didn't prepare for anything else. We don't have a choice."

Siena's gaze drifted from John, and then back to Andino. "What will happen if I don't go?"

"They have several vehicles outside at the moment. We can safely assume each one has a driver, obviously, but likely more. What do you think?"

No.

Her heart broke all over again.

"I'm sorry," Andino murmured.

Siena shook her head, and quickly wiped away the tears that slipped down over her cheeks. "No, it's okay."

It really wasn't.

She could only imagine what life was going to be like for her once she left this house. She had not only attacked her brothers in order to help John, but also betrayed her own family. They had probably found her father's body by now, and put things together seeing as how they found her with John.

This was bad.

For her, it was going to be really bad.

Moving off the bed, Siena headed for the door with slow steps. Every single inch of her screamed to turn back around, and hide in the bed with John.

At the door, Andino stopped her with a hand on her shoulder.

"This isn't over," he told her. "Know that this is only temporary."

"I don't know anything, Andino."

All she wanted was John.

Andino nodded once. "We'll finish this."

She didn't ask how.

She didn't want to know.

"How fast?" she asked.

"That, I don't know."

Siena looked back at John. "They can't ever hurt him like that again, Andino. No one can ever hurt him or use his own mind against him ever again."

The man stared at her for a long while, saying nothing. Like maybe he had found something he hadn't even been looking for.

Siena knew what it was.

Loyalty.

Like him, her loyalty was sparse and carefully hidden. She didn't offer it freely, and only to a select few.

John was one of them.

He would always be.

"Ever," Siena repeated.

"Never," Andino agreed.

CHAPTER TWENTY-ONE

JOHN STUMBLED from the bed. A muddy sensation filled up his mind. A medication-induced fog had nothing on a manic break. The exhaustion that came on a person when the mania finally left was unlike anything else.

A hell he would wish on no one.

Not even his worst enemy.

It was like a thousand pounds of rocks had slipped into his body to replace his muscles and bones. Cement had been used in place of his blood.

Walking was a chore.

Breathing was too much work.

Being alive was troublesome.

John moved down the stairs of his home, grateful that somehow, he had been brought home—or made his way—to a familiar place. It made this process so much easier to understand. He felt less out of place, even though not a single thing in his life currently felt right.

He took the stairs carefully, navigating one after the other with heavy feet while he held onto the banister. The quiet chatter coming from the kitchen drew his attention in that direction.

He recognized the voices. Andino, and his father. However, there was one voice missing. One voice that he wanted to hear the most.

In the haze of his memories of the week and night before, John distinctly remembered one person standing out the most above all others.

Siena.

Where was she?

Why wasn't she here?

He was sure that she had been in bed with him the night before. His eyes had cracked open, though they felt like someone had taped them shut, and he had seen her lying next to him.

That had not been his mania.

He had not imagined her there.

So, where was she?

John stumbled into the kitchen. Instantly, the gazes of his father and cousin darted his way. Lucian stood from the table first, and then Andino quickly followed suit.

"John," his father said. "How are you feeling?"

In Lucian's eyes, John could see the questions his father didn't ask. Things about his mind, and what was currently going on up in there.

John didn't know what he would say if his father did ask. His thoughts were slower, and his mind was not warring between emotions, and trying to process them. He did not have so much shit muddling up his brain, even if it did still feel muddy in ways.

It was better.

Not like it had been.

"Where is she?" he asked.

Lucian looked at Andino, and then back to John. "Who, son?"

"You know who."

He was not playing this fucking game with them.

Andino took a step forward. A hesitant step. He had a right to be hesitant, John knew. After the weeks and weeks of mania, anyone had a right to look at John in that moment with a little bit of hesitancy.

"Siena?" Andino asked.

Is this twenty fucking questions?

"Where is she?"

Andino swallowed hard. A nervous tic his cousin tried his best to hide, but never quite succeeded with his family. "John—"

"Where is she?"

His roar reverberated through the home. The sound made his head ache even worse, and his heart hurt like nothing fucking else. His soul was slipping from his fingertips, and he couldn't grab it. He couldn't hold on to it.

All he wanted was to hold on to it.

"Where is she?"

"We had no choice," Andino said.

"No choice," John echoed.

What did that mean?

What did that mean for her?

What did that mean for him?

What did that mean for them?

"They sent for her," Andino said.

"We had no choice," Lucian confirmed, "unless we were willing to have them come in on us unprotected, and we were not. Not with you in the midst of a mental break, John. We wouldn't have been able to get some kind of backup here in time to help."

John nodded, but the action felt robotic. Just an action his brain told his body to do, but not something he had actually wanted to do.

Silently, he turned around and left the kitchen. He wasn't quite sure how he made it back up the stairs, but he did. Soon enough, he was in his bed once more. The blankets suffocated him, but he liked it just fine that way. He brought them tighter around himself, until he could barely breathe at all.

The darkness seeped in through his mind, and spread through his body like poison.

He didn't want to move.

He didn't want to breathe.

He didn't want to see.

He didn't want to feel.

He didn't want to be.

This was what the mania was like when it finally broke.

A dark nothingness that settled deep within John's body and psyche. A harsh emptiness that left him lonely, and so out of touch with everything, and everyone. His body ached, and his mind screamed into blackness.

A depression that almost nothing could fix.

Or, that's how it felt.

John wasn't sure how long he stayed like that before he felt a hand touch his shoulder over top the blanket. The blanket was tugged away just enough for him to see his father looking down at him.

Lucian tried to give him a smile, but it didn't feel true. Nothing could be true.

"It'll be okay John," his father said. "Another one of those things for us to figure out."

"Will it?"

How could it be?

"We'll handle it, John. We always handle it."

John thought about how easy it would be to fix this problem forever. How simple it would be to take away the one issue that constantly brought his father and the rest of his family so much heartache, and so much trouble.

Him, that was.

He thought of the gun in the bedside drawer. He knew what gun metal tasted like. It wouldn't be the first time he tried to swallow a bullet.

Wouldn't it be easier?

He thought so.

He also knew those thoughts—those self-harming thoughts—were not entirely his own. And if he didn't speak up to deal with them now, they would only get far worse.

John looked up at his father. "I'm sorry I hurt you, Dad."

With words.

With violence.

With more …

Lucian shook his head. "You always see these things far differently than the rest of us, John."

Maybe.

"Tell her I'm sorry I had to go again."

Lucian frowned. "What?"

"Siena. I'm always leaving her with no explanation. I promised I wouldn't do that anymore."

"We'll fix this, John."

"Sure."

For now, though …

He had to fix himself.

• • •

"Are you not interested in talking with me at all today, Johnathan?"

The white-haired, bespectacled therapist rarely ever sat down during his sessions with John. The man liked to move, and it was a little disconcerting for him. Especially considering John liked to look at people when he talked to them. See their eyes, and gage their words when they spoke.

His therapist at Clearview Oaks Facility was everything John was not accustomed to. And yet, John looked forward to this hour every day with Leonard.

"I don't know if I want to talk, no," John admitted. "I haven't done much of that today."

He hadn't talked a lot at all since he voluntarily admitted himself into the place. That was three weeks ago.

The first week was hell.

Suicide watch all the way.

They didn't put him in a padded room or anything, but they did the next best thing. They took everything and anything away from him that could be used as a tool to harm himself. Shoelaces, plastic, bed sheets, and more. They even gave him clothes with double sewn hems and no elastics so that he couldn't pull them apart. When he ate breakfast, someone had been sitting beside him, and he was forced to use a spoon.

For everything.

Even a steak.

All in all, the facility was nothing like a psych ward at a hospital. It was more open, and the staff was welcoming. The grounds were beautiful when he had finally been allowed outside on the second week. His time was spent between his private room, therapy, and roaming between different activities. The expensive facility toted everything from a spa, to a state-of-the-art gym.

"I've noticed you don't rapid cycle," the man said.

"No, I'm not a rapid cycler."

"Ever?"

"In mania, maybe."

Leonard nodded. "That would make sense. In general, though, you don't find yourself rapidly cycling between highs and lows daily or even weekly?"

"No, not generally. That's more common in bipolar women, isn't it?"

"Typically, but I have seen it in men, too. I was curious. Give me a one to ten on the depression today," Leonard said. "One being good, and ten being the worst. As always."

"A four, maybe."

"We don't deal in maybes, John."

Of course, not.

"Five."

Leonard nodded like that was more the answer he expected. "Good. Another couple of days and we'll start weaning the antidepressants away."

And begin a new mood stabilizer regime.

John knew how this worked.

What he liked the most about this facility was that his therapist listened. He looked over files from John's history, and saw the facts staring him in the face. He didn't deny those facts, or try or push too many different choices on John.

He didn't need a constantly changing martini of medications. His disorder was most stable when he only had to take one or two.

"So," the therapist asked as he rounded the couch, "are you going to talk with me today, or not?"

"We talk," John said.

Leonard tapped the top of his nose, and then pointed the same finger at John. "Safe topics, sure. But not what brought you here, or the things that drove you into your latest manic spiral. You have to deal with all of that so then the next time—"

"I'm prepared."

"Yes," Leonard said with a smile. "Exactly."

"Do I have to?"

Today was just one of those days for John. He was tired, and would much rather be in bed than doing anything else. That's why he settled on a five and not a four for the depression.

"I think today is a good day to talk, John. You see, you have a visitor coming. I was forewarned by your father during our last phone call that you would greatly like to see this woman who is coming later today. So, I am absolutely not above using the means I have at my disposal to get you talking."

He had no reason to believe it was *her*, and yet, something inside knew it absolutely was her.

Siena.

John's throat tightened at the thought.

"Blackmail, you mean," John said to Leonard.

The therapist chuckled. "Well, that's a language you understand, isn't it? Men like us always understand the language of blackmail."

Men like us.

Criminals.

Living in shades of gray, and never black and white.

John knew there was a reason his father suggested this facility, and pushed his son to take the opening when it was offered. Something other than the prestigious name, expensive price tag, and privacy it offered.

"Talk?" Leonard asked.

"If I answer one, can I ask one?"

The white-haired man smiled. "I can't promise to answer, John."

"Yeah, me either."

"Tell me, I know you struggled to agree to voluntarily check yourself in this facility. Why is that?"

John swallowed the knot in his throat. "Because everything I have worked to keep from the public would be exposed."

"Being bipolar?"

He only gave a nod. "My turn. Who are you?"

The man raised one thick eyebrow. "A man who used to be someone entirely different, John."

"And my father knew who you were before?"

"It's my turn."

Shit.

"Yeah," John said, "I guess it is."

"Why hide your disorder?"

"Would you want to be known as the disgrace of your family?"

Leonard coughed gently. "Is that how you see your disorder?"

"Bit self-deprecating, isn't it? That typically isn't my style."

"And yet ..."

John shrugged one shoulder. "It's my one thing."

"Have you ever taken a good look around at your family, Johnathan? Have you looked at the structure of support and unconditional love they've built around you? Do you know that your father calls me every day just to make sure you have had *one* single good day? I know that it is sometimes easier to alienate yourself away from those you love because it's simpler."

"I hurt them. All the time."

"Not all the time."

That was up for debate.

And not one John wanted to have.

"My turn," he said.

"Go ahead."

"Mafia, or otherwise?"

The therapist flashed a grin that spoke of years long gone, and a younger man. "Otherwise."

"Hmm."

"Your father tells me you've met a woman—love, he said. He believed you to be in love."

"Just how much have you talked to my father?" John asked.

"More than you care to know. Old friends, so to speak. You don't recognize me at all, do you?"

John's gaze narrowed. "For business, or otherwise?"

"I diagnosed you, Johnathan, after your first severe manic episode."

Jesus Christ.

John could do nothing but stare at the man. Leonard simply stared right back, unmoved. He wasn't quite sure how he felt knowing that he was staring at the man who had changed his life forever with a simple diagnosis. He didn't know whether to be grateful, or something else entirely.

"It's been over ten years," the therapist said, tipping his head to the side a bit as he eyed John, "and of course, you were in a very bad place. They opted not to treat you in a facility back then, and so I referred them to someone who would go in-home."

"It's been a little over thirteen years, actually, and I begged them not to put me in a place."

"I know. Now, about the woman."

"Siena," John murmured. "Yeah."

"Do you think the change in your emotional circumstance and just her in general might have … had an impact on edging you toward the hypomanic stage?"

"No."

"Not at all?"

"If anything, she held me back for longer," John admitted. "I feel like I fucked up at the end with her—that she's going to feel like I didn't do enough to keep her with me after everything she did for me. At first, when I realized they had sent her back to them, I was still in a state of suspension; between the manic break, and the heavy depression. I should have gone after her. I should have—"

"Should or could?"

John met the therapist's gaze. "I wish I had."

"You checked yourself in here being suicidal, and low functioning. You were fresh off a mental break, and certainly not in any position to be going to war with anybody for a woman, John."

"How do I tell her that?"

Leonard raised one thick brow. "I don't think you'll have to tell her anything. If she is a good woman, she will understand your situation."

"She is."

"Pardon?"

"A good woman," John clarified.

Leonard smiled. "Then, you've talked yourself out of that problem. Haven't you?"

"Maybe."

A bit.

"Hmm," Leonard said. "Your turn."

"Specialty?"

The man smiled widely, clearly understanding John's question without further details. "Cocaine, actually. Smuggling, specifically. See, I am a hobby pilot, John. I think you might call that a—"

"Side-hustle. Nice."

"It served me well over the years. On you, though, how do you feel about this ... Siena?"

John barked out a laugh. "Her, or love?"

"It has to be both, doesn't it?"

Leonard was right, of course.

John knew it.

"It's hard to grasp the concept that someone loves me the way she loves me," John said quietly.

"Self-deprecating again."

John shook his head. "No, I just never thought that was going to happen. I didn't look for it—this disorder ruins so many things for me when I bring people close because they can't handle it, or I shove them away."

"And she ...?"

"Kept coming back."

"And what does that mean for you?"

"My biggest fear with people is that once they know—or see what this is really like for me—it becomes John *with* bipolar. She just sees me."

"John."

"She only sees me."

Leonard ticked a finger in John's direction. "Well done, John."

"My turn?"

"Your turn."

• • •

Siena's gaze was only on John as she entered the facility after being checked in by one of the nurses. The white dress she wore made him think she looked like some kind of angel gracing his life.

Funny.

She had always been like that for him.

A saving grace.

Right up until the end.

The rules of the facility were clear when it came to patients and visitors. Hugs were okay, but any romantic displays were not appropriate or encouraged. Patients were there to get healthy, not go on a date.

Even knowing it might be a mark against him, or another long chat with Leonard about walking the right lines, John grabbed hold of Siena the second she was close enough for him to do it. He dragged her close, wrapped his arms around her, and kissed her hard.

The way her lips curved into a sweet smile sent his racing heart slowing down to a more settled tempo. All those nerves finally drifted away. She was still his peace, it seemed. His one place of calm inside a continuous storm of chaos.

He had been worrying nonstop since he found out she was coming. He knew in that second that his worries had been for nothing.

"John," she whispered.

He kissed her nose. And then her eyelids. Finally, her mouth again.

Someone cleared their throat nearby.

The warning was clear.

John ignored it.

Siena cupped his face with her hands, and she drew him in close again. Not to kiss, but just to stare in his eyes for a moment.

"You look better," she said.

He laughed.

Damn.

It felt so fucking good to laugh.

"I feel better," he admitted.

She smiled.

A bright, beautiful smile.

Lighting up his life just like that.

John had a million and one questions for Siena, but the nurse that was closing in said he needed to put a bit of distance between them. It'd be a fucking shame if they took her away from him before he even really had her again.

"Come sit down with me?"

Siena nodded. "Of course."

The visiting area was not closed to just the indoor areas. They were allowed to go outside, but the heavy snow falling down didn't look particular warm today.

Siena took a seat next to John on the white leather couch. Her fingers found his, and wove tight.

He had done so much in a very short period of time. He had done so much to her.

"I'm sorry," he said.

Siena peered over at him. "Never do that, John."

"What?"

"Apologize for being you. I never want you to do that with me."

"You do understand everything that happened, and what I did, right?"

"I know."

"So—"

"John," she said, leaning in close so all he saw was her, beauty, and life. "You know I love you, don't you?"

Yeah, he knew.

"How could I not, now?"

Siena nodded. "I always will."

"I'm still sorry."

Not for killing her father, but for everything that came before.

Matteo got what he deserved.

Simple as that.

Siena patted his cheek. "Let's talk about anything other than all of that. I don't have much time. It was hard enough just to get the time away to be here, John."

"Yeah, about that."

"What?"

"How?"

He had been told—during the one visit from Andino—that Siena was being heavily controlled by her brothers. His cousin hadn't explained much more, only that he had a line of contact occasionally.

Siena smiled slyly. "I took up yoga. It gives me an hour or two a couple of times a week to get away. I sneak out the back."

"How tight of leash do they have you on?"

Her brothers, he meant.

Siena frowned. "So tight it's killing me."

He appreciated her honesty, but … *fuck*.

"It's okay," she added quickly. "It's not forever."

He didn't know how.

He didn't know anything that was happening beyond these walls. His father and Andino made sure to keep him in a place where he was simply dealing with himself, and nothing else. John knew they were making the right choice in that regard.

If he didn't take care of himself first, then bad shit happened.

And what happened leading up to this moment could never happen again. Or, he was going to try his hardest to make sure it didn't happen again to this severity.

"How bad is it?" he dared to ask. "The streets, I mean. The families."

He didn't know if she would tell him.

He wouldn't blame or push her if she didn't.

Siena's eyes drifted down to their connected hands. "It's bad."

"How bad?"

"It's war, John."

ACKNOWLEDGMENTS
&
A NOTE

One of my first memories as a young child (about four or five) was of one of my mother's manic episodes. One memory of many. One episode of many. These never lessened—they were never managed with medications or otherwise. Her choice. And herein lies the difference between my experiences with this disorder, and how I chose to approach it in this book.

And I always thought that someday, I wanted to go there in writing. So, I finally have. Mental illness needs a voice, too. The louder the voices—the more voices in a chorus —the less stigmatized it becomes. The more likely people are to come forward, and admit they too are one of many who have felt silenced because of judgement, shame, or otherwise.

The more people get the help they need.

From disorders like bipolar, to depression, anxiety, eating disorders, addiction and more ... pretending it doesn't exist helps no one.

Thank you to the man who saw my need and silent screams for help, and gave me the strength to find my voice. The voice I needed so I could carry these words on to more people. In life, in writing, and with myself.

To my editor, Eli, and her husband, Mark, I know it's been a rough go this last while for you two, but I love you so much. Thank you for everything you do for me, and for being my biggest supporter and fan.

To Shonda L. who was the sensitivity reader of mine I brought in on this book ... thank you, hon. And you are so amazing. You're only going to get more amazing. Give your Ace a hug for me. I hope she knows how lucky she is to have a mom like you.

Many thanks to Mignon for the covers for this series. To Tracy for proofing. And London for putting a buzz in my ear to get me to write these books a little faster, and listening to me rant. Also, Sasha … even though I know life is rough right now on your side of the world, you still think about me. That means the world, love.

To my readers—more to come, loves. Thank you for being on this journey with me.

To my spouse, and my four boys … another one down. Thank you for being mine.

Bethany-Kris

ABOUT THE AUTHOR

Bethany-Kris is a Canadian author, lover of much, and mother to four young sons, one cat, and three dogs. A small town in Eastern Canada where she was born and raised is where she has always called home. With her boys under her feet, a snuggling cat, barking dogs, and a spouse calling over his shoulder, she is nearly always writing something ... when she can find the time.

Find Bethany-Kris at her:
WEBSITE: www.bethanykris.com
BLOG: www.bethanykris.blogspot.ca
FACEBOOK www.facebook.com/bethanykriswrites
TWITTER: www.twitter.com/bethanykris
INSTAGRAM: www.instagram.com/bethany.kris

Sign up to Bethany-Kris's New Release Newsletter here:
http://eepurl.com/bf9lzD.

OTHER BOOKS

John + Siena

Loyalty
Disgrace (coming soon)

Cross + Catherine

Always
Revere
Unruly

Guzzi Duet

Unraveled, Book One
Entangled, Book Two

DeLuca Duet

Waste of Worth: Part One
Worth of Waste: Part Two

Standalone Titles

Effortless
Inflict

LOYALTY

Donati Bloodlines

Thin Lies
Thin Lines
Thin Lives
Behind the Bloodlines
The Complete Trilogy

Filthy Marcellos

Antony
Lucian
Giovanni
Dante
Legacy
A Very Marcello Christmas
The Complete Collection

Seasons of Betrayal

Where the Sun Hides
Where the Snow Falls
Where the Wind Whispers

Gun Moll Trilogy

Gun Moll
Gangster Moll
Madame Moll

The Chicago War

Deathless & Divided
Reckless & Ruined
Scarless & Sacred
Breathless & Bloodstained
The Complete Series

The Russian Guns

The Arrangement
The Life
The Score
Demyan & Ana
Shattered
The Jersey Vignettes

Find more on Bethany-Kris's website at www.bethanykris.com.